LIE DOWN

WITH

DOGS

LIE DOWN
WITH
DOGS

A Laurel Highlands Mystery

LIZ MILLIRON

LEVEL
BEST BOOKS

First published by Level Best Books 2022

This novel is entirely a work of fiction. The names, characters and incidents portrayed in it are the work of the author's imagination. Any resemblance to actual persons, living or dead, events or localities is entirely coincidental.

Liz Milliron asserts the moral right to be identified as the author of this work.

Author Photo Credit: Erin McClain Studio

First edition

ISBN: 978-1-68512-138-9

Cover art by Level Best Designs

This book was professionally typeset on Reedsy.
Find out more at reedsy.com

To lovers of retired-racer greyhounds and all the people who work to find forever homes for these beautiful, loyal, gentle, animals.

Praise for LIE DOWN WITH DOGS

"Liz Milliron's best novel yet! Love in the time of murder, with a fascinating and sharply-written insider's view of greyhound racing and its abusers and desperate hangers-on. Don't miss it!"—Peter W. J. Hayes, Derringer and Silver Falchion-nominated author of the Vic Lenoski mysteries.

"*Lie Down with Dogs* is another fast-paced tightly-plotted mystery from Liz Milliron. Highly recommend!"—Bruce Robert Coffin, award-winning author of the Detective Byron Mysteries

"*Lie Down with Dogs* is a compelling mystery that keeps you guessing, as a murder investigation draws us into the tawdry, cruel, and in this case, deadly underworld of illegal dog racing."—Kerry K. Cox, author of the Nick Tanner Crime Thriller series

Chapter One

Assistant public defender Sally Castle looked at her boss and put her hands on her hips. "Ciara Delmonico's business barely makes a profit. She covers her bills, but she has a minuscule bank account balance. Because of that, she doesn't qualify for representation? She can't afford a private defense attorney, Bryan. The cost will bankrupt her."

Bryan Gerrity, the Fayette County Public Defender, removed his glasses and polished the lenses with a soft cloth. "Sally, we've been through this before. I don't make the rules. I only enforce them. Mrs. Delmonico has a job and money in the bank—"

"Neither of which give her an exorbitant amount of cash."

"Regardless, both are sufficient to disqualify her." Bryan replaced his glasses. "We seem to be having this conversation more frequently. A couple months ago it was that woman from Somerset County. Last month it was those teenagers arrested for shoplifting. Who were caught on CCTV, I might add."

Sally's response was swift. "Black teenagers who were getting a lot more hassle than white kids arrested for the same offense."

Bryan held up his hands. "That's not my point."

"Then what is your point?"

"I believe you got both parties legal representation with your friend, Ms. Dunphy."

"I did." And Kim had been incredibly reluctant to take both cases, as none of the defendants could afford the kind of fees she wanted to charge. Sally had guilted her friend into accepting them. She couldn't do that forever.

Bryan steepled his fingers and stared.

"What?"

He didn't speak for a long minute, and when he did, the words came reluctantly. "Sally, what's changed with you?"

"What do you mean?"

"When you came here five years ago—"

"Four."

Bryan sighed. "All right, four years ago, you were eager to help people. You knew how things worked, what the rules were, and you accepted them. Most importantly, you understood that we can't help everybody. That's not our job."

Sally didn't like where she thought Bryan was heading. "My motivation is still to assist people, Bryan. You know, make sure everybody's rights under the law are protected, guilty or innocent."

"I'm not denying that." He sat forward. "But in the past year, especially over the past few months, you've gotten...well, reckless isn't exactly the word, but I can't think of a better one."

"Excuse me?"

"You push the edges. You handed off that case in July to Ms. Dunphy, yet you stayed involved."

She shook her head. "At the client's request."

"Tell me you weren't secretly happy about it." He leaned back. "You and I have had more arguments over potential cases in the last four months than we ever have. I've always given you a long rope, but Sally, this has got to stop."

The words were out of her mouth before she could think. "I quit."

Bryan paused and blinked. "Excuse me?"

"I can't do this anymore, Bryan." The logical part of her brain shrieked at her to stop talking and take it back, say she'd misspoken, but she didn't. The words tumbled out of her mouth, despite her better judgment telling her to shut up, but the more she spoke, the more the speech felt right. "It's not...how do I put this? It's not the job. Doing the job, I mean. The mechanics or dealing with low-income clients. Even the repeat offenders."

"Is it me?"

"You? Oh God, Bryan, definitely not." Sally leaned on the chair in front of the desk. "You're the best boss I've ever had. I mean that. It's more..." She paused, searching for words. "I'm tired of the rules telling me who I can and cannot represent. They stick me with people like Ethan Haverton and keep me from deserving people like Ciara Delmonico."

"Haverton did wind up getting his just desserts."

Sally waved off the words. "You know what I mean. Bryan, if I stay, I wind up calling Mrs. Delmonico and telling her 'Sorry, you'll have to bankrupt yourself for a decent attorney or settle for a second-rater because your job disqualifies you.' If I go..."

"You don't have to make that phone call." Bryan rubbed his face. "I can't talk you out of it?"

"No."

"When are you leaving?"

"I kind of want to go now. Before common sense asserts itself and talks me out of it."

"I don't know, Sally. It's a hasty decision. Definitely out of character for you."

"Please don't do this. I know it's not normal for me, for how I make decisions. But if I take time to think, I'll let you talk me out of it. Or worse, I'll talk myself out of it. I need to rip off the Band-Aid, so to speak."

He looked at her. "You have any vacation remaining?"

"About two weeks' worth."

He stood and gathered some papers from his desk. "Take the two weeks. Think about it and take your time. Make sure you know what you're doing. Leave your office, all your stuff. I won't make any moves. If at the end of the two weeks you change your mind, let me know, and you can come back, no questions asked."

Sally got to her feet. "And if I don't?"

Bryan stopped in front of her and shook her hand. "Then I wish you all the best."

* * *

Pennsylvania State Trooper Jim Duncan stepped out of the Uniontown barracks into the brilliant September morning sunshine and looked up at a perfect blue sky liberally streaked with white clouds. He noted that the temperature was pleasantly warm, without a trace of humidity. Even nature was striving to make his last day at the barracks pleasant.

Fellow trooper Aislyn McAllister came up beside him. "How does it feel? Your last day, I mean."

"You make it sound like I'm leaving for good." Duncan adjusted his campaign hat. For the last fourteen years, going to work had meant donning the gray uniform and wide-brimmed hat of the PSP. Would he feel naked without them?

McAllister nudged him. "Last day of patrol duty. A free weekend and what, next week you report to Criminal Investigation?"

"Monday morning, bright and early."

"I can't believe they only gave you the weekend."

"It was my idea. Nicols wanted to give me more time, but I'd rather keep working." He wasn't changing employers, just positions within the same organization. No sense delaying that first day.

"Are you ready?"

"As I'll ever be. Sally insisted we go shopping. She said I couldn't wear the same suit and shirt five days a week, so we went to Pittsburgh a couple weeks ago. I should have just given her my sizes and let her shop for me, seeing as she made all the final decisions."

McAllister laughed. "Boss, had it been up to you, you would have bought five new white shirts, a black tie, and maybe another gray sports coat. Sally just wants you to look good at the new job. I'm constantly telling Tommy-Boy what he can and cannot wear together."

It would have been faster and nobody would have said a thing, either. But it made Sally happy and saved him the chore of doing it himself, so why fight? "Well, you'll be happy to know that I have all sorts of choices and everything goes with almost everything else. It's the adult version of those

4

clothes for kids."

"You mean Garanimals? My mother loved those. " McAllister unlocked the door to a marked Ford Interceptor. "Be honest. You gonna miss this?" She waved her hand at the parking lot.

"Some of it. I'll miss you, Porter, the others in the barracks. I'll miss driving around and seeing the county, all of the people. I will not miss shift work or working holidays where you learn exactly how many ways alcohol can screw up a family celebration, like this past Fourth of July." He searched the parking lot for his own car.

"Boss. I'm flattered." She batted her eyes and fluttered her hand in front of her face, a mock picture of girlish charm. "I bet Sally is happy you'll be on a more normal schedule."

He barked a laugh. "She's already got my first three weekends scheduled with stuff to do."

McAllister grew serious. "We'll miss you too, Jim. Thanks for everything. I mean it."

"Come on, McAllister. Lighten up." He walked backwards to his vehicle and spread his arms. "I'm not leaving the county. Who knows, maybe we'll meet up over a scene sometime."

* * *

Sally returned to her office and collapsed into her chair. She looked around. *What am I doing?*

In all her life, she'd never made such a rash decision. It wasn't her style. She weighed the options, wrote lists, gathered opinions from people she trusted, then made a choice. By doing things that way, she knew she wouldn't make a move she couldn't live with, or one she'd wind up reversing because she hadn't taken the time to think it through. But standing in front of Bryan's desk, it was as if her subconscious, which had been pushing for a change without her even realizing it, had finally asserted itself.

Criminal law was her passion, as it had always been. First on the side of the prosecution, wanting to uphold the laws of the Commonwealth and protect its citizens, then jumping the aisle to make sure every defendant got a fair shake, regardless of income level. That wasn't the problem.

It was all the rules she had to deal with that made her want to pull her hair out. She'd had plenty of conversations over the last six months with Jim, even with Tanelsa Parson, a fellow assistant public defender, about how unfair it was.

Suddenly, her decision didn't feel so impetuous.

She gazed around the room. Bryan had said to take the time and not bother packing, but Sally didn't think she could face it if she had to return to the courthouse to retrieve her belongings. It was better to make a clean break of it now. All she needed was a decent-sized box. She'd ask Doris...no, she wouldn't. The knowledge that Sally was leaving would break the older woman's heart. This was something Sally had to do by herself. There wasn't that much to pack, to be honest. A few pictures, her framed law school diploma.

It's time to move on to something else. Kim had offered her an opportunity to do just that in July, and Sally had turned it down. She knew if she called her friend, she'd have a new job in a hot minute. But was that really what she wanted? Working for Kim would undoubtedly come with a whole new set of rules.

First things first. Find a cardboard box.

She was busy sorting through the contents of a desk drawer, deciding what to take, when a tap on the doorframe interrupted her.

"Knock knock." Tanelsa Parson stood in the doorway, clad in her usual elegant, yet understated, court attire. Tanelsa dressed better than anyone Sally knew. Of course, her wife, Lisa, was a high-end fashion buyer. That helped.

"What's up?" Sally swept aside the papers on her desk.

Tanelsa strolled over and leaned on the visitor's chair. "I just got back from a meeting. The whole office is buzzing, and Doris is going through boxes of tissues like we have an unlimited supply. Are you really leaving?"

"Yes." Sally snapped a rubber band around a collection of her favorite pens, ones she'd brought to the office, and dropped them into the box.

"Damn." Tanelsa pulled out the chair and sat. "What precipitated this move? It's awfully rash for you, isn't it?"

Sally told her friend about Ciara Delmonico and the logic behind the decision to leave the public defender's office. "I'm tired of having to tell good, hard-working people I can't help them because of some stupid rule made up by a bureaucrat who doesn't understand that just because you have a job doesn't mean you have money."

"You want to make your own rules. But Sally, have you really thought this through?"

"Well, yes and no."

"What's that supposed to mean?"

"Exactly what I said." Sally stacked a couple of picture frames to protect the glass. "I didn't plan to come into work today and turn in my two weeks' notice. But Tanelsa, I've been dealing with these thoughts since the spring. You know that; I've talked to you about them. Have I made detailed lists and outlined all the possibilities? No. Has the thought been rolling around in my head for a while? Obviously yes. I wouldn't have told Bryan I was quitting otherwise. I'm not that impulsive."

"True." Tanelsa thought a moment. "You think private practice will let you pick and choose your clients?"

"I know it offers more options."

Tanelsa crossed her legs. "Even if you do pro bono work, Sally, you need paying clients to keep the lights on. You need to build a client list, too. And rent a space, and market yourself, and—"

"I know all that." Sally rifled through a stack of legal pads, looking for protected information. Finding none, she put them back in a drawer. "I'm not an idiot, Tanelsa. I don't expect this is going to be easy. I've never been afraid of hard work, though."

"I never said you were. I'm only trying to make sure you know what you're getting into." She eyed Sally. "You going to call what's her name? Kim?"

"Maybe." It would be a logical place to start. "Bryan told me to take my remaining two weeks of vacation to think about it and let him know."

"Sounds like what Gerrity would do. He's a fair kind of guy." She stood.

"If I can help you in any way, even if it's having you over for dinner because the fridge is looking bare, you have my number. Not that Jim will let you starve, but sometimes you need a little girl time."

"Thanks, Tanelsa. I appreciate it."

Tanelsa gave her shoulders a tight squeeze and walked to the door, where she stopped and turned. "Just make sure you explore your options, Sally. All your options. Going with your gut isn't necessarily a bad thing, but it's hard to build a satisfying life on spur-of-the-moment decisions. Also, remember that sometimes the devil you know is better than the devil you don't. I'll make sure no one poaches your office stuff until you've made your final decision."

Sally didn't say it, but she was pretty sure her mind was made up. "Got it."

Tanelsa took another step, stopped, and turned again. "Also, remember one more thing."

"What?"

Tanelsa pointed, her deep-red nail polish gleaming in the light. "If you decide to strike out on your own, once you're up and running, you promised me a partnership."

Chapter Two

Jim stared at Sally as smoke from the grill rose to the early evening sky. "You did what?"

Sally sat on the back step, absently scratching Rizzo, Jim's golden retriever, behind his ears. "I quit. At least, I think I did."

"What does that mean?"

"Don't let the meat burn." Sally stood, brushed off the seat of her pants, and went inside. She set about tossing the salad with such vigor that bits of lettuce and carrot flew out onto the counter. A moment later, the door banged, and the sound of a platter against wood reached her ears. The tangy smell of seasoning and wood smoke tickled her nose.

"Sally, did you quit or not?"

She felt Jim's presence behind her. "I...yeah." She told him about her conversation with Bryan, but didn't turn around. What if he was looking at her like she was insane?

Jim laid his hands on her shoulders. "Stop punishing that salad and look at me." He turned her gently, then tilted her head up so his eyes bored into hers. "What brought this on?"

"Why are you grilling me like I was a suspect? I thought you'd understand." He was confused. She could see it in his eyes. But at least he wasn't looking at her, or talking to her, like she had completely taken leave of her senses.

He pulled her close. "Nope, don't understand at all. Actually, that's not true. I kind of get it. You're an idealist. You want to change the world. You can't do that in a government agency, and that's what the public defender's office is. All of that makes sense." He kissed the top of her head. "The spur of the moment decision, that's what baffles me. Not your typical modus operandi, if you catch my drift."

She took a moment to enjoy Jim's warm, comforting embrace, then pushed away. "I rather surprised myself, to be honest. I was talking to Bryan, and all of a sudden, the words were out of my mouth, and they sounded right. Hell, they *felt* right, which is more important, I guess. So no, I don't need two weeks, although I'll give Bryan the respect of taking them."

"You won't get into trouble?"

"No. If I leave today, I'd get the money in a lump sum. This way they, don't owe me anything." She paused. "Making up my mind isn't the problem."

"It's deciding what to do next," Jim said. He released her, picked up the salad bowl, and went to the table.

"Precisely." She got two bottles of dressing from the fridge and sat. "I mean, I don't want to give up law and, oh, become a cupcake lady or something."

"Well, that's a start." Jim laid a perfectly cooked Delmonico steak on her plate. "I can't envision you as a cupcake lady anyway."

"I don't want to go back to prosecution. I don't want to join a big firm, and I don't want to switch legal fields. I'm not going to join a big personal injury firm, for example."

"All good to know. I think I'd have to break it off with you if you became an ambulance chaser."

She swatted his arm. "You're terrible." She took a bite, savoring the flavor and tenderness of the meat. "The way I see it, I have two choices. I can join Kim, or I can strike out on my own."

"Sounds reasonable."

"I don't know which way to go. And I have to make up my mind quickly."

Jim took a swallow of beer. "I was gonna ask about that. How are your finances?"

"I have some savings, so I'm good for, oh, about a month. I need to let my landlord know if I intend to renew my lease by the end of September."

"I thought your lease renews in March?"

"It does, but I have to give them six-month's notice of renewal. That's not the issue."

"What is?"

"When I signed, my income had to be three times the rent. Working in the public defender's office, it wasn't a problem, but if I go private, I don't know how that will work out or if it won't matter because I'm a current tenant."

"I can't imagine them kicking you out. You've never been late on your payments or anything, right?"

"No, but there was that whole stalker thing last winter." Not like it had been her fault, and Jim had cleaned the door pretty well, but she wouldn't be surprised if the leasing company used that as an excuse to terminate her contract, especially if she was unemployed at the end of the month.

Jim hesitated, then said, "Well, if worse comes to worst, you can always move in with me and Rizzo."

He'd tried to sound casual, but Sally detected the nervousness underlying his words. "That's very sweet, but I wouldn't want to impose." They'd been together for less than six months, and she'd spent a number of overnights and weekends in Confluence. Moving in, however, was an entirely different level in their relationship. If she told her mother she was moving in with Jim, Louise Castle would be at the printers the next day to get wedding invitations done and setting up appointments to get a dress chosen and fitted. Sally had enough on her plate with her career plans, or lack thereof.

"It wouldn't be an imposition. Hell, Rizzo would adore the extra attention." The dog lifted his head at the mention of his name and thumped his tail on the floor. "Stay down, doofus. I'm not talking to you. Anyway,"—he turned back to Sally—"tell me your thoughts. Maybe talking it out will help put things in order."

This was one of the things Sally liked most about him. He hadn't reacted to her announcement with panic or outrage that she'd done such a crazy thing. Just a calm acceptance and working on a plan forward. "I'm going to enjoy the weekend," she said. "You're taking two days yourself, right?"

"Yep."

"Monday morning, I'll call Kim. She might not want me anymore."

He grinned. "Fat chance. At least, not if she's smart, and I got the impression stupidity is not one of her failings. She'd be a fool to turn you down, if that's what you want to do."

"I'll do some research to figure out what my expenses would be if I decided to open my own practice. Office costs, advertising, that sort of thing. I can't run a law office out of my apartment, that's for sure."

"But you could run it out of here. I wouldn't mind." He gave her a sideways look.

What had brought this on? She and Jim had never discussed living together. Then again, he was thirty-seven, she was thirty-five. They were too old to bother with an elaborate courtship. He'd done all that with his first wife and it hadn't mattered in the long run. Maybe this was his way of saying, "Let's get on with it." How would she feel, waking up next to him every day for the rest of her life? Pretty damn good.

She brushed her thoughts aside. One major life decision at a time. "I'll keep it in mind. New topic." She took another bite of steak. "Are you ready for Monday? Clothes laid out, all your gear ready, everything in order?"

"It's only Friday night, Sally. Aside from my gun and badge, I don't have any gear." He paused, and wrinkles creased his forehead.

What was he thinking? "You want to make a good impression, right?"

"Yes, mother." His face cleared, and he dodged her playful slap. "I will have all my ducks in a row by Sunday night. But first, that empty weekend you mentioned." He stood, pulled her to a standing position, then moved closer. His fingers traced her jawline, and he kissed her, long, slow, sensual. All thoughts of job hunting, leases, and what she was going to do next with her career evaporated, burned away by the warmth of his touch as his hands slid under her shirt. "Neither of us has to get up early," he said, voice husky. "How about we start by sleeping in?"

"Oh, Trooper Duncan." She tugged his shirt out of his jeans and trailed her fingers up his back. "I don't think there's going to be a lot of sleeping involved tonight, do you?"

Chapter Three

Monday morning, Duncan stepped out of his unmarked Ford sedan into another blaze of September sunshine and adjusted the holster under his armpit. It had been a morning full of jarring notes. Instead of dressing in the gray uniform he'd worn for over a decade, he had slipped on his new suit and shoes. No twenty-five-pound duty belt to wear. He felt physically unbalanced. He'd had to focus on driving to the newly built Troop B headquarters in Eighty Four, Pennsylvania, where the Criminal Investigation section was located, instead of the familiar Uniontown barracks. A fresh crop of faces had greeted him, including the Troop B captain, and Lieutenant Leslie Ferguson, a woman in her late forties, her silver-streaked brown hair in a no-nonsense cut, and whose personal energy, direct brown-eyed gaze, and blunt way of speaking belied her short stature. Lt. Ferguson was maybe a couple inches taller than Aislyn McAllister, but her presence seemed to loom over everyone in the division.

The only common characteristic between his old situation and the new one was the coffee. Not horrible, but not up to Duncan's exacting standards.

Thoughts of Friday night skittered through his mind. He hadn't let Sally know how shocked he'd been at her decision to leave the PD's office. No, shocked was the wrong word. He knew, from the way she'd talked since spring, this was coming. He'd expected more notice, that's all.

He arrived at the crime scene and focused on the task at hand. All Ferguson had said was that it was his partner's turn to catch a case, and since she was in court, he had to handle it for now. At least it should feel more normal, even if he was dressed like a civilian.

Duncan took a moment to survey the property. The plain box house on the outskirts of Markleysburg needed a fresh coat of paint or a serious power wash. The windows were liberally streaked with dirt and grime. Straggly, overgrown bushes nearly choked off the front entrance. It definitely needed some TLC, but he wouldn't describe it as ramshackle.

The most notable characteristic of the place had nothing to do with the visual appeal. It was the smell. Sweet and stomach-churning, it promised that whatever was inside was way beyond simply unappealing.

There was a black panel van parked in the garage, which was located slightly behind the house at the end of the drive and leaned to the left, as though shifted off its foundation. A chain-link fence, between five and six feet high, enclosed a patch of yard with grass that had been torn up in chunks. A dog's water bowl was in the corner, but the animal was nowhere to be seen.

A uniformed trooper came out of the house. "Well, I'll be damned," she said as she took off her campaign hat and ran her hand through her blonde curls.

"McAllister. I told you we'd meet up at a scene."

"I'm sorry, do I know you? You do sort of look like this guy I used to work with." She cracked a grin and snapped her fingers. "Why, it's Jim Duncan. You clean up pretty good, Boss. Turn around and let me look at you."

"Wiseass." But Duncan obliged her with a slow three-hundred-and-sixty-degree turn. "Am I acceptable?"

"Whoo-eee. Pinstripes, wingtips, and is that a regimental tie? I'm surprised Sally let you out of her sight looking like that and didn't drag you off to a fancy dinner up in the 'Burgh instead." McAllister smirked. "First day, first body. You don't waste time, do you? Where's your partner? I thought you'd have one of those."

"She's tied up, so it's just me for now." Duncan again shifted the shoulder holster. "Damn this thing."

"No belt holster?"

"I'm trying something new. Why don't you tell me what you've got?"

"In here." McAllister led him inside the house, which was only slightly less

14

dirty than the outside. None of the rooms were well furnished, and what was there looked like the victims of rough use. Everything had a thin coat of dirt, and the dust bunnies were the size of jackrabbits. "The call came in early this morning, around eight. Neighbor woman complained of a stench. Like rotting meat, she said. You can see that the houses aren't exactly on top of each other, but they aren't ridiculously far apart. I noticed it as soon as I got here."

"As did I."

"I showed up and found a John Doe in an advanced state of decomp in the front room." McAllister paused and held out a pot of Vick's. "This doesn't work worth a damn, but you might as well give it a try."

Duncan nodded, smeared some of the jelly under each nostril, and stepped through the door. He immediately gagged. If the odor was this bad with the medicinal goo, what was it like without it?

A young man wearing white coveralls worked over an object barely identifiable as a human body in the middle of the low-end-carpeted floor. He looked up as the troopers entered. "Hey, I didn't know Jim Duncan had a brother. I have to say, you dress better than he does."

"Very funny, Burns. Stand-up comic, that's you." Was everyone going to comment? *Probably just the people who know me.*

Tom Burns merely spread his hands. "It's one of my many talents."

Duncan cast a glance at the bloated body, which was lying face up and was undoubtedly the source of the smell. "What do we have?"

"A bloody mess, and I mean that literally and figuratively." Burns narrated, pointing as he spoke. "Your John Doe is a male, approximately five foot ten, and I'd guess two hundred and twenty pounds."

Duncan inched closer. "He looks heavier."

"That's the bloat. You can see here and here that there is significant skin slippage." The deputy coroner indicated the areas he referenced. "Rigor has come and gone, and lividity is fixed, from what I can tell."

Duncan made notes as Burns narrated. "When exactly did the call come in?"

McAllister answered. "A neighbor reported a high-pitched whine and a 'stink of rotting meat' at seven fifty-two this morning. I found the victim, cleared the house as fast as I could, then called for a wagon and the techs."

At that very moment, a piercing sound rent the air. It wasn't a howl, more like a whine and it sent shivers down Duncan's neck. He'd never heard such a thing. It didn't track with the cry of a child, but it pierced his soul. Definitely a living creature in distress. "McAllister, find the source of that sound. The backyard tells me there's a dog somewhere in this place. Did you find it?"

"No, but like I said, I rushed through the house and barely took the time to make sure no one else was here."

"Go look. Now."

She nodded and left the room.

He nodded at Burns. "Go on."

"Now, based on what I see with my external exam, bloat, decomposition, yadda, yadda, I'd say you're looking at a victim who has been here for possibly a week. However, we had those ninety-degree days at the end of last week. The windows in the house were shut, and there's no air conditioning." He rubbed his nose. "Heat like that in an enclosed space with little ventilation would significantly speed the decomposition process. Because of that, your victim could have been here as little as thirty-six hours. But I think you're going to find it a shade longer. Call it a gut instinct."

Duncan inched around the body and studied the brown stains on the blue carpet. He pointed "You said literal bloody mess. I take it the large stain is the literal part?"

Burns nodded. "Yep. You can see it's under the victim and has pooled around him. From what I can tell from this angle, he was shot, multiple times, in the chest. I haven't tried to roll him yet. The minute I do..." He mimed an explosion with his hands.

Duncan understood immediately. Movement would rupture the rotting tissue and send gases billowing everywhere. "You're going to have to, you know."

"Just putting it off as long as possible, now that the photo shoot is done." Burns sat back on his heels and rubbed his chin. "Oh, and I haven't found any identification in any pockets on the front of the body. Once I muster up the determination, I'll check in the back, as well as look for exit wounds. By the amount of blood on the floor, I think there's at least one."

McAllister poked her head through the doorway leading to the rooms at the back of the house. "Boss, you're gonna want to see this." Her voice was tight.

Duncan looked up. Whatever had snagged the young trooper's attention, it was beyond the usual level of bad. "Let me know about the exit wounds. And wait until I'm out of the room to touch him."

"Coward," Burns said, but he waved Duncan off.

He followed the path McAllister had taken. Behind him, he heard the thump of the body being rolled, Burns gagging, and a muttered oath. A cloud of noxious fumes chased Duncan from the room.

He found McAllister in the very back of the house in what might have been a mud room or something similar. The sour scent of urine hung in the air. In the corner stood a wire cage, with a pile of blankets in it. A tremulous cry, filled with sadness and need, was coming from the lump of fabric. "Don't tell me that's a child in there," he said.

"No, thank God. I don't think I could handle that."

The black blanket on the top of the pile moved. Duncan blinked to adjust his eyes and noticed it was staring at him.

It was the dog.

He could tell at once the animal would be tall, at least thirty inches at the shoulder. Its long legs were splayed beneath it, a thin, almost rat-like tail flopped over them. Two huge, liquid brown eyes gazed out of the slim head, ears pinned back against the skull, and the long, slender mouth opened to show yellowed teeth, some big enough to take a good hunk out of someone's flesh. He inched closer and the dog scrabbled back into the far corner of the cage. The coat should have been a glossy black. Instead, it had a dull, unhealthy patina, covered with dust. Small insects buzzed around the dog and the blankets. He crouched down. The dog's hip bones jutted, and the ridge of its spine was evident. Even in the low light, each one of the animal's ribs was visible against the skin. Heat rose in Duncan's face, and he tasted bile in the back of his throat.

"The minute I saw it, I called animal control," McAllister said. Her voice was strong, but sounded as sick as Duncan felt. "Poor thing didn't even howl when it heard us."

He examined the padlock on the cage. "Get the bolt cutters from your car."

"Boss, you sure? If that animal was used in dog fighting, it could bite you."

"It's a greyhound." The hound let loose another piteous whine, the pink tongue stark against the dirty blankets.

"You sure?"

"Yes. A couple years ago, I was up in Market Square, downtown, and there was an adoption group there. They aren't very vocal, and they make terrible guard dogs, which is probably why no howling. This poor thing is malnourished, but it's a greyhound. They aren't temperamentally suited for fighting."

McAllister hesitated. "Any dog will bite if it's provoked."

Yet another mewling cry ripped through Duncan's heart. "You hear that, McAllister? Does that sound like an animal that's been provoked?" The bars of the cage were too close together for him to reach in and touch the hound. "Go get those cutters!"

She left and returned with the tool minutes later. Wordlessly she handed them over.

Duncan stood and snipped off the lock. The cage door swung open, but the greyhound didn't move. Duncan knelt on the floor. "It's okay. You're all right." He kept his voice low and soothing, and held out his clenched fist for the dog to sniff.

McAllister took back the cutters. "Boss, your pants."

"Damn the clothes. I can always send them to the dry cleaners." He leaned forward, still holding out his hand. "It's okay. You're safe now."

The greyhound let out another cry but also thrust its slim head forward, the nose quivering as it sniffed.

"That's it. Come on out. That's a boy."

The dog crept out of the cage, inch by inch. McAllister uttered a string of curses under her breath. Up close, the hound looked even worse. "What kind of…filth would do that to a living creature?"

"I don't know." He grabbed the water dish from the corner. "Fill this with water and bring it back."

She took the bowl and left.

Duncan took out his phone and snapped pictures of the greyhound, which was now on its feet. Wobbly, but it stood, cringing, and the whip-like tail tucked between its legs. When McAllister returned and set down the water dish, it drank greedily, splashing water everywhere, including all over Duncan's pants. "Intact male. The thigh muscles are prominent, but he's way underweight. This dog should probably be at least eighty pounds, and I'd be shocked if he's sixty-five." The dog paused, licked its muzzle, and returned to its task.

"If he's so underweight, why is there so much muscle on his legs?"

"Not sure." Duncan lightly touched the coat. He could see dry skin and small hairs came off the dog even at the soft contact.

McAllister snorted. "Are those tattoos in his ears?"

Its thirst finally sated, the greyhound took a tentative step toward its rescuer, allowing Duncan to reach toward the ears.

"Boss, um, I don't know that much about dogs, but isn't having the ears back like that a warning sign?"

He pummeled his brain to remember what the rescue group volunteers had told him about the dogs. "Not in greyhounds. Better aerodynamics. Look at his head, his body. This dog is built for speed." He folded back the right ear, then the left. McAllister was right. There were tattoos in both ears, each a string of numbers and letters. Duncan pulled out his phone and snapped a picture of each. "These mean something. I just don't remember what."

At that moment, an animal control officer entered the room. "Someone rang?" He sucked in his breath at the sight of the pathetic-looking greyhound. "Aw, shit. Where'd you find him?"

"That was awfully fast," McAllister said.

"I was in the area. What's the deal with this poor guy?"

Duncan stood and waved toward the cage. "There. The blankets stink of urine. Who knows how long he's been lying there. There's a water dish in the corner of the cage, but it's bone dry. No idea how long it's been that way, either."

The animal control officer took a step forward, but the greyhound flinched, cried, and huddled near Duncan. "Looks like you've made yourself a friend," the officer said. He coaxed the dog forward and slipped a collar on him. "Come on, buddy. Let's get you out of here." He tugged the leash, but the dog didn't move and cast a mournful look at Duncan.

He reached out for the leash. "Here." He led the greyhound from the room, keeping up a soothing patter. "I'll be right back," he said to Burns, who glanced at the emaciated dog and nodded.

Outside, Duncan and the control officer loaded the greyhound into the back of the officer's truck. As they shut the door, it let out another series of cries. "What'll happen to him?"

"I take it the owner is the dead guy inside?" the officer asked.

Duncan nodded. "I need to confirm that, but I presume so. I don't want to see the dog destroyed."

"I have a friend who works with a greyhound group up in Pittsburgh," the officer said. "Let me give him a call. Assuming nobody comes forward to claim him, I might be able to get him in with my friend's group. After we clean him up and make sure he's healthy, and isn't a danger to dogs or humans, that is."

Duncan pulled a card out of his coat pocket. "If you have any trouble, please call me. I have a dog of my own. Good thing the owner of this one is already dead."

The control officer took the card. "Amen to that. I'll keep you posted."

He got into the truck and drove off. Duncan couldn't see the greyhound, but he was sure the sound of its cries wouldn't soon be forgotten.

Chapter Four

On Monday morning, Sally treated herself to the start of her two-week vacation by sleeping in, which meant she was up at seven instead of five-thirty. After her morning run, she took a quick shower and headed out to meet Kim for a late breakfast.

Since the weather was good and the coffee shop where they were meeting wasn't more than half a mile away, Sally walked. Saturday's mail had brought a reminder that her lease was due to be renewed, which, if she signed it, included a statement of income. She was sure if she contacted her landlord, they'd make some kind of accommodation or give her an extension. After all, she'd been a reasonably good tenant for the past four years. On the other hand, the place had limitations, like any rental. And it was an hour's drive away from Jim.

Thinking of that led her to Jim's seemingly off-hand statement of Friday night. Did she want to move in with him? It was an interesting question. She mentally ticked off his good qualities. He was kind, patient, loving, and had what her father always said was the most important trait in partner: a steady job. He didn't snore and didn't hog all the hot water in the shower. As for bad qualities, he was stubborn and had a maddening need to see factual evidence before he'd make up his mind. He did hog the bed covers, maybe not intentionally, but it happened. He liked his routine, that was one thing she was sure of. After all, he'd been single for a long time, longer than his first marriage had lasted. How would he handle living with another person? He made accommodations for her when she spent the night, but she'd essentially been a houseguest. Jim had the type of personality that he'd go along with the quirks of a guest, but if she moved in that wouldn't be the case anymore. How would he feel when those behaviors became permanent?

Of one thing, she was absolutely certain. Rizzo would lose his doggy mind and be overwhelmed with joy if his second-favorite person was around more often.

The coffee shop loomed ahead and Sally spotted Kim's Audi parked at the curb in front. There'd be time to ponder Jim's proposal of a shared living space later. Sally needed to be on her A game, if for no other reason than she wouldn't put it past Kim to use the current work situation to dupe her friend into a law partnership.

The bell on the door jangled as Sally entered and she saw Kim's vivid red hair over the top of one of the armchairs arranged in front of the cold fireplace. A moment later, Kim peered around the chair back and waved. Sally pointed at the register and held up five fingers to indicate her need for caffeine and sustenance before she took a seat.

A few minutes later, armed with a large latte and an orange scone, Sally sat. Based on Kim's attire, a charcoal suit over a pale pink shirt and glossy black pumps, she was headed to court after the meeting. A half-empty cup of coffee that had been liberally doused with milk and a napkin covered in crumbs was in front of her, evidence that she'd been there for some time. She snapped shut the folder on her lap and stuffed it into a brown leather messenger bag at her feet. "Just doing some prep work for later while I waited." She gave Sally the once over. "Look at you, embracing the unemployed life."

"Why wear a suit when I'm going to meet a friend?" Sally had opted for a cotton v-neck shirt, dark jeans, and sneakers that morning. This wasn't a business meeting. Well, it was, but not one that required getting dressed up. If Bryan was going to insist that she take her vacation, she was going to be comfortable.

"I didn't get the impression this was a simple let's meet for coffee thing." Kim picked up her cup. "How are things going so far?"

Sally tried a sip of her latte. Finding it still too hot to drink, she broke off a piece of scone and popped it in her mouth. "Kim, it's been two days, and those two days were the weekend. Give me a break."

"Hey, you called me, remember? I figured you were hot to make your move."

"I'm not in a hurry." She thought of the notice about whether she intended to renew her lease. "Then again, I don't want to waste this time, either."

"It's definite, then? You're leaving your job?"

"The limitations that irritate me aren't going to disappear in two weeks." Sally brushed crumbs from her hand and tried the latte again. Still hot, but she'd manage.

Kim sat back, one leg over the other, foot bouncing. "And I'm one of your options, huh? What makes you think I haven't changed my mind?"

"That's why I wanted to talk to you. Is the offer still open? If it is, then yes, this is one choice."

Kim studied her for a long moment, not saying anything and looking like she was weighing ideas. She seemed to come to a decision because she suddenly sat up straight. "Yes, the offer is still on the table."

"Okay. First question, where have you set up your office? You took a temporary lease in Uniontown, but are you staying there?"

"Probably. It's downtown, not far from the courthouse, and there are other practices nearby. It's near the Housing Authority, and it has good foot traffic. I plan to put a sign in the window facing East Main, maybe drum up a little more interest."

Sally knew the spot. Yes, it was convenient to the courthouse as well as a couple bail bondsmen, which meant Kim's practice would be front and center for anyone looking for legal representation. "Second, what kind of clients have you taken so far?"

"I've had the ones you sent me, which includes the woman from a couple months ago, the teens, and this most recent case. Fayette County is not exactly a mecca for high rollers, but I've landed a couple of good-paying jobs from people who have vacation homes down here. Drug possession charges and the like. A smattering of middle-class folks with charges that are small time, but after all, that depends on your perspective, doesn't it?"

Sally understood. When that possession charge could cost you a job or a house, it was as serious as an arrest for first-degree murder. "How much latitude would I have to pick my own clients?"

"I knew you'd ask that." Kim drummed her fingers on the armrest. "I know you've got a bit of a...let's call it a crusader thing." She held up a hand. "Meaning you don't want to turn someone away who needs help, but can't afford my rates. I get it. I'm willing to give you some leeway on that. But"—she jabbed a red-lacquered nail at Sally—"I can't have a situation where my billable hours are paying for your charity work. You're going to have to bring in your share of the rent, so to speak."

Sally had figured on that. "Understood. Will you do a two-week trial period?"

Kim's eyes narrowed. "What do you mean?"

"I don't want to lock myself into a situation where I'm going to be as unsatisfied as I am now."

"Liking the work, not thrilled with the restrictions."

"You got it." Sally paused to take a drink and break off a large piece of scone. "Here's my proposal. I come to work for you for the next two weeks. After that, we can evaluate and see if this arrangement is going to be suitable for both of us."

"Two weeks isn't a lot of time."

"Hey, if we haven't gotten enough work, I'm willing to extend the trial period. But I will not make a move unless I have a reasonable expectation of satisfaction with where I'm going. Understood?"

Kim said nothing, but Sally could easily imagine the gears turning in her head. After a long pause, she nodded. "Okay, fine. I can work with that. As a matter of fact, I already have the perfect case for you."

"Oh?"

"Yeah, the Delmonico woman you sent my way. Work that for the next two weeks, see where it goes, and we'll talk." She glanced at the clock. "I have to go. Meeting with a client in fifteen. You have any other questions?"

"Not at the moment." Sally held out her hand, and they shook. "You want me to come in today? I can go home and get changed."

"Nah, swing by the place and pick up the paperwork. Take today to read it. Feel free to use the office. I'll see you tomorrow." Kim tossed her a key.

Sally held it up. "Where do you want me to leave this?"

"Keep it." Kim winked. "They gave me two." She bent and picked up her purse and bag. "This is going to be fun, Sally. I promise." She turned and strutted out the door.

Sally sat back and sipped her latte. She had no doubt working with Kim would be interesting. What she didn't know was whether it would give her the freedom she was looking for.

* * *

Duncan sent McAllister to canvas the neighborhood and talk to any neighbors who were home on a Monday morning. While the crime scene team dusted and collected evidence, he searched the house for any clues to the identity of his victim.

As he passed through the front room, he noted Burns struggling to zip the body into a heavy black bag. The intensity of the overripe stench had ratcheted up. "You need any help with that?"

"I got it." Burns expertly adjusted the position of the limbs so he could close the plastic over the unsightly contents. "As soon as you can, open the windows. That'll help with the smell."

"Understood." Duncan looked at the tech currently dusting the window frames. "You got that?"

"Loud and clear," the tech said. "Believe me, we will be letting some fresh air into this place as soon as we can."

Duncan turned back to Burns. "You'll call me with the autopsy details?"

"Of course." The deputy coroner maneuvered the bag onto the waiting gurney, secured it, and popped it up. "Oh, my preliminary exam revealed what I believe to be three gunshot wounds to the upper left chest. I think we'll find that to be the cause of death. I only found one exit wound, though. That tells me there might be a bullet somewhere in this place." He waved a hand. "I've let the techs know, but keep your eyes peeled."

"Will do. Thanks, Burns. Talk to you later."

Burns grunted and wheeled the body out of the house.

Since the technicians were still combing the front room, Duncan snapped on a pair of nitrile gloves and made his way to the bedroom at the back of the house. Every room he passed through had the same air of neglect. Not a place that was run down, necessarily, but one where the resident hadn't expended much beyond the bare minimum in terms of keeping things clean. He spotted dirty plates and a pot that had contained what might have been chili in the sink as he went through the kitchen. Perhaps the remains of John Doe's last meal. Mold had not yet had time to take things over, but the mess drew flies and had a crusted appearance that made Duncan sure it was at least a couple days old.

The back bedroom was neat, but exhibited the same shabby aspects of the rest of the furniture. The bed was made, covered with a thin, brown spread, maybe purchased at a discount store. Pillows that were flat from use. The furniture was at least a decade out of date and in need of a good scrubbing and polish. Duncan checked the closet and pushed open the lightweight folding doors. Clothes hung in a row. No business attire, but again, shirts and pants that came from a low-end store. A pile of work attire was folded and laid in a stack on the floor. The tan twill was heavy and stained, especially at the knees, leading Duncan to conclude that the owner worked some type of manual labor, maybe in a barn. There were a number of t-shirts, some more faded than others, with the logo of Blue Mountain Racetrack on the front. The name was unfamiliar, and Duncan made a note to search for it.

Finding nothing of interest in the closet, he moved on to the dresser. The drawers contained underwear, socks, and an assortment of shirts, including a couple of polos with the Blue Mountain logo on the chest. Was it the victim's place of work? The top of the dresser held little: a tray with some loose change, a battered hair brush, and some type of hair gel. Finally, he hit pay dirt and found a beat-up black leather wallet in a chipped bowl on the corner of the dresser. He flipped it open. Less than twenty dollars in cash, a grocery store rewards card, and a Pennsylvania driver's license. He pulled it out. Allowing for the distortion of death and decay, the picture looked like it would match the victim. "Otto McDonough, age thirty-nine," he said to himself. Otto had dark hair and eyes. The height and weight on the card seemed a good match for the victim. The license indicated McDonough was approved for commercial vehicles and the address matched the Markleysburg house. Duncan pulled an evidence bag from his pocket and dropped the license in. The wallet also held a couple of credit cards in the name of Otto McDonough. He put the wallet and contents in another bag, sealed them, and filled out the chain of custody information.

An inspection of the kitchen yielded little more than the dirty plates and utensils he'd noted on his way through and a refrigerator that contained more cheap beer than food. "Where's the dog food?" he asked under his breath. No bags of kibble, no treats, nothing. What had the poor animal eaten? Given how emaciated the dog had looked when Duncan had found him, the answer was probably "not much."

He returned to the front room, where the crime scene techs had finished dusting the window frames and opened them to let in the outside air. "You guys find a bullet?" he asked.

"No, we're still looking," the female tech responded.

Duncan stood where the body had been found. There were drips of blood across the floor. McDonough had not fallen where he'd been standing when he was shot. Duncan studied the patterns, trying to visualize the victim as he staggered around post-shooting. The window glass was unbroken, which it would have been if the victim had been standing in front of them. The same went for the mirror on the far side of the room and a lamp with a glass shade straight out of the '80s standing on a table in the front corner. "If there is one, I'm guessing it's in this area." Duncan swept his arm in the direction of the wall that divided the front room from the hallway, including the fireplace. "Given the lack of broken glass in the other parts of the room. Have you searched that side?"

"Not yet. This place is a dump of physical evidence. Have at it, but be careful," the tech said.

Duncan examined the facing on the fireplace. No nicks, no dents where a bullet might be lodged. He moved over to the wall, working back and forth. Luckily the paint was a pale color, which should make a hole stand out like a Maglite glare in a dark room. After a few back and forth passes, he saw it. "I think I got it."

The tech came over, labeled the hole and snapped the appropriate pictures. Then she used a knife to dig at the spot. "Nice find, Trooper," she said as she dropped the slug into Duncan's palm. "Saves us some work."

The bullet was intact, not misshapen, and perfect for a ballistics comparison. Duncan gathered it had come from a decent-sized weapon, not some petite little peashooter. He placed it in an evidence bag and labeled it. "You're welcome, but keep your eyes open. There may be more if—"

He was interrupted by the entrance of McAllister, who deftly stepped around the technicians.

He held up a finger to her. "As I was saying, there may be more if the suspect fired additional shots that missed our victim." He stepped over to McAllister. "That was fast."

"Late Monday morning, not too many people at home." She lifted her campaign hat, wiped her forehead, and replaced it. "According to the lady across the street"—McAllister pointed through the window—"the resident is Otto McDonough. She's not sure of his age, maybe late thirties or early forties. She described him as a big guy, with thinning hair he slicked back 'because, obviously, he doesn't know when to let it go.' I thought that was a reasonable description of our victim."

"It also matches the driver's license I found. Go on."

"The house is a rental. McDonough has lived here for about three years. He used to work at Blue Mountain Racetrack in West Virginia, but the neighbor believes he lost his job at least a couple months ago because he's around a lot more than he used to be."

"That also fits. I found a lot of shirts with that logo in the closet and dresser." Duncan wished all of the victim IDs he had to do were this easy. "Did she know who owns the house?"

"No, but he doesn't live in Markleysburg."

"We'll get his name from the property records. By the way, what kind of racing does Blue Mountain do?"

McAllister's lips thinned. "Greyhounds."

Chapter Five

As suggested, Sally went home to get her car, then drove to Kim's new office. It was a modest building nestled between two other law firms, one a personal injury outfit Sally was familiar with and the other specializing in family court cases. Sally let herself in. The decorating was rather bare bones, with a couple of chairs and a magazine rack in the waiting area, a kitchenette-type area that held a coffee station with a single-cup brewer, a dorm-sized fridge, a laser printer, two rooms clearly meant for the attorneys, and a small room with a square table and two chairs, probably meant for client conferences.

Both desks had blotters, ergonomic chairs, and places for clients to sit. One office looked more lived in, with a couple of pictures and Kim's framed diplomas on the wall. But even the desk in the unused room was well-stocked with office supplies, and empty frames were already affixed to the wall. *All it needs is an occupant*, Sally thought, as she dropped her purse on the surface. The natural light was better here, and there was a little shelf near the window, perfect for holding a plant or two. A brand-new, three-drawer metal file cabinet in matte black occupied the corner.

Since the cabinet was empty, Sally went to the other office, which was a shade larger, but not as airy. Files were stacked everywhere and jammed into a filing cabinet that was the duplicate of the first one. At least they appeared to be in alphabetical order, but the folders didn't hang very neatly. Doris would have a fit. Sally felt a little lump in her throat as she thought of the secretary. She wouldn't miss the restrictions of the public defender's office, but she would miss the people.

Less than fifteen minutes later, Sally had located the Delmonico case file, which she took to her office. *The second office*, she corrected herself. Or her temporary office. There was no use getting too comfortable in the space if the possibility existed she might not stay. She went to the fridge and found it stocked with bottled water, so she grabbed one and returned to sit and read.

The defendant, Ciara Delmonico, was a forty-two-year-old divorcée who worked from her home as a bookkeeper-slash-accountant. She had a number of clients, including several nonprofits located in multiple counties in southwestern Pennsylvania. She had no prior offenses, little credit card debt, and a good credit rating, if a slim bank account. The mortgage on her modest home, located in Uniontown, was up to date, all taxes paid by escrow. She owned an older car, long ago paid off. She did not have children. Her spending patterns were not outside the means of a woman who ran a modestly successful business.

Sally pulled her cell phone from her purse and dialed Ciara's phone number. After a few rings, it went to voicemail. "Mrs. Delmonico, this is Sally Castle. I would like to talk to you about your case. Please call me back." Sally gave her number, repeating it twice. Then she flipped to the complaint.

According to the charge, Ciara had stolen from one of her nonprofit clients, River City Hounds. Information provided by the district attorney's office showed record books with highlighted discrepancies. It wasn't a large sum, but to a small charity, it was. *Everything is relative.* She vehemently denied the charges. "If she stole from them, where is she keeping the money?" Sally said, paging through the records. After a few minutes, she found what she was looking for. An account had been opened at a local bank slightly less than a year ago. The name was Helen Delgarde, but the social security number belonged to Ciara. According to the prosecutorial material provided during discovery, the account had been opened in the name of Ciara's deceased mother. However, a search of Ciara's home failed to turn up a social security card or driver's license that could have been used in the transaction. "No way she opened those accounts without ID. Not in this day and age," Sally said. She was talking to herself. She made a note to buy a potted fern or something. At least then she could say she was speaking to it, maybe like those people who believed talking to plants helped them thrive.

Her phone buzzed. "Sally Castle speaking."

"Uh, Ms. Castle? This is Ciara. Ciara Delmonico? Returning your call?"

"Yes." Sally pushed aside the paper. "I've taken your case, and I'd like to meet with you to discuss the background. Can you come to my office or would you rather meet somewhere else?"

"I don't understand. I hired Ms. Dunphy, the woman you referred me to."

Right. Ciara couldn't magically know everything that had happened lately. *Rookie move, Castle.* "I'm sorry, let me start over." Sally explained her departure from the public defender's office. "I've gone into partnership with Ms. Dunphy, and she asked me to take over your case. I'd like to talk to you and get up to speed."

"Oh, I see." Ciara paused. "I don't know how to put this delicately. How much will this change cost?"

"What did Ms. Dunphy quote you?"

"She gave me a discounted rate of one hundred and fifty dollars an hour."

"I'll honor that." Sally grabbed a pencil and did some quick calculations. "In addition, I won't bill for phone call or email exchanges or mileage for travel within Fayette County. If I have to go outside the county, I'll only charge half the federal mileage rate. Does that sound fair?"

"More than fair. Thank you so much." Relief colored Ciara's tone of voice. "I don't want to be a charity case, but as you might imagine, things are tight."

Sally tossed aside her pencil. "Perfectly understandable. Now, about the meeting. Are you available?"

"Yes, I can be there in half an hour or so."

Sally hung up. Aside from the initial foot-in-mouth stumble, that had gone okay. She straightened the desk blotter. She'd have to buy a computer for work, or at least use her personal laptop for the time being. While she waited, she familiarized herself with the office layout. Where Kim kept extra supplies, the location of the restroom, and, most importantly, where the coffee was stored. Sally was on her second cup when Ciara arrived.

"Hello?" she said, voice uncertain as she stood in the half-open door.

Sally went to her doorway and waved. "Hello. In here." She returned to her desk. "Have a seat. Can I get you something to drink? We have coffee and water." She made a mental note to stop and pick up additional beverage choices on her way home.

"Water is fine." Ciara perched on the edge of the visitor's chair. She wore a pair of chino pants and a button-down shirt, both of which were in desperate need of a hot iron. She wore no makeup and her short hair was tousled, but not enough to hide the clear half-inch of gray root against the reddish-brown.

Sally got a bottle from the fridge. "We don't have glasses, sorry," she said as she handed it over and added drinkware to her mental shopping list.

"This is fine." Ciara twisted off the cap and took a drink. "What do you want to know?"

"Ms. Dunphy's notes are pretty good, but I'd like to hear it from you. I might pick up on something new." Sally resumed her seat, picked up a pen, and turned to a fresh page of her notebook.

The other woman took a swallow of water, recapped the bottle, and looked for a place to put it. She took a proffered coaster and set it and her drink on the desktop. "Well, um, I'm an accountant. At least, I have an accounting degree. I work on my own, doing the books for a number of people and a few nonprofits. That includes keeping their accounts and filing their taxes."

"Where is your degree from?"

"Slippery Rock."

"Good school." Sally jotted notes. "How long have you been doing this?"

"Over twenty years. I built my business through word of mouth. That's what makes this so distressing."

"Is that how you came to do the books for River City Hounds?"

"Yes." Ciara twisted and untwisted the cap to the water. "The treasurer at RCH is a friend of one of my clients. She, my client, recommended me."

"How long has RCH been a client?"

Ciara scrunched her forehead. "Uh, four years? No, five. I'd have to check my files to be positive. Except I don't have them. They were confiscated by the cops."

"Right, for evidence." Sally looked up. "In all the years you've been in business, have you had any complaints?"

"Not about my services." Ciara's shoulders twitched. "Oh, people gripe about their taxes—either they have to pay, or they don't get as big a refund as they'd like. But nobody has ever accused me of cheating." Tears built up in her brown eyes.

Sally looked around for a box of tissues. Seeing none, she pulled a travel pack from her purse. Her shopping list was growing. "What happened?"

Ciara dabbed at her eyes and took a shuddery breath. "It was right after Memorial Day this year. RCH wrote a check for something, I don't know what, and it bounced. It shouldn't have. According to the records I gave to the treasurer, they had a nice bank balance with plenty of funds to cover the check. That's what I told them when she, the treasurer that is, called. That's when she told me the bank informed them their balance was low. I said that couldn't possibly be true. She told me they had an outside accountant go over the books, and he found all sorts of discrepancies for the past year. She accused me of embezzling money from the group and said she was calling the police." Her voice broke, and the tears leaked out. "I swear, Ms. Castle, I didn't do it. Once word got out, well, my other clients started pulling their books and asking for audits. I've had to justify every decision I've made for the past ten years! And I never did anything wrong!" She sobbed and covered her face.

Sally let her compose herself before continuing. "When was the last time RCH was audited?"

"Oh, I don't know. It's a private group, and they don't have a lot of money, so I don't think it's a regular thing for them."

Interesting. "Did they, the prosecution that is, offer you the opportunity to make restitution?"

"Make resti...what?"

"Did they say you could just pay back the money and the charges would be dropped? In cases like this, it isn't an unusual course of action to avoid the expense of a trial."

"They didn't, but it doesn't matter. I didn't take the money in the first place, so I certainly don't have it to give back."

Sally tapped her pen on the pad. Someone had hurried straight to court on this one. Why? "Other than RCH, has anyone filed charges against you?"

"No, but…" Ciara tried to get her voice under control. "There have been threats. People are saying they want audits, even if they just did one, or that's not something they usually do. Accounting, especially for a business, can be complicated. For example, there are multiple methods for how you value inventory or whether you use accrual or cash accounting. Several of my clients have accused me of choosing a method because they think it made it easier for me to skim money."

"Did you?"

"No, I didn't. They don't have any proof, either." Ciara's expression turned insulted, and she got to her feet. "Frankly, Ms. Castle, if you're not going to believe me—"

"I didn't say that." Sally pushed forward the pack of tissues. "These are questions the prosecution is going to ask if we go to court. I want us to be prepared." She jotted down a few more notes. "If we go to trial, I'd want our own independent accountant to go over your records and evaluate them."

Ciara dropped back down. "You keep saying 'if we go to trial.' What other options do I have?"

"That depends on your goal for these proceedings." Sally leaned forward and clasped her hands. "Tell me, what are you hoping for as a conclusion to this case?"

Ciara raised her chin. "I want to be cleared. I want to go back to my business. I enjoy it—the work, the people…everything."

Sally paged through the file. "You've been arraigned, and I see you entered a plea of not guilty. What happened to the lawyer you had at the arraignment?"

"I fired him. He kept pushing me to accept a deal." Ciara snorted. "I won't do that, Ms. Castle. I won't go to jail, or wind up with a conviction record, for something I didn't do."

Sally stared her client in the eye. "If that's the case, then yes, your best option might be to go to trial."

Chapter Six

I t was early afternoon before Duncan finished with the scene at the house in Markleysburg. He returned to HQ in Eighty Four, intending to find the property owner and hopefully connect with him for an interview that afternoon.

He entered the building and immediately encountered Lt. Ferguson. "Afternoon, L-T."

"Duncan." She gave him a brisk nod. "What did you find out there?"

"One very ripe corpse."

She nodded toward the kitchenette. "Drink?"

He followed her over to the communal pot. Finding the selection of pods unappealing, he decided to skip it and instead got himself a bottle of water from the vending machine. Lt. Ferguson had gotten herself a Diet Coke and was already standing next to his desk when he returned.

"Preliminary details?" Ferguson had a clipped way of speaking, as though she wanted to use as few words and little energy as possible so she could expend them elsewhere. It made Duncan feel like his new boss didn't like him much, but he shook off the feeling as irrational. Ferguson barely knew him. "Definitely a homicide. The deputy coroner found what he believes are three GSWs to the chest. I recovered one bullet from the scene, lodged in the drywall. It's intact, so it should be good for ballistics analysis. Not that it'll necessarily match anything, but they'll be able to run their tests."

"Caliber?"

"Unknown, but my wild-ass guess is a .38 or a 9mm. I own a .45, and it didn't strike me as big enough. But again, the tests might prove me wrong."

"ID?"

Was she acting this way because he was new? *Stop being paranoid.* "I found a wallet in the bedroom with a license that identified the victim as Otto McDonough." He consulted his notes and relayed all the information he'd learned at the scene to Ferguson.

"Next steps?"

"I plan to run background on McDonough for the usual. Criminal record, credit score, employment, relatives. I'm also going to do a property search to determine who the owner of the Markleysburg house is and hopefully interview him. Or her, as the case may be. If I find McDonough's employer and next of kin, I'll set up interviews there, too. One other thing." Maybe if he demonstrated his competence, she'd loosen up.

Ferguson motioned him to continue.

"We found a dog at the scene, a greyhound. He had tattoos on both ears, so I think he's a racer. I called animal control to take charge of him. But Blue Mountain is a dog track, so with any luck, they'll be able to shine some light on why McDonough had a dog."

Ferguson gave a brisk nod. "Carry on." She strode away.

"Ma'am, yes, ma'am," Duncan said under his breath. He booted up his computer. Was he going to have to earn his stripes all over again? *Yes, you jackass. Now get to work.*

Minutes later, Ferguson returned, this time followed by a woman wearing a black jacket and slacks and a pale blue button-down shirt. "Duncan, this is Jenny Cavendish. You two will be working together." Ferguson turned to the other woman. "I sent Duncan over to the Markleysburg scene earlier while you were with the Washington County DA. He'll get you up to speed." She left.

Cavendish studied him, brown eyes cool. "I see you've met Fire-away Ferguson," she said. Her dark-blonde hair was twisted into a bun at the nape of her neck.

"Excuse me?" Used to working solo for most of his time on patrol, he'd half-hoped that would continue. No such luck. The police work didn't worry him. He knew how to handle that. Learning to work with another

38

trooper, all the time, *that* worried him. Would they get along?

"Our nickname for the L-T, not to her face, obviously." Cavendish gave a faint grin. "Because of the way she speaks, all clipped words and tone. Like a verbal firing squad."

"Then she isn't that way with just the new people. I was afraid she didn't like me." He entered the search parameters for McDonough's background check and started the process, then did the same for the property search.

"Oh no. She's like that with *everyone*. Wait, I take that back. We did have a trooper in here last year. She used very elaborate sentences with him." Cavendish paused. "He lasted four months, then transferred over to Troop A out in Greensburg."

"You mean as long as she's peppering me with short sentences I'm fine?"

"Something like that." Cavendish looked at the computer screen. "What's the deal with the Markleysburg victim?"

Once again, Duncan recapped everything he'd learned. "It was a stinker. Decomp was pretty bad."

"Gotta love those. We need to interview the neighbors, see if there are any witnesses. Then see if there is any information on McDonough in NLETS or NCIC."

Duncan pushed down a flash of irritation. "I had a canvass done already. Few witnesses." He told her about the woman across the street who McAllister had interviewed. "I started the checks right before you arrived."

Cavendish waited a moment. "And?"

He read at the computer screen. "Nothing." Using the International Justice and Public Safety Network, he could get a pretty good picture of McDonough's criminal history. "No outstanding warrants, terrorist activity or drug connections. Looks like he has a mid-80s Chevy pickup and a black panel van registered in his name, both of which were at the house."

"Physical evidence?"

"Almost too much, but who knows how much is useful? They were still processing things when I left."

Cavendish looked down again to read. "He was a maintenance worker at Blue Mountain."

"He had a greyhound at his place. I don't think he took very good care of it. I didn't find any dog food on the premises, just a freezer full of raw meat. Pretty low-quality cuts, too. I know dogs are carnivorous, but raw meat and nothing but?" He paused. "The techs also found jars of canine vitamins, syringes, and packets that, according to the labels, were anabolic steroids."

She straightened. "I guess I'll get on a property search for the house."

He picked up a printout from his desk. "Also already done." What did she think he'd been doing? This was not starting well if she was acting as though he was a rank amateur. "House belongs to Robert Bevilacqua, age fifty. Lives in Connellsville. Near my old barracks."

She took it, read it, then handed it back. "Have you called him yet?"

"That was next on my list."

"I'll do it." She sat at a nearby desk and looked up. "I hear you spent a long time on patrol."

"Fourteen years." Duncan was more than aware that most troopers, with his time on the job, had either been promoted or taken other positions. Did she think he lacked initiative because he'd spent so much time in uniform?

Cavendish gave him a long look. "CI isn't like patrol."

"I'm aware of that."

She paused. "You like whiskey?"

"I do. Is that an invitation?" Was he wrong about her?

"It's a tradition to take new guys out for a drink. Besides." She turned to her computer screen. "I like to know who I'm working with."

* * *

Before Ciara left, Sally asked her to write down a complete list of her accounting clients, individuals as well as any organizations. People she could call as witnesses for the defense. Sally made a note to ask Kim about any expert witnesses she might know who could rebut the prosecution's witnesses, as well as provide an independent assessment of Ciara's books and show they were in good order. At least Sally hoped that's what a second look would result in. If her witness agreed with the prosecution, she and

Ciara would have to have a long talk.

Next, Sally filed the paperwork necessary to obtain Ciara's confiscated records to turn over to the forensic accountant once that person was hired. Task complete, Sally settled in to make phone calls to Ciara's clients. The questions she asked were always the same, and there wasn't much variation in the answers, either. "Were you satisfied with the service you received from Ciara Delmonico?"

"Oh, gosh, yes," replied the man at Children's Welfare Resources of Fayette County, one of the other nonprofits Ciara had been the accountant for. "She was extremely professional, friendly, and always had our taxes done on time. And she kept her fees in line with what a small organization could afford, not like some other independents we contacted."

"You never had any suspicions or qualms about the results?"

"No, never. Everything always balanced and made sense, even to me." He chuckled. "I'm not the biggest math-whiz out there."

"I understand. You never had any problems with the IRS or your annual audits?"

"No."

"When you were told of the charges brought against Mrs. Delmonico by River City Hounds, and that your books might be inaccurate, what was your reaction?"

"Honestly? I thought it was a joke." He paused. "I've known Ciara for almost ten years. I've recommended her to my friends who were looking for an accountant. When the district attorney contacted me and told me Ciara had fiddled with the books from that dog group, and she might have done the same with ours, well, I thought he had called the wrong person. He assured me he hadn't."

"Do you do regular outside audits?"

"We have to. Our last one was this past January. Came through clean as a whistle." He hesitated again. "Do you think they're wrong? The DA? How can that be?"

"Anything is possible," Sally said. "Tell me, did you ever have problems with your bank balances? Checks that bounced and shouldn't have? The cash reserves not being what you expected?"

"I...no, not really. Well, there was one time I went to write a check, and I was surprised our bank balance was lower than I thought, but I talked to Ciara, and she explained why I'd been wrong. At least"—he faltered—"it seemed like a logical explanation at the time."

"I'm sure it did. Thank you. I may be in touch again later if I have more questions." Sally hung up.

Sally made ten phone calls, and every conversation was a variation on what the representative from Children's Welfare Services had told her. Everybody trusted Ciara Delmonico. Several of them said they'd only severed the relationship because of the risk of the criminal charges. If Ciara was cleared, they'd hire her back in a heartbeat. That alone made Sally suspicious of the prosecution's claims. Ciara might have been able to pull the wool over the eyes of some of her clients. But could she have swindled over two dozen people and organizations without anybody getting wind of it? In Sally's opinion, it was unlikely.

The sound of footsteps and a knock on the door interrupted her thoughts. "How's it going?" Kim asked. "Are you settling in okay?"

"Yeah, I'm fine. It took me a while, but I finally found the most important thing, the coffee." Sally rested her arms on the desk and gazed at her friend. "You stocked my favorite blend?"

Kim winked. "Let's just say I was following the recommendation from *Field of Dreams*. You know, the baseball flick."

"If you stock it, she will come?"

"Something like that." Kim leaned on the doorframe. "Anything else?"

"Not right now. Except for business cards. Where are they?"

"I have a box of generic ones." Kim beckoned and went to the supply closet.

Sally followed and took a small white box from her new partner. "How plain?"

"You'll have to write your name on them and a personal phone number if you want to use one." Kim closed the door. "How's Mrs. Delmonico looking?"

"She insists she's innocent and wants to go to trial." Sally went back to her desk.

Kim followed. "You think she's got a chance?"

"After talking to all these clients, I do." Sally waved her hand at her pages of notes. "Not one of them had a whisper of suspicion, not one. I think a large-scale successful fraud could swindle quite a few people. I mean, look at the Ponzi schemes and shenanigans that go on in the corporate world. But this is one independent accountant, not a woman with huge resources behind her. You're going to tell me she rooked over this many individuals and organizations, some of them very educated individuals, without a glimmer of trouble? I don't buy it."

"She could have been very crafty." Kim read over the notes. "You get a copy of the prosecution's evidence?"

"I'm working on it. By the way, do you know a forensic accountant I can use for a rebuttal witness?"

Kim furrowed her forehead. "Let me look into it, and I'll get back to you." She glanced around the office and turned a piercing gaze on Sally. "What do you think of your first day in private practice?"

Sally had expected the question. She was also determined not to give a definitive answer until she'd completed more than a few hours' worth of work. "I can tell you one thing."

"What's that?"

She lifted her mug. "The coffee is better."

Chapter Seven

I
t was close to two-thirty in the afternoon when Duncan finished what turned out to be a pleasant drive to Connellsville. Now that he didn't drive the Interceptor with the PSP markings, motorists didn't hit the brakes when they saw him coming. He had to fight the instinct to issue citations.

Once they arrived in Connellsville, they found Bevilacqua's address. He parked in the gravel drive and took a moment to study the house. A plain, Shaker-style two-story brick building with white trim around the windows, typical for the area. About the right size, with good features, for a family of four or five, but according to the records, Bevilacqua lived alone. A dusty sedan in the garage said the owner was home.

Cavendish rapped on the front door using the slightly tarnished brass knocker. After a wait of a couple minutes and another knock, a male voice said, "Hold on a minute. I'm coming." The door opened to reveal a man whose forehead reached the level of Duncan's chin. A thick shock of gray hair nearly obscured his eyes. He looked like someone who used to have an athletic build, but he'd lost the battle against the paunch around his middle. "Yes, can I help you?" he asked, tilting his head up.

The troopers showed their badges. "Trooper Cavendish, this is Trooper Duncan. Are you Robert Bevilacqua?" Cavendish asked.

"Yes. What's this about?"

"Do you own the property at 4329 Friendsville Road in Markleysburg?"

Duncan wouldn't have been so direct, but Cavendish was senior. He'd let her run the show. This time.

"Yes." Bevilacqua's forehead creased. "What's the asshole done now?"

"May we come in?"

Bevilacqua hesitated. Then he pushed open the storm door. "I guess. What's this all about?"

They entered the cool interior of the house, and Duncan glanced around. The furniture was modern, all glass and chrome, and too much of it crowded the room. It felt like it belonged in a different type of dwelling. "Thank you," he said. Maybe he didn't understand Cavendish's style yet, but her tone sounded rude. "Is there somewhere we can sit?"

"I'm sorry, Trooper...Duncan, is it? Am I in trouble?"

"No, sir. But there has been an incident at your Markleysburg property."

"What kind of incident?"

Cavendish spoke. "Your tenant, Otto McDonough, is dead."

Bevilacqua blinked a couple times and rubbed his chin. "I'm, well, I don't know what to say. Holy shit. Dead how? Did Otto have a heart attack or something?"

"Someone shot him." Cavendish, it seemed, didn't pull her punches. "We're treating the case as a murder."

Her bluntness made Duncan feel—not uncomfortable, but a little off-balance. They could talk about tactics later. For now, he watched the other man's reaction.

Bevilacqua paled, opened his mouth, closed it, and swallowed. "When... when did this happen?"

Duncan spoke. "Sir, it's really better if we have this conversation sitting down."

"Sure, sure. In here." He led the way to the front room. An oversized leather sectional stood in front of the windows. Two matching armchairs crammed against the wall facing it. A glass-topped coffee table with a chrome base occupied the space in the middle, positioned on a plush area rug with a geometric design in black, dark red, and cream. The entire arrangement left little room for maneuvering. "Have a seat." He waved at the couch and dropped into a chair.

Briefly, Duncan wondered why all this furniture was in one room. He took a seat. "Thank you. We found Mr. McDonough this morning. However, we believe he'd been dead for some time. A few days at least, maybe more, based on the condition of the body."

Cavendish narrowed her eyes, but sat next to him.

Bevilacqua looked like he wanted to vomit. "Condition of the...you mean he was, um..."

"Decomposing rapidly." Duncan removed a notebook from his jacket pocket. "Yes. We aren't sure of the exact time of death, not yet. When did you last speak to Mr. McDonough?" He clicked open his pen.

"Uh, let me think." Bevilacqua rubbed his chin. "His rent is due the last day of the month, and I received August's check." He clasped his hands behind his head. "It's been at least a couple months since I've seen him, though. I only go out there if there's a problem."

"You're sure he wrote the check?" Cavendish asked.

"Pretty sure. I mean, I'm not a handwriting expert, but I didn't notice anything about the check or the envelope that made me think he hadn't."

"You don't take direct payments?"

"You didn't know Otto." Bevilacqua gave a small smile. "He wasn't technologically savvy and preferred checks. Antiquated, I know."

"You have more than one rental property?"

For a moment, Duncan felt he'd been shouldered aside. Didn't Cavendish believe he could ask questions?

"Yes, I'm in the real estate business. As a matter of fact, we're sitting in one of my properties. I um"—he flicked a bit of lint from his jeans—"I needed a place on a temporary basis and this house was available. Usually, I live in Pittsburgh."

That would explain the amount of furniture. "Where in Pittsburgh?" Duncan asked. He'd show her he knew how to handle himself.

"I used to have an apartment in the Cultural District. Are you familiar with the new apartments on Penn Avenue up by Heinz Hall and the Benedum? That's where I lived until very recently. Quite a difference from Connellsville, if you get my drift."

"Why aren't you there now? Seems silly to be living in a place you could be getting income from." Unlike Cavendish, Duncan kept his tone mild, inviting confidence.

Bevilacqua's face and voice were bland. "I don't have tenants for this house, which means my cash flow is reduced."

"You don't plan to stay here long-term then?"

"Not once I can find a new place in Pittsburgh. The city is more my style, if you know what I mean." He ran his hand over the armrest. "Why are we talking about me? Didn't you have questions about Otto?"

Cavendish said nothing, but tilted her head to scrutinize her partner.

Duncan noted the man's shift away from himself and detected a note of unease. He made a note to follow up on Robert Bevilacqua's background. "Tell me, how well did you know Mr. McDonough?"

Bevilacqua relaxed a bit, bringing his hands down so he could examine his nails. "As well as any landlord knows his tenants. Which is to say, barely at all. I knew what he put on his rental application and the contract, and not much more."

"Did you know where he worked?"

"He was a groundskeeper at Blue Mountain Racetrack down in West Virginia."

"He took care of the dogs?"

"Oh, heavens no. Not directly, that is. As far as I know, he only did maintenance around the track, mowing the lawn, probably general upkeep. I don't think he had anything to do with the animals, except maybe cleaning out the kennels." Bevilacqua clasped his hands and settled one leg over the other. He looked definitely more at ease.

"Would it surprise you to know we found a dog at the scene?"

Bevilacqua raised his eyebrows. "Very, considering Otto wasn't a pet person. That and he never notified me he had a dog. I allow animals, but the resident has to sign a contract rider and pay an extra deposit."

Duncan lifted an eyebrow. "You're sure it was a pet?"

"What else could it be?"

Duncan made a note. "How long has he rented from you?"

If the landlord had any other questions about animals, he didn't seem keen to ask them. "Five or six years, maybe? A while now."

"Did you know him before then?"

"Hell, no. I put an ad in the paper, he answered it. His credit checked, he had money, his references were clean, I rented him the house. The end."

Duncan gazed at him. "You didn't talk to him outside your relationship of landlord and tenant? I mean, you didn't hang out for a beer or see him at work?"

He snorted. "No. I doubt Otto McDonough and I have the same taste in, well, anything really. We had a business relationship, nothing more. I didn't call him socially, only saw him if he reported a problem, which he rarely did, and I didn't mix with him at work because I don't care for dog racing. It bores me."

"You're unaware of anyone who might have had a gripe against Mr. McDonough?" Cavendish asked. "Anyone he might have argued with?"

Bevilacqua spread his hands. "Haven't got a clue. Sorry."

Duncan stood. "Well, thank you for your time. If you think of anything else, anything at all, please give me a call. Doesn't matter if you think it's important or not. If it has to do with Mr. McDonough, I'd like to hear it." He handed over a business card.

Cavendish followed suit. She didn't say anything, but gave her own card.

Bevilacqua took them and stood. "Understood, but don't hold your breath waiting for me to be in touch." He ushered them out.

Back in the car, Cavendish said, "What's with all the please and thank you bullshit?" She clicked her seatbelt.

"I find people are more cooperative if you show some common courtesy." He started the car and pulled out.

"Good luck with that." She glanced at him. "What's your takeaway?"

"It seemed that the relationship between the two men had been straight-up business, landlord and tenant," Duncan said. "But he's too casual. Call me a cynic, but there's something else in play there."

She twitched a shoulder. "You may have a Boy Scout's manners, but at least you also have instinct."

Duncan bit back a response and drove.

CHAPTER SEVEN

* * *

Since Sally had not taken her laptop to the office, she went home to do some more computer research. Also, she'd have access to snacks while working from her apartment.

Once there, she poured herself a glass of iced tea, sliced up an apple, and went to her office. The case file from Kim had contained all the official records and background checks, but she wanted to know more. She'd learned the hard way that clients didn't always tell the whole story.

Ciara had a simple website, professional-looking but obviously done by herself or a low-cost builder. No flashy graphics, special effects, or fancy features. Just a few black and white pages, with Ciara's photo, professional credentials, and a contact page. It had come up near the top of the search results, though, so Ciara must be doing something right to get herself so highly ranked.

Sally went back to her list of search results. There were a few hits on review sites, the online Yellow Pages, and a site listing accounting professionals in the area. Sally looked at the ratings. Ciara had a solid four stars out of a possible five. Not bad. After all, not everybody would be thrilled with the services provided. As a t-shirt Sally had once seen said, "You can't please everyone. You're not pizza."

She skimmed the list of comments. Most repeated what she'd heard this morning and praised Ciara's professionalism, speed, and friendliness. Sally paid particular attention to the one-star reviews. A few were clearly cases of sour grapes and seemed to be people who felt they'd been owed a refund, or a bigger one, than they'd gotten. Those Sally brushed off. But two others hinted at something more than an irritation about the size of their checks. "This woman made everything very confusing," a review wrote. "I have a small business. It can't be that complicated. It seemed like Mrs. Delmonico deliberately mixed everything up as though she wanted me to not know what was going on." Another reviewer had a similar complaint. "My nonprofit makes way less than twenty-five grand a year and something that should have been way simple wasn't. Got the definite impression she tried to be shifty. WOULD NOT RECOMMEND."

Sally clicked through the usernames, looking for any helpful identifying information. The problem with review sites was the users could be as anonymous as they wanted. The first review, from A.S. Webber, fell into that category. The profile had nothing beyond the name, not a location, not a business, email, or phone number.

She went over to the second reviewer. This one held a little more information. The name was only listed as N. Weaver, but at least the person had listed a location, Uniontown. N. Weaver had also listed his, or her, title: Director of Finance at Fayette County Farmers Co-op. Jackpot.

She opened another tab and in no time had located the website for the co-op, which appeared to be an association for small farmers in the county. Some of the members barely qualified as farms in Sally's mind, more like oversized backyard gardens that produced way more food than the owners could consume. The co-op provided a way to unload the leftovers and avoid food waste. She located the main phone number on the Contact page and dialed. Almost immediately, a message played, saying the number was out of service.

Next up she looked into River City Hounds. The Pittsburgh mailing address listed only a post office box, but also listed a phone number and an email address for general information. Sally took several minutes to look at the photos of the dogs on the site. They were beautiful animals. A page titled "Find a Friend for Life" showed at least six dogs in various colors, black, dark red, a fawn, and several striped ones the description referred to as "brindle." Another page, called "Winners," showed all the dogs that had been adopted with their new families.

Stop wasting time. She clicked to the About page, found the names for the board of directors and a phone number, which she dialed.

After three rings, a woman answered. "River City Hounds, Annie speaking. How may I help you?"

Sally glanced at the page. Annie Norquist. "Yes, hi. My name is Sally Castle. I'm..." She stopped. She no longer worked with the public defender's office. "I'm looking for the person who handles your finances. Can you help me?"

"Patricia? She's our treasurer. May I ask what this is about?"

Another check of the website listed the woman as Patricia Dennister. "I'm an attorney representing Ciara Delmonico in her fraud case."

There was a long pause. "Oh," Annie finally said.

On second thought, maybe she shouldn't have called. Too late now. She pressed on. "Are you a volunteer with the rescue?"

"We're an adoption group," Annie responded, a bit automatically. "No. Well yes. I'm the president of the board."

"I see. I'm preparing Mrs. Delmonico's defense, and I'd like to get some background information. Is now a good time?"

"Well, um." Annie felt uncomfortable; that came across the phone quite clearly. "I don't...I don't think I should. I didn't have much to do with the finances anyway. Sorry."

Sally found it hard to believe that the president of an organization wouldn't know about its finances, but she let it pass. "Understood. Could you give me a number to contact Ms. Dennister?"

"I'm sorry," Annie said again. "I just...I don't think that's advisable. I mean, I wouldn't give out Pat's information to anyone regardless, but in this situation...I'm sure you understand." A deep bark sounded over the line.

"Of course. I understand completely." Sally had a thought. "I've been looking at your website. They are lovely dogs." Maybe if Annie relaxed, she'd be more willing to talk about Ciara.

Now off the topic of finances, Annie's voice warmed. "Oh, we think so. So gentle and loving. Big couch potatoes, too, despite their reputation for speed."

"Too bad I live in an apartment. No space for a big dog."

"You'd be surprised. They do well in apartments, mostly because they sleep so much and are generally quiet. A couple walks a day is all they need."

Sally laughed. "Are you trying to sell me?"

"Habit. I apologize."

"No problem." Sally paused. "If you speak to Ms. Dennister, would you please mention I called?"

The guarded tone immediately came back to Annie's voice. "Oh, um, certainly. I...Ciara...well, I shouldn't say anything. As I said, I wasn't really involved anyway."

Sally said goodbye and clicked off. What an odd conversation. What kind of president was uninvolved in her group's money?

Pushing aside the question, Sally turned to any researcher's best friend: the internet. But it turned out a lot of Patricia or P. Dennisters lived in the Pittsburgh area. Contacting all of them would be foolish. She went back to the RCH website, found the email address link, and clicked it to send a message asking that Patricia contact her in regards to Ciara. Of course, the prosecution had most likely warned the group against talking to the defense. Sally'd been foolish to think they would. It would explain Annie's hesitation earlier, although not her thin excuse of not knowing anything about the money situation. If she'd simply been advised not to speak with defense counsel, why not say that and be done?

Sally shut the laptop and returned to the kitchen. She'd just have to cross her fingers and hope Patricia Dennister was the type of person who didn't listen to her lawyer.

Chapter Eight

Duncan and Cavendish made it back to HQ a little before four o'clock. He checked a map. It would take twenty to thirty minutes, at least, to get to Blue Mountain. He called the track, but as expected, the manager or anyone who might be able to give him information about Otto McDonough had left for the day. They would go first thing tomorrow morning.

Cavendish shut down her computer. "You ready?"

He looked up. "I suppose. There's nothing more to be done."

She shrugged. "There's a fine line between hitting it hard and brown-nosing."

Her cool tone stung. Did she think he was only working hard to impress her? "I've never been a clock-puncher."

"I didn't say you were." She stood and grabbed her keys. "Follow me. Or not. Your call."

Part of him wanted to make his excuses and head home. But right from the time they'd been introduced, Duncan had a niggling suspicion Cavendish viewed him, or at least his abilities, with skepticism. The last thing he wanted was to come off as not wanting to be part of the new team.

The parking lot at Whiskey & Rye was nearly full, a good sign. Duncan nabbed one of the few remaining spots and met Cavendish by the door. "Before we go in, what's the specialty?"

"Booze or food?"

"This time, just drinks."

"It changes daily." She went inside and over to the bar. A large, hand-

53

lettered chalkboard proclaimed the day's selections. "Pick your poison. What do you like?"

He studied the board. "What've they got?"

A young man dressed in a W&R t-shirt and jeans had come over while they were talking. "Evening, Jenny. Who's the new guy?"

Cavendish pointed. "Frank, this is Jim Duncan. He's our latest FNG. Jim, this is Frank Gilmartin. He's our favorite bartender."

FNG? Okay, he was the freaking new guy, at least to this section, but did she have to say it to the bartender? He shook hands with Gilmartin. "What's your recommendation?"

Gilmartin waved at the board. "Our list is extensive. But, if this is your first visit, I recommend our oak-barrel-aged single malt. Good taste, smooth finish. I've never had a complaint."

"Sold."

Cavendish ordered the same, and they mingled with a few other troopers from HQ for a bit. But it didn't take long for Cavendish to maneuver him away from the guys and toward a table. "Let's sit down. Oh, I forgot to mention, tradition says first round is on you. Sort of an initiation."

Of course, it was.

Cavendish lifted her glass. "Welcome to the Troop B Criminal Investigation Division, Trooper First Class Duncan."

Did he detect a bit of sarcasm when she said the rank? Or was he reading too much into things? He'd never been sensitive about his relatively low rank considering his time-in-service before. Cavendish seemed to have a knack for bringing all his unacknowledged insecurities to the front. "Thank you." He took a sip. The whiskey was as smooth as Gilmartin had promised. He approved. Good thing he had to limit himself to one.

She leaned back. "So tell me. Fourteen years as a patrol officer and still a trooper. Couldn't you get promoted?"

I knew it. She took the lengthy service as an indication he didn't have the chops. "I never tried. When the promotion cycle came around, we didn't have an opening in Uniontown, and I didn't want to go where the corporal positions were open."

"You liked Fayette-nam that much?" she asked in a tone of disbelief.

"As a matter of fact, I do." He didn't rebut her unsaid accusation. Blowing his own horn would make it look like he was apologizing for his career. He'd rather let his work speak for itself. "Popular place."

"Good food, good drinks, what do you expect? Don't change the subject." She pierced him with her icy blue eyes. "Why the sudden move to Criminal Investigation?"

"It's not that sudden. I had the opportunity to be involved in several incidents that went beyond normal patrol duties over the past couple years. I decided I liked it."

She took a drink and studied him over the rim of her glass. "What makes you think you can cut it?"

He took his time answering. *Two can play this game.* "Those incidents I mentioned? They were murders. I got the job done. If I can get it done in uniform, I'm sure I'll be equal to the task in CI."

Her expression didn't change, but she did narrow her eyes a touch. "I guess we'll see about that."

* * *

Sally flipped the page of a magazine and looked at the clock. Almost six and no sign of Jim. He'd texted her earlier to tell her about after-work drinks, but he'd be home by five-thirty. She hadn't heard anything since. Hopefully he was okay.

As if summoned by thought, she heard the rumble of his Jeep as it pulled into the driveway. A couple minutes later, his footstep sounded in the kitchen. Beside her, Rizzo lifted his head, then went back to snoozing. She set aside the magazine.

He came into the living room. "Sorry I'm late. I had to clear my head."

She got up and crossed to him. A person who didn't know him well might miss the minute lines on his forehead and the tension in his shoulders, but she didn't. "What's wrong?" She put her hands on either side of his neck. *He's tighter than a drum.* "Didn't things go well? Wait. Go get into sweats, I'll

55

get you a beer, and we'll talk."

Minutes later, they were seated on the couch, Rizzo stretched in front of them. Jim took a long pull from a bottle of Edmund Fitzgerald porter. Sally turned him so she could massage his back. "How'd it go? And don't tell me fine. I've rarely seen you this wound up."

He told her about the murder scene, the decomposed body, and the maltreated greyhound.

"Trust you to get assigned a homicide on your first day. But that's not what's got you all knotted up," she said.

"No, that was all routine. But I'm pretty sure my partner thinks I'm a dunce."

"Oh, come on. It's been one day. She doesn't even know you yet."

He told her about Jenny Cavendish, her veiled references to his being a patrol officer for over a decade, and how he had felt second-guessed all day. "Well, I won't say you're imagining things. I know you better than that. But isn't it possible you're reading something that isn't there? Maybe it's your nerves coming out."

He turned to face her. "I'm not nervous. Hell, why should I be? I'm not a rookie."

"But this is a new assignment for you. All the familiar faces aren't there. Instead, you have to learn to work with a whole new cast." She leaned against the back of the couch, head against her palm. "I don't care how much time you've been a cop. It's natural to be a little antsy going into a different environment."

"I don't have any doubts about my ability." He set down the bottle. "Although Cavendish sure as shit seems to. And Ferguson, although she wasn't as bad."

"Then you'll just have to prove them wrong." She leaned over to kiss him.

He brushed back her hair. "Will do, Counselor. Enough about me. You had a big first day yourself."

She recapped her day, including as much as she was ethically allowed to about Ciara Delmonico and her case. "Funny. You said your victim had a greyhound?"

"We found one at the scene. There seems to be a question about whether it was a pet or not. Why?"

"It could be a coincidence. I mean, Ciara's charges involve a greyhound rescue group, and your victim had a dog. And worked at a dog-racing track." She nibbled a fingernail. "But you know how I feel about coincidences."

"The same as I do." He got up and took the empty beer bottle to the kitchen.

Sally followed. Looking to change the subject, she asked, "What do you think will happen to that poor dog?"

"He'll be taken care of. The Animal Control officer is going to try and get him placed with an adoption group."

"I bet he's beautiful."

"He will be, once he's gotten a vet check and eaten a few dozen healthy meals." After one last kiss, he let her go and headed for the stairs. "I'll be right back. I need some of that body cream you have. I think I have a raw spot from the damn shoulder holster."

She darted around him and grabbed his hands. "I'll give you a hand."

He lifted an eyebrow. "What about dinner?"

She leaned in and kissed him, and pulled him up the stairs. "It'll wait."

Chapter Nine

Duncan inhaled the heady aroma of freshly brewed coffee as he entered the kitchen. "I could get used to this."

Sally, seated at the table, paper, and breakfast in front of her, didn't glance up from her reading. "Get used to what?"

"Coming down to have my coffee brewed and ready." He poured a travel mug full. He'd have to invest in a thermos and take the entire pot with him. Well, almost the entire pot. Sally would rightly take her share.

"Despite last night, I have not decided to move in. The coffee is made because I wanted some." She lifted her cup and gave him a sly wink.

"Then I guess I have to come up with a more persuasive argument. Are you going to drive back to Uniontown later?"

"I have to. That's where my office is. Plus, I need fresh clothes."

"See you tonight?"

"That's the plan."

"At this rate, you might as well move in." He watched her closely. She never passed on an opportunity to spend the night. Why the reticence to make it permanent? Unless she was fine with things the way they stood. But damn, it felt nice having another warm body beside him all night. One that didn't shed long golden hairs all over the sheets.

She stood and came up beside him, put her arms around his waist and kissed him, hard. Then she stepped back. "Jenny Cavendish doesn't know how good she's got it."

"That's what I'm planning to show her." He adjusted his tie. "I'll have plenty of opportunity today. We need to go to talk to the folks at the dog track and do some follow-up on the landlord. What about you?"

"Kim's only got me on the one case, so I'll probably spend the day learning about Ciara's work with RCH. What was the name of the track?"

"Blue Mountain Racing."

"I'll keep my eyes open for a connection. Oh. And I'll make pasta for dinner if you grill some shrimp."

"Your place or mine?"

She tilted her head to the side. "You are the one with the grill."

"Deal."

Cavendish was not at her desk when Duncan arrived at HQ. Yesterday, he'd ended feeling he was on the defensive. He had no intention of spending day two the same way. By the time she came in five minutes later, he had a plan for the day.

She set her purse and a stainless-steel travel mug on her desk. "Arriving extra early doesn't earn points, you know."

He met her gaze, determined to stay calm. "I've only been here five minutes, maybe ten."

She drummed her fingers on her chair, and her nails clicked on the aluminum frame. "Let's talk about what we need to do today."

"I thought about it while I was waiting." He pushed over the sheet of paper on which he'd jotted his thoughts. "What do you think about starting with the race track? That could take most of the morning. Then we can spend this afternoon getting a little more background on the victim, as well as checking into Robert Bevilacqua."

Cavendish read the notes with a look of grudging admiration. "Sounds logical to me. I'll drive."

They arrived at Blue Mountain Racing about forty-five minutes later. The track was located in West Virginia and just across the state line. The parking lot was nearly empty at nine in the morning. Shutters covered the ticket windows, but a gate at the side stood open. Maybe the employee entrance. He took a moment to survey the landscape. Gravel lot, neatly painted buildings, a smudge of mountain scenery in the background. It probably looked very different at night.

Cavendish headed for the open gate. "You coming?"

He followed. Once inside, he called, "Hello? Anybody here?" Somewhere off to his left, he could hear running. Four feet, not two, judging from the sound. Maybe a training track. Directly ahead, he saw the grandstand, and a long, low building off to his right. The relative silence unnerved him. Aside from the running and a few human voices, he heard no indication of animals.

A young woman leading a slim, muzzled red dog exited the building to the right. "Morning. Can I help you?"

The troopers showed their badges. "We're looking for someone in charge," Cavendish said.

She nodded behind her. "Track manager is in there. Ask for Gary Conaway." She led the dog, who had not made a peep throughout the conversation, toward the sound of voices.

Duncan and Cavendish entered the building. The main room held rows of kennels, nearly every one of them occupied by a greyhound. The color variety was stunning. Not a single dog barked as they wandered down the row, but pairs of large, brown eyes followed his movements. At the end of the building, they found the office. An older man who looked like he spent a good deal of his time outdoors sat at the desk, shuffling papers and comparing them to a computer screen. "Left the gate open again, did they? This is the kennel, not the track, and the first race isn't until this afternoon."

Duncan held out his badge wallet, as did Cavendish. "We're not here for the racing," he said. "Are you Gary Conaway?"

The man looked away from his sheets and blinked. He studied the badge. "Pennsylvania State Police? Kinda out of your area, aren't you?"

"Little bit." Duncan tucked away the wallet. "Are you Mr. Conaway?"

"That's me. What can I help you with?" He held out a massive hand.

"Do you have an employee named Otto McDonough?" Duncan asked.

"Used to." Conaway leaned back. "We fired him, late May? Early June? Something like that."

"Why'd you let him go?" Cavendish asked.

"Because he did a crap-ass job." Conaway snorted. "All he had to do was clean the kennels, make sure the dogs had clean crates, keep the water bowls full, and sweep the building twice a day. The third time Heather—she's one of my trainers—complained of empty bowls and crates that smelled of urine, I gave him his walking papers."

"We saw the crates as I walked through," Duncan said. He was determined not to let Cavendish take over the conversation, as she almost had yesterday with Bevilacqua. "Not much in them to clean."

"Little bit of carpet-like lining, that's all."

"Can't be all that comfortable for the greyhound."

"Don't tell me you're one of those anti-racing folks." Conaway leaned forward. "We take care of our dogs. They're clean, well-fed, and we have a crack vet staff. I'd say most folks in the racing world care very much for the dogs they breed, or own, or train. It's a different world. Not better, not worse, just different."

Duncan held up his hands. "I'm not here to discuss the merits of greyhound racing with you. We want to know about Mr. McDonough."

"He was a lousy employee. Lazy, a slob, a little too fond of cheap booze, and if there's one person here who looked at these dogs purely as a commodity, it was him." Conaway reached for a toothpick. "What's he done now? He in trouble up in Pennsylvania? Can't be something he did here, or I'd be talking to a West Virginia trooper."

"He's dead. Shot." Duncan watched for a reaction.

Conaway stared for a moment, open-mouthed. "Damn."

Cavendish removed a notebook from her pocket. "Did anybody here at the track have a gripe with him?"

"Nothing serious enough to kill him. I mean, none of the trainers liked Otto because of the sloppy way he took care of the dogs. Most track employees gave him a wide berth. But murder? No, can't think of anybody who hated him that much."

"He had a dog at his house," Duncan said. "A greyhound. Did you have anything to do with that?"

"Absolutely not." Conway's face reddened. "We don't give away our retired racers to barely adequate employees. They go to reputable adoption groups.

If a dog is very successful on the track, he or she might go for breeding."

"This one looked to be in pretty bad condition. Male, black. He'd be a beauty if he was in shape."

"You could be describing one of a dozen dogs."

"His ears were tattooed." Duncan held out his phone.

"This is useful information. Let me see." Conaway put on a pair of reading glasses and looked at the pictures. "Every dog gets two tattoos. This one is the dog's birth month, the second digit of the year he was born, and his assigned birth order. From this, I can tell your boy is about five and a half years old, and the third one in his litter to be tattooed."

"What about the other one?" Cavendish asked.

"That's his litter registration number. It's assigned by the NGA." Conaway pulled forward his keyboard. "The National Greyhound Association. Racers are purebreds, but they're registered with the NGA, not the AKC. Using this information, I can tell you all about your dog, including his lineage, who owned him, and where he raced. I can even get you his racing record." He tapped away on the keyboard. When the results popped up, he sat back. "Well, I'll be damned."

Duncan studied him. "What?"

"Johnny's Pixelated. That's the dog. He used to be one of ours. He retired last March. Good racer. He ran the max, until age five." He rubbed his chin. "What the hell was he doing with Otto? We sent Johnny to the folks at the Wheeling Island adoption kennel, but last I heard, he ended up with a group out of Pittsburgh."

"Could there have been a mistake?"

"I suppose, but that's a damned big mistake."

A vision of the caged, emaciated animal flashed in Duncan's mind. "I don't think McDonough was keeping Johnny as a pet." He described the conditions of the dog and its so-called home to the track manager.

Conaway's face grew darker with every word. "Son of a bitch. He raced him. Otto raced Johnny, I mean. I'd lay money on it."

"But if the dog retired—"

"Not anywhere legal, mind you. But the cage, the freezer of raw meat, jars of vitamins, steroids, that tells me Otto doped the dog. Probably for illicit racing." Conaway stared at the screen. "There was a big story down here last spring. They even arrested someone."

Cavendish looked up. "What happened?"

"One of the volunteers, a guy who helped transport the hounds, cherry-picked ex-racers meant for adoption to use in illegal racing. Looks like the bastard got Johnny." He stood. "Let's go talk to Heather."

"Before we do that, would you print off the information on the history?" Duncan asked.

"Sure." Conaway hit print, waited a minute, then handed a sheet to Duncan. Then he led the way out of the kennels, past an area that looked like a divided exercise pen, and toward the sound of pounding feet.

Perhaps half a dozen dogs sprinted around a track, coats gleaming in the sun. Duncan had never been much of a fan of animal racing. Not dogs, horses, or even the guinea pigs the kids raced for fun at county fairs. But the sight of the greyhounds thundering down what appeared to be packed sand inspired awe. Lured by a bit of fluff, the six sets of legs worked so fast, it looked as though the animals flew, barely touching the ground. The whiplike tails streamed behind them, lean bodies and heads laid out in a straight line, every set of eyes fixated on the fake rabbit.

"Amazing, aren't they?" Conaway asked when he noticed Duncan's stare. "I could go into long, boring details, but you are seeing pure athleticism. The entire body is form serving function. These dogs were born to race."

"Why are they muzzled?"

"To keep them from hurting each other. The lure gets the prey drive going. Last thing we need is a pack of hounds fighting each other over a bit of fake fur on a trolley." Conaway glanced around, put his fingers to his lips, and whistled. "Heather! Come over here when you're done."

The dogs streamed across the finish line and eventually came to a halt. They panted, sides heaving, tongues clearly lolling out of the long mouths, even with the muzzles. "Hold on, Gary." Heather turned out to be the woman who had directed Duncan to the office. She checked a clipboard, talked to a couple of helpers who led the dogs away, then trotted over. "What's up?"

63

"This is Troopers Duncan and Cavendish, from the Pennsylvania State Police. They have some questions," Conaway said.

Duncan nodded toward the track. "That was…amazing. Do they race every day?"

Heather shook her head. "A dog races only once or twice a week, and these dogs won't go today. Sprints only. They're off to drink up now and have a good, long sleep. But I don't think you came all the way from Pennsylvania to talk about dog racing."

"No." Cavendish shot her partner a dirty look. "Do you remember a man who used to work here named Otto McDonough?"

Duncan refrained from shaking his head, but barely. Unbelievable. She was going to hold a bit of curiosity against him?

Heather made a face. "Yes, unfortunately. I'm glad we fired him. Talk about a poor excuse for a human and a lousy worker to boot."

Conaway broke in. "Someone shot him. You remember Johnny's Pixelated?"

"He was a sweetie. Good racer, too," Heather said.

"Otto had him locked in a cage," Conaway said. "Know about that big scandal last spring?"

"Of course. Disgusting."

"Johnny must have gotten caught up in it. I thought they'd found all those dogs and rescued them, but guess not."

Duncan would have preferred to deliver the information about Mc-Donough. From a glance, he could tell Cavendish thought the same. But he rolled with it. "You both keep saying this Johnny had a good racing record. Why didn't the owner breed him?"

"There are multiple levels of racing," Heather said. "Johnny ran at the B level. He had a fair amount of success, too. But breeding is expensive, and Johnny wasn't quite good enough for that."

Duncan looked at Heather closely. "Do you know anyone who would have wanted to harm Mr. McDonough? Or why he'd have a dog in his house?"

Heather's shock was genuine, no doubt about it. "As for your first question, sure. Everybody here would have liked to thump Otto between the eyes at one point or another. He couldn't be trusted with the simplest tasks, and it made double the work. It put the dogs in danger, too. You said his killer shot him?"

"Three times in the chest."

The young woman shook her head, setting her hair swaying. "I don't think anyone disliked him that much. He wasn't worth the time. Once the track ownership fired him, we all basically forgot about him"

"What about the dog?" Cavendish asked.

"I don't know why he'd have Johnny. As dogs retire, they're sent to the WIGAC, at least here in West Virginia."

"I'm sorry, the what?"

"The Wheeling Island Greyhound Adoption Center. Trainers, like me, are the people who work to place dogs who come off the track, or any adoptable dog, with groups. Unless the owner decides to breed, of course. From the WIGAC, they are adopted or go to other groups to be placed with families." She bit her lip. "I remember putting Johnny into the transport van myself. I was so happy, imagining him with people who were gonna love him."

Duncan had heard all sorts of horror stories about greyhound racing. Much like horse racing, dedicated activists believed the industry was cruel and inhumane, dogs treated as nothing more than commodities, pulled from active racing for not being fast enough. But he had no problem believing the people in front of him loved their hounds and wanted the best for them. Heather looked to be on the brink of tears. The expression on Conaway's face made Duncan think Otto McDonough had gotten off easy, despite being murdered. "Can you think of any reason, no matter how unbelievable, Johnny wouldn't have made it to retirement?"

She dashed a hand across her eyes and took a breath. "Just like that guy this past spring, someone in between the WIGAC and a second adoption group could have redirected the shipment. Or even just one dog. As I said, Johnny had a fairly successful racing career at his level. His owner had no interest in breeding him, but he won quite a bit. If Otto wanted a dog to race illegally, Johnny would be a good candidate. I suppose he could have used bribery to get himself a retired hound. It sounds fantastic to say, but"—she paused—"I can't think of another explanation."

"Thank you." Duncan made a note. "Do you happen to remember the name of the adoption group slated to take delivery of Johnny? Or was he adopted through the state center?"

"Oh yes." Heather glanced at her boss. "He went to River City Hounds up in Pittsburgh. I spoke to the president myself. I remember telling her whoever adopted Johnny would get a wonderful dog."

Chapter Ten

After arriving at the office, Sally contacted the district attorney's office and asked about possible appointment times to talk to the prosecutor. Jim's words echoed in her mind. She wasn't sure what was holding her back. She spent most of the week at his place. If she took him up on the offer, she could eliminate the need to either pack a bag of clothes or stop at her apartment before heading to work. She felt at home at his place. She loved Rizzo and Jim was easygoing, she could easily see herself happy living there. The only thing that wouldn't change was her driving time.

But it all felt so fast. Sure, they'd known each other for two years, but the romantic relationship was new. Then again, neither of them were youngsters, fresh out of school. Her mother would be semiscandalized, but when had that ever stopped Sally from doing anything she wanted to do?

She pushed the decision from her mind. She could analyze her turbulent emotions later. She called her client. "What does your schedule look like tomorrow morning?"

"Until this is over, I'm wide open. Why?"

"I'd like to schedule a meeting with a representative from the DA's office. Does ten o'clock work?" A sudden thought struck her. "I'm sorry, I should have called you first. But I wanted to make sure to get on his calendar."

"It's okay. As I said, I don't have anything else to do. But why would we meet with him?" Ciara's voice sounded puzzled.

"I want to hear what he has to say and what, if anything, they'd give as a plea bargain. I know you said you didn't want one, but I want to hear any offer for myself."

"If you say so." Ciara spoke a bit slowly. "I'll be there."

Sally hung up the phone. The information she'd requested yesterday had not yet arrived. She'd interviewed enough of Ciara's other clients to know which ones would make good defense witnesses. The RCH treasurer had not called back.

She went to get a second cup of coffee and returned to her desk, where she pulled up the group's website. Once again, she spent a few minutes looking at pictures. "They're so beautiful," she said, as she heard the front door open.

"Who's beautiful?" Kim asked as she went to her desk.

"The greyhounds." Sally scrolled down the page. "Come here and see."

Kim kicked off her shoes and walked over to stand behind Sally to look. "Um, they're just dogs."

"Yeah, but look at them. Have you ever seen such a striking animal?"

"Meh. I'm not a fan. Too much poop to clean up. At least cats do their business in a box." She got herself a cup of coffee and came back to sit in front of Sally, stirring the pale brown liquid with a bamboo stick. "Is this about Ciara? Are you spending billable time looking at dogs?"

Sally pulled back, stung. Surely she could take five minutes to look at pictures, couldn't she? "I'm not spending hours goofing off and passing that on to our client. Yesterday I interviewed Ciara and some of her other clients. I've got a list of potential witnesses." Sally tapped the legal pad next to her. "I also spoke with the RCH president and asked to get in touch with their treasurer, but I haven't received a call from her. Of course, later I thought that maybe the prosecutor warned them off, but it was worth a gamble."

"Why talk to them?"

"I might be able to persuade them to settle and avoid litigation."

Kim sipped. "Did the president pass on the message, or do you think the request went into the circular file?"

"I'm not sure." Sally doodled on the pad. "She acted kind of squirrelly. The president, I mean. Annie...wait a sec." Sally clicked over to the web page that listed RCH's board of officers. "Annie Norquist."

"How so?"

"She didn't want to speak to me, which I can believe because I'm representing the woman who allegedly ripped them off. But when I asked for her version of the incident, she said she didn't have much to do with the finances. Not that she'd been advised against talking."

Kim lifted an eyebrow. "Well, there's not having much to do with them, as in she doesn't write the checks or balance the books, and there's not being aware of anything. Which is it?"

"I don't know." Sally navigated over to the Events page. "Looks like the group will be at Market Square today for some local vendor event the city is holding. RCH calls it a meet and greet."

"Where you adopt one?"

"I don't think so. I mean, there's a link to an application here, and they say someone will call and interview you before you're matched with a dog. Maybe it's come meet the hounds and get to know them. A little advocacy, a little fundraising." Sally checked the clock. "They'll be there starting at noon. It's not quite ten now."

Kim stood. "You thinking of going up to the city, maybe catch someone at this event? Is this billable?"

"Why not? They'll have a harder time brushing me off if we're face to face." Sally looked up at her friend. "And I'm charging Ciara half the federal rate of out-of-county mileage, as well as honoring the rate you quoted her."

"Good." Kim walked to her desk, but stopped and turned at the archway. "Just one thing. Don't be a sucker and come home with a dog."

* * *

Duncan slipped off his jacket and sat down at his desk. Cavendish dropped a clipped stack of pages in front of him. "More on the victim, McDonough. What do you think about the trip to the track?" she asked

"That greyhounds might be the fastest animals I've ever seen. Watching them run was incredible."

She scoffed. "I meant about what Conaway and the trainer said."

"Interesting that River City Hounds is the group who should have taken delivery of Johnny's Pixelated. A friend of mine is representing a woman in an embezzlement case involving the group." He reached out for the paper. "What are you reading?"

"More background on the victim." Cavendish passed over half the stack. "You think there's a connection?"

"I don't know. But it's quite a coincidence that the name has cropped up again. By nature, I'm suspicious of coincidences."

She went back to reading. "Good to know."

He knew she was evaluating him. Had the roles been reversed, he'd have done the same. But he wished he understood the criteria she was using for judgment. *All I can do is my job.* He paged through the reports without speaking. Cavendish had scorned anything he'd said that didn't directly relate to the job. If she wanted small talk, she could start it.

She didn't.

Several minutes later, though, he broke the silence. "Looks like our boy had a car accident about three months ago. Damn, he killed a kid."

She looked up. "Where did the accident occur?"

"Markleysburg, last April." He ran his finger down the page. "McDonough admitted to drinking, but his blood alcohol tested under the limit, although just barely. It had been pouring, bad visibility. He claims he never saw the kid dart across the street. From what it says here, a state police investigation cleared him of any wrongdoing."

Cavendish tilted her head. "What was the kid's name?"

"Michael Fisher, age seven. Lived right in the town."

"Is that all?"

He kept reading. " There is a write-up of an altercation between a guy named Kyle Sullivan and McDonough a couple weeks later. No charges were filed, but according to witnesses, Sullivan got pretty hot under the collar. Called McDonough a murderer."

"What did he do in response?"

"Nothing serious, according to the report. Just said he was sorry the kid died, but he didn't do anything wrong, and maybe parents should keep better tabs on their children during heavy rains. Then he stormed off." Duncan noted Sullivan's name and address. "Sullivan lives just outside the town limits. I'll try and get an interview, maybe this afternoon."

Cavendish looked at the clock on the wall. "It's noon. I'm going to run out for lunch. See you in an hour." She grabbed her jacket and left.

Duncan watched her go. No invitation to join her, no offer to bring something back. No doubt the jury was still out on him as far as Jenny Cavendish was concerned.

Chapter Eleven

S ally timed it so she arrived in Pittsburgh's Market Square around one-thirty. People filled the area, a large, brick courtyard ringed by a one-way street, shops, and trendy restaurants, even on a weekday afternoon. The event appeared to be some sort of fair, judging by the collection of pop-up tents, each one featuring an artist. Collections of paintings, pottery, handmade jewelry, and clothing tempted her from every angle. She didn't see any dogs, so she strolled among the vendors, browsing and keeping her ears open for the sound of barking.

After ten minutes, she stopped at a tent featuring a selection of ceramic jars and called over to a young man working there. "Excuse me, maybe you can help me."

"Sure thing," he said. "What do you want the jar for?"

"Oh, no, sorry. These are lovely, but that's not my question." She set down a squat blue container decorated with flowers. "I thought a dog group was here, but I haven't seen them yet. Do you know where they are? Or if they're here at all?"

"Oh, you're looking for the greyhounds." He pointed off to a corner of the square masked by tents. "Over that way. You can't miss them once you get there. The hounds are pretty big."

"Thanks." She picked the blue jar up again. "On second thought, I'll take this one." After all, the guy had been helpful. At least she could buy some of his stuff.

After she'd paid for her purchase, she slung the fabric shopping bag he'd given her over her shoulder and headed to the far corner. Once she cleared the aisle, she saw a group of people clustered around a table. One of them moved to reveal a long white table with a placard on it that read "River City Hounds" in black script edged in gold. Four dogs were grouped around the table, three standing against people and one lying on its side, accepting belly rubs from the small girl kneeling beside it.

As Sally walked up, a woman turned to greet her. "Hello! Come to meet the hounds?"

"As a matter of fact, yes. I've been looking all over for you. I'm surprised. I thought for sure I'd hear the sound of barking. You know, excited dogs with all these people."

The woman laughed. "Doubtful. Greyhounds are usually calm and aren't very vocal."

A tawny gold dog with deep brown eyes and a patch of white on his chest came over, sniffed Sally's pants, and promptly leaned against her with unexpected force. "Whoa," Sally said as she staggered a little.

"Rascal must like you." The woman held out a hand. "I'm Annie."

Sally scratched Rascal behind his velvety-soft ears. Hopefully, the group didn't have more than one Annie. "Ms. Norquist? My name is Sally Castle. I'm representing Ciara Delmonico, your former accountant. We spoke on the phone."

The open, friendly expression slid from Annie's face. "I told you. I don't think I should talk to you."

"I understand. But hear me out. I'd like to talk and hear your side of the story. Mrs. Delmonico is quite insistent she isn't guilty."

"I'm not really the best person." Annie stepped back, but her range was limited by the length of Rascal's leash. The big dog didn't move and didn't look like he wanted to. "I told you on the phone. I didn't have a lot to do with the finances."

"I know, but I find that hard to believe. You're the group's president, yes? Wouldn't you have to know about the money as part of the job?"

"Well, of course." Annie tugged the leash, but Rascal just blew out a horsey-sounding breath and continued his lean. "I mean, I approved expenditures as part of the board, and I knew roughly how much money we had. But I didn't work closely with Mrs. Delmonico or know specifics. You'd have to talk to Pat Dennister, our treasurer."

The woman holding leashes for two other dogs, a reddish one with black stripes and a black one, turned. "Did I hear my name?"

Sally could tell from Annie's expression that she'd rather have turned Sally away without letting her know Pat Dennister was in attendance. "Yes. Pat, this is Sally Castle. She's, um, well...."

Sally held out her hand. "I'm Ciara Delmonico's attorney."

Pat had a firm, brisk handshake. "Pleased to meet you. Damn shame about Ciara. I still can't believe it." Pat looked to be in her mid to late fifties. Slim of build, she stood slightly taller than Sally, with blue eyes and close-cropped silver hair. Her facial expression said "friendly, but no-nonsense." She didn't present herself as a woman who would mince words.

"What can't you believe?" Sally asked.

Annie tugged Rascal's leash, and he grudgingly moved. "I'll leave you two to talk." She walked the dog over to a new group of visitors.

Pat glanced at her dogs, both of whom were calm. The striped dog walked over to a passing couple. Pat deftly untangled the leashes. "Wouldn't have believed it about Ciara," she said. She wrapped both leashes around her hand. "I've volunteered with RCH for fifteen years, ever since we started the group. I've worked with two different accountants. Ciara was our second. She was damn good at her job, always polite and very efficient. She didn't own a hound, but she loved them. If I hadn't seen the proof with my own eyes, I'd say someone had made a mistake."

The black strolled over to Sally, who obliged her with a chin rub. "What happened?"

"You already know if you've talked to Ciara."

"I've heard her side. I want yours. Maybe there's a way to resolve this without going to court."

Pat thought for a moment and shrugged. "I probably shouldn't, but I say cut the red tape. If this helps avoid a trial, I'm all for it."

Sally liked this woman. The conversation shouldn't happen someplace as casual as a greyhound meet and greet, but her instincts told her that Pat wouldn't play games and switch her story, or go running to the prosecutor.

"We called Ciara as usual to do our taxes last February," Pat continued. "Everything went fine, routine like always. We met our tax obligations for the feds, the state, and had a nice cushion in the bank. When Ciara handed over the paper, I filed it away without even looking at it. I used to work in a bank, so I know just enough to be dangerous as the saying goes. I'd gone over the records with Ciara earlier and I was satisfied with everything."

"What did your auditor say?"

"We don't get an audit every year." Pat rubbed her nose. "It's not required. We don't have enough money and they're expensive. We had one last year, though, and there were no major issues."

"Then what?"

"About, oh, May I think, I wrote a check to cover the transport of some dogs. Didn't think anything of it. A few days later, I get a form letter from the bank. The check had been returned for insufficient funds. Then I got a phone call from my contact at the adoption kennel saying the check had bounced, but the dogs had left, and could I straighten this out. I called the bank, because we ought to have had plenty to cover the check. That's when I found out our balance was way down. I called a board meeting, naturally."

"Who in your group has access to the bank account?"

"Just the board. Me, Annie, Mary Lou Evans, she's the vice president, and Sue Hensen, she's our secretary."

"You're sure?" Sally felt a nudge on her hand and looked down. The striped hound poked her long nose under Sally's palm while the black continued to lean.

Pat chuckled. "Mitzi and Di like you. Anyway, I'm positive. That's the way we've always done it." Pat shifted on her feet. "No one admitted to making any withdrawals or payments. We called the bank, got the information from them. I called Ciara and asked for an explanation. She stood by her work and didn't know where the money went. So I called the cops and turned everything over. I'd say about a month later, end of June, some guy from the district attorney's office called. They'd run the records through a forensic accountant, I think that's what he called it. The accountant showed me his report. That's when the explanation started going over my head, but the bottom line was somebody had been tapping into the account since February. He asked a lot of the same questions you did."

A little girl holding a dripping ice cream cone walked by, and the striped dog trailed after her, tongue licking her long jaw.

"I think someone sees a free snack coming," Sally said.

Pat chuckled. "That kid looks about ready to drop that cone, and Mitzi knows it. She's no dummy." She watched the dog, but continued talking. "I told the cops the only person besides the board who'd had access to the account since February was Ciara."

Pat's story more or less tallied with what Ciara had said. "You said Mrs. Delmonico has worked for you for a while with no issues. Why do you think she decided to do this?"

"No clue. She never seemed like she needed money. I mean, she's not wealthy, but she's not hard up either. At least not that I knew about. And as I said, she loved the dogs."

"Was it a board decision to file charges?"

Pat wrinkled her nose. "Yes, but the vote was close. It was Sue's idea. She said we shouldn't let ourselves be taken advantage of and convinced the others to go along with her. I was the holdout."

Interesting. "Did you know Mrs. Delmonico continues to say she's innocent?"

"I do. I'd love for that to be true." Pat faced Sally, her face earnest, and ran her free hand over her hair. "Somebody took our money, Ms. Castle. I might not have understood the language, but when that accountant showed me his reports, I saw it plain as day. The only people who have been near our account since February are the board and Ciara. The other women have been cleared. That leaves Ciara. You tell me. Who else could it have been?"

Sally looked at Mitzi, still gazing hopefully after the child with the dripping ice cream cone. It was a good question. Kim would say it wasn't her job to answer it.

But Sally knew her conscience and sense of justice wouldn't let her leave it alone.

* * *

Michael Fisher's parents had left Markleysburg after the accident, but Duncan tracked them down at their new address in Pittsburgh. He didn't get a lot of information out of the phone call he made.

"They put it down as a no-fault," Mr. Fisher said, voice tinged with anger and disgust. "Yeah, it was raining hard. Yeah, Mikey shouldn't have darted out in the road like he did. But isn't a motorist supposed to have control of his vehicle?"

"I understand Mr. McDonough had been drinking," Duncan said.

"Not enough to warrant a DUI," Fisher spat. "Who the hell makes up those limits anyway? My son was killed. Doesn't that count for something?"

Duncan couldn't do anything more than offer his sincere condolences, which always sounded hollow. He'd caught enough of these types of calls as a patrol officer and dealt with his share of distraught family members. He refrained from telling Mr. Fisher that nothing, even when criminal charges were filed, would ever be enough. Instead, he thanked the man for his time and hung up.

Next, he looked up Kyle Sullivan but the National Law Enforcement Telecommunications System, NLETS, contained no information. He worked at one of the lumber yards in the town of Eighty Four.

Cavendish returned, holding an oversized soft drink cup from a fast food restaurant. "Did you even go to lunch?"

"I grabbed a sandwich." He told her about the conversation with Mr. Fisher.

"Not that helpful. What's the next step?"

Why did she keep asking? Why not offer a suggestion? Duncan brushed off the thought. "An interview with Kyle Sullivan."

They drove to Eighty Four and Sullivan's employer, where they showed their badges and asked to speak to Sullivan. They waited in a small, plain conference room for about fifteen minutes while someone fetched Sullivan.

Duncan's first impression of Kyle Sullivan was of a human stick. He topped Duncan by about two inches, without an ounce of fat on him. Duncan's father would have called him "stringy." Sullivan wore the plain flannel shirt, tough cargo pants, and reinforced boots of a laborer. The bones of his wrists stuck out prominently. A rugged type, more than capable of holding his own in a fight, a trait communicated through the strong grip of a callused hand. His plain face had a puzzled expression. "Troopers Duncan and Cavendish? They said you wanted to talk to me."

Duncan indicated the table and chairs. "Have a seat. Don't worry, you aren't in trouble." He sat.

Sullivan slid onto a chair. "That's good to know."

Cavendish took a seat next to Duncan and pulled out a notepad. "Mr. Sullivan. Do you know a man named Otto McDonough?"

Sullivan didn't twitch. "Unfortunately, yes."

"From where?" Duncan asked.

Sullivan ran his tongue over his lips. "I had a fight with him last spring. Is that what this is about? I'm surprised he remembers it. As I recall, he was pretty drunk."

"What was the fight about?"

The other man paused. "McDonough ran over a kid in town. It should have been a DUI and murder or whatever you call it. But he got off. I called him on it, we argued, exchanged a few punches, and that was it." He looked from Duncan to Cavendish and back. "Why? Is he claiming something else? It was months ago. Give it a rest."

Duncan fixed him with a stare. "Mr. McDonough is dead. Someone shot him in the chest."

Sullivan didn't twitch. "Well, I'll be damned. Guess there's such a thing as karma after all."

Duncan glanced at his notes and then focused on Sullivan. He looked relaxed, not particularly worried to be talking to the police. "Where were you last week Wednesday through Friday?"

"What, you think I shot him over a fist fight from five months ago?"

Cavendish looked up. "Just answer the question, please."

Sullivan's face showed no emotion. "I worked days all last week. You can check with HR, they've got my schedule."

"Where were you at night?" Duncan asked.

"Oh hell, I don't remember. Friday night, I went out drinking, I remember that. We always go at the end of the week. Wednesday and Thursday, I went home and watched TV."

"Where were you over the weekend?"

"I went fishing on Saturday with one of the same guys I went drinking with Friday night. We were up on the Casselman to try our luck with small mouth. Sunday, I bummed around the house. Again, completely alone. Sucky alibi, but it's the truth."

Duncan pushed forward his notebook. "Understood. If you'd give me the names and phone numbers of the men you were with, I'd appreciate it." He watched while Sullivan wrote. "Do you own a gun?"

Sullivan finished and shoved the notebook across the table. "I own several. Two .22 rifles, a shotgun, and two handguns. One is a Smith and Wesson .38, the other a Glock 21. All of them legally purchased and licensed."

"I didn't say they weren't." Duncan paused. "Just one more question, Mr. Sullivan. Did you know Mikey Fisher personally?"

Cavendish glanced at Duncan, then transferred her gaze back to Sullivan.

He'd been in the process of pushing himself up using the table, and his hand slipped. "Of course I did," he replied, words soft. "It's a small town. Everybody knows everyone. Mikey was a good kid." His voice caught on the last sentence.

"Thank you for your time, Mr. Sullivan. We'll be in touch if I need anything else."

Sullivan recovered his poise and left the conference room. He didn't look back.

Chapter Twelve

The first thing Duncan did when they returned to HQ was to file requests for the complete report on McDonough's accident, while Cavendish put through the paperwork to get business information on Blue Mountain Racing. Then he looked up everything NLETS and the FBI's National Crime Information Center had on Robert Bevilacqua and Kyle Sullivan. It wasn't a lot. Neither man had any outstanding warrants, were fugitives, or had terrorist or drug connections.

Next, he searched for information on the greyhound scandal he'd heard about from Gary Conaway. According to the news articles he found, it had happened pretty much as described. A man who volunteered as a driver to transport greyhounds from the central Wheeling adoption center to various adoption groups in West Virginia and southwestern Pennsylvania had been arrested, charged, and convicted of taking select dogs and diverting them before they reached their final destinations. The dogs had been purchased by a number of people, mostly in West Virginia, and raced at an off-the-books track near the state line. Once the WIGAC got wind of it, the West Virginia State Police, local law enforcement, state animal control, and the adoption folks took down the operation in a sting. The net result was several people in West Virginia were arrested and jailed, and the track was shut down.

"How on earth did they miss McDonough?" Duncan muttered as he scrolled through the article.

Cavendish didn't spare him a glance. "What are you muttering about?"

"This greyhound thing we heard about. I was wondering how McDonough missed being picked up."

Her gaze flickered in his direction, but she quickly returned to staring at her computer screen. "Do you think it matters?"

"I'm not sure, but I'd like to know if only to tie off a loose end. He got that dog somehow."

She made a noncommittal noise in her throat. "Have we gotten the victim's financial records?"

"Yes. I'm looking at them now." Cavendish might not think the greyhound connection was important, but Duncan preferred to make sure it wasn't before dismissing it. McDonough lived in Pennsylvania. Perhaps that was what allowed him to slip through the cracks and avoid prosecution. He must have kept Johnny, hoping to find another illegal racing operation.

He picked up the financial report on McDonough. But before he could start reading, his desk phone rang.

"Trooper Duncan? This is Heather Arden, from Blue Mountain. We met this morning."

"What can I do for you, Ms. Arden?"

"A protest group is outside the track gates."

"As irritating as that may be, there's not a whole lot I can do from Pennsylvania. I suggest you call the nearest police department in your area."

"No, no." She covered the phone to speak to someone, then returned. "We've taken care of that. But seeing them jogged my memory. You asked about people who argued with Otto. Well, this happened a couple weeks before we fired him. The same protest group showed up. I use the term 'group' lightly. It's really about three people. On this particular day, they poured ketchup or something over a couple cars to simulate blood, in addition to the usual picketing and signs and garbage."

Duncan could imagine the scene. "Not racing fans, huh?"

"Hardly. Anyway, most of us know to park our cars in a back lot behind a fence to avoid this kind of thing, but that day, Otto had been late, and he parked out front. I mean, he'd been later than usual. When he left, his car was a mess. He started a screaming match with the protesters, mostly with the woman in charge. She called him a murderer, he called her a bitch, blah,

blah…you know how it goes. At the end of it, she said he deserved a bullet to the head for what he'd done, and if he had any decency, he'd go home and do it himself. Then she said if he was too chicken to do the deed himself, maybe she should help him."

Duncan scribbled notes as Heather talked. "Do you know this woman's name?"

"Bethany, I think. Or Beth Ann. She comes out at least once a week. Her most distinguishing features are a potty mouth and bright purple hair. I get the impression from the few times we've, um, spoken that she's not too bright. But she's very into protesting animal cruelty in all forms. I've only ever seen her in cotton clothes, and I doubt she eats anything that isn't flax seed. A friend of mine, who is a vegetarian, calls people like her 'militant vegetarians.' You know, you go out to lunch with them, and they get offended if you order a hamburger."

"Got it." He'd come across people like that when he went fishing, but fortunately, he'd never had his car doused in a condiment.

"Anyway, I thought you should know. Sorry I didn't remember this morning."

"That's all right. You called when you did. How did Otto take all this?"

"As you might expect." Heather covered the phone again, said something, and came back. "To say he was mad is an understatement. If he'd approached his work with as much energy as he put into arguing, he might still have a job. Hey, I have to go. Did that help?"

"Yes. One last quick question. What's the name of the group?"

"Humans for the Proper Treatment of the Environment, Animals, and the World. I know, it's a mouthful, and it doesn't even make a good acronym. We just call them the nut jobs. If that's all, I really have to run."

Duncan thanked her, told her to call with any other information, and hung up. He looked at the name scrawled in front of him. Bethany, or Beth Ann, had threatened to shoot McDonough, a clearly unethical action. He wondered how murder fit in with the group's mission. One more thing to research. He turned his attention to Otto McDonough's bank records.

A mere fifteen minutes of study told him McDonough had as much success as a dog owner as he'd had at his career at Blue Mountain. "Johnny's Pixelated might have been a good racer, but McDonough was a crap owner," Duncan said.

Cavendish lifted her head. "How so?"

"The only deposits into the account were his salary from the track." Duncan highlighted rows of payments to meat vendors, as well as online pharmacies where McDonough might have bought the steroids and other doping materials. "There were no cash deposits or transfers of money into the account, and his bank balance dipped into the red several times over the last couple of months." In fact, Duncan couldn't find a deposit made after McDonough's last paycheck.

"Maybe he stored his winnings elsewhere."

"Could be." It took several minutes of studying the highlighted rows for Duncan to notice something else that was missing. Payments to Robert Bevilacqua. "He also hasn't paid his landlord," he said.

"Duncan, Cavendish," said Lieutenant Ferguson, who'd come up beside him. "Status on McDonough."

Cavendish sat back. "We've talked to his landlord, his former employer, and one other guy." She gave a quick overview of the conversations with Bevilacqua, the folks from Blue Mountain, and Kyle Sullivan.

"You'll get Sullivan's guns for ballistics?"

"Working on it."

Duncan spoke up. "His financials are a mess." He told Ferguson about his findings.

Ferguson thought a moment. "Next steps?"

Cavendish might be a doubter, but at least Ferguson was talking in rapid-fire dialog, reportedly a good sign. "We're going to talk to the former owner of the dog we found, who also happens to be the breeder, and see if he knows anything, and we're still waiting on the ballistics report. Also"—here he shot a glance at Cavendish—"I want to go back to Bevilacqua. He says McDonough paid his August rent, but I can't find a record of any payments for several months."

"He was behind on his rent?" Ferguson asked.

"That's what we need to ask."

She nodded. "Keep me posted." She walked off.

Cavendish scowled. "You didn't tell me about the landlord."

"I didn't have a chance to." Duncan kept his tone mild. "The L-T wanted an update."

Her expression relaxed. "So based on what you found, McDonough was a big loser at the track, or he's hiding his money."

"Correct." Duncan tapped the bank records. "And either he paid his rent from the hidden stash, or Mr. Bevilacqua is lying."

* * *

Sally returned to Uniontown at two-thirty and went straight to Kim's office. "Question," she said, standing in the doorway. "Are you using PATCH for criminal background checks?" The Pennsylvania State Police offered the Pennsylvania Access to Criminal History service online. As a member of the county government via the public defender's office, Sally had enjoyed a direct line to the criminal records for suspects. As a private citizen, she'd have to find another source.

Kim looked up. "I have a subscription to Tracer. Highly recommended by private investigators, skip tracers, and other attorneys. And it doesn't cost a fortune." She scribbled her login information on a sticky note and handed it over.

Sally went to her desk and opened the Tracer website. She'd never heard of it. Hopefully, it was as least as good as her former options.

Tracer turned out to be better. Within half an hour, she had information on all of RCH's board members. Annie Norquist did not have a criminal history and possessed a good credit score. Her taxes and mortgage were up to date. Sally checked the woman's address. It was a modest house in a decent neighborhood, consistent with Annie's income. Sally looked up. "Where are your subpoena forms?" she called over to Kim.

The other woman pointed at a wall of filing cabinets. "Second cabinet, third drawer down."

Sally took several forms from the drawer and returned to her work. She completed one for RCH's bank records. In her public defense days, the forms had been pre-stamped with a judge's signature. Now she'd have to get one in person.

Kim wandered over. "What are you doing?"

"Checking into the RCH board members."

Kim narrowed her eyes. "Are you billing our client for your detective work?"

If Kim was going to make Sally justify every little thing, the arrangement was not going to work. "Part of constructing a defense is showing reasonable doubt, isn't it? How can I do that if I don't know anything about the other people who had the opportunity to take from the RCH bank account?"

Kim pondered this. "Don't go overboard." She walked away.

Sally suppressed a sigh. Bryan had given her more leeway than Kim seemed willing to. She stood and grabbed her purse. "I'm going to the courthouse. I won't be long."

Kim didn't answer.

At the courthouse, Sally headed for the chambers of a friendly judge, where she explained her need and got the required signature on the court order. She returned to the office, faxed the form to the bank, and went back to her search.

But an hour later, Sally had to concede defeat. Tracer had not turned up anything more serious than a five-year-old citation for possession of marijuana, no intent to sell, for Sue Hensen, the vice president.

Her cell phone rang. The caller ID showed the name of a well-known Pittsburgh bank.

"Ms. Castle, this is Tyler Randolph. I'm calling in response to your subpoena."

Sally grabbed a pen and her legal pad. "Go ahead."

"There are five signatories on the River City Hounds account." He listed the names of the current board members. "The last one is Lynn Moss."

Sally paused. "Who is she?"

"I don't know. But she's authorized on the account. Have a good

85

afternoon." Tyler hung up.

Sally double-checked the RCH site. She searched in Tracer. Nothing. Pat Dennister hadn't mentioned that name. What the hell had happened to Lynn Moss?

* * *

Duncan stood in front of the vending machine debating his choices. He rarely drank soda, but he needed a sugar and caffeine hit for the afternoon. He'd selected a Coke and was wiping the top of the can clean with his handkerchief when his phone buzzed. It was a text from Sally: *Meeting Tanelsa for drinks. Will probably be late.* He sent back a thumbs-up and returned to his desk.

Cavendish had gone somewhere. A quick glance at his desk told him ballistics weren't back. He was waiting on requested background information. He'd called Robert Bevilacqua, the victim's landlord, but the call had gone straight to voicemail. Stymied on all other fronts, he decided to look up the protest group from the racetrack.

When he'd heard the name Humans for the Proper Treatment of the Environment, Animals, and the World, he'd suspected the group wasn't one of the more polished organizations out there. A quick glance at the website confirmed it. "Who uses these crazy fonts?" he asked.

Cavendish chose that exact moment to appear. "Yowza," she said, dropping the stack of paper in her hand. "That is truly awful. My niece could do better web design, and she's seven. What the hell are you looking at?"

In addition to the nearly unreadable title font, the site featured bright colors and flashing graphics. "It's the website for the group Heather called about earlier. Definitely not a pro job," Duncan said, sipping from his Coke.

"You really think this Bethany or Beth Ann person is a serious suspect?"

Duncan couldn't miss the challenge in her voice. "She threatened the victim. I think it needs to be checked out."

Cavendish studied him a moment. "Have you found her?"

"I just started looking. Heather said we'd know her by the bright purple hair."

Cavendish shrugged. "That shouldn't be too hard to find." She pulled her chair around to sit next to him.

He scrolled down the page. Lots of pictures, but no one with bright purple hair. He tried another page, labeled "Wanted List." This one listed all of the target organizations for the protesters, presumably ones that didn't meet the group's standards. It included logging companies, waste management, a couple of animal rescues, a local horse racing track, and a few local farms. The protesters accused each organization of a crime, which seemed to be everything from animal abuse to pollution to failure to recycle or compost. His gut told him probably none of the companies had actually broken the law. More like Humans for the Proper Treatment didn't like the methods used. "They're an equal-opportunity protester, it seems."

"Is there anybody they do like? I bet half the businesses in southwestern Pennsylvania and northern West Virginia are there." She read for a moment. "There, third from the bottom. Blue Mountain Racetrack."

Duncan looked. Sure enough, there was the track, the associated crimes named as animal cruelty as well as water pollution and failure to recycle. "Water pollution?"

"From waste disposal, either food or animal. No pictures on this page, though. Try that one." She tapped the screen.

Duncan clicked over to the page marked Events. He scrolled through the pictures until one caught his eye. "There she is. Heather was right. The hair is unmistakable." The woman in question was young, late twenties, or early thirties. She had short spiky hair dyed a color that was certainly not any shade of purple found in nature. In the picture, she was clearly screaming, mouth open, fist in the air, brandishing a sign that read, "Earth H8ter." There was a caption under it. "Bethany protesting farm waste management," Duncan read.

"No last name?" Cavendish asked.

"No."

She stood. "Not making it easy to find her, is she?"

"No, she isn't." Too bad Heather hadn't mentioned a last name.

"Let me try something." Cavendish went to her phone and dialed the phone number listed on the Contact page. "Yes, hi," she said a moment later. "I'm looking for Bethany. She gave me a flier at your farm waste protest, and I want to talk to her about it. She really got me thinking." Pause. "Oh, she isn't? Do you know where I could find her?" Another pause. "Well, when will she be in your office? Oh? Well, what's your next protest event? Maybe she'll be there. Uh-huh, okay, yeah, thanks, bye." She hung up. "The group doesn't have an office so to speak. The guy wouldn't give me contact info, but they'll be picketing at the Meadows tomorrow at five. She should be there."

"Uh, thanks, I think."

She stood and stretched. "No problem. It's a rookie mistake, thinking things always have to be complicated."

He swallowed a retort. Rookie move? If she'd given him thirty seconds to think he could have come up with the idea.

Before he could say anything, one of the admins came and dropped a manila folder on his desk. "Duncan, Cavendish. Here's your ballistics report." The admin left.

Duncan snatched the envelope. Petty, maybe, but his hackles were still up over the rookie mistake comment. He pulled out the report and scanned it.

"Are you going to share with the class?" Cavendish asked.

He handed over the paper. "The bullets that killed McDonough all came from a .38. No matches in the system."

She dropped her superior tone and took it. "Didn't Sullivan say he had a .38?"

"He did. Guess we'll be talking to Mr. Sullivan again." Good thing Sally had already said she'd be late. As it turned out, so would he.

88

Chapter Thirteen

Duncan put in a quick call to the lumber yard where Sullivan worked and learned the man had left early. "In fact, he clocked out shortly after you talked to him, Trooper."

"Do you know where he went?"

"Said he had a migraine and was going home."

Duncan checked the clock. Slightly after three-thirty. It would take at least an hour to drive to Markleysburg. If Bethany's protest had been happening tonight, he might have put talking to Sullivan on his to-do list for tomorrow. "Fancy a drive to see Sullivan?" he asked his partner.

She gave him a long, neutral stare. "A five-month-old fistfight is a weak motive."

"Yes, it is. But he has means and opportunity."

"And you want to be thorough, is that it?"

"Don't you?" He couldn't keep an accusatory note from his voice. But maybe he shouldn't. He was convinced she didn't think much of his skills. Maybe he needed to play the same game.

He half-expected a retort, but it didn't come. "You're driving," she said as she left the room.

The sun hung low in the sky by the time they reached their destination. Duncan adjusted his shoulder holster and straightened his jacket as he studied the house in front of him. Nothing fancy, just a solid square painted light blue, with a neatly trimmed yard. The porch and a handicap ramp were fresh pressurized lumber. The two-tone Chevy truck in front of the garage was a few years old, but clean and obviously well maintained. Through the open garage door, Duncan could see a variety of tools and a set of sawhorses. The whole picture belonged to a man who knew his tools, and prized organization and method.

Duncan knocked firmly on the front door. No answer. He tried again, this time announcing his presence. Still no answer.

"Maybe he's not home," Cavendish said. "He could have walked some-where."

He walked around the house. No one was in the garage. A quick peek at the truck showed a square of orange on the interior of the door, indicating the vehicle was unlocked. Markleysburg was hardly a high-crime area, but several of the tools inside the garage appeared valuable. The backyard was as neatly mown as the front, with another newly built handicap ramp leading up to a small deck. But no people.

He returned to the front door. "Kyle Sullivan? This is Trooper Duncan from the state police. I'd like to talk to you."

This time, the door opened. Sullivan's clothes were disheveled, as though he'd dressed in a hurry. The shirt was buttoned incorrectly, and his fly was undone. His hair stuck up at all angles and his eyes were red. "Yes?"

"This is the third time I've knocked."

"I was…asleep. Allergies. What can I do for you?"

"Your boss said you left with a migraine," said Cavendish.

"It's all part of the allergy thing." He ran the back of his hand over his nose.

"May we come in?" Duncan asked. "By the way, the barn door is open, if you know what I mean."

"Oh, uh, right." Sullivan fumbled with his zipper and fixed his shirt. "Sorry, the place is a mess. I've been zonked out on Benadryl." He pushed open the door.

"Your allergies didn't seem to be bothering you when we spoke earlier." Duncan stepped inside. His host wasn't kidding about the state of his house. A few empty beer cans and a pizza box were on the coffee table. A hand-knitted afghan trailed from couch to floor. Used tissues were everywhere. The far wall held a number of framed pictures. The haphazard condition of the interior didn't match the exterior.

"I, uh, forgot to take a second pill." Sullivan followed him.

Duncan stepped over to look at the photos on the wall. A few were of Sullivan and an older couple. Parents? Another one, hanging at a lopsided angle, showed the same couple, but obviously from years before. "You're missing some photos." He waved at blank spots on the wall.

"Oh, yeah." Sullivan rubbed a hand through his hair, making it stand up even more. "I had friends over a while ago. They were horsing around and knocked some of the pictures off the wall. A few frames broke."

"These your parents?" Cavendish asked.

"Yeah." Sullivan picked up the pizza box and cleared off a chair. "Have a seat."

"Thanks." The troopers sat, and Duncan took another look around the room. Cluttered and messy, but not truly dirty. Sullivan's eyes looked pretty bloodshot. "It must be pretty bad to send you home."

"Huh?"

"Your allergies."

"Oh, right." The man continued cleaning, picked up the pizza box and cans, and took them to the kitchen. The sound of cabinets and running water sounded, then he returned with three glasses. "I, uh, it's the, um, oak trees for me. Every September. It's a killer. Water?"

"Thanks." Duncan accepted the glass, but put it on the coffee table.

Cavendish waved off the offer.

Sullivan sat on the couch and took a long drink. "What can I help you with?"

"We have the ballistics report back from the crime scene. Otto Mc-Donough was shot with a .38."

Cavendish crossed her legs. "When we talked this morning, you said you owned a .38."

"I do." Sullivan's eyes were wary over the edge of his glass.

"Do you have it?" Duncan asked.

"Why wouldn't I?"

"Just asking." He glanced at Cavendish. "We'd like to take it for ballistics comparison."

"Am I a suspect?"

Cavendish hadn't moved. "It's standard practice. You had an interaction with the victim, you didn't like him, and you own a gun of the same caliber that killed him."

"Do I have to let you?" Sullivan looked from one to the other.

Duncan waited before answering. Sullivan's reluctance didn't mean he was guilty. But it was puzzling. "No. But we can get a court order, and you won't be able to refuse that."

"You get it back when we're done. If it's not the murder weapon, that is," Cavendish said.

Sullivan placed his half-empty glass on the table and rubbed his hands on his jeans. "Right. I'll go get it." He left.

Duncan stood. "I'll go with you." He followed Sullivan to the basement.

"Who are the ramps for?" Duncan asked as Sullivan fiddled with the lock on the safe.

"What? Oh, my mom. She had a stroke not that long ago, and now she's in a wheelchair. I put the ramps in for when she visits." He opened the door. "Here they are." He reached in.

Duncan stopped him. "Allow me." He snapped on a pair of nitrile gloves. Inside the safe were two rifles. Duncan examined them. Just as Sullivan had told him, they were both .22s. On a shelf next to the long guns were the Glock and the .38. He picked it up, made sure it was unloaded, then dropped it into an evidence bag. "As my partner said, we'll get this back to you as soon as we're done, assuming it's not a match."

"Right." Sullivan closed the safe, and they returned to the living room.

Cavendish stood by the wall, studying the pictures. "Looks like you're close to your parents. Do they live nearby?"

"My dad died several years ago." Sullivan scuffed his shoe on the carpet. "Mom moved out of town, but she visits a lot. It's getting harder for her to get around, that's why I put in the ramps."

Duncan held out his hand. "Once again, thanks for your cooperation."

"How long do you think this will take?" Sullivan asked.

"It's hard to say." Cavendish turned from the wall. "A lot depends on how backed up they are. But we'll be in touch as soon as we can."

Sullivan watched them go, a stiff expression on his reddened face.

Back in the Interceptor, Duncan put the bag in the backseat. "Talk about rapid onset allergies. He was fine when we saw him at the lumber yard."

Cavendish clicked her seat belt. "Could something at work have triggered it?"

"I guess." Duncan put the car in gear and drove off. Sullivan worked in a lumber yard, and it was very likely oak wood was around. But something about that felt wrong.

* * *

Before Sally left the office, she called Tanelsa. "How about meeting for a drink? It'll be nice to see you."

"Are you buying?"

"Of course."

"Meet you at five."

Sally arrived at the bar on East Main early enough to order two glasses of a locally-made merlot, one for her and one for Tanelsa, as well as a plate of tapas to share. She snagged a booth near the front window and killed time by scrolling through the RCH website, looking at pictures. Each time she checked the captions. But there was no mention of the elusive Lynn Moss.

The snapping of fingers interrupted her. "Earth to Sally," Tanelsa said, sliding into her seat. "I said hello and asked if you'd been waiting long. What's so interesting? Shots of half-dressed firefighters?"

"Oh, please. I'm looking at greyhounds." She held out her phone. "Did you know that the Egyptian pyramids have pictures that strongly resemble greyhounds?"

"Fascinating." Tanelsa handed back the device. "Since when have you been so interested in dogs?"

"It's not just them. It's for this case I'm working. I came across a name of a woman who used to volunteer with the group, and I was looking to see if there were pictures of her."

"Any luck?" Tanelsa picked up a glass. "Is this mine?"

"It is. And no, I didn't find her." Sally dropped the phone into her purse. She'd look for Lynn Moss tomorrow.

Tanelsa popped a piece of flatbread slathered in cheese into her mouth. "How is the private sector is treating you? You didn't say much on the phone."

Sally sipped her wine. "I suppose it's fine. I mean, I'm not terribly busy, but that's by design. I'm sure if I decided to jump in with both feet, Kim would load me up with cases. Naturally, I miss the courthouse, you, Doris, the others. It's nice setting my own hours and picking my clients."

Tanelsa studied her over the rim of her glass. "That sentence is just begging for a 'but' on the end of it."

"I don't know that where I am is exactly what I'm looking for. I'm still reporting to someone else." She selected a piece of flatbread.

"How does Jim feel about the change?"

"I don't think he sees much of a difference. Not in the work. I've spent more weeknights with him. He likes that." Sally hesitated. "He asked me to move in with him."

Tanelsa barely reacted, aside from a slight narrowing of her eyes. "What did you tell him?"

"I told him I could only handle one life-changing decision at a time."

"Sounds reasonable."

Sally picked at a spot on the table. "The problem is I want to do it. Live with him, I mean. I don't even mind the commute from Confluence to Uniontown. But not right now. Argh." She buried her face in her hands. "Why does everything have to happen at the same time?"

"Because that, my friend, is life." Tanelsa took a sip. "What's up with the Delmonico case?"

"It's early days. My client is adamant that she's innocent. What I don't understand is why it's gotten this far."

"What do you mean?"

"It's the kind of thing where I'd have expected settlement and restitution if she's guilty. Or she'd call someone to audit her work and prove she's innocent. But instead, they went straight to the police."

Tanelsa topped off her glass. "You called a forensic accountant?"

"Kim's going to get me a name." Sally swirled her wine. "Pat Dennister, she's the RCH treasurer, told me the whole thing stunned her. But the more I think about it, the more it feels forced."

"What do you mean?"

Sally met her friend's gaze. "I don't know. Like someone *wants* Ciara Delmonico to be found guilty. No matter what."

* * *

Later that night, Sally stood in Jim's kitchen and listened to him recap his day. Once he finished, she turned and salted the water for the fettuccine. "Jim, don't you think you're overreacting? How can anyone in her right mind doubt your abilities?"

Beside her, Jim skewered the shrimp that would go with the fettuccine. "Sally, those were her words. Rookie mistake. I am not a rookie."

"Well, you are at this job."

He paused in his work. "Whose side are you on?"

She laid a hand on his shoulder. "Yours, of course. I'm trying to look at it from Jenny's perspective. In her eyes, you're fresh from patrol and a newbie investigator. How long did she work with her previous partner?"

"She didn't say. She hasn't told me anything about herself." He brushed marinade over the shellfish, picked up the tray, and went outside.

She added pasta to the pot and adjusted the heat to a simmer. Then she followed him. "Have you asked?"

"Been a little busy with this murder." He laid the skewers over the hot coals. "Except for drinks last night, she goes out of her way to exclude me. She went out for lunch, and not only did she not ask me along, she didn't offer to bring anything back. What am I supposed to take from that?"

It did sound off-putting, and Sally couldn't blame him for feeling the way he did. Jim had been fairly popular at the Uniontown barracks, where he'd also had a reputation as a top performer. Naturally, he'd anticipate a certain level of respect at his new job. After all, they didn't let just anyone into Criminal Investigation. There was an interview process. "Give it another shot. Tomorrow, try and get her to talk. After all, didn't McAllister hold out on you when you first met?"

"Yes."

"And look how that turned out. In the meantime, just keep doing the best you can. If Jenny Cavendish is at all reasonable, she'll see your value sooner or later."

He flipped the skewers. "One can only hope. Hey, what do you know about allergies?"

"I'm not a doctor, nor do I play one on TV, if that's what you're asking."

"Not exactly." He told her about Kyle Sullivan's claim of oak sensitivity. She frowned. "Well, I don't find it odd that he'd get a migraine, or at least a severe headache. But with plants, you're sensitive to the pollen, not the wood itself."

"That's what was bothering me! I knew it was something. Not sawdust, pollen."

"And it's the wrong season for oaks. That would be spring."

He removed the shrimp from the grill. "So the story he gave his boss is bullshit." He went inside, and she followed.

She tested the fettuccine. It was perfectly cooked, so she picked up a colander and drained it. "Why lie? I mean, I can see him fibbing to his boss if he didn't want to be at work this afternoon. But why you and Cavendish? It's not like you two would tattle on him in."

"I don't know. But it will be interesting to see what ballistics come up with when they test his .38." He took the food to the table. "You know what? Let's eat in the backyard. I'm tired of being inside." He left with the plate of shrimp, Rizzo trailing closely.

They took seats at the picnic table. Rizzo sat in the grass, on the alert for dropped goodies. A cool evening breeze rustled the leaves on the trees, and the water of the Casselman River sparkled under the rays of the setting sun through the branches. Sally slid four fat, perfectly grilled shrimp off a skewer and onto a mountain of noodles, then drizzled olive oil over them.

"You know, if the police thing doesn't work out for you, I bet you can get a job as a grill master in one of the local restaurants."

"Thanks, but no thanks." He filled his own plate. "I think food service might be a tougher gig than being a cop." He swirled up some pasta. "Your turn. How was your day?"

They talked as they ate, and she shared what she'd learned about RCH and the extra officer.

Jim held a forkful of pasta above his plate. "RCH is the group that should have taken Johnny's Pixelated."

"The dog you found at McDonough's house?"

"Yes. His name hasn't come up, has it? Or has anyone mentioned the whole illegal racing scheme?"

"No, but I haven't asked. It's not relevant to my client. At least not that I can see."

"Do you think they knew they were supposed to take delivery of Johnny? Or just a certain number of hounds?"

"I really have no idea. My recommendation would be to call them and ask."

"You've spoken to some of the board members, right?"

"The president and treasurer. But not about the mechanics of how the dogs get to them, just about the pending litigation."

He chewed and swallowed. "Do you think they knew about the illegal racing and covered it up?"

"No way." She pulled the tail off her final shrimp and dropped the tail onto her plate. "Money issues aside, those people love their dogs. I absolutely do not believe they'd knowingly let a retired racer go to an unscrupulous owner, and no way would they condone the kind of treatment you described. And based on what I do know, I can't see how it would tie to the embezzlement case I'm working." She looked at Rizzo, who lay next to them, head on his paws. "Anyway, if you really want to know more, I'll give you the phone number for Annie Norquist. She's the group's president and can probably answer all your questions. Just don't ask about money because she clams up as soon as you mention it."

97

"Not interested in money. Just the dogs." He swirled up some pasta. "Back to you. I hope you're thinking what I'm thinking about this Moss woman."

"That she could have stolen from RCH? Oh, you bet. I'll be jumping on that line of inquiry first thing tomorrow."

"Good." They finished the meal without any more shop talk. Jim pushed aside his empty plate. "Are you spending the night?"

"That was my plan, unless you don't want me to."

"Nope, fine by me." He studied her. "Sally, you know this is ridiculous right? Move in. You spend most of your time here. Tell your landlord you're not going to renew your lease in March."

She twirled her fork in her food. "What happens the first time we have a fight like we did last spring?"

He snorted. "I doubt that will happen. We know what we did wrong, and we learned our lesson." He put down his fork and folded his hands on the table. "I like having you here. Rizzo likes having you here. You like being here. What's the problem?"

She pushed aside her plate. "It does seem like the perfect arrangement, doesn't it?"

"But you're still not going to move, are you?"

She took his hand. "At the risk of sounding like a romance novel cliché, it's not you, it's me. I admit the prospect of waking up next to you for the foreseeable future is pretty satisfying. But there's so much going on in my life right now, and I can't do it all at once. Thank you for the offer. My heart wants to say yes, but my head is telling me to slow down, and I feel like I have to listen to it. I'm not saying no, but I am saying not right now."

Jim said nothing for a long second and sat there, assessing her with an inscrutable expression. "Well, I can't say that doesn't make sense. Consider the discussion tabled. For now."

Chapter Fourteen

Wednesday morning, Duncan arrived at HQ with two cups of coffee. Cavendish was already at her desk. "A little late this morning, aren't you?" she asked without looking up.

He set one of the cups in front of her. "Medium roast, two creams correct?"

She startled. "You got it." She pulled back the tab and sniffed. "Nice. Thanks."

He sat down. "I think we may have gotten off to a rocky start."

"Is this your peace offering?"

"Sort of." He blew on his own cup. "I'm not bringing you coffee every morning. I realize I'm new to this whole investigative thing. But I have a lot of experience. I may have been in uniform, but I know how to do this job. I only ask that you give me the chance to prove it to you. Deal?"

She studied him. Her face was a mask and gave no hint as to her thoughts. *I'd hate to play poker with her.* Duncan waited, determined to let her speak first.

"Fair enough," she said after a few moments. "Got a plan for today?"

"I want to follow the dog angle." He paused, and when she didn't say anything, he continued. "There's no money to trace, at least not that we've found. But I'm intrigued enough by the illegal racing thing that I think it's worth pursuing."

"What's your angle?"

"Number one is always money." He wanted a whiteboard to jot down his thoughts, but he didn't see one around. Instead, he grabbed a yellow pad. "McDonough could owe someone. Or maybe he was trying to get paid."

She leaned back, coffee in hand. "Either way, he failed. Conflict ensues, and he's shot."

"Correct." He wrote a second bullet point. "Next, I'm thinking a person in the racing industry could have taken serious issue with the whole illicit racing scheme."

"Which we don't know happened."

"I've got a guy who might be able to help with that." Duncan made a note to talk to Eddie V, his primary source in Confluence. As a bookmaker, Eddie would know where to go to confirm McDonough's participation in any off-the-track operation. "Let's assume he was. Something like that couldn't have gone over well with the legitimate operations."

"Conaway? Or someone else at Blue Mountain?"

"Maybe, but I'd also like to talk to the Johnny's Pixelated's former owner. His name is Max Renner, and he also happens to be the breeder. People at the track might be angry, but the owner might have more skin in the game. After all, the greyhound was his property. I know he wasn't compensated once Johnny retired, but if he's one of those owners who is invested in his dogs, I can't see him taking abuse lightly."

"It's definitely worth asking." She set down the cup. "What about this protester? Beth Ann with the purple hair?"

"Bethany." Duncan wrote a third bullet point. "I want to talk to her as well. She had a confrontation with the victim and threatened him. Might have ended at words."

"But maybe not." She regarded him with an even stare. "Are ballistics back on Sullivan's .38?"

He glanced in his inbox. "No. By the time we finish the interviews, it might be." He wrote Sullivan as a fourth bullet and circled the list. "That's a solid list of suspects."

"It is." She tapped her fingers on the desk. "Where does Renner live?"

"West Virginia. I called him on my way in, and he's home. He's expecting us."

"Then let's go. I'll drive." She stood. "Thanks for the coffee."

"Don't mention it."

When they arrived, Cavendish drove through a simple wrought iron gate with the words *Renner's Farms* worked above the arch. Rolling fields of deep green grass stretched on either side of the neat gravel road. In a fenced area, Duncan could see a couple of greyhounds outside for what seemed to be daily exercise.

She parked next to a long, low building. Max Renner, the man who identified himself as the owner of the farm, had said he'd meet them in the kennel, but there were several buildings on the property, and Renner had failed to specify which one to go to. Reasoning that the stately Victorian farmhouse on the property was not a place to keep and whelp dogs, Duncan headed to a low building off to the left, Cavendish beside him. The door was open, but he knocked on the frame. "Hello? Mr. Renner? Trooper Jim Duncan, from the Pennsylvania State Police. We talked on the phone."

"In here," a deep voice answered. Around the corner, a trim man with silver hair, dressed in jeans and a plaid work shirt, stood pouring a thick slurry into several feeding bowls. He looked up briefly. "Chow time. Just give me a sec." He added what looked like pasta and another liquid to the bowls, then carried them over to a pen where several puppies crowded around the gate.

"Looks like they know exactly what's going on," Duncan said. "This is my partner, Trooper Cavendish."

Renner nodded a hello. "Anybody who says a dog can't tell time has obviously never had one bother him for meals."

"Amen to that. I have a golden retriever. God forbid I be a minute late with breakfast or supper."

"Exactly." Renner deposited the bowls in the pen, then backed out as the puppies charged the feeding station. He latched the gate, gave it a firm tug to make sure it was closed, then held out a hand. "Max Renner. I was surprised to get a call from the Pennsylvania State Police. What can I help you with? On second thought, let's go sit in my office. It'll be more comfortable." He led the way down the building to a room with a metal desk, three serviceable chairs, and a filing cabinet. The walls were covered with photos of greyhounds as well as several ribbons, many of them blue.

Duncan took the seat nearest the door. "All these pictures are of your dogs?"

"Yep." Renner waved at the walls and sat. "I've had more, of course, but these are the most successful, the ones I bred. The ribbons and plaques are from awards they've won."

"Looks like you've been fairly successful." Cavendish scanned the pictures.

"I've had my share." Renner's gaze held pride, but more than that as he studied the photos. Affection? Maybe. "You mentioned on the phone you wanted information about a particular hound?"

"Yes," Duncan said. "A black male named Johnny's Pixelated. The track manager was able to give me some information when he looked up the dog's ear tattoos."

"I remember Johnny. He raced right here in West Virginia, up at Blue Mountain. Had a pretty good career. Not good enough to breed, but decent."

"Do you know anything about the adoption?" Cavendish asked.

"Not really." Renner leaned back. "The trainers generally handle that. Take Johnny, for example. I knew he'd reached the top age. I talked to the trainer, made the decision to let him go, and she handled the rest."

"I see." Duncan consulted his notes. "Do you know a man named Otto McDonough?"

Renner's face didn't change. "No, name doesn't ring a bell. Should it?"

"He worked at Blue Mountain."

"Not as a trainer."

Duncan's curiosity reared its head. Renner's words had been a statement, not a question. "How do you know that?"

"No big thing." Renner brushed dust from his desktop. "I know all the trainers up at Blue Mountain is all. There isn't one named Otto."

"He might have been new."

"I was up there a couple weeks ago, and Heather, that's the girl in charge, didn't mention any new hires. I don't talk to the maintenance staff. Keeping those kennels clean is track business, not mine."

"You don't care about the well-being of your dogs?" Cavendish asked.

"I didn't say that." Renner's voice turned sharp. "I'm not dumb, Trooper.

I understand how it is. People against racing think owners and breeders and trainers view these animals merely as moneymakers. Dog isn't making money? Get rid of it." He jerked his thumb over his shoulder. "I suppose there are people out there like that. I'm not one of them. Hell, look around you. Would I have all these pictures if I didn't care about my animals?"

"You said earlier these were your winners."

"Sure, but I didn't breed all of them. Take Flash over there." He pointed at the photo of an elegant red dog. "She won exactly two races. Broke her ankle in a freak accident when she jumped out of her crate at the kennel. Never healed right. But she ran like the wind, poetry in motion. Won those races by a couple lengths. I bred her. She was one of the most affectionate dogs I ever owned. She developed osteosarcoma at an early age. Broke my heart when I had to have her euthanized."

Duncan rose to examine the pictures. "She's beautiful." He noted the names on the frames. "Every one of these names seems to have something to do with photography. Why is that?"

"It's a hobby of mine. I took all these pictures myself."

"Then Johnny's Pixelated is from…what?"

"My oldest son is named John. Pixelated is how digital pictures get when you blow them up too much." Renner smiled. "Back to the question at hand. What does a maintenance worker have to do with one of my hounds?"

For the second time, Duncan noted Renner's words. "We found Johnny in a cage in McDonough's house. He didn't look good. I wondered if you knew anything about it."

Renner's face became abnormally still. His eyes flashed, and his mouth thinned. "No, I don't. Describe what you mean by not good."

"Thin. You might say emaciated. But we also found steroids on the premises. We don't know for sure, but we think McDonough may have obtained Johnny to race him illegally."

"You've arrested him, right? This McDonough character?"

Cavendish folded her hands on her lap. "No."

"Why the hell not?"

"Because somebody killed him. Shot him last week, as far as we can tell."

"Huh. Well, good."

Duncan raised an eyebrow. "Excuse me?"

Renner clenched his hands. "I probably shouldn't say this, you being police officers and all, but I think it's good he's dead. Because if he wasn't, and he had abused one of my dogs, or any dog, I'd be tempted to shoot him myself."

* * *

Sally arrived at the courthouse fifteen minutes before her meeting. She thought briefly about stopping downstairs to see her former colleagues but reasoned that any conversation with them was likely to take way more time than she had. Instead, she headed for the district attorney's office on the first floor.

Ciara was already there, dressed in a neat blue skirt and a lightweight cotton twin set. She and Sally had discussed the image they wanted to present to the DA, one of an earnest businesswoman. From the clothing to the jewelry, Ciara had hit the nail on the head.

"You look nice," Sally said after she'd checked in with the receptionist and took a seat next to her client.

"I didn't know about the necklace. They are pearls, after all." She fingered the irregularly-shaped white beads at her neck.

"But it's a freshwater string. Nice, tasteful, not excessive. If you'd walked in wearing a three-rope choker of perfect round ones, we'd have a problem. Those are fine." Sally checked her phone for the time.

At precisely ten o'clock, one of the assistant district attorneys appeared and led them into a conference room. Both women declined the offer of beverages. Sally indicated Ciara should sit beside her, on the opposite side of the table from the ADA. "Neil, nice to see you," she said.

"I heard you'd jumped ship for the private life," he replied. "Now I see it's true."

"Gotta love the courthouse rumor mill. Let's get down to business." Sally unsnapped her briefcase and removed Ciara's file. "What kind of offer are you making?"

"What would you like to hear?" Neil didn't lose his friendly expression, but the shift from pleasure to business was clear in his voice.

"A dismissal of all charges."

"Oh, come on, Sally."

Ciara looked ready to speak, but Sally laid her hand on Ciara's. "My client has maintained her innocence throughout this entire proceeding. Five other people had access to the bank account during the same period. In fact, they still do." She pushed over a sheet of paper.

Neil tugged his jacket. "We've investigated and cleared the other signers on the account."

"Including Lynn Moss? She's not listed on the current board, yet the bank records indicate she's a vice president with the group."

"I'm sure it's sloppy paperwork on the part of River City Hounds, leaving her on the account. Groups like these aren't always on the ball with those things." He didn't take the paper.

"Neil, don't be a hard ass. I've seen Ciara Delmonico's financials, there's nothing there. She lives modestly, drives an old car, no big expenditures during that period. You have the same amount of evidence against her as you do against these others. None."

He leaned forward. "We have an analysis by an independent forensic accountant that shows irregularities in the way Mrs. Delmonico handled the books and tax filings for River City Hounds for last year, which were filed this past spring. Irregularities that could easily allow her to make off with the majority of the group's funds. You should have received all that in discovery."

"I did." Sally wetted her lips. "This is too small an affair to go straight to court. What's the deal on the table?"

Neil sat back. "Mrs. Delmonico pleads no contest on the charges. She makes full restitution to RCH and a suspension of her accountant's license for two years."

Ciara shot to her feet. "I can't possibly pay that amount back, and besides, I didn't take their damn money!"

"Ciara, I know you're upset, but please sit down." Sally looked at her opponent. She'd haggled many a case with Neil when she worked for the public defender. "She doesn't have the money, Neil. If you suspend her license, she can't work. If she can't work, how do you expect her to make restitution?"

"She can work," he replied. "Just not as an accountant."

Ciara, who had resumed her seat, looked ready to cry.

"That's your best offer?" Sally asked.

"Best offer," he said.

She looked over at Ciara, who shook her head. "No deal, sorry," Sally said. "My client is innocent. See you in court."

Chapter Fifteen

Duncan parked outside the coroner's office around eleven o'clock. "You should have been at the autopsy." Cavendish buttoned her jacket, voice neutral but gaze accusatory.

"You didn't see the body. It's not one you would have wanted to attend." He headed for the door. "I know the deputy coroner well. We'll get a full report." He opened the door.

"You know him from where?" She entered the building. "Accident scenes?"

"We've worked together several times. Tom Burns is a little strange, but he's one of the best."

Burns was in his office, headphones on, typing what looked like a report. An open can of energy drink and a half-empty bottle of soda rested on the desk next to the wrapper for a fast-food breakfast sandwich.

"Knock, knock." Duncan tapped on the doorframe.

Burns looked over, pushed pause on a small black machine next to him, and removed the headphones. "Man, I expected you yesterday." He glanced at Cavendish and back to Duncan, unspoken question in his eyes.

"Burns, this is Trooper Jenny Cavendish, my partner." *Please don't be a wiseass.*

Burns must have heard the telepathic plea. "Pleasure. I assume you want the details?" He got up and pulled a folder out of a nearby filing cabinet.

"I'm already pretty sure I know cause and manner of death. Nobody shoots themselves three times in the chest."

"The voice of experience, that's you."

"I'd love a time of death, though."

107

"On that one? Be real." Burns snorted and leafed through the folder.

Duncan pulled out his notebook. "Hey, a guy can hope."

"Just call me the killer of dreams." Burns shook his head.

Cavendish appeared content to observe, but her eyebrows did raise a fraction at the banter.

The younger man glanced at her, then focused on Duncan. "We're calling this one at thirty-six hours or more. Forget about body temperature. It must have been a hundred degrees in that house. We know that lividity was fixed, but normally there's no way you get that amount of decomposition in twelve hours. However, the conditions would have sped the process considerably. Therefore, the coroner is saying more than thirty-six hours, but admits there is a chance it could be less." He tossed aside the folder.

"Is there anything you *can* tell us?" Duncan picked up the report.

"Oh, sure." Burns held up a finger. "We looked at the bugs present."

"Bugs as in insects?"

"Correct. We found flies, mites, and a few maggots. No beetles. That leads us to think the corpse was between three and five days old."

Duncan counted the days back. Wednesday through Friday. "What else?"

Burns held up a second finger. "Stomach contents were fries and a burger. The victim's blood alcohol content was .09"

"Food consistent with a lunch or dinner, and he'd been drinking."

"Also correct." Burns laced his fingers behind his head. "That's it."

"Let me get this straight." Duncan reviewed his notes. "The victim was definitely shot, making it homicide by person or persons unknown. You to think the victim died anywhere from three to five days prior to discovery, probably midday to evening based on the nature of his last meal. But it's all a wild-ass guess because of the condition of the body and the circumstances under which it was found."

"Precisely, Sherlock. No wonder they made you a detective." Burns twisted off the cap of the soda bottle and took a slug. "Anything else I can do for you?"

Duncan put away his notebook and left without giving him an answer. The laughter that followed him out told him Burns hadn't expected one.

* * *

Ciara's breakdown started as soon as they left the meeting. The poor woman was going completely off the edge, convinced the whole thing was over before they'd begun. "I can't go to jail."

"You won't," Sally told her, trying for the soothing approach. "I know their approach, now I get to build mine. They have an expert who says your work is suspicious. I'll…we'll get our own analysis that will say otherwise." *We, not I.* It was another difference to get used to.

Ciara wrung her hands. "But that doesn't prove anything. And it sounds expensive."

"Our firm has one on retainer." Kim had said that, right? *I hope she did.* "It's built into our rates. The burden of proof is on them. I know what I'm doing." The task would be harder than her confident tone implied, but she needed Ciara to stay in one emotional piece. Sally sent her client home with the recommendation to get out of town for a couple days, maybe go to visit friends or family.

As soon as she got back to the office, she went to Kim's desk. "Please tell me you have a forensic accountant on retainer."

"Retainer? No. But I might know one." Kim reached for her phone. "You need one for the Delmonico case?"

"Yes. Damn it. I told Ciara the hourly rate would cover the cost." Sally dropped into a chair. "The prosecution says the work Ciara did for RCH this past tax season is suspicious. Needless to say, I want a second opinion."

"All is not lost." Kim didn't look up from her scrolling. "First, tell me about the meeting with the DA."

"Completely unacceptable." Sally recounted the details.

"Not surprised you passed on that offer." Kim tapped the phone and set it down. "I sent you the name and contact info for someone who should be what you need. Find out her rates, we'll figure out a number, and let Ciara make the call."

"This was so much easier when I worked for the government." Maybe she should go back to Bryan.

Kim's answering grin was lopsided. "What's your next move?"

"I need to find out more about Lynn Moss. She's still on the bank account as an approved signature, and her title is listed as VP, but she's not on the website. It could be a simple error, and it most likely is, but she had means and opportunity. Therefore, I need to know more about her. Thanks for the contact."

"Any time. Let me know if you need something else." Kim returned to her work.

At her desk, Sally fired up her laptop. She was holding off buying a new machine until she had a better grip on her future career plans. She could hear the cash register cha-chings as she tallied the costs of private practice. Maybe some of it was tax-deductible. *I need to talk to a financial advisor.* Later.

She went back to Tracer, and it didn't take long to create a picture of Ms. Moss. The service had a lot of information in one place, no running from point to point to get a clear vision, which was a definite plus. Why couldn't it be a simple decision? *There are always rules, girl. You have to decide which ones you want to work under.*

Lynn was divorced and currently worked as a secretary for a medical records company in Pittsburgh. Her house had been listed in her name as well as her husband prior to March of this year, when it switched to hers alone. Based on that, it was likely she'd gotten the house in the divorce settlement. Her previous job had been with an orthopedic surgery practice in Shadyside, and she had changed jobs last February. Ms. Moss had experienced some financial trouble in the early part of the year, including falling behind on her mortgage, but her financial picture looked decent now, albeit with a slightly lower credit score. Not a terrible one, just lower.

She picked up the phone and called Pat Dennister, who was willing to give her a few minutes. *Thankfully.* "Do you know a woman named Lynn Moss?"

"She used to be our vice president. She did great volunteer work for the group. Unfortunately, we parted ways this past February."

Sally reached over for a legal pad. "What do you mean by that?"

"We had to remove her from the board." A dog barked in the background. "Hold on a second." There was a clatter as the phone was set down, Pat's faint voice rebuked Mitzi, and then there came the sound of a dish being filled with water. Finally, Pat returned. "Sorry about that."

"That's the first I've heard one of those dogs make a peep."

"I was holding a snack, and I didn't give it up quickly enough." Pat sounded resigned, but amused. "Where was I?"

"You were explaining why Ms. Moss left the group."

"Right. She argued with someone at one of our Christmas events last December. Somebody passing by said greyhound racing wasn't all that bad, and Lynn took issue with it. She caused a scene. We talked about it and removed her from the board."

"Is she still a volunteer with the group?"

"No. It happened again in February. Different event, same kind of argument. That was when we told her she couldn't volunteer with us unless she followed the rules, and she quit."

Sally wrote all this down. "I'm a little surprised. I would have thought RCH would be against racing."

"It's our policy to be completely neutral about the racing industry," Pat replied, voice serious. "Our sole objective is to get the dogs to their forever homes after their days on the track are done. I'm quite aware our members have personal opinions, but that's what they are. Personal opinions. As an organization, we don't take any position with regards to racing, and we don't discuss the subject at our events. That's why we're an adoption group, not a rescue. Rescue implies we are saving greyhounds from a negative situation."

"But I'm sure Ms. Moss was expressing just that, her opinion."

"It doesn't matter." Pat paused. "When one of our volunteers is at an event, they are representing us to the public. You have to follow the rules, and those are that RCH is neutral on racing."

It sounded harsh to Sally, but then again, if Lynn Moss had been a long-time volunteer and a board member, she ought to have known the standard operating procedures of the group. "If Ms. Moss is no longer a volunteer and lost her board position, why wasn't she removed from the bank account?"

"She was. I do that myself. Although this time, I was going on vacation and didn't have time to get it done, so Annie said she'd take care of it for me."

"Ms. Norquist must have forgotten or not gotten to it then, because Ms. Moss is still listed as an approved signer, according to the information I received."

"Aw, hell." Pat snorted. "I knew I should have taken the time to do it before I left. I love Annie to death, but sometimes she's so scatterbrained she'd forget to feed her dogs if they didn't complain. Guess I should get down to the bank and take care of that. Which means I need to get in touch with Lynn. Thanks for letting me know, Ms. Castle." Pat said goodbye and hung up.

Sally laid down her phone and stared at the screen in front of her, which displayed Lynn's address and phone number. Pat had been concerned about cleaning up the group's bank records, but had failed to see the more significant side of the discovery. Lynn Moss had means and opportunity. The DA might have dismissed the possibility, but in Sally's mind, it was one more witness to call for Ciara's defense.

* * *

Outside the coroner's office, Cavendish paused next to the unmarked Interceptor. "Interesting guy. And relationship."

"You have to know Burns. He's not clinical. But if there'd been anything relevant that could help us, he'd find it." Duncan got into the car.

She followed suit. "Exactly how do you know this guy, Burns?"

"It's a long story."

"But you trust him."

He placed the key in the ignition and turned to her. Once again, her expression was unreadable. "Yes. I told you. He's one of the best."

Her stare was different this time. Less flat doubt, more considering. "I looked up the details on that illegal greyhound racing case. If you're right, and McDonough diverted a dog, what do you think was the best opportunity?"

"The driver, Dan Overbeck. He was the prosecution's star witness."

"Why him?"

"Less oversight. He also worked with the Wheeling adoption center. He was perfectly placed to divert a hound before it was sent to another destination." Duncan started the car.

She thought. "Where does he live?"

Duncan thought he detected a reluctant hint of admiration in her voice. *Score one for me.* "Overbeck lives in Pennsylvania, just over the state border from Wheeling. Should take us about an hour to get there. I called before we left HQ to make sure he would be at home and willing to talk."

Cavendish waved a hand. "Then let's go."

They arrived at the house at about eleven-thirty and knocked on the door, which was opened within minutes. He introduced himself and asked, "Are you Daniel Overbeck?"

The man who greeted him was thin, his jeans cinched tightly with a wide leather belt, the plaid shirt hanging off his torso as if he were a scarecrow. "That's me. Who the hell are you?"

"Trooper Jim Duncan, Pennsylvania State Police." He introduced Cavendish. "I called earlier. About the greyhound racing."

Overbeck licked his lips. "I've told all I know. It's in the trial records."

"We're not really interested in that case. We're investigating a murder that might be connected."

"I don't have anything to do with a murder."

"We didn't say you did," said Cavendish.

Overbeck pointed. "He said—"

"I said it *might* be related." Duncan studied him. Nervous, but there were two cops at his door, one of whom had said the word 'murder.' "The victim had a greyhound with him, one that was supposed to go into retirement and adoption. He may have been connected to the illegal racing. Or not."

Overbeck seemed to consider, then he pushed open the door. "Fine. Come inside. Can I get you anything?"

"If you have coffee brewed, that would be great. Otherwise, just a glass of water." Duncan surveyed the interior of the house as they proceeded to the kitchen. Plain. Spartan, even. He seated himself on a simple wooden chair at a scrubbed table that showed definite signs of age. "You live alone?"

Overbeck placed a cup of black coffee in front of him. "Yep. Not married, no kids, obviously. You want milk or creamer?"

"Black is fine." Duncan took out his notebook and pen.

Cavendish sat and waved off the offer of coffee.

Overbeck topped off his own mug and sat. "What do you want?"

Duncan removed a picture from his pocket and slid it in front of Overbeck. "I realize the features are distorted, but do you recognize this man?"

He frowned and picked it up, the overhead light gleaming off a bald spot on the back of his head. "He looks dead."

"He is," Cavendish said. "Do you recognize him?"

There was a moment's pause, and Overbeck shook his head. "No. Who is he?"

"His name is Otto McDonough. He worked at Blue Mountain Racing doing maintenance."

Overbeck handed back the picture. "Is that why you think I knew him? I dealt with the trainers at the tracks when I picked up the dogs for the Wheeling adoption center. Occasionally, I volunteered to drive them from the center to other locations."

"We thought you might have known him because he was in possession of a retired racer when we found his body," Duncan said. "A dog that was supposed to go to an adoption group in Pittsburgh, according to the information we've gathered."

"You think this guy, McDonough, bought the dog off me?" Overbeck scratched his ear.

"Possibly. How did the operation work?"

"I told you. It's in the court records."

"Indulge me. Please. I'm not asking for anything outside of your agreement with the West Virginia authorities."

Overbeck brushed hair off his forehead. "I worked at the big adoption center in Wheeling. The trainers contacted the center when they had retired racers ready for adoption. I picked them up and helped sort them, deciding which one went where. Part of the packet is the dog's history and family tree, so I had access to the records, the family history, and could pick the good ones. You know, those who'd had a decent racing career." He stopped.

Duncan took notes, but didn't stop watching Overbeck. "Then what?"

"I'd offer them to buyers online. Usually through dark web sources, so it was harder to trace."

"Did you use Tor?"

"The Onion Router, yes. This would be done before Wheeling contacted other groups to tell them what dogs were available so they could work to get them placed. Sometimes, not often, dogs were spoken for because a group would know it was retiring, but if it was a good dog, I was able to gloss it over, explain why it wasn't available after all."

"You said buyers contacted you through the dark web?" Cavendish asked.

Overbeck's shoulders twitched. "You know how it works, right? No names, just handles. DogLover23 or RacingMaven4Evr, that type of thing. They picked their dog, I'd provide information on how to pay me, and we'd arrange delivery."

Duncan raised an eyebrow. "I take it you didn't take cash or credit."

Overbeck chuckled. "Nah, I mostly used Bitcoin. More anonymity that way."

Duncan took another drink. "Payment before delivery?"

"Most of the time. If I had a repeat buyer, someone with a good record of payment, they got more leeway. New buyers had to pony up first, unless they were vouched for by an established contact."

He didn't volunteer for the love of animals, Duncan thought. "You never used names."

"Nope. I didn't ask theirs, they didn't know mine. Better that way."

"But when you got caught, you knew enough to make yourself valuable." Cavendish's voice dripped scorn. "After all, contacts are made through Tor, but the actual transaction is done by text. And then you'd have to deliver the goods. You can't mail a dog, right?"

"You sound like someone who has some experience in these matters."

"Not as much as others, but I know enough."

Overbeck gave a sly grin. "Always cover your tracks. My old man taught me that. In many cases, not all, the information I had was enough to connect usernames on Tor with real-life identities."

Duncan swallowed his distaste. *Your old man probably bootlegged whiskey.* He tapped the post-mortem picture of McDonough. "Are you sure you don't recognize this man? We've traced the greyhound we found at his house to Blue Mountain. According to their head trainer, the dog retired last March, and she thought he was bound for Pittsburgh."

A thick silence filled the room as the men stared at each other. Finally, Overbeck broke eye contact and picked up the photo again. "I might know this guy. Hard to tell. People look a lot different when they're alive. But he might have bought a dog."

"You keep any records? After all, it would be in line with your father's advice, cover your tracks. Plus, I know several buyers were arrested through this investigation. They missed McDonough, but they had to have ID'd them somehow. Which meant you had sufficient information to help with that."

Overbeck ran his tongue over his lips. "What's in it for me if I answer your question?"

Cavendish muttered something.

Duncan didn't spare her a glance. "Nothing. I told you, We're only here looking for information on a murder." He folded his hands and waited.

The silence lasted almost a full minute. "I kept a ledger of who bought what dog and for how much—which online handle, that is. I never listed anybody by name." Overbeck said. "The cops in West Virginia chased down at least half a dozen of my buyers. Could be this guy wasn't one of the ones they identified."

"You're positive you don't know him." Duncan didn't raise his voice but challenged his quarry with his stare.

Overbeck tried to maintain the connection but broke it, his gaze drifting to the left before he brought it back to Duncan's face. "I told you. He sort of looks familiar. That's the most I'll say."

"All right." Duncan replaced the picture in his pocket. "If you change your mind, and realize you do recognize him, I'd appreciate a call."

Cavendish leaned forward. "One last question. Where were you last Friday between the hours of six and ten?"

Overbeck didn't blink. "I had dinner with a friend. A lady friend. We went back to her place for…dessert."

Cavendish looked like she wanted to follow up, but Duncan put a hand on her shoulder. He slid a business card across the table and paused. "By the way, how much?"

"Excuse me?"

"How much did you charge for each dog?"

The card sat on the table, a small rectangle of white. "Anywhere from five hundred to seven hundred and fifty dollars. I couldn't get my hands on the big moneymakers. They went for breeding. But I knew about how much money a moderately successful racer made for his owner. By my calculations, five Ben Franklins was a cheap investment for a dog that could make thousands."

"But the racing wasn't legal."

"Trooper, you surprise me." Overbeck arched an eyebrow. "The illegal part is what made it so profitable. No fees to tracks, no vet bills, none of the little things that eat into the profits of legitimate racing."

"All your buyers agreed, did they?"

Overbeck didn't move. "They did. At least they paid."

Once again, Duncan's gaze bored into the watery blue eyes of the man across the table. "What if the buyer didn't hold up his end of the bargain?"

The eyes took on a hard glint. "Best case, they didn't get their dog. Worst case? Well, I'm not gonna go there. That's a different discussion, one I'm not willing to have in my kitchen with an officer of the law."

Chapter Sixteen

Instead of spending more time inside on the phone, Sally decided to take advantage of the superb weather and go to see Annie Norquist in person. She lived in Shaler, slightly north of Pittsburgh. If she kept charging a reduced rate, she might have to do more phone work. *I'm not only going to work for low-income defendants, though.* She needed to start a spreadsheet and see what her break-even point was.

The leaves had not yet begun to change, but the sky was a clear blue, and while the sun coming through the windshield of Sally's Camry was hot, the brutal heat of August had given way to friendlier temperatures. She cranked the radio and spent the drive time planning how to approach the president of River City Hounds, especially since the woman had already proven to be a bit skittish when talking about anything other than the greyhounds themselves.

Annie's house, a modest split-level, was nothing special, but it was located on the top of a hill overlooking the valley, without anything impeding the fantastic view. The gravel drive, wide enough for two cars, led to a garage on the side of the house that held a dusty blue SUV. An eight-foot-tall board fence prevented Sally from seeing the backyard, but it appeared to completely enclose the space. She went to the front door and knocked.

Annie opened the door a few moments later. "Yes, can I help you?" She was dressed in worn sweatpants and an RCH T-shirt, hair held back by a blue bandanna. She held yellow rubber gloves and the knees of her pants were wet. "You look familiar."

"Sally Castle. We met at your event in Market Square."

"Why are you here?"

"I may need to call you as a witness in Ciara Delmonico's defense, and I have a few questions. May I come in?"

Annie hesitated, then pushed open the door. "This is the last time. We'll go to the back. Please, take off your shoes. You can put them on the mat or carry them with you."

Sally looked around at the living room. The furniture was unspectacular, probably bought at a discount store or on clearance. An oversized dog bed was in the corner. "Where's your greyhound?"

"Rascal is in the backyard." Annie pointed through an archway. "This way."

Sally followed her through the house, which was as plainly furnished as the front room. She noticed a handsome sideboard covered with silver frames, each one holding the picture of a different greyhound. "Are these all yours?" she called.

Annie turned. "Were. Those are all the dogs I've owned over the years. All of them are across the Rainbow Bridge now, well, except Rascal here." She nodded at a frame.

In the backyard, Rascal had been sniffing along the fence line, but he loped over to greet Sally, tail waving as he energetically sniffed all over her. "He's a lot more active than the last time I saw him." The tail banged at her legs as he circled. "Ouch. It's like being flogged." Maybe talking about the dog would make Annie open up.

"Rascal, place." Annie pointed at an oversized cushion in the shade. Rascal took a few more sniffs, then went to flop down. "You've come into his territory. He has to give you the once-over." She waved at the bench. "Have a seat. What more can I tell you?"

"I want to talk about Lynn Moss." Sally removed a legal pad from her briefcase. "I spoke to Pat Dennister earlier. She told me Ms. Moss used to be your vice president, but was asked to leave the group because she violated your neutrality policy regarding racing."

"Yes, that's right. We all felt awful about it, of course. Lynn hadn't done anything serious. It was just an argument, not like she'd gotten into a physical fight or worse. But if you suspend the policy for one person, you might as well not have one."

"What was Ms. Moss's reaction?"

"Lynn wasn't happy, but she understood. At least that's what she said."

"Did you know she's still an approved signer on your bank account?" Sally watched the other woman's face.

Annie gave a small frown. "That's odd. Pat's usually very diligent about keeping the books clean. We definitely got her name off of the website."

"Pat told me that you volunteered to take care of it while she was on vacation."

"I don't...oh." Realization flooded her face and her cheeks turned a faint pink. "I remember, I did tell Pat to go on her trip and I'd go to the bank. But then Rascal tore a dew claw, and I wound up at the vet. The whole thing pushed the bank out of my head. Pat didn't return for two weeks, and by then, I'd completely forgotten about it."

Sally studied her. Annie was trying to sound calm, but her gaze kept drifting off to the left. Sally flipped through her notes. "According to the information I have, Ms. Moss was in a car accident early this year."

"Yes. Someone t-boned her at an intersection. I believe the other driver was texting and blew the stop sign."

"Was she badly injured?"

"Her back was messed up for a while. I remember she couldn't even walk Cassie. That's her hound. Cassie has some of the nicest leash manners you'd ever see, but even the gentle pressure if she stopped or turned when Lynn wasn't expecting it was torture." Annie snapped her fingers and Rascal came over. She ran her hand down his back.

"Did it heal? I assume so, if she was at events later in the year."

"Yes, but it was aggravating, I know that." She scratched Rascal under the chin. "All she could say, though, was how thankful she was Cassie hadn't been in the car. She probably would have been killed."

Sally paused. "Have you talked to Ms. Moss since she left the group?"

"Yes. Lynn and I are good friends," Annie said. Rascal went back to his bed, and she crossed her arms, leaning them on the table. "We take Rascal and Cassie down to a place on the Allegheny River once a week and meet for drinks. They have a patio, so the dogs can lounge while we eat and talk."

"How's she doing now?"

Annie picked at the table. "Good. She changed jobs right around when the accident happened. And she got divorced. She and her ex always had massive fights about finances. She's pretty happy. She misses volunteering, but then again, every time we meet it's like an event because people always want to pet the dogs and ask questions."

"Do you ever talk about the missing money? I mean, did you tell her about it?"

"I didn't have to." Annie brushed the tabletop. "She read about it in the paper. She was just as shocked as anyone else."

Sally glanced over at Rascal, who was half on and half off the bed, his head on the concrete, which struck her as a highly uncomfortable position, but it didn't seem to bother him in the slightest. She refocused on her hostess. "You never thought she knew more than she ought to? She never asked questions about the situation that surprised you?"

Annie pushed back her bandanna and gave Sally a stoney look. "I know what you're thinking, Ms. Castle. You think Lynn could have taken that money, and that's what you want me to say. If you think I'll smear a good friend just because you put me on the witness stand and make me swear an oath, think again."

* * *

After Duncan left Overbeck's house, he tossed the keys to Cavendish. "Mind driving?"

She caught them. "Why?"

"I need to make some phone calls."

She shrugged. "Fine."

In the car, he called HQ, to see if any information on Robert Bevilacqua's financial history was in. It wasn't. His second call was to Aislyn McAllister, to arrange a meeting so they could review the notes she'd gathered from the day McDonough's body was discovered.

"Who were you talking to?" Cavendish asked.

Duncan put away his phone and told her. "Lunch is on me."

She pulled into the parking lot of the Gray Line Diner shortly before one. A favorite gathering place for troopers, on and off duty, Duncan had brought McAllister here right before her field training stint with him had ended. That had happened almost a year ago. He wondered if she remembered.

Inside, he spotted her almost immediately, a glass of yellow liquid in front of her.

"Boss, over here." She waved.

He pointed at the soda. "Let me guess. Mountain Dew?"

"You know me so well." She looked around. "Is this your partner?"

Duncan made the introductions and took his seat. "Let's order first."

McAllister sized up the other woman. "You don't know how lucky you are, you know."

"How so?" Cavendish reached for a laminated menu.

"Boss is the best." McAllister's voice was matter-of-fact, as though she was sure Cavendish shared her opinion.

She studied the younger trooper for a moment. "Jury is still out." Then she turned her attention to choosing her lunch.

McAllister turned to Duncan and raised her eyebrows. He gave a tiny shake of his head. A few minutes later, the waitress came over and took their orders, a turkey club for McAllister, grilled chicken for Cavendish, and a burger for Duncan.

McAllister pulled out her notebook as soon as the waitress moved off. "I don't know what more I can tell you about the scene that day. But hey, never turn down a free lunch, right?"

"Right." He took out his own notes. "I want to go over the order of events. See if we can narrow down a time of death, since the autopsy is useless on this one."

Cavendish said nothing.

Again, McAllister shot him a puzzled look. "Where do you want to start?"

He didn't answer the unspoken question. "You canvassed the neighbors that day. When was the last time someone saw McDonough?"

She blew out a breath. "The woman across the street saw him Wednesday afternoon, late. She thinks it might have been somewhere between four-thirty and five. That's when she normally gets home. He was unloading bags from the back of his van."

"According to his phone records, he received a call on his cell at seven-thirty Thursday morning. The call lasted twenty minutes, and the geolocation puts it in Markleysburg. I'm going to guess it was his house."

"He was at home and answered the phone that morning."

"Someone answered the phone." The waitress brought out the drinks and told them the food would be ready shortly. McAllister switched her straw to the new glass.

Cavendish finally spoke up. "Maybe the killer answered the call."

"And talked for twenty minutes?" Duncan shook his head. "I doubt that."

"Who was the caller?"

"Number belongs to a pay-as-you-go phone. The kind you can buy for fifty bucks just about anywhere."

McAllister tapped the table. "That's not helpful."

"That it isn't." He glanced at his partner. She looked like she was uninterested in the conversation, but he was sure that was an act. *It's like she's grading me or something.* He almost said something, but decided to keep talking to McAllister. "You said he was spotted in the grocery store Thursday afternoon around two."

McAllister consulted her notes. "Then on Thursday night at approximately seven-thirty, the guy who lives across the street and up two saw lights come on at the victim's house. He also noticed a dark-colored car in the drive, or he thinks it was red. Four doors, not 'fancy,' whatever that means. The witness admits it could also be brown, but doesn't think it was blue or black. Of course, being a civilian, he didn't write down or remember the license plate number."

Cavendish tilted her head. "You're quite thorough."

McAllister lifted her chin. "My FTO taught me that the details provided by the responding trooper could make or break an investigation."

Duncan swore the air crackled with tension between the two women. Over him? Cavendish couldn't know he'd been McAllister's FTO. "That's the start of the window. I don't have any information on him being seen after that night. From you or anyone else."

The sandwiches arrived. McAllister took a bite, chewed, and swallowed. "I made some follow-up visits and can confirm that the previous Thursday night was the last time he was seen."

"Who asked you to go back?" Cavendish asked.

"No one. I didn't consider the canvass complete until I'd made my best effort at contacting everyone I could."

"You don't look like you've been on the job long. Who taught you?"

There was no mistaking the challenging look on McAllister's face. "The guy sitting next to you."

Cavendish pivoted slightly. Her expression shifted, just a touch, from stoney to thoughtful.

McAllister, I owe you. He hoped she could read his mind. "Do you remember if the lights were on or off when we found the body?"

Maybe she could, because she gave a small nod of acknowledgment. "I'm pretty sure they were off. What are you thinking?"

"He was shot Friday morning after the sun came up and there was enough light to see?" Cavendish asked.

He paused. "Maybe, but the killer could have turned off the lights Thursday night. Think about it. You just shot a guy. It's dark. You don't want him to be found quickly. Would you leave the lights on all night?"

Cavendish muttered a curse. "That means we could be looking at as much as a twelve-hour span for the time of death."

"Burns said he's pretty sure the body sat at least over the weekend based on the, uh, evidence." He eyed his burger.

"You mean the maggots." McAllister grinned. "Boss, don't tell me that makes you squeamish. If so, you're in the wrong line of work."

"Touché." He took a bite and thought. "Eight Thursday night to eight Friday morning."

Cavendish frowned. "What makes you say that? The Friday time, I mean."

"The newspaper was still on the doorstep. We can call and find out when morning delivery is, but I bet it's sometime between six and eight. If the killer had left after that, there'd be enough activity in the neighborhood that someone would have seen a person, or at least a car, at the house." He took another bite of hamburger. "That is still a pretty sucktastic window of opportunity. I'd like to make it narrower."

McAllister wagged a fry in his direction. "But it's a hell of a lot more than what you had."

"Thanks for the assist."

"Never too busy for you, Boss." She paused. "Question for you."

"Yes?"

"You're paying the tab for lunch, right?"

"I already said I would. You are giving up time to help me out."

"Good." She waved to catch the waitress's attention. "Because they're advertising fresh apple pie and I want dessert."

* * *

After Sally left Annie's house, she stopped at the forensic accountant's office to drop off the RCH tax information. "I have to clear this with my client, but I'm in the area, so I'll drop the material off now. If she wants to proceed, I'll give you a call."

"Good enough," the man said. "If she doesn't want to hire me, you can come get it, or I can FedEx it back to you."

Outside, she slipped on a pair of sunglasses. Through gaps in the buildings, she could see boats bobbing down the Allegheny River, enjoying the warmth of an Indian summer day. She stood on the sidewalk as people dressed in business attire, some jabbering on phones, slipped around her. Things hadn't changed much since the days when she worked for the Allegheny County District Attorney. *I could go back to prosecution. They'd take me in a heartbeat.*

No, definitely not an option.

She wandered down to the river walk, where a light breeze tossed the leaves on the trees. She paused to allow a few joggers to pass, found a bench, and sat. Her landlord had emailed her a reminder about her lease that morning. Why hadn't she already done that? She'd been telling Jim the truth when she said she wasn't ready to make the move to Confluence. Whether she drove to see him, or commuted from his house, she wasn't saving any time or gas. In fact, a move gained her almost nothing.

Except I'd be living with Jim.

She shook her head and stood. "Enough woolgathering." She was in Pittsburgh. If Sally intended to call Lynn Moss as a witness, she needed to learn more about the woman. Sally pulled up the address of Lynn's current employer on her phone and drove there. Lynn wasn't working, and the receptionist wouldn't say anything other than Lynn Moss was an employee.

Next, Sally looked up Lynn's former employer, the orthopedic surgery. The practice was in Shadyside and was open until five. She'd be dropping in unannounced, but sometimes those were the best interviews.

Given typical Pittsburgh traffic, it took her longer than expected to get to the office, and it was after one thirty by the time she walked through the door. "Afternoon," said a perky receptionist. "How can I help you?"

"I need to speak to someone."

The young woman reached for a plastic clipboard. "Are you a new patient?"

"No, I'm looking for information on a former employee. Her name is Lynn Moss."

Instantly, the open expression on the receptionist's face became guarded. "Ms. Moss doesn't work here any longer."

"I know that." Sally identified herself. "Ms. Moss is a potential witness for me."

"I'm not the person to talk to."

"Who is?"

The receptionist shifted. "I don't know, but not me. I also don't think you'll get anyone here to talk to you without a court order. Good day." She slid the glass divider on the desk shut, got up, and walked away.

Sally looked around the waiting room. It was clean and comfortable. Two patients waited, one on his phone and one browsing what had to be the moderately current magazines ubiquitous to every doctor's office. She left, got back into her Camry, and headed home.

She hadn't expected a lot of information, especially from the former employer. But the orthopedic surgery receptionist had shut down hard and fast. Not only that, she'd used the words "court order," and that wasn't a normal reaction to a simple question. All of it told Sally one thing.

Lynn Moss had not left under congenial circumstances.

Chapter Seventeen

When Duncan and Cavendish returned to HQ at two, Duncan checked the contents of his inbox, looking for the ballistics report on Kyle Sullivan's .38. "Damn it."

She sat and unlocked her computer. "What?"

"I hoped we'd get lucky and ballistics would be back. No such luck." He dropped into his chair.

She looked over at him. "Why does Trooper McAllister call you boss all the time?"

"It's a running joke." He briefly told Cavendish about the training stint the previous year, leaving out the gritty details of the Trafford case. *She doesn't need to know about that.* "I stopped trying to make her give it up."

"She thinks very highly of you."

He didn't meet Cavendish's gaze. He didn't want to see her expression or watch her weighing and measuring him. "I guess so."

"It says a lot about you." Her words, and her tone of voice, made him look up. Cavendish seemed thoughtful, as if she regarded him in a new light.

Enough of this bullshit. He would do his job and let the chips fall where they may. "I think we need more background on Sullivan. He doesn't feel right."

Cavendish rested her arms on her desk and leaned forward. "You don't buy his story?"

"I think there's a connection we don't know about that prompted that confrontation. I also think he lied about the allergy attack."

"There's no oak pollen in the fall. I wondered if you caught that."

"I did." He waited for a comeback.

But it didn't happen. She turned back to her screen. "I'll check the usual sources. What about this greyhound business? McDonough definitely had a dog, and that wasn't a pet. You think he was still racing it?"

"Yes. Or trying to find a new place to do so."

"Where?"

"I don't know, but I know someone who might." One man knew more about any illegal gambling in that little corner of Pennsylvania than anyone else. Eddie V, Confluence's resident bookie.

"You have a snitch already?" Now there was definitely a note of admiration in her voice.

"I wouldn't use those words around him, but yes." Duncan would bet good money Eddie knew where to get action on the dogs, either locally or across the state line. He glanced at the clock. No use visiting Eddie for another couple of hours.

One of the administrative staff he'd met yesterday passed his desk and dropped off an envelope. "Financials related to your murder investigation," she said.

"Thanks." He picked up the envelope and slit it open.

Cavendish got up and rounded the desk. "That is a record turnaround time. Who'd you bribe?"

"No one. These are for Robert Bevilacqua. Somebody must have been bored." He set down the envelope and pulled out a sheaf of paper.

They split up the papers for review and read in silence for a good fifteen minutes. "Mr. Bevilacqua is an interesting guy," Cavendish said, laying down her share.

"Everything he told us when we saw him in Connellsville was sensible. And yet..."

"It set your spidey-senses tingling." She skimmed each sheet, laying it face down on the desk as she finished. "Based on the stuff here, no wonder."

"Exactly." There was no doubt Cavendish was a competent investigator. A thought struck him. *It's not that she doubts I can investigate at all. She's not sure if I can meet her standard.* "Bevilacqua told us he owned several real estate properties, which is true. Most of them, these four, are in Pittsburgh. Then there's the one he's living in and McDonough's house in Markleysburg. You can see from this that the Pittsburgh properties are the most lucrative."

She nodded. "Makes sense. Outside of the areas around the resorts, you don't find a lot of luxury rentals in the Laurel Highlands."

"From what I've read, it also looks like the property in Connellsville has been empty for some time. At least four months."

"I saw the same thing."

"When we visited, he admitted he usually resided in Pittsburgh. He'd only moved to that house because it was empty, and he found himself in financial difficulties."

She scanned the reports. "That's an understatement. These bank balances don't belong to a successful landlord."

Duncan passed over another sheet. "He filed for bankruptcy protection at the end of the summer. Chapter 11. According to this, his payment plan is still under review. Prior to that, he barely scraped by. At least that's what it looks like. Then in April, something else happened to push him over the edge."

Cavendish looked up from her reading. "What?"

"Otto McDonough stopped paying his rent. I'm looking at his accounting, and that's the last time Bevilacqua recorded a payment from his tenant."

"That must have hurt."

He passed over more paper. "Within six months, Bevilacqua was broke. After the filing, he sold his Pittsburgh condo. Looks like he sold his car, his bank account is awash in red ink, and he hasn't made a payment on any of his credit cards in months. In fact"—Duncan rummaged in the paper until he found what he was looking for—"his bankruptcy plan includes the sale of two of his properties."

"He put the squeeze on one of his remaining tenants. Otto McDonough." She handed back the file.

"It makes sense. Bevilacqua was treading water until McDonough stopped his payments. I did some rough math." He handed her a sheet of figures and calculations. "If Bevilacqua collected the money he was owed, he'd be able to pay off most of his debt. If McDonough resumed payments, Bevilacqua might have enough to move back to Pittsburgh, at least if he waited a few months. It would be ideal if he also could rent the Connellsville house, but McDonough seems to be the difference between doing okay and being destitute."

"The two men argue, Bevilacqua loses it, and pops his tenant? Then he freaks and leaves."

"Something like that."

She pursed her lips. "No, I don't see it. How much can you possibly get for that dump?"

Duncan paused to look for the payment amount. "It's…holy shit, McDonough's rent is seven hundred and fifty dollars a month."

"Get out of here." She snatched the sheet.

Seven-fifty times six was four thousand, five hundred dollars. Pricey for a run-down residence in a tiny town. Math had never been his strong suit, but even he could see that amount of cash would have more than covered the bills. "Makes you wonder why, doesn't it? I know that's cheap by Pittsburgh standards, but down here? Seems like a lot."

She set down the paper. Any doubt she might have been harboring appeared to have disappeared. "Here's another thought. He says he's in property management. Why Markleysburg? I mean, if he had multiple houses in the town, I might understand, but one property way out here in the boonies? Also, it doesn't make sense to kill a guy who owes you money."

He gathered up the sheets. "Bevilacqua may have believed that with McDonough dead, he'd get at least the money owed in a death settlement or whatever. You know, deducted from any cash McDonough may have had when he died."

Cavendish cocked her head. "I'm not sure it really works that way."

"I'm not either, but all that matters is if Bevilacqua believed it. Or at least thought he had a chance." Duncan opened a can of Coke he'd bought that morning and tossed back a gulp of the lukewarm soda.

She sat back. "Then Bevilacqua is our prime suspect?"

"That's a bit much. We need to talk to him again, get some answers to those questions. I also want to find out more about Kyle Sullivan, the guy who threatened the victim over the kid. Plus, we have to talk to the protest group, and we have to learn what was going on with his illegal greyhound racing." He wondered if Johnny's Pixelated had gone to an adoption group. He made a mental note to call animal control and check up on the matter.

Her expression turned thoughtful. "Nice work."

The compliment caught him off guard. "Thanks." What did she expect him to say?

She locked her computer and stood. "It's already two o'clock. Let's go back to the Markleysburg house, see if we spot anything else? There might be new witnesses, ones we haven't talked to."

He followed suit. "Sounds like a plan. Who's driving?"

She tossed the keys on his desk. "You are, rookie."

He smothered a retort and grabbed them. Just when he thought he'd earned some respect.

* * *

Sally checked the dashboard clock in her Camry. She did some quick math on the billing for the case. *I've got a little wiggle room.* She decided to drive to Lynn Moss's house. According to the information from Tracer, she lived in Penn Hills, a suburb to the east of the city. In the middle of the day, it shouldn't take too long to get there.

Lynn's house was in a small development off Frankstown Road, one of the main arteries from the suburbs into the city. The houses were small, the yards were neat. Here and there, Sally saw red and gold signs proclaiming pride in the local high school football team. Most of the houses were brick, some red, some yellow, but there were no sidewalks. In the middle of the day, few cars and fewer people could be seen.

Sally parked in front of Lynn's home, a two-story with white shutters and a small garage off to the side. No car stood in the driveway, and the door was down. Sally walked to the front and rang the bell. No answer. She rang again. The blinds covered the windows, and a ribbed square of fabric on the door prevented her from peeking in, but her rings remained unanswered, and no sounds came from the house.

Sally strolled around to the garage and peered in the dusty windows. No car, but the walls displayed panels of pegboard that might have once held tools. When a car was inside, there wouldn't be much room. She saw a push mower, a watering can, and a set of long-handled shears in the corner. She checked out the backyard, the grass green and in need of a trim. There was a patio with a metal table that held a collapsed umbrella and four white chairs with faded cushions. The yard was not fenced, and Sally saw no way to tie up a dog. If Lynn still owned a greyhound, she had to walk it or take it someplace for exercise. She returned to the front of the house.

While she inspected the back, a middle-aged Black woman wearing gardening gloves and holding a small pair of clippers came out into the yard next door.

"Excuse me. Do you live here?" Sally pointed at the house next to Lynn's. The woman nodded.

Sally introduced herself. "Do you have a minute? I have some questions, if you don't mind speaking to me."

The woman waved her clippers. "As long as you're not selling anything."

"I promise I'm not." Sally stopped well outside the range of the curved blades, just in case. "I'm looking for Lynn Moss. This is her house, isn't it?"

"Yes, but she's not home right now. She doesn't generally get home until five-thirty." She paused. "You said you were a lawyer. Is Lynn in trouble?"

"She could be a witness in a case I'm working on. I want to ask her a couple of questions. Tell me, has she lived here long?"

The woman squinted at her. "Got any ID?"

Sally showed her driver's license and her old Fayette County Courthouse identification.

The woman nodded, apparently satisfied. "Lynn and her husband have lived here, oh, has to be ten years now. Well, until their divorce. He's gone. She's still here. My name's Myra Hunter, by the way."

"Pleased to meet you, Ms. Hunter." Sally nodded toward the house. "You have lovely roses."

"Call me Myra. Thank you. It's been a good summer for them."

Sally wanted to keep the conversation on Lynn and hoped Myra wouldn't get sidetracked.

Myra rubbed her chin. "I know she was in trouble of losing it, the house, last spring. This was after her accident, which was in January."

Sally itched to take out a notepad, but sensed that might make her new source clam up. "I heard about that from a friend of hers. It sounded awful."

"Oh, it was. Messed up her back fierce. She couldn't even walk her dog, poor thing. Lynn, not the dog. She has one of those retired racers. Beautiful animal."

"A greyhound."

"Yeah, that's it. Anyway, I remember talking to Lynn and her saying how if something didn't happen soon, she wouldn't be able to pay the mortgage. I'm not positive, but it sounded like she missed a few payments. She couldn't work because of her back, see."

"That's what I've been told." Sally glanced around the neighborhood. "Her friend said she came into some money, though."

"Well, there was the divorce settlement. Then oh, must have been March or so, I saw her at the Giant Eagle and asked how things were going. She said an aunt had died and left her some cash, so she'd be able to pay off her bills. Between the house and the medical payments, she had to have been floundering. Why, the prescription costs alone had to be staggering."

"Prescriptions?"

"Pain killers, as I understand. For her back. Matter of fact, I think she's still taking them, poor dear."

"Why do you say that?"

Any reservations Myra may have had seemed to be gone, because she talked freely. "We had a windstorm a few weeks ago, and one of her trash bags ended up in my yard. I could tell when I tossed it in my can, there were a lot of prescription bottles in it. I asked her if she were okay, and she said they was old, but Lord, there sure did seem to be a lot of them."

"I see." Was Lynn an addict? Sally knew it wasn't an uncommon story. A person took pain pills for an injury and was soon hooked. Opioid addiction could be expensive. Maybe Lynn had stolen from River City to fund her need for meds. "The accident must have made it hard for her to work."

"It did. She's a secretary. Sitting or standing, she can't do it long. But you're right. In fact, she lost a job shortly after the accident. She worked for a doctor's office or something. It might have been a few months later, say April or May. She said they let her go because she couldn't work the hours anymore. But she's got a new position and says they're much more understanding."

"Well, that's good. When you're hurting like that, having a compassionate employer is important."

"Amen."

Sally checked, but Lynn's driveway remained empty. "It doesn't look like I'm going to catch her today. Would you do me a favor?"

"I can try."

Sally handed a business card to Myra. "Next time you see Lynn, would you ask her to call me? Tell her it's about the money problems at River City Hounds, and I'd appreciate a little of her time."

Myra took the card and slid it into her pocket. "I will. You have a good evening."

"You, too. Thanks for your time." Sally went back to her car and started it. Before she drove off, she stared at Lynn's neat house. Money problems that mysteriously went away. An accident resulting in severe injuries, which might have led to an opioid addiction. Everybody assumed Lynn's money problems started with the divorce and were resolved with the settlement and an inheritance. It seemed Lynn had encouraged that belief.

But what if the money had come from RCH's coffers instead? *Reasonable doubt.* That was all she needed to raise. And if Myra was right, and she could get Lynn on the stand to make the story more than hearsay, she could easily do that.

Chapter Eighteen

Duncan and Cavendish pulled up in front of McDonough's Markleysburg house around two-thirty.

"This neighborhood isn't any less grim when you aren't showing up for a dead body," Cavendish said as she buttoned up her jacket.

"Markleysburg isn't attracting high-tech businesses like Google and undergoing urban renewal."

"You got that right." She looked up and down the semi-deserted street. "Where do you want to start?"

"Let's check the scene again." It wasn't that he doubted McAllister's skills or thoroughness, but he might be able to shake a few more details loose if he went in person.

The house was still boarded up, yellow crime scene tape over the door. He wondered if the house would be able to be cleaned enough for another resident or if anyone would even want to live there once they learned of the previous tenant's fate.

They removed the tape enough to let themselves in. The stench of rotting flesh was mostly gone, but the interior still stank of mold, mildew, and the lingering scent of death. "Should we split up?" he asked.

"Makes sense. We'll finish faster. I'll check upstairs, you do the first floor." She took the stairs two at a time.

Once again, Duncan made a detailed search of the premises, but it turned up nothing new. The cage where he'd found Johnny's Pixelated still stood in its corner, but all the steroids and other doping materials were gone. Mercifully, the freezer still hummed, so the meat inside had not thawed and rotted. He examined the cuts. They didn't seem to be high quality, nothing he'd put on his grill for human consumption, but probably deemed acceptable for a dog whose only purpose was to make its owner some money. He sure wouldn't feed Rizzo this stuff. He tossed the frozen blocks back and slammed the freezer door.

The crime scene unit had been thorough. Very little remained in the house and nothing that looked helpful. All of McDonough's personal papers were gone, catalogued and in envelopes back at HQ. He'd had a laptop, but that was also absent. Duncan made a note to contact the tech guys and see if they'd been able to recover anything useful.

He went back to the living room where they'd found the body, stood in the middle, and revolved in a slow three-hundred-and-sixty-degree turn. The place was a cesspool, and he was sure once the fingerprint reports and information on the rest of the physical evidence came back, it would be a mess of unknown prints, fibers, and the detritus of a man who simply didn't believe in clean living in any sense of the word. No, the house had yielded all it was going to.

Cavendish reappeared in the doorway. "Find anything?"

"No. You?"

"Zilch. Except for mold and mildew, and I don't think those will be helpful."

They let themselves out and had replaced the tape over the door when he heard a voice behind him. Down in the street, an old man shuffled, leading a scruffy dog on a leash. "Excuse, me, sir?"

The man stopped and squinted. "Who are you? The cops said we wasn't supposed to go in there. And I ain't no sir, thank you very much. I worked for a living."

"It's okay, we are the cops." He held out his badge for the man to see. "This is my partner, Trooper Cavendish."

She showed her ID.

The dog sniffed at Duncan's ankles, stump of a tail wagging frantically. He watched the animal carefully. In his experience, small dogs could be just as aggressive as large ones, maybe even more so. But all the mutt did was lift his leg. Duncan jumped to the side.

"Henry! Stop that. For chrissakes, take a piss somewhere else." The old guy tugged the leash. "Sorry about that, Officer. Guess he likes you and wants to mark you as his own."

"I think my dog might object to that." Duncan glanced at his clothes, but Henry had missed.

The old man wheezed a laugh. "Guess he would at that."

"Are you a resident of this neighborhood? Did you know the man who lived here?" Cavendish asked.

"Sure do. Name's Ben Hastings. I live 'round the block." He pointed. "Yeah, I knew Otto. Surly cuss. Henry took a dump in front of his house once, and Otto nearly lost his fool mind. This ain't some hoity-toity neighborhood, for God's sake, and I clean up after him anyway."

Duncan took out his notebook and a pen. "I take it Otto wasn't what you'd call a good neighbor then."

"Oh, he was all right, I guess." Ben scratched his cheek while Henry sniffed the weeds along the street. "Mostly, he kept to himself. Never had no big parties, no loud music, none of that crap. But he never had a friendly word, no matter how often I saw him when I was out walking Henry. I got the impression that he didn't much like dogs. Which is funny 'cause I think he had one himself. Big black thing."

"Yes, we found a dog on the property. You saw Otto with it?"

Ben hawked and spat. "If you call loading a crate into that van of his, yeah, I saw him. Poor thing, all skin and bones. I wonder if Otto ever let it outta that damn cage."

Henry moved over to sniff Cavendish's shoes, and she sidestepped away from him. "We think he might have been involved in illegal greyhound racing."

"Yeah, that don't surprise me." Ben spat again. "Otto struck me as the kind looking to make a buck. I never found dog racing that interesting, keeping those poor beasts for sport, but least it's clean, and they get fed and stuff. Rules, you know?"

Duncan pulled pictures out of his pocket. "Did you ever see any of these men around the house, maybe talking to Otto?"

Ben threw a quick glance at his dog, but Henry was exploring the area around a storm sewer and looked content. He shuffled through the pictures. "Well, that there is Kyle Sullivan. He lives here in town. He tangled with Otto once or twice over Mikey Fisher. That was a crock of shit, if you ask me. Otto shoulda been charged with something in that boy's death."

"Do you recognize anyone else?"

Ben pursed his lips. "This guy." He shook the picture of Max Renner. "He came by once. Otto wouldn't let him on the property. He got real mad, said he'd be back, and if Otto didn't 'give him back' he'd be sorry."

"Give who back?" Cavendish asked.

"Guy didn't say, sorry. Otto looked like he knew, though. Least I thought so. I was walking Henry and making sure he didn't take another dump on Otto's grass, so I wasn't paying real close attention."

"When did this happen?"

"Oh, I don't know." Ben scratched a stubbled cheek. "End of August, maybe? I'm thinking it was before Labor Day 'cause I remember it being hot as hell. Definitely not much later than that."

"Got it. Thanks." Duncan put the pictures back in his pocket. So much for Renner's statement he didn't pay attention to the track maintenance staff. "One more thing. Kyle Sullivan's argument with Mr. McDonough."

"Arguments, you mean. There was more than one of 'em."

Duncan waved in acknowledgement. "Why was he so upset? I mean, the death of a little kid is serious, and I live in a small town myself so I know that kind of incident is going to rile a lot of folks. But Mr. Sullivan seems particularly angry. Do you know why that would be?"

Ben raised his eyebrows. "Don't you know?"

"Know what?"

"Mikey Fisher was Kyle's half-brother."

* * *

It was nearly four o'clock before Sally returned to Uniontown. She decided

139

to swing by Ciara's house to update her on the state of the case and for a general check-in. The last time Sally had seen Ciara, the woman had been a bundle of nerves. It would help her to know progress was being made, even if it didn't look like it.

But when Sally arrived at Ciara's house, the door to the garage was open, and it was empty. Maybe the car was in for service or Ciara had gone out. After all, she wasn't on house arrest. Two empty garbage cans laid at the curb, their topsy-turvy positions indicating the sanitation department had emptied them that day, but Ciara hadn't been home to carry them back inside.

Sally went to the front door and rang the bell. No answer. She waited a minute, then rang again. Nothing. Leaning over, she peered in the front window, where the curtains had been pulled aside, affording a clear view into the house. All the lights were off with no people visible. Determined, Sally knocked a third time.

A voice came from behind her. "If you're looking for Mrs. Delmonico, she's not home."

Sally turned to see a teenage boy dragging the trashcans from the house next door back from the curb. He wore a faded black t-shirt with some band logo and ripped jeans. His dark brown hair flopped in his face, which didn't hide the eyebrow piercings. A silver hoop was in his right nostril, and a black gauge stretched his left earlobe. "Thanks. You live next door?"

"Yup. Me and my folks." He pointed at the house. "Anyway, she's not here. Drove off this morning, early. Came back around noon, changed her clothes, and left again."

"I don't suppose you talked to her before she left."

The youth shook his head. "Nope. She put her garbage out first, though. Then took off like a bat out of hell, as my mom says." He heaved the plastic cans into the garage, pulled an e-cigarette out of his front pocket, and puffed.

"Any idea where she went?"

He blew out a stream of smoke. "What's it to you?"

"I'm her attorney."

"Then shouldn't you know?"

140

Sally bit back a sarcastic response. "Not if she didn't have a meeting with me. I don't keep tabs on her around the clock."

"Maybe you should." He puffed on the device.

"What does that mean?"

"Just that you should keep in touch with your clients a bit better. You know, so you can find 'em when you want 'em." He smirked.

God save her from wise-ass teenagers. "If you don't know where she is, thanks." She turned to go back to her car.

The boy's sly voice called her back. "I don't know *exactly* where she is, but I might have a guess."

She faced him again. "Oh really? Where?"

"What's it to you?" he asked again as he puffed.

At that moment, Sally would have given almost anything to have Jim with her. He would have put this kid in his place. Instead, she was just going to have to channel her inner police officer. "If you're trying to get me to offer you money, it's not going to work. I don't pay for information like this because while it would be helpful to know where Mrs. Delmonico is right now, I can always call her." She played a hunch. She walked up close to the boy and took a deep breath. Underneath the fruity smell of whatever he was vaping, she detected the faint, yet definite, smell of weed. "How old are you?"

"Sixteen."

"Huh. Last I heard, you had to be twenty-one to purchase nicotine products in this state." She sniffed, exaggerating the action. "And while I know Pennsylvania has decriminalized marijuana possession, you have to be a legal adult, eighteen, for that to apply."

"So?" His voice cracked a bit.

"I have a friend in the state police. Maybe I should call him, ask him to have a talk with you and your parents. You know, explain the dangers of vaping and marijuana use." She pulled out her phone and tapped a few numbers.

"Shit, no, wait." He reached for the phone.

She snatched it away. "You can tell me where you think Mrs. Delmonico is, or I can complete this phone call. Your choice."

The kid bit his lip for a second and then said, "Screw it. I saw Mrs. Delmonico when she got home. She looked stressed. She came out at noon, and she was yelling on her phone about money. Least I'm pretty sure."

"Did you hear what she said?"

The kid frowned. "Something like how she only needed a couple hundred, and she was good for it. She must have been really into her call because she pulled out of her drive crooked and nearly took out her garbage cans."

If Ciara wasn't working, she'd definitely need money, but the scene the teenager painted slid a finger of doubt down Sally's back. "When was this? When she left the second time?" Ciara had been stressed this morning, but not run-over-the-trash-cans stressed.

"Dunno. Lunchtime maybe? We had a half-day at school. I got home before one and saw her leave."

That meant Ciara had left shortly after the meeting with the district attorney. She'd definitely been rattled. "Okay, thanks." She turned to go.

"My mom thinks she's got a gambling problem. Maybe that's why she needs cash."

The words stopped Sally in her tracks. "What makes you say that?"

"Last week, I overheard my mom and Mrs. Delmonico talking. See, we'd gotten some of her mail, and one of the pieces was a card from Rivers Casino. It was a special for 'frequent guests.' Anyway, when Mom went to return the mail, she got into her advice-giving mode, saying how there were programs to help people and stuff. She said the numbers were right on the billboard advertising and how there was no shame in admitting you had a problem, blah, blah, blah."

"What, you went with your mother?"

"No. I was cutting the grass. I may have, you know, fiddled with the string on the trimmer a little bit." He held up his hands. "What? I get hounded by my mother all the time over my hair, and friends, and clothes. It was sorta nice to see her going off on someone else. Least until she caught me and told me to either trim the edges or go inside."

Sally's analysis of Ciara's financials hadn't turned up any significant debt that could be attributed to a gambling addiction. Then again, maybe she wasn't going into debt, but she blew any so-called extra cash at the card table. There could be any number of reasons Ciara had hidden her habits. Anything from not thinking it was relevant to shame. But if she had a gambling debt, it was certain the prosecution would bring it up, and that meant Sally needed to get in front of it. She pulled out her phone and dialed. "Ciara, we need to talk. Please call me back as soon as you can." She turned to walk back to her car.

The teenager ran in front of her. "Hey, in TV shows, the informant always gets something for helping out." He held out his hand.

"You want something in return, huh?"

"Heck yeah."

"Then here's some free advice." She jabbed her finger at the e-cigarette. "Stop vaping. It's worse for your health than smoking."

Chapter Nineteen

Sally returned to the office. Kim was still there, but she wore a coat and held her keys, sure signs of leaving. "I have a problem," Sally said.

Kim buttoned her coat. "I'm sorry to hear that. If it's professional, we can talk tomorrow morning. If it's personal, I can't help you."

"I think we should chat now."

Her law partner paused, her hand frozen on her coat. "This doesn't sound good."

"It's not." Sally got a cup of coffee and proceeded to tell her the latest news about Ciara. "She doesn't need the money for me, that's all I know. If she's in debt I don't know about, it could really hurt her defense."

Kim groaned. "Okay, let's think about it a minute. All you have is the word of a sixteen-year-old kid. That can't be reliable. Have you talked to Ciara?"

"I've called three times in the last half hour. Each time the call goes to voicemail." Sally plopped down in her chair.

"Maybe she's busy. I mean, it's a Wednesday afternoon. She could be anywhere."

"Such as?" Sally knew she sounded snappish, but her nerves were taut after the failed attempts to reach her client. *If I can't lose my temper a little with a partner, and no one else around, when can I?*

"Don't bite my head off, sister. I understand you're frustrated, but be rational." Kim ran a hand through her red curls. "She's a professional. At least she has been up to now. What would she normally be doing on a business day?"

Sally looked at the time on her phone. "Right about now I'd be expecting her to be wrapping up her work day. She could have had a late meeting with a client. She might be closing up shop and heading home for dinner."

"Logical. She also could be at a personal appointment. Maybe a doctor or something."

"We were done at the DA's office by twelve. The kid said he saw her at one. It's now"—Sally checked the time again—"a little after four-thirty. That's an awfully long doctor's visit."

Kim lifted her arms and let them fall. "I tried." She paced. "Okay. So the client might be holding out on us. What do you propose we do?"

"Obviously, I have to talk to her. But she didn't confess before now, so I'm not terribly hopeful she'll come clean. Then again, I can't spend her money, or ours, on a snipe hunt looking for answers." Sally stared into the inky liquid in her cup. "I'll call one more time. If I connect, I'll ask her to come in tomorrow, when I can impress on her the seriousness of the situation and urge her to tell me what's going on."

"If anything *is* going on."

"Right." No longer interested in the coffee, Sally went to the kitchenette and poured it away. She returned to pick up her purse and keys.

Kim held open the front door. "What if she refuses?"

"I'll tell her I might have to re-evaluate whether we can represent her." Sally stepped out into the warm evening and squinted against the setting sun. "I'm all about helping people. But I'll be damned if I'll get blindsided in court."

* * *

Duncan scrolled down the Events page of the website for the Proper Treatment of the Environment, Animals, and the World while Cavendish talked on her phone a few paces away. The protest group listed a gathering at the Meadows racetrack tonight from five to seven. *Perfect.* He could go to the track then head over to talk to Eddie V.

Cavendish came back, phone in hand. "Renner isn't answering. I left a message saying we needed to talk." She nodded at him. "What are you looking at?"

"Website for the protest group. I'm going to try and catch Bethany at this event, then head over to my informant. I can drop you at HQ."

"You aren't going without me, rookie."

He'd made himself a promise that he wouldn't get angry, but her condescending tone shattered his resolve. "Time out. I'm new here. I got that. But I'm not a rookie. Not in the traditional sense of the word."

She gave him a cool stare. "You are to me."

"Maybe. But that doesn't mean you get to insult me. Call me Jim, or pal, or even FNG. But I'd appreciate it if you'd stop with the R word."

"Don't worry. I will."

He took a breath. "When?"

"When I decide you aren't one." She walked off to the car without a backward glance.

He watched her go, hands clenched at his side. *If you think you're going to get me to quit over your bullshit attitude, think again.* No wonder she hadn't had a partner when he arrived.

He drove to the Meadows. When he pulled into the parking lot, he could see a small cluster of people near the entrance, including a woman with violently purple hair.

"Nice call," Cavendish said. "Ten to one that's Bethany."

Duncan grunted a response and parked at the far end of the lot. He got out and shut the door.

It must have slammed, because Cavendish positioned herself in front of him, barring his way. "What's eating you?"

He took in her matter-of-fact tone. He'd rarely heard brown eyes described as cool, but hers were as they evaluated him. Did she really not know? "You are." He rubbed his chin. "I'm not sure what you expect out of a partner. But I know what I do, and this isn't it. I've tried to be patient and understanding, but I really can't figure out what you want from me."

She tilted her head. "Just keep doing the job." She turned. "How do you want to do this?"

Whatever Cavendish wanted, she wasn't going to tell him. *Do the job.* "I think we need to talk to her alone, or as alone as we can get her in this situation. I don't want to get into a pissing match with a bunch of activists."

"Agreed. I think we can separate her from the group without too much trouble. Let's go."

They approached the small knot of people holding signs. As they came closer, a woman with long red hair and a pierced nose moved in front of them. "We're not leaving, so if the noise is interrupting your evening of depravity, too bad," she said, thrusting her chin forward.

Duncan held up his hands. "I'm not going to ask you to leave."

"Changed your mind? Come to join the fight for animal rights? These horses should be running free, not tethered to a cart for the enjoyment of people. They don't deserve death just because they don't run fast enough for their human overlords."

"To be honest, I'm not a big fan of horse racing. I have better places to spend my money. We want to talk to Bethany."

The women gave him a squinty, suspicious look. "What for?"

He pulled out his badge wallet and showed it to her. "We have some questions."

Wordlessly, Cavendish held out her own badge.

She puffed up and raised her voice. "We got a right to protest here. We're not interfering with business. The Constitution says we have the right to peaceful assembly."

A couple of other protesters moved to her side, gripping their signs and looking daggers at him.

Duncan didn't bother pointing out the fact they were on private property, which meant the Meadows could have them removed, and the right to peaceful assembly only applied to government property. Now was not the time for a civics lesson. "We're not here to break up your evening. We want to talk to Bethany on an entirely different matter."

Bethany pushed forward through her fellows. "What do you want to talk about?"

"Otto McDonough," Cavendish said.

She tossed her head. "I have no idea who that is."

Cavendish crossed her arms. "He worked at Blue Mountain Racing. You decorated his car with ketchup not that long ago."

"Pig." Bethany snorted. "He's another one making his living off the sweat of poor innocent animals who are forced into a life of servitude and slavery."

"He's also dead."

"Good." Bethany's eyes flashed in the setting sun.

Duncan stepped to the side, discreetly nudging the red-haired woman back to the rest of the group. "Ms.…. I'm sorry, I don't remember your last name." A fib, but trying to be casual might soften her attitude.

"Carlyle."

He replaced his badge in his jacket. "Ms. Carlyle. We want to have a peaceful, non-confrontational conversation about a murder victim. If you want to make this difficult, we can certainly oblige you. Just answer a couple of questions, and we'll be on our way without disrupting your gathering."

Bethany glared at him for a long moment. Then she thrust her sign at a fellow picketer and said, "Hold this for me. I'll be right back." Without another word, she stomped off toward the parking lot. She stopped about ten feet away and whirled around. "Ask your damn questions."

Duncan and Cavendish followed. Once there, Duncan took out his notebook. "I've been told you had a confrontation with Mr. McDonough not that long ago. Is that true?"

"Sure is. I told him he was a piece of filth and should be shot for what he's done to those poor dogs."

"Who covered his car in ketchup?" Cavendish asked. "You?"

"Nah, that was someone else." Bethany smirked. "It pissed him off, though. Serves him right. If he didn't want to be a target, he should've parked somewhere else. Most of the track staff know that. Not my fault he's a dumbass as well as a pig."

Duncan eyed her. "Did you volunteer to shoot him?"

Her tone became slightly less belligerent. "Why would I do that?"

"The story we have is you told him he should shoot himself, and if he wasn't up to the task, you'd help him out."

"I don't remember exactly what I said." Bethany's gaze shifted to the ground. "Why does it matter if he's dead?"

"Because someone shot him," Cavendish said. "Three times, to be exact."

She crossed her arms and stared at the troopers. "Like I said, good."

Duncan studied the defiant pose. With the outrageous hair, crossed arms, and angry words, Bethany wanted people to think she didn't care. But the look in her eyes, that of a frightened rabbit, and the slight tremor in her voice betrayed her. "Ms. Carlyle, do you own a gun?"

"No."

"Anybody you know own one?"

She licked her lips. "I think a couple of the guys have handguns. I know they like to go target shooting. One of them hunts, so he has a rifle."

He lifted an eyebrow. "Your group is against animal cruelty, but you hunt?" The definition of irony.

"I'm a vegan. But yeah, a couple guys hunt. They aren't in it for the trophies, though. It's about food. It's not the same as exploiting animals for sport, or using the inhumane practices of big agra, companies that stuff their animals full of drugs and slaughter them in warehouses."

"I see." In other words, they couldn't give up their love of a good venison steak. "Where were you last Thursday?"

"What time?"

"All day."

Cavendish took out her own notepad and a pen.

She paused. "I'm a student at Pitt. I had class until two-thirty. After that, I attended a meeting of the Environmental Activist club until five."

Out of the corner of his eye, he saw Cavendish write. "And after that?" he asked.

"I met a friend for dinner, and we, uh, hung out."

"Anyplace in particular?" Cavendish didn't look up.

"His place in Pittsburgh. I was there all night."

She didn't offer any further details, and Duncan didn't ask. He figured he had a pretty good idea of what went on at the friend's house. "We need the names and phone numbers of any people you were with and your professors, so we can corroborate your story. Don't forget your Thursday night hangout buddy. Don't worry, we're not interested in what you were doing, just confirming you were there." He held out his notebook.

She scribbled down several names and thrust the book back at him. "McDonough really was a pig. I think he owned a greyhound and raced it. I'm positive it was illegal, and I'm pretty sure he abused the dog, too."

"What makes you say that?"

"He made a comment once about how at least he didn't have to put up with us 'at the other place.' And Josie, that's the redhead, saw him once in a store. His cart was loaded up with cheap meat and steroids, the kind they use to dope animals for racing."

"I know about the bust in West Virginia."

"He must have found another place. When he said that, it was after the arrests from earlier this year."

"You know where it is?"

She shook her head. "No, but if you find it, let me know. I'll organize a protest. We done?"

"Yeah, thanks."

Bethany strode off, not giving Duncan and Cavendish a backward glance.

He'd been right. McDonough had found another off-the-books racing operation. Eddie wouldn't be involved in dog racing. But he'd definitely know where to look.

They walked back to the car. Cavendish opened her door. "I'm going with you tonight. To talk to your snitch."

"No, you aren't."

"I'm the senior partner. If I say I'm going, I'm going." She got in the passenger side.

He slid into the driver's seat. "No, you're not." He held up a hand. "Someday, I'll introduce you. But I'm not going to risk you putting his back up. Not when his place will be full."

She shook her head. "His place? Who is this guy?"

"He's a bookie in my town and he runs his own gambling parlor. He's helped me out a couple of times. He also has a doorman, Stanley, who could easily play linebacker for the Steelers, and he doesn't like strangers. You want to meet Eddie. Fine. But not tonight. I want to keep Eddie in a good mood."

For a moment it seemed like she was going to argue, then she shrugged. "Have it your way. How are you going to make this guy talkative?"

Duncan started the car. "I'm going to bring a friend."

Chapter Twenty

A round eight o'clock that evening, Duncan pulled into the gravel lot outside the cinderblock building that served as Eddie V's place of business. He'd spruced the place up over the summer, applied a fresh coat of light gray paint to the walls, and installed a new steel door. Things must be good in the gambling racket. As he put the Jeep in park, he turned to Sally. "Thanks for coming."

She didn't face him but picked up her bag from the floor. "No problem. I'm shocked you asked."

"Eddie likes you. He's more talkative when you're around. Hell, I think Stanley likes you, too. He certainly doesn't give me as hard a time when I've got you on my arm."

She laughed. "I wouldn't be so sure about that. I don't think Stanley likes anybody."

Under the sodium lights of the parking lot, he could barely make out the worry lines on her forehead, but they were there. "Are you okay?"

"Yes. Why do you ask?"

"You've been awfully distracted this evening. The waitress at the Lucky Dog asked three times for your order before you answered."

She closed her eyes and half-laughed. "I'm just tired. Not physically, emotionally. I can't get into specifics, but there may be more to the Delmonico case than she initially told me. I know everybody lies, but I'm kind of sick of it."

"Ah." He got out of the Jeep, rounded it, and opened her door. "Has it ever

152

occurred to you that maybe you're burnt out on criminal law?"

She got out and used the sideview mirror to touch up her lipstick. "I don't have any other skills, Jim. If I'm not a lawyer, what am I?"

"You have lots of skills. And if you aren't practicing law, you're still a strong, smart, beautiful woman who can do anything she sets her mind to." He kissed her. "Fortunately, you don't have to make that decision right now. In fact, you probably should put it from your mind. Eddie might like you, but you still need to be on your A-game. You ready?"

She checked the contents of her purse. Was she stalling? "As I'll ever be."

Hand in hand, they approached the steel door, which looked exactly like the old one, except it was cleaner. Duncan pounded on it and waited.

A minute later, the cover of the slot at the top of the door snapped back to reveal a pair of eyes so dark they could be black. "Duncan. What do you want?" asked Stanley, the doorman-slash-bouncer.

Duncan waved at Sally. "I need to talk to Eddie. She's along to say hi and make me look good."

Stanley's eyes shifted. "Rumor has it you're a detective now."

"The PSP doesn't have a detective rank, but other than that, rumor is right."

"That why you're in a suit? Or you here for entertainment?"

"When have you ever known me to gamble? Tell Eddie we're here, will you?"

The cover slid over the viewing slot.

Sally shivered. "You think he'll see us? We've never come here this late before." She waved at the dozen or so cars parked in the lot. "How many people do you think are here?"

"Anywhere from one to two dozen. Eddie likes to limit the number of people in the house at one time. Keeps things easier to manage." He eyed her. "You want my jacket?"

"No, I'll be fine unless he leaves us standing out here."

The heavy door swung open. Stanley, dressed in all black with a heavy truncheon hanging off his belt, waved them in. "He'll see you in the office."

The first thing Duncan noticed once he was inside was the lack of smoke.

"Eddie implemented a no smoking policy?" he asked as Stanley led them down the hall.

"Someone pointed out that he'd get more business if the room didn't smell like an ashtray, so we installed one of those high-end air filtration systems. Sucks up the smoke like a vacuum." Stanley reached a door, knocked twice, and opened it. "Here they are. Call if you need me."

Duncan and Sally entered a small office. Seated behind a dark wood desk that took up half the room was a grossly fat man. He chomped an unlit stogie, and his red hair gleamed in the harsh LED lighting. The diamond in the stickpin holding his dark blue tie winked in the light. Duncan noted that the suit was top of the line, obviously tailored for its wearer's girth. Business must be very good indeed. "Evening, Eddie." He glanced back as Stanley closed the door.

Eddie held out both hands. "Pretty! It's been too long. Where have you been hiding?" His high, girlish voice held a note of genuine pleasure.

Sally blew him a kiss. "If you got out once in a while, Eddie, we'd see each other more often."

He waved her off. "I'm a fat man, Pretty. We don't move around much." He switched his calculating gaze to Duncan and removed the stogie. "You look like you're ready for a night on the town, Trooper. Or do I call you detective now?"

"I'm still a trooper first class, just with a different job description. And a different daily uniform."

A sly grin spread across Eddie's face. "Did she take you shopping? I don't think you could look that good on your own. Of course, the word is you two have all but moved in together. The new living arrangements suit you."

"Enough about my personal life." Eddie lived in Confluence. Of course, he knew about Sally.

"It's always business with you." He shook his head. "How do you put up with it?" he asked Sally.

She shrugged. "He has his good points."

Eddie laughed and clapped his hands. "To business! What needs can I fill for you this evening? Stanley tells me you have questions. Normally, I'd tell you to come back during business hours, Duncan, but I wanted to see Pretty."

Duncan knew bringing Sally had been a good move. He pulled Mc-Donough's picture from his inside jacket pocket. "What do you know about greyhound racing?"

"Aside from the amazing speed of the dogs, I know it's boring. Who wants to watch any animal, dog or horse, run in a big circle? Not my thing. No style, no finesse. At least with poker or blackjack, there's some strategy."

Sally cocked her head. "There is?"

"Sure." Eddie waved his stogie. "It's a psychological game, you against the house. Some people get hooked on the adrenaline rush. So much so they'll steal from their mother for a fix."

Sally pursed her lips.

She's thinking about something, Duncan thought. But now wasn't the time to corner her. He handed the bookie the picture. "You know this guy?"

Eddie tilted it to get a better look. "No. He's not one of my customers. Who is he? He doesn't look very well."

"Guy by the name of Otto McDonough. He's dead. Someone popped him, we think last week."

"You think?"

"We found the body Monday, but it was ripe. I've managed to narrow it down to a twelve-hour window from Thursday night to Friday morning. There was a greyhound on the property, badly treated at that. Our suspicion is that McDonough was involved with illegal racing."

"The West Virginia operation. I heard about it. And you want to know if there's anything going on in Pennsylvania."

"You got it."

Eddie clamped down on the cigar again. "Off the top of my head, I don't know anything. Let me make some calls. Can I keep this?" He waggled the photo.

Duncan nodded. "I appreciate it."

Eddie folded his hands across his enormous stomach and cocked his head. "And is there anything I can do for you, Pretty?"

* * *

Sally paused. Was there? She only had a teenager's overheard conversation and that wasn't very reliable. But what if he was right and Ciara had withheld information? It could be a time bomb for the defense. "Would you be willing to answer a hypothetical question?"

Eddie studied her. "That depends. What are you going to hypothetically give me?"

She blinked. "Excuse me? You answered Jim's question without getting something."

Jim stepped back. "Leave me out of it."

Coward. She glanced at him, then turned back to Eddie.

"You need to talk to your beau here. If you want something from me, you have to give up something." He finally lit a match and put it to the cigar. The smoke wafted up to a grate in the ceiling and disappeared, leaving only the stink of dirty socks. "Duncan and I have a working arrangement. Goods don't have to be exchanged every time. You, on the other hand, are new."

"But you like me." She'd heard the worse a cigar smelled, the higher quality it was. Eddie must have a way to get the good ones.

"Liking has nothing to do with business, Pretty." He folded his hands over his generous midsection.

She glanced at Jim. What was she supposed to do now?

He held up his hands. "This is your show. How much and what you say is up to you. If it were me, I'd give the man a bone."

It wasn't exactly helpful advice. "How about I ask my question, and you tell me what it's worth?"

Eddie grinned. "You're getting the hang of it."

Her thoughts whirled. "How does a casino work? In the movies, people hand over a fat wad of money and get a stack of chips, but is that really how it works?"

"I'll answer this one for free." Eddie tapped ash into a crystal tray. "More or less. Casinos don't do credit. They will give you a cash advance on a card, but I hear the fees are astronomical. If you belong to a member club or whatever that particular place calls it, you may be able to put money on account. When you're out, you're out. Now this is just for in-person casinos. Online is an entirely separate model and one I'm not as familiar with."

"I'm not interested in online. Are you a cash operation?"

"Yes. I'm old-fashioned. You hand me a hundred dollars, I give you chips."

She drummed her fingers on her arm. "And you're more, shall we say, lenient when it comes to extending credit, right? If, for example, someone needs just a little bit more for the night, you'll take an IOU."

Eddie wagged a plump finger. "That's where you're wrong, Pretty. No pay, no play. That's my policy."

She couldn't but *tsk* in disbelief.

"It's true." He puffed. "I won't deny that some of my competitors would gladly let a customer sink herself in a hole, fronting them money, and then send someone like Stanley when they couldn't pay. That's not my business model. It is also not the way the big boys play. I told you, there are people out there who will max out their credit cards, take their kids' college funds, or steal from their mothers to get a gambling fix. That's how they find themselves in a hole." He licked his lips. "You have a client with a gambling problem."

"I didn't say that."

Eddie puffed the stogie. "You didn't have to. I'm obese, Pretty. Not stupid."

She stayed silent.

Eddie laughed. "I'm sure you're a tigress in the courtroom, Ms. Castle. But like you and our law enforcement friend here, a large part of my success rests in the ability to read people. Plus, I love to play poker. And you, my dear, need to work on your poker face."

"Thanks for the advice." She could hear the tightness in her voice. "Now, what do I owe you?"

"I'll give you one on the house. You didn't ask for any information you couldn't have gotten elsewhere." He leaned back. "Besides, this is a new game for you, and this is your first hand. You didn't do too badly. A good effort should be rewarded."

Sally faced Jim. "I'll be in the car."

Out in the parking lot, she leaned against the Jeep and looked up at the sky. A thick carpet of stars stretched before her, with only a few wispy clouds here and there. What the hell had she been thinking? She was a lawyer. She had no business pretending she could negotiate with a source the way Jim could.

She exhaled, letting the tension bleed out of her. She needed to talk to Ciara and find out if the hearsay conversation was true. Until then, everything was moot.

Chapter Twenty-One

Duncan got to HQ the following day and passed through the kitchenette to grab some coffee. Like barracks brew everywhere, it wasn't quite up to his standard, but he needed the caffeine. Someone had brought donuts, good ones. As he stood over the box, pondering the merits of glazed versus cream-filled covered with powdered sugar, Ed Loughlin, another member of the CI division entered. "Hey, Ed," Duncan said, reaching for a powdered circle.

"Morning. I'd think twice about all that white stuff on a navy blue suit. Especially if you have any interviews today," Loughlin said as he popped in a single-serve coffee pod in the machine and pushed the blue button.

"Good call." Duncan settled for the glazed.

"How is it going?"

"Pretty good. Quite the change from breaking up bar fights and responding to domestics."

Loughlin chuckled. "I bet. How is it with Cavendish?" He took his mug and sipped, his gaze fixed on Duncan.

Duncan paused. The way Loughlin was staring at him, he got the feeling he was supposed to give a specific answer. But what? No matter how frustrated Duncan had been over the past three days, he didn't feel comfortable trash-talking his partner. He stalled by taking a bite. After he'd swallowed, he said, "Okay."

"Really." Loughlin drew out the word.

"What's that supposed to mean? Why wouldn't it be?"

Loughlin checked to make sure no one was around, but he also dropped

159

his voice. "Cavendish has a reputation for being a hard-ass. Word on the floor is she's run at least three partners out of the section."

"If that's the case, maybe they didn't belong here."

"Don't give me that." Loughlin scoffed. "I've heard her, grilling guys on every little detail. Did you do this, that, and the other thing? Did you dot all the i's and cross all the t's? For Christ's sake, I've never met such a cold fish. The section goes out to celebrate something, she has one or two drinks, and leaves. It's the job, the whole job, and nothing but the job." Loughlin's voice dropped again. "If you ask me, she's trying too hard to prove she fits in a man's world."

Was this what Cavendish had to put up with? If so, no wonder she had been so distant and demanding. "You know, I've worked with some outstanding women troopers over the years."

"As have I."

"But it's still a male-dominated field. Even with the strides that have been made, it's my experience that a woman has to do twice as much to prove she's half as good as a man in this job." Duncan's thoughts flashed to McAllister. "I had a female trainee last year. I tell you, there's nobody I'd rather wade into a crowd of drunks with. She's damn good at the job."

Loughlin held up a hand. "So is Cavendish."

"Then maybe you should try treating her the way she deserves instead of belittling her behind her back."

Duncan walked off. He'd been fairly confident his new partner was testing him. He'd thought it was just about seeing if he had the chops for investigation. But maybe it was also about seeing if he was a man she could respect as a human being. And who would respect her in return.

* * *

Sally arrived at her office armed with coffee and determination.

"You look like you're ready for battle," Kim said from across the hall. The rooms faced each other through archways. Pocket doors were available to ensure some privacy, if needed, but leaving them open allowed the women to talk without being on top of each other.

Sally set down her Starbucks to-go cup on her desk and fired up her laptop. "I am. I decided to assume what Ciara Delmonico's neighbor told me is true. She needed money badly enough to have a phone conversation where she didn't care who heard her. I want to know why." She sat and shuffled Ciara's file to the top of the pile of documents on her desk.

"And if she won't tell you?"

"Then I will respectfully suggest that she needs to find other representation. I can't work with someone who won't be honest with me." She looked at the clock. "I finally got in touch with her last night around ten, and I arranged to meet here this morning. She should be here any minute."

Kim shut her laptop and picked up her coat. "I'd love to see this. I don't think I've ever seen you in attack mode. But I have to be at the courthouse by eight-thirty. Maybe take video?"

"I'm pretty sure that's frowned upon. Besides, I want her to talk, not clam up."

Kim shrugged into the coat. "Then I want a play-by-play when I get back. Good luck." She grabbed her briefcase and left.

Not five minutes later, the door opened, and a timid knock sounded. "Hello? Ms. Castle?" Ciara called.

"In here." *Calm, professional, and firm*, Sally reminded herself. Haranguing her client wouldn't help, but neither would accepting half-truths.

Ciara appeared in the office doorway. She held her own coffee. Crumbs dotted the front of her sweater and betrayed a hurriedly consumed breakfast of some kind of pastry. "Has something happened? I didn't think we were gonna meet until the trial started, or at least just before then."

"Things have changed." Sally indicated the chair in front of her desk. "Please, have a seat. I'd offer you something to drink, but it looks like you've taken care of that."

Ciara sat, eyes wide, a mouse caught in the stare of a hungry cat.

"Ciara, do you know when is the worst time a lawyer can discover a client's secret?" Sally waited for an answer, but none was forthcoming. "In the courtroom. After the trial has started. If I know about something beforehand, I can come up with a strategy. That's true of just about everything. But if I don't know about it, and the prosecutor springs it on me when a witness, or, God forbid, the defendant, is on the stand, it's harder to respond. Do you understand?"

"I think so." Ciara fidgeted with her sweater. "I mean, it makes sense. You want to know what's coming."

"Correct." Sally continued to stare over her fingers. "I went to your house yesterday. I was concerned when I couldn't get in touch with you. When I got there, you were gone, but I did talk to your neighbor. Or, more accurately, your neighbor's son."

"David? I can't imagine he said anything interesting."

"Except he did." Sally leaned forward. "He told me about a phone conversation he overheard earlier that afternoon. You were asking for money. In his words, you looked and sounded pretty upset."

"I...I don't know what you mean," the bookkeeper said in an unsteady voice. "Yes, the meeting with the DA was unnerving. But you knew that."

"Was he right? About the conversation. Were you asking for money?"

"It's nothing. I was talking to a friend, that's all."

"Then you did ask for money. What for? We've agreed you won't be billed until this case is settled. I've seen your financials, and you assured me you are temporarily solvent. Meaning you can pay your bills. Why would you need a couple hundred dollars in cash?"

Ciara licked her lips. "It's not a big deal. Just some...stuff I need to take care of."

Inwardly, Sally sighed. It would have been so much easier if Ciara was willing to be honest. "If you can't tell me, then I'm sorry. We can't work together." *This is definitely a benefit. If I were still in public defense, I'd have no choice.*

"But...but you said you could help me!" Ciara's eyes shone.

"Only if you are honest." Sally leaned forward. "Ciara, whatever it is, it's okay. We can deal with it, if you tell me right now. But I can't represent someone knowing she's not being forthright and that she's hiding something. It's bad for me, my partner, and honestly, it's bad for you. I urge you to tell me what is going on."

Ciara was silent for what felt like forever. Then she slumped. "I needed the money because I wanted to go to Rivers Casino."

"You like to gamble."

"Yes. It's my stress relief. I go up there, have dinner, and spend a few hours at the slot machines. Sometimes the table games, but mostly slots. I sit there with a drink in my hand, pulling the lever, listening to the bells and whoops, and let it all wash over me. I can almost feel the stress leaving my muscles."

Sally straightened a stack of papers. "How often do you go?"

"Almost every weekend."

"How many times do you leave with more money than you started?"

If possible, the woman's voice softened. "Almost never."

"You are going out, on a regular basis, and losing almost every time. Is that correct?"

Ciara nodded.

But Sally had seen the background information. Ciara wasn't in heavy credit card debt, and her bills were paid. "Where's the money coming from?"

"I have a rainy-day fund." She sipped from the coffee cup, the contents of which had stopped giving off steam. "When I do a job, I put seventy-five percent of it in the bank. The rest I keep in cash. That's my money to play with. Until recently, it was enough. I'd take that, and when it was gone, I would leave."

"What changed?"

Ciara closed her eyes. "I don't know. My mother has dementia. My sister and I share the responsibility of caring for her. But this past January, my sister got sick and couldn't help. I was taking all my extra time to care for Mom. I fell behind during tax season so I had to work late to make sure all my clients got their stuff filed by the April deadline. The stress was killing me. So I went more and more often."

Sally waited for her to continue.

"Pretty soon, my 75-25 split wasn't enough. I skimped on the grocery bill, gave up my newspaper subscription, pawned some antique jewelry, anything I could do to get a few dollars more." She let out a sigh. "But it never seemed to be enough."

"I have to ask. Did you take money from your clients, specifically RCH, to fund your gambling habit?"

Ciara's eyes popped open. "No, I swear it. Ms. Castle, you have to believe me." Tears trickled down her cheeks. "I dug one hell of a hole, I know that. I didn't know how to get out. I still don't. But even when I was losing everything, I still had my integrity. That was important to me."

Sally handed her a box of tissues. "I'm pretty sure this is why the DA wouldn't give you a better plea offer. I don't know it for sure, but that's my suspicion. He's going to argue that cutting corners wasn't enough and you decided to take from your clients. He believes he's got you dead to rights. You see that, don't you?"

Ciara dabbed her eyes. "I always told myself just one more night. Whatever happened, I'd quit." She blew her nose. "What are you going to do? Can you still help me?"

The addict's lie. "Let me think." Sally tapped her pen. "The fact remains that you're still not in debt. Not enough, that is. We can get out ahead of the gambling issue somehow. I'll talk to my partner and see if she has any ideas. You said you pawned items?"

Ciara nodded.

"We'll want to show you made concessions in your personal life instead of taking from your clients. I've also found a forensic accountant who can go through the RCH tax filings and give me his opinion. I strongly suggest we proceed with hiring him."

"That sounds expensive." She gulped. "But if it shows I didn't steal, it'll be worth it."

"He isn't cheap, but given what I suspect is going to be thrown at you, we don't want to cut corners." She folded her hands. "Is this it? Is there anything else you've been holding back?"

Ciara's hair came loose as she shook her head. "No, I promise. I haven't held anything else back. I'm sorry I wasn't honest in the first place."

Sally tapped her laptop to wake it up. "I found out before trial, and that's what's important."

Ciara twisted the tissue until it ripped. "Thank you. I don't know what I'm going to do about the gambling. That's where I was earlier, when you called. I was in the casino. I saw your number on the caller ID, but I didn't want you to hear all the noise. I was too embarrassed."

All of Sally's previous frustration melted as she looked at her client's haggard face. "One more thing. I suggest calling the eight-hundred number on the billboards or the one you see on TV. In fact, here." She did a quick search on her computer and turned the monitor toward Ciara. "Call this one. It'll help your defense if we can show you are in recovery before we get to trial. If it comes to that."

Chapter Twenty-Two

Duncan left the break room, stopped at his desk to grab his notes, and went to a conference room with a whiteboard. Once there, he dropped his jacket over a chair, loosened his tie, and rolled up his sleeves. He grabbed a colored marker and started to write.

Cavendish found him fifteen minutes later. "What on earth are you doing?"

"Going old school." He continued to write facts on the board. "I have a column for each suspect. Facts are in black, firm guesses in blue, pure speculation in red. Then I draw arrows to connect things. The visualization helps me cut away the noise and focus on what's important."

"Interesting idea." She came up beside him.

He waited for a snarky comment, but got nothing. Maybe she was too intrigued.

Instead, she took her own marker and started writing. "Do any of these people, aside from Sullivan, own a .38?"

"Not legally. I couldn't find anything in the database. Long guns aren't registered, but we aren't looking for a rifle." He tapped the board. "Overbeck used to have a Glock ml, but he sold it last spring. I found the transaction paperwork, all clean and aboveboard."

She tapped her chin with the red marker. "Bethany Carlyle looks weak. I mean, I never thought she was our best suspect, but seeing all this, she's way down the list. Yeah, she argued with the victim, may even have conspired to pour ketchup on his car and threaten him. But no means, no opportunity."

"Plus, her story checks out." Duncan held out his notebook. "At least so far. She was definitely up in Pittsburgh at college when she said she was."

"All day Thursday, until what, five?"

"Closer to five-thirty. Confirmed by the advisor to the environmental club. I had a message from him this morning. Now, I haven't been able to track down the friend she said she spent the evening with. He might be a little freaked at returning a phone call from a state police officer, if what I suspect went on really did."

"Ah, youth." Cavendish rolled her eyes. "Like we care in this context. But if everything is kosher up until five-thirty, what are the chances she lied about the evening?"

"Everybody lies about something, but point taken. A better argument is her lack of access to a weapon and the fact it would take what, two hours for her to drive to Markleysburg and two hours back home?"

"What does she drive?"

"A silver Prius, a newer model. Which nobody mentioned, and it's a distinctive design. It would have been noticed."

"Not quite goodbye Bethany Carlyle, but she goes to the bottom of the list." Cavendish waved at the other columns. "Why do you have the phone call from the burner in Overbeck's column?"

"I figured of all the people on our radar, he was the one most likely to use a disposable phone. But that's a wild-ass guess on my part, which is why it's in red. Unless he confesses to the call, we'll never know if it was him or not."

"Smart thinking." She chewed her lip. "Is that everything?"

Was it his imagination, or was this conversation going better than the previous ones? Cavendish sure sounded more like a partner and less like someone out to prove he was just another rookie who couldn't cut it. He grabbed another set of reports. "Not quite. Of the remaining suspects, Overbeck has the wrong car. He drives an older pickup, red. Same with Renner. He has a new GMC Sierra."

"The old guy with the dog, the one who put Renner on the scene, did he mention a car?"

"No, but we didn't ask."

"I'll take care of that. Motive?"

"You saw how he feels about his dogs. What if he found out McDonough was illegally racing, and worse yet, doping, one of the puppies from Renner's farm? Remember, he said he wanted 'him' back."

Cavendish looked slantwise at her partner. "You think 'him' was Johnny's Pixelated?"

"I do." Duncan drew a line from Renner's name on the board to McDonough. "He cared enough to confront the victim. He doesn't own a .38, but I'm sure he could get one. But nobody saw his car the night we think the murder happened, and the confrontation with McDonough was prior to that. Means, motive, but weak opportunity."

She stepped back, turned, and rummaged through the rest of the papers. "What about Overbeck?"

"He sold McDonough a dog. We know that much. We have his statement that payments were all Bitcoin, but he wouldn't surrender a dog without payment."

She glanced up. "Or unless the buyer was a repeat or vouched for by an established customer. How much do you know about Bitcoin?"

"Just enough to be dangerous." Duncan twirled a marker. "Dark web folks love it because it's so anonymous, and from what I've read, you can turn it into cash pretty easy. The tech guys are still working on tracing McDonough's activity."

"Remember what Overbeck said about customers who didn't pay? I don't think he'd have any problems confronting a buyer who didn't pony up."

"Hopefully, the techies will unearth the truth about that, too."

She nodded. "That leaves Sullivan and Bevilacqua. What do we know about them?"

He rubbed his chin, then tapped the board. "Here's where it gets interesting. Sullivan could have walked to the scene. He lives in town. He has a powerful motive."

"His half-brother's death."

"Precisely. And he owns a .38. I wonder if we can lean on ballistics. Get them to hurry up with that report."

"That reminds me." She tossed the marker from hand to hand. "The report is in. Sullivan's gun isn't our murder weapon."

Damn it. "As for Bevilacqua, he went bankrupt because of McDonough. There's no registered firearm to his name, but get this." He handed over another sheet of paper. "He drives a brown Saab sedan."

"The witness your former trainee interviewed said he saw a dark red or brown four-door car in McDonough's driveway that night." She looked up. "Are you thinking what I'm thinking?"

"We wondered why Bevilacqua would own a house in Markleysburg. He lied about the rent payments, and he lied about not seeing or hearing from his tenant since August. I'm thinking it's time to pay Mr. Bevilacqua another visit."

She set down the marker. "Nice job, Duncan."

She used my name. Maybe he'd turned a corner. "Thanks. Of course, it always helps to have a partner to go over it with." He grabbed his jacket and headed for the door.

But not before he noted the look of admiration on her face.

Chapter Twenty-Three

S ally's phone rang around eight-thirty—her cell, not the landline. Ciara had left not five minutes earlier, after calling the gambling addiction help-line. A glance at the screen told Sally it was Pat Dennister. What could she want? "Hello, Sally Castle speaking."

"Ms. Castle, this Pat, from River City Hounds. How are you?" The older woman sounded hesitant. "I hope I didn't call at a bad time."

"No, I'm between tasks, so your timing is perfect. What can I do for you?"

"I've been thinking. I'd like to talk to you a little more about Lynn. I…well, my first thought was I had no business blabbing, which is why I didn't mention anything when we talked before, but I hashed it out with my sister last night. I think I could help her. And you and Ciara."

Sally mentally calculated the drive time. And cost. Could she charge this to the case? Should she? She had not considered this aspect of working for herself. "When and where would you like to meet?"

"I'm already on my way to Uniontown. Call me crazy, but I figured you'd jump at the chance to help your client, so I started driving. I should be there in half an hour." She paused. "If I was wrong and you didn't want to talk, I could always turn around. Also, I thought if I called from the road, I'd find it harder to chicken out, if you understand me."

In other words, Pat Dennister didn't feel confident in her decision. "I understand completely. How about you meet me for a late breakfast? We can talk over coffee and pastries." Sally had already eaten, and Pat probably had as well, but the cozy emotions associated with food had a way of making difficult conversations easier.

170

"Okay. Where?"

Sally rattled off the address of the coffee shop in downtown Uniontown where she'd met Ciara. "See you soon." She hung up.

"Meeting someone?" Kim asked from behind her.

"I didn't hear you come in. I thought you were at a consultation." Sally drained her coffee.

Kim blew the hair off her forehead. "My client flaked out and wrote down the wrong time. I had to reschedule. Who was that on the phone?"

"That was Pat Dennister, the accountant from RCH. She wants to get together."

"What do you think she'll say?" Kim went to the single-cup coffee machine and selected a pod.

Sally stood and started gathering her things, raising her voice so Kim could hear. "Not sure. She mentioned helping Lynn Moss and Ciara, but she sounds as though she isn't sold on talking to me. I don't know how talking to me will help Lynn. It could help me decide if I want to call her as a witness, though." Sally considered taking her laptop but decided to leave it behind. "I'll keep you posted." She shouldered her purse and left.

She'd grabbed a table in the back corner of the shop where she could sit facing the door. Pat entered almost exactly at nine. She spotted Sally immediately and headed for the table. "Good morning. I've been sitting in the parking lot for five minutes, trying to work up the nerve to come in. I almost chickened out."

"I'm glad you didn't." Sally took in Pat's appearance. Her hair was mussed, face drawn, and there were worry lines around her mouth that hadn't been there the last time they'd spoken. "First things first. Food and caffeine. I don't know about you, but I'm starved." She hadn't been when she walked in, but the smell of baking had changed that.

It didn't take long before they were back at the table, steaming cups and iced cinnamon rolls in front of them. "Thanks for suggesting this," said Pat. "I've been too nervous to eat much lately, worrying over what I should do."

"My pleasure." Sally pulled off a piece of roll. "Have you heard anything about Johnny?"

The mention of the dog seemed to relax the other woman. "He's good. Animal control is going to be sending him to us by the end of the week, maybe as early as tomorrow. Good food and love are all he needs. He'll be ready for adoption in no time."

"I'm glad to hear it. Will you take him?"

"I'll probably foster him, me or Annie. But he'll be looking for his forever home. Why, are you interested?"

"I might be." *One more reason to just move in with Jim. He has the space for a second large dog.*

"If so, go to our website and fill out an application. Get the ball rolling." The decision to start the conversation with the abused greyhound had worked. Pat visibly relaxed as she talked.

Sally couldn't put off the real purpose of the meeting forever, though. "You said you wanted to talk about Lynn, that it could help her and Ciara. What did you mean?"

Pat gripped her mug. "Don't you want to take notes or something?"

"No, let's just chat. I can go back and write things down later."

Pat sighed and stared at her mug. "How much about Lynn do you know?"

"She was in an accident that messed up her back. I know she had to quit her job and had money problems. She almost lost her house in Penn Hills. She also got divorced earlier this year. Between the divorce settlement, a new job, and a small inheritance from an aunt, she seems to be back on her feet."

"That's mostly true."

"What do you mean, mostly?"

Pat stalled with a sip of coffee and a bite of roll. "It's true she was in an accident, got divorced, had money problems, and almost lost the house. I don't know about the inheritance. I haven't spoken to her in some months. But she didn't quit her job. She was fired."

"I heard she's a secretary, now working at a medical records company, right?"

"Correct. I believe she has a degree in nursing, but she's switched fields." Pat nibbled on her breakfast.

CHAPTER TWENTY-THREE

"Do you know why she got fired?"

Once again, Pat hesitated, overly focused on her coffee. "Yes."

Sally waited. She'd had tentative witnesses like Pat before, and if pushed too hard, they clammed up.

"After the accident, Lynn was on medication. For the pain, you know." Pat tore a napkin into small pieces as she spoke. "I don't know if it was Vicodin or oxycodone, but it was powerful stuff. She joked about how if she didn't need it so much, she could make a small fortune selling it on the street. A month or two rolled by. I figured the prescription must have run out. I mean, doctors usually only go thirty days on that stuff, right?"

"I don't know, but I wouldn't be surprised."

"It was right around when she got heated at one of our events. To be honest, the whole thing took me by surprise when it happened, because Lynn had been with our group for a long time, and such an outburst was out of character. But she'd been edgy for a while. Anyway." Pat paused. "She made a comment about needing to go get her pain pills. I asked if she still needed them and she practically bit my head off, saying how I didn't understand. It had been a terrible ordeal, and who was I to judge. I wasn't judging. I was worried."

"You thought she'd gotten hooked."

"That or her doctor had messed her up more. But then," Pat shifted, "she left her job. She brushed it off, like it was no big deal. She *said* it was because she couldn't be on her feet, but then I saw it."

Sally drummed her fingers on the table. "What?"

"We were out to lunch. She popped a pill, then went to the bathroom. While she was gone, her bag fell on the floor, and the pill bottle rolled out." Pat looked at Sally, her eyes filled with worry. "The doctor's name was from the practice where she used to work, but I'm pretty sure the date was after she left."

"Naturally, you wondered why a physician she used to work for was writing prescriptions for her after she was no longer employed there."

Pat nodded, eyes huge.

"Do you know if she was seeing any of those doctors?"

"No, she went to a different place. I remember because she recommended them to me when I mentioned another friend of mine was looking for an orthopedic surgeon." Pat paused. "She came back from the ladies', saw me with the bottle, and, well, it got ugly. I asked if she'd taken it, if that's why she lost her job. She exploded. She said I couldn't possibly understand, she was under a lot of stress, in a lot of pain, and no one had one ounce of compassion. I urged her to get help. She stormed out. That was the last time I spoke to her." She stared at the pile of napkin bits in front of her.

Sally rolled around the details of what she'd heard in her head. Opioid addiction was expensive. Lynn could have been on the edge financially because of her pills. It might even have contributed to the breakup of her marriage. And when the money ran out, she stole. "You think the inheritance—"

Pat didn't lift her head. "May have been the money from RCH, yes. She needed to cover her debts and fund her habit, so she took from the group. If that's the case, I don't know how to feel. Of course, I'm angry she stole. But on the other hand, if that's really what happened, she needs help. Ciara shouldn't get in trouble for something Lynn did. Aside from talking to you, I didn't know what to do."

"Yet you didn't say anything when Ciara was arrested."

The older woman hung her head. "I know, I'm sorry. I should have. I figured the cops would have known about Lynn, they'd have found out in their investigation, so they obviously knew something I didn't. Who was I to say otherwise? But I should have. Best I can do to make up for it is what I'm doing now."

Sally sat back. She'd come to this meeting intending to put Lynn Moss on the stand. But maybe the witness she needed to call was Pat Dennister. "Thank you for speaking to me. Here's where it gets tricky. Are you willing to appear as a witness for the defense and say what you just told me under oath?"

"How does that help anyone?"

"It helps Ciara because I can offer your testimony to raise reasonable doubt. It helps Lynn because maybe she'll get the medical treatment she needs if her problem is out in public."

"But she'll go to jail."

There was that. "Perhaps not. The RCH board still has the option to drop charges or agree to restitution as long as Lynn gets treatment. Or some other solution that doesn't involve a trial and incarceration."

Pat paused, then nodded. "Yes. I'll be a witness for you."

Sally pulled out her phone and set it between them. She opened the voice memo button and tapped record. "Let's go over that again."

Chapter Twenty-Four

D uncan waited in the front lobby, the keys to an unmarked state Interceptor in his hand. Cavendish had made a detour to the bathroom. When she appeared, she said, "We need to see someone here at HQ before we head to Connellsville."

Duncan put the keys in his jacket pocket as he followed her. "Oh?"

"Got a call from the tech guys. They have some information for us about McDonough's dark web activity." She glanced at him. "By the way, did I see you talking to Ed Loughlin earlier?" She kept her voice casual, but the light in her eyes was suspicious.

"Yes, we debated the relative merits of different donut varieties."

"That's all? You didn't talk about anything else?"

"Like what?"

She glanced at him out of the corner of her eye as she strode down the hallway. "You are the new guy. It's natural he'd ask how you were doing."

He could tell it was another test. He refused to rise to the bait. "He did. I told him things are fine. I didn't have much to say, to tell you the truth. It's been less than a week. I'm still settling in."

She seemed to relax a bit and halted before a closed door. "This is our stop."

Inside the Staff Services department, they made their way to the technology desk. She rapped on the counter. "Troopers Cavendish and Duncan. Here about the Otto McDonough investigation."

A slim young woman with dark hair confined to a bun beckoned. "Tina Silverio. Come on back."

Duncan and Cavendish gathered around her desk, topped by a half-eaten breakfast sandwich in a plastic shell container, a bottle of sparkling water, and a computer monitor. "What's up?" Duncan asked.

Silverio pushed aside the food and pointed at her monitor. "Your victim wasn't the greatest guy in the world."

"We knew that." Cavendish leaned against a nearby table. "Most citizens who are on the up and up don't resort to dark web activity and pay for purchases with Bitcoin."

Far from being taken aback, Silverio nodded. "Well, that used to be true. Not so much anymore. Lots of legit companies accept Bitcoin. But it's still the cryptocurrency of choice for today's criminal. The anonymity makes it perfect for all sorts of schemes. The way it works is—"

"I don't mean to be rude and I'm sorry if you take it that way," Duncan said, breaking what he was sure would turn into a full-on lecture about the inner workings of Bitcoin. "We don't need to know exactly how it works. We know that it's anonymous, hard to trace, and lets people pay for items that might be, shall we say, embarrassing if they showed up on a normal credit card or bank statement. I assume you were able to learn something about Otto McDonough's activity."

Silverio didn't seem put out. "Eventually." She brought up a screen filled with numbers. "I'll spare you the technical details about packets and encryption and junk. Last spring, your victim made contact with this person, RunningMan38, to purchase a dog."

Duncan leaned forward to read. "That would be Dan Overbeck. He sold retired racing greyhounds that were supposed to go up for adoption."

"There's some blah-blah about the details, and you can see here where they arrange for payment."

"What was the price?"

"It would have been equivalent to"—Silverio tapped on a calculator—"seven-hundred and fifty dollars USD."

He looked at Cavendish. "We should check and see if McDonough had access to that kind of cash."

She made a note on her phone. "Could be why he didn't make his rent payment, at least that month. The money went to buy the dog."

Duncan turned back to the tech. "Overbeck said he didn't deliver unless he was paid. Did you find that transaction?"

"Well, that's where it gets interesting." Silverio switched to another screen. "There's no payment record at all, not through Bitcoin. Could they have changed their minds and used a different cryptocurrency?"

"No, it was Bitcoin," Cavendish said. "At least that's what Overbeck told us."

"But he also said repeat customers, or new ones who were vouched for by repeat customers, got a grace period." Duncan paged through his own notebook. "When was the purchase talk?"

Silverio switched back to the first record. "Mid-January of this year with the agreement made by the end of the same month."

"Okay, here." Duncan held out his notes for his partner to read. "The West Virginia racing operation was busted in February. I'll bet you anything there was a delay in payment when Overbeck was arrested, and that whole circus played out."

"Makes sense." She turned to Silverio. "But you said there's no record at all."

The tech shook her head. "Nope. I mean, this stuff is tricky, and criminals come up with new ways all the time of hiding their transactions. But we can't find any record of any kind that indicates your victim paid for his purchase."

Duncan put his notebook back in his pocket. "McDonough got the dog, no question. We found it at the scene. Overbeck said he didn't take cash, only Bitcoin. I can see where payment would be delayed because of the West Virginia case. But I'd bet good money, no pun intended, that he went looking for payment when the dust settled."

"Looks like he didn't get it." Cavendish chewed her lip. "What was it he told us? About what would happen if a customer stiffed him? Something about how he didn't want to tell that to a cop, right?"

Duncan once again turned to the columns of numbers. "Tough shit. He's going to tell us anyway. Right after we talk to Mr. Bevilacqua."

A grin spread across her face. "You know what, Duncan? I think I like your style."

* * *

Duncan and Cavendish arrived in Connellsville in a blaze of Indian summer sunshine. Bevilacqua's property looked almost abandoned. No noise came from inside, and the closed blinds gave the windows an empty, almost dead, feeling. The whole atmosphere was not helped by the complete lack of landscaping.

Cavendish surveyed the street. "I bet the kids skip this place on Halloween."

"No doubt." Duncan mounted the front steps. "Connellsville does have a little notoriety, though. They filmed parts of *Silence of the Lambs* here all those years ago. It's still a talking point. Or was that Perryopolis?"

"I don't know." Cavendish took up a position behind her partner. "Even that house doesn't feel this creepy."

Duncan made a noncommittal noise. He knocked on the front door. No answer. He knocked again. "Mr. Bevilacqua, Troopers Duncan and Cavendish from the State Police. We need to speak with you."

Still no answer.

He took a step back. "Is he at home?"

"Hold on." Cavendish jogged over to the garage. "Car is here. And get this. It's a dark brown Saab sedan. That's consistent with the witness statement."

"Dark red, maybe brown."

"This particular color might have a reddish hue in low light. Let me check the plate." She went to the state car and returned a couple minutes later. "The Saab is registered to Robert Bevilacqua, all right. Shall we try a third time?"

Duncan turned to the door, and this time he didn't knock. He pounded. "Robert Bevilacqua. State police. If you're in there, open the door."

Still no sound, but this time, the door popped open.

"Do we go in?" Cavendish asked.

"He may be hurt. I think we have to. But not blindly." He drew the Glock from his shoulder holster. He heard Cavendish do the same. "Let's go."

Guns at the ready, they entered. The first thing Duncan noticed was a familiar coppery scent. "Do you smell that?"

She grunted an assent.

"That can't be good," Duncan said. "Coming from the front room?"

"That's my guess." Cavendish tipped her head toward the door off the left side of the small entranceway. "Shall I?"

"Ladies first. I'll be at your six."

They entered the room. The lamps were off and the blinds shut out most of the sun, giving the room a dim atmosphere despite the bright outside light. The unmistakable metallic tang of blood hung in the air, dark red stains on the thick white rug.

Cavendish made her way around the massive sectional sofa and uttered a string of profanities.

"What is it?" Duncan asked. But that amount of swearing could only mean one thing.

"He did not go for a walk." Cavendish holstered her gun.

Duncan moved up beside her and looked. Bevilacqua's body was splayed on the leather, two holes in his chest. Blood soaked the front of his shirt, and his eyes fixed, unseeing, on the ceiling. On the floor beside him lay a gun, a .38 by the look of it. Duncan lowered his Glock. "Well, shit."

* * *

Armed with the new information from earlier, Sally called Lynn Moss's former employer. Depending on how the conversation went, she might be able to add another witness to her list. She doubted she'd learn anything, but sometimes people surprised her and talked, if only because an unexpected call from a lawyer jarred them from normal behavior. After introducing herself, she said, "I'd like to speak to your office manager or someone who can talk about personnel matters."

The young woman on the other end of the line sounded cautious. "What is this regarding?"

"A former employee of yours, Lynn Moss."

"Please hold."

During the wait, while Sally listened to the bland music played by doctor's offices nationwide, she doodled on her notepad. Nobody else she'd spoken with had mentioned Lynn's potential problems with painkillers. Then again, they might not know. If they did, maybe they didn't want to discuss it. Nobody *wanted* to talk about addiction.

Just as Sally had decided no one would pick up the phone, the music stopped. "This is Leslie Dunworthy," the man said. His voice was clipped. "You have questions about Lynn?"

"I do." Sally pictured an older person, especially a man named Leslie. Fussy, and he probably wore a suit with a bow tie. "My name is Sally Castle—"

"Yes, Dina told me." Leslie didn't sound angry, but he definitely didn't want to mince words. "I'm sorry, who are you again, and why do you want to know about Ms. Moss?"

Sally repeated her credentials.

"Are you representing Ms. Moss?"

"No, but I may need to call her as a witness in my client's defense, and I need you to confirm some information that is in my possession."

"I see." He waited a second. "What is it you want to know?"

"First, can you tell me whether Lynn Moss was, in fact, an employee of yours until roughly February of this year?"

"That is correct."

"Why'd she leave the practice?"

Leslie's tone turned prim. "I'm not at liberty to say. Under the law, I only have to confirm she worked here."

"I understand that." Sally fought back a sigh. Mr. Dunworthy was not going to be startled into giving up information without a fight. "It has come to my attention that Ms. Moss was fired from her job for stealing opioid painkillers. Is that true?"

No answer.

"Mr. Dunworthy, this can be an easy conversation or a difficult one. I already have the information. All I'm asking is for you to corroborate it."

"I'm under no obligation to speak to you."

"Right now, no. However, I subpoena you as a witness, and you'll have to answer the question. In court, before a jury. I'd rather not take that route."

Another pause. Then Leslie spoke. "I'm sorry, Ms. Castle. I've told you all I'm going to. If getting a more detailed answer is that important, I'm afraid you're going to have to get your court order. Good afternoon." He hung up.

"Shit." Sally dropped her phone on the desk.

Kim stuck her head through the door. "Problem?"

"Why can't people make this easy on me once in a while?" Sally yanked open a drawer. It was empty. She opened a second one, which was also empty "Just answer the damn questions instead of making me jump through hoops? Do they really think if they refuse, after I tell them I'll get the information anyway, I'll give up and go home?" She went to a filing cabinet, but still didn't find what she was looking for.

Kim chuckled. "Probably. But are you surprised?"

Why are they so out of reach? It wasn't how she'd set up an office. "No, not really." She went to the closet, got the paper, and returned to her desk.

"Who's playing hardball now?"

Sally brought her friend up to speed on the latest developments in Ciara's case, including Lynn's potential painkiller addiction.

"Wowza." Kim leaned against the wall. "If you're right, this Moss woman had at least as powerful a motive as Ciara, maybe more. And if she was still on the bank account, she could have drained the funds." She paused. "So that's it. There's our reasonable doubt."

"Yes." Sally put the finishing touches on her affidavit. "I'm going to run over to the courthouse and see if I can find a friendly judge." She stood, put the form in a folder, grabbed her purse, and headed for the door.

"Then what?" Kim asked. "Call the DA, see if he'll negotiate now."

"I will." Sally stopped, her hand on the doorknob. "But I need to track down Lynn Moss, too."

"Why? We've done our part."

Yes, they had. "I can't, Kim. I have to give Lynn a chance at redemption."

CHAPTER TWENTY-FOUR

Kim pushed off the wall. "She isn't the client. Ciara Delmonico is."

"I know. But it isn't how I work. I wouldn't be able to live with myself if I don't talk to Lynn." Justice wasn't saving one person and throwing another to the dogs. In that moment, Sally realized her true mission was justice and not only for the woman who was paying her.

"Who's going to foot the bill for this?"

Sally yanked the door open, tired of answering that question. *Which only means this isn't the place for me.* She needed something that allowed her to be her own boss and not be constantly defending her decisions. "If necessary, I will."

Chapter Twenty-Five

While Cavendish made the rounds, talking to Bevilacqua's neighbors, Duncan phoned in a request for a search warrant. While he waited, the other members of the death investigation team, the CSI techs, and the deputy coroner, showed up and began their work. Approval for the search and a promise to deliver the paper copy of the warrant arrived shortly thereafter.

Legal requirements fulfilled, Duncan searched the house. Every room in the place was crammed with furniture, knickknacks, and assorted junk. The desk in the office was filled with paper, all stored in a haphazard manner with no immediately intelligible system. Same with the files on the laptop. There was only the single Documents folder, with no organizing structure, no pattern to the file names. Just scores of documents and spreadsheets. The accounting software Bevilacqua used to track the income and expenses for his rental properties was moderately more organized, but still a mess. It would take hours to read through it all and separate the wheat from the chaff.

He turned his attention to the email. Once again, nothing was sorted, but at least Duncan could filter by date or sender to apply a semblance of order to the chaos. Almost immediately after doing so, he saw a number of messages to and from Otto McDonough. A quick skim told him that most referred to delinquent payments, probably the rent on the Markleysburg property. A few, however, referred to a "deal" and accused McDonough of reneging. Duncan would read those in more detail when he returned to the office.

The filing cabinets held an assortment of unpaid and overdue bills. One folder held rental agreements. "Pittsburgh, Pittsburgh, Pittsburgh," Duncan muttered.

Cavendish appeared in the doorway. "Are you talking to yourself?"

"They tell me it's not an issue unless I start answering myself, too."

"So I've heard." She stepped into the room. "Good grief. Didn't the man know how to file anything? How'd he ever find what he was looking for?"

"Organized chaos? It's not my thing, but I've known people who I'd swear were completely disorganized yet could lay their hands on any given object within minutes." He flipped through the rest of the papers in the folder. "But this doesn't make sense."

She held out her hand. "What?"

He gave her the folder. "This is apparently all of Bevilacqua's rental agreements. At least as far as I can see. There are contracts for all of the Pittsburgh properties going back five years. But nothing for this place or the Markleysburg house."

Cavendish wrinkled her forehead as she looked. "Here's a contract dated two years ago for this address. Stuck between another one, go figure. We can call the tenant, but I'm going to guess he didn't renew and moved out. You're right, though. Nothing for Markleysburg." She looked up. "How long did McDonough live there?"

"I'd have to look at my notes, but I seem to recall it's been a few years."

"Then there should be a contract. At least based on the time period for all the others." She slapped the folder against her palm and looked around. "Are we taking all of this?"

"I think we have to. How else are we going to know what's important?"

She groaned. "You talked to the deputy coroner yet?"

"No. Flip you for the privilege."

She pulled out a quarter. "Heads." She flipped the coin and slapped it on her forearm. "Shit, tails. Oh well. I'll start bagging and tagging all this crap."

"Once I'm done with the body, I'll help. What did you learn from the neighbors?"

Cavendish plopped in the desk chair and began her task. "A fat lot of nothing. Most of them said Bevilacqua was an odd duck and the general consensus was that he was gay. No proof of that, mind you. He had few visitors and mostly kept to himself. No rowdy parties, no incidents."

"What about in the last twelve to twenty-four hours?" They didn't have a time of death yet, but it was a good window to start with.

"Nada. One guy said he thought he saw a pickup truck in the drive. But he lives over half a block away and admitted the truck could have been in a different driveway. The residents on both sides of this place own pickups."

Helpful, but not. "I'll be back as soon as I can." He went downstairs to the living room.

Tom Burns knelt on the floor, engrossed in his examination. "We have to stop meeting this way," he said, not looking up.

"If that happens, it means one of us is out of a job." Duncan nodded toward the couch. "What have you got?"

"Victim is a white male, approximately forty years of age. I'd put his weight in excess of two-hundred pounds. Height, oh, about five-ten? Based on the condition of his hands, I don't think he's ever done a day's worth of manual labor in his life." Burns adjusted the paper bags over the victim's hands.

"What about the wounds?"

"Two." The deputy coroner pointed to the chest. "Nice, tight grouping. No exit wounds. We'll find out which one was the kill shot when we open him up."

"Any other observations?"

"I don't see any obvious defensive wounds. There are no powder burns on skin or fabric, so the shooter was most likely some feet away." Burns tilted his head. "Based on the position, I think it likely he staggered back and fell onto the couch. His legs are hanging off the edge, the torso kind of slumped against the back and armrest. Nobody lies down like that and stays there."

Duncan agreed. "Early estimate on time of death?"

"Really?"

"Humor me."

Burns blew out a breath. "He's not in full rigor, so less than twelve hours. Livor mortis isn't set, so again, eight to twelve hours." Burns demonstrated by pushing lightly on one of the dark spots where blood had settled. It turned white.

"But both have started, so what, at least two hours?"

Burns nodded. "I'd say so. Unofficially?"

"Yes?"

"This place is shut up pretty tight, but if he'd been dead any significant amount of time, he'd be drawing flies. My inclination is to go with the later TOD estimate."

Duncan glanced at his watch. It was noon. Time of death was as early as four a.m., possibly as late as ten. He and Cavendish had arrived somewhere between ten-thirty and eleven that morning. They hadn't seen anybody, so the killer had either just left or was long gone. "Thanks. Do you know where the gun went?"

Burns aimed a thumb at the doorway behind him. "They took it that way. See you at the autopsy?"

"Maybe. But either Cavendish or I will definitely be in touch."

"Speaking of your partner, how's it going?" Burns gave him a knowing look.

McAllister talked about what happened at the Gray Line. "Everything's fine." Duncan left in search of the crime scene tech who'd bagged the evidence. "Hey, can I see the gun we found on the floor?"

The tech handed over the bag. "It's a Colt 1911 loaded with .38 super. Nice condition. Been fired recently. The magazine holds seven rounds, six are missing, and the deputy coroner says two of them are in the victim. We haven't found the other bullets. Could be the clip wasn't full. But that's not the interesting part."

"What is?" Duncan turned the bag over in his hands.

"Someone tried to file off the serial number. They didn't do a very good job, though. It's hard to read, but it's there."

Duncan handed it back. "I want ballistics on this compared to the McDonough murder from earlier this week. Give me that number." The tech read it off, and Duncan wrote it in his notebook. "I know it's asking a lot, but is it possible to get the ballistics by tomorrow?"

The tech sighed. "I'll ask the team, and I'm sure they'll do their best."

Duncan nodded his thanks and went back inside to the living room. "Anything else?" he asked Burns.

Burns zipped the corpse into a heavy black bag. "Not from an exterior exam. I'm sure more will be forthcoming." He looked around. "I didn't mean to pry. Earlier."

"I know. Keep me posted." Duncan looked at the other crime scene tech in the room. "You find any other slugs?"

The tech shook his head.

Leaving them to their jobs, Duncan headed back to the second floor, taking the stairs two at a time. He took a moment to watch Cavendish, who was methodically sorting paper. *She's good. I can't be the first partner to see that.* Or maybe he was. "How's it going?" he asked.

Cavendish paused in her work. "There are pack rats, and there is Robert Bevilacqua. No joke, I found a box with bank statements going back at least twenty years. Not in any chronological order, mind you." She waved. "This is a mess."

Duncan related what he'd learned from Burns and what he knew about the weapon.

"Think the ballistics will match?" Cavendish asked.

"I'm hopeful. A filed serial number. Tells me someone didn't want that Colt traced back to him. Or her."

"Or it's a plant."

He rubbed his chin. "Maybe, but I think it's more likely they abandoned the gun because they think it can't be traced back."

"We shall see. What else do you have to do?"

"Nothing."

"Good." Cavendish thrust a stack of evidence bags at him. "Start packing."

Chapter Twenty-Six

Sally parked her Camry in front of Lynn Moss's home in Penn Hills. After the failed attempt to get information from her previous employer, Sally had placed a call to Lynn to see if she was home. There was no way Sally was driving to Pittsburgh, yet again, only to discover her target couldn't be found. But Lynn had answered. Sally pretended to have a wrong number and hung up. Now all she could do was hope Lynn didn't go anywhere during the hour and a half drive north.

She used the drive to start a mental spreadsheet. What would it take to go solo? She didn't intend for all her clients to be *pro bono* cases or even reduced rates. But she needed flexibility. Not just *what* she billed but when. Take this trip. Instinct told her Lynn Moss was as much behind the eight ball as Ciara was. Hell, if she looked closer, she'd probably find Lynn was the type of client she wanted the ability to defend, too.

The question is whether I can find the sweet spot. I'm sure it's out there.

Lynn's garage door was open this time, and a black Ford Fiesta hatchback with a "Greyhounds make greyt pets" sticker on the back bumper was visible from the street. It had to be Lynn's. Sally rapped on the front door and waited.

After a few moments, it opened to reveal a woman wearing faded jeans and a sweatshirt that read "I failed Fostering 101." Her dark blonde hair was in a short pixie cut. Her face was devoid of makeup, showcasing faint purple smudges under her brown eyes and tiny lines at the corners of her mouth. "Who are you?" she asked in a low voice.

"My name is Sally Castle." She held out one of her temporary business cards and wished she had something more official, like her old courthouse ID. "I'm a defense attorney representing Ciara Delmonico. Are you Lynn Moss?"

"I am."

"I want to speak to you. I drove up from Uniontown and hoped you'd spare me a few minutes."

"You should have called first. You've wasted your time and gas. I don't have anything to say about Ciara." Lynn pushed the door.

Sally reached out and stopped it. "Do you have anything to say about River City Hounds?"

"No." Once again, Lynn attempted to close the door.

Sally held firm. "Ms. Moss. I really think we should talk. You need help. I think I can provide it. Please give me fifteen minutes. After that, if you still want me to go I will."

Lynn ran her tongue over dry lips, perhaps considering her options. Finally, she seemed to make a decision and opened the door. "Come in. Put your shoes on the mat, please."

Inside, Sally took off her heels and placed them on a black plastic rectangle inside the door. The room was plain, the furniture solid and the tweed fabric a bit dated. A giant dog bed occupied a whole corner, where a reddish greyhound lounged, half on and half off the cushion. It looked at Sally with solemn brown eyes. "What a beautiful dog," Sally said. "Is it a he or a she?"

"She. That's Cassie." Lynn eased down onto the couch, as if the act pained her, and patted her knee. Cassie scrambled to her feet and trotted over. "Go say hello to our guest."

Sally held out a hand, and Cassie nosed it with her long muzzle, but lost interest quickly and returned to her bed. "Not a people dog, huh."

"She can be aloof. It's nothing personal. If you had a treat in your hand, it would be a completely different story." Lynn brushed back her hair. "Quite honestly, I don't know what I can tell you about Ciara. I was gone long before all the hoopla started with the accounts."

Sally set her bag on the floor. "But you did know her."

"Yeah, of course. I mean, I didn't talk to her as much as Pat, the RCH

190

treasurer, but I knew her."

"How long did you volunteer with the group?"

"I don't know." Lynn bit her lip. "Seven or eight years? Not as long as Annie or Pat, but a good while."

"Then you should have been aware of RCH's neutral stance on racing."

"Stupid rule, but yeah. I knew. I was having a bad day in the first place, and the guy pushed me over the edge. You had to be there to understand."

"Try me." Sally studied Lynn's face. Sally knew her time was ticking, but it was important to establish trust with this woman. Otherwise, the whole conversation was a bust.

"I never liked racing. Never. Most of the time, I kept my opinions to myself. But last spring, there were just a couple of stupid people, and I guess I couldn't stay quiet any longer. I blew my top. After the second time, Annie told me I couldn't be a volunteer any longer. I'd been having a difficult time, and it was one of those days."

"Did it make you mad?"

Lynn shrugged. "A little, but I got over it. Every time I take Cassie out in public, it's like doing a meet and greet. People don't see greyhounds very often or know anything beyond the fact they are fast. Now I get to educate people, and I don't have to pretend to not have a stance on racing."

Time to move on. "You had an accident earlier this year. I'm told it messed up your back pretty badly. Did that contribute to the blowup?"

Lynn shifted on the couch. "Yes, and I'm still in a lot of pain. You're right. The day of the argument was a bad one. I suppose if I hadn't hurt so much, I would have kept my cool."

"You take anything for it? The pain?"

"Ibuprofen." Lynn's gaze was fixed somewhere over Sally's shoulder.

"They didn't give you anything stronger?"

"Oh, well, yeah. At first, I had oxycodone. But, um, docs don't like to leave you on that too long. I wish they'd give me another script. The ibuprofen is shit." She fiddled with the fringe on a throw pillow. "You got a problem with me wanting stronger meds?"

"Of course not." Sally paused a beat. "Someone told me you lost a job

191

because you couldn't stand. Too much stress on your back."

"They wouldn't accommodate me, so I quit." Lynn moved again, but this time she winced.

"You didn't think about suing them? They have to make reasonable accommodations. That's the law."

Lynn's gaze drifted to a spot over Sally's right shoulder. "I didn't bother. It wasn't worth my time and I didn't want to pay for a lawyer. Besides, I found a new place."

Sally knew from Jim, and experience, that people had a tendency to look off to the left when they weren't being entirely truthful. *Careful now.* "Ms. Moss, did you really leave your job? I've heard differently."

Lynn flushed. "I quit. I've been in a lot of pain, Ms. Castle. And neither you nor anybody else has the right to judge anything I might have done. Do you know what it's like to feel like your body is on fire every time you take a step? To be unable to do the things you enjoy, like walk your freaking dog, because the effort brings you to tears? Do you?" Her voice rose with every word, and she clutched at the afghan on the couch, knuckles white from the pressure.

"I'm not judging anything." Sally kept her voice low and calm. "I'm only telling you what I've heard from others. This is why I like to talk directly with people. To clear up any misunderstandings."

"Could you excuse me for a sec?" Without waiting for a response, Lynn got up and left the room.

As Sally waited, she could hear cupboard doors open, running water, the clink of glass, and another sound. The rattle of pills? How was she going to bring this woman around to telling her the truth? Despite the anger, Sally's impression was Lynn also harbored some guilt. Over stealing from the group? Or from letting Ciara take the fall? Or both? Sally wanted to be frank. She wanted to say she knew about the addiction. *But that would make her even angrier, she'd throw me out, and I'd lose my opportunity. I want to help her, not piss her off.*

Shortly thereafter, she came back. "Sorry about that. I had to get a drink."

"No problem. Tell me about Ciara."

Lynn rubbed her hands on her pants. "She did our taxes. More accurately, she helped us fulfill our tax reporting duties. I was never quite clear on the details, Pat handled all that, but the two of them kept the IRS off our asses, that much I understood."

"Did you like her?"

Lynn shrugged. "Of course I did. She seemed smart, competent, didn't rob us blind for her services. And she was fond of the hounds, although she couldn't adopt herself. That's always a plus. You know, getting along with your clients."

"Right. Were you surprised when the allegations were made against her?"

"Yeah, I guess." Lynn fidgeted a bit. "I always assume everybody is innocent, you know? She sure fooled me."

Sally tapped her pen on the pad. Her gaze flitted around the room.

"You know what? This is a mistake. I'd like you go leave now." Lynn pulled herself up.

"It hasn't been fifteen minutes, has it?"

"It's almost time for Cassie's walk. Greyhounds are such creatures of habit. If I'm late, she'll drive me nuts."

Sally glanced in the corner, where Cassie again lay half on and half off the bed, flat as a flounder, tongue lolling out of her mouth. The greyhound did not look the least bit concerned about a delay in her walk. However, Sally decided against continuing. Lynn's body language screamed discomfort, and Sally suspected it wasn't all physical. Talking about Ciara made her uncomfortable. *Because she thinks Ciara is guilty or because she knows Ciara is innocent and has been hung out to dry? And it's Lynn's fault?* Sally leaned toward the latter, but again, if she overstayed her welcome, she would only shoot herself in the foot. She picked up her bag and headed for the door. Lynn trailed.

Sally slipped on her shoes and turned. "Ms. Moss. I understand that things may not have gone well for you recently. I want you to know that I am not your enemy."

Lynn gripped the door. "Aren't you trying to get Ciara off?"

"I am defending Mrs. Delmonico because I believe she is innocent. But that does not mean I'm trying to foist guilt off on someone else." She met the other woman's eyes. "I want this whole situation to come to an amicable ending and for everyone to get what she needs. Do you understand what I'm saying?"

Lynn's knuckles turned white. "Goodbye, Ms. Castle."

Sally left. Once in her car, she sighed. If she went to the DA with the information she had, it was pretty certain charges against Ciara would be dropped. Kim would count that a win. But Lynn Moss would pay the price.

For Sally, that wasn't a win at all.

Chapter Twenty-Seven

Sally had navigated her way to Monroeville when she received a call from the forensic accountant. The analysis of the tax information was complete. She pulled up the address on her GPS and headed over.

The accountant, Harriette Masterson, met her at the door. "Good afternoon. I've got everything set up in my conference room." She led Sally to a room with an oval table covered in papers. "Your client is well organized and detailed. I approve."

That didn't mean non-criminal, though. "I'm more interested in whether or not her methods are legitimate," Sally said.

"Of course. This summarizes my findings. You'd want to submit it along with my detailed analysis, of course." Harriette handed her a typed page. "There were no irregularities with the numbers or the calculations. What Mrs. Delmonico reported in terms of tax responsibilities, income, outflow, and year-end bank balance were accurate."

"Good to hear."

"As to the way she prepared the statements and the accounting methods she used, I would not have chosen to value things the way Mrs. Delmonico did. However, her methods are legitimate."

Sally skimmed down the text. "Is there a difference between how you'd do it? I mean, would RCH wind up with more or less money?"

Harriette pointed at the report. "I address that in the final paragraph. The group ends up with slightly less in noncash assets, under Mrs. Delmonico. No doubt that's why she chose to do it that way, and it's not a bad decision for this kind of client. The tax responsibilities are the same. Since RCH doesn't make in excess of twenty-five thousand dollars, there is no liability to the IRS. They don't owe the Commonwealth of Pennsylvania anything either."

Sally lowered the paper to look at him. "Then why would you do it differently?"

Harriette spread her hands. "In my experience, groups are more likely to be audited, particularly by the feds, when the reporting is done the way Mrs. Delmonico chose to do it. Again, it's not wrong, and it's not illegal. But given the nature of the organization and the volunteers, I'd simply choose to limit any potential for audit as much as I can. As I said, the money difference is negligible so, in the end, it really doesn't matter." She folded her hands on the table.

Sally finished her scan of the report. If what Harriette said was correct, Ciara hadn't benefitted at all. So why did the DA think differently? She'd have to re-read the discovery materials and compare the findings. "Thank you. Both for the analysis and the speed. I appreciate it." She looked at the piles. "Is all this for me?"

"I laid it out in case you wanted to review it here. If you don't, I'll get a box and pack it up." She stood.

Once the packing was complete, Sally took the cardboard bank box. "Thanks again. You can send the bill to me at the address on my business card. I'll take care of it. If we're unlucky enough to get to trial, I'll be in touch."

* * *

Duncan and Cavendish left the scene, carrying boxes of evidence. Burns had departed, and although the techs would be at it for a while, neither trooper believed there was anything more they could do in Connellsville. Most of the neighbors had either seen nothing or weren't home, aside from the one mention of a pickup. But when Duncan had gone back with a picture of Sullivan's truck, the witness shrugged. "Maybe. It was pretty muddy, and like I said, it could have been in a different driveway. Plus, the sun was in my face, so I didn't get a real good look. Sorry."

They arrived at headquarters and took the papers and Bevilacqua's laptop to a conference room. Cavendish pointed at the computer. "Are you going to take a crack at that before we hand it over?"

"Yeah. I found that short exchange with McDonough, but I want to see if there's more. And I'm going to take a quick look at the numbers. I'm not a genius, but something might pop out." Too bad McAllister wasn't there, with her accounting degree. Maybe he could call her.

Cavendish nodded. "Let me check my desk, grab a can of Coke, and I'll be back."

Duncan decided to focus on the laptop first. It was clear the dead man hadn't been big on privacy. The machine wasn't locked. *All the better for me.* He scrolled through the email messages, looking for more exchanges with McDonough, or anything that might explain why he'd decided to buy and rent a house so far from his residence. Finally, he located a chain of messages that matched McDonough's email address. But before he could read further, Cavendish re-entered the room, a single sheet of paper in one hand, a Coke can glistening with condensation in the other. "You're going to love this." She handed him the sheet.

He took it. "What?"

"Remember how we'd pretty much decided Bethany Carlyle, the protester, was out of the picture because of the drive time to and from Markleysburg?"

"Yeah."

She dropped into a chair. "I figured I'd make sure, and I checked to see if she had an EZPass. And whether it had any recent activity."

"Does she?"

"No. But." Cavendish raised a finger. "Her friend does, the one she spent the evening with. And guess who exited the Turnpike at the Somerset toll plaza at 6:34 p.m. a week ago, the night we figure McDonough was murdered. And he drives, drum roll please, a dark red Chevy Malibu."

Duncan slapped the desk. "No friggin' way."

"Way."

197

"That girl is pissing me off."

"You and me both." She stretched and took a sip of soda. "Looks like we'll be talking to Ms. Carlyle again. But that's for later. Did you find anything yet?"

"Sort of." He turned the laptop so his partner could see the screen. "There's another email exchange between the two victims, this one from earlier in the year. Before McDonough stopped his rent, but after he obtained Johnny. See?"

Cavendish read aloud. "Nice job last night. You're on a roll. When do I see my cut?"

"We wondered why Bevilacqua had the Markleysburg house. Try this on for size." Duncan leaned back. "What if he was renting it to McDonough in exchange for a cut of the race winnings?"

"Interesting. But we don't have any proof the two men knew each other prior to the rental agreement or that Bevilacqua knew about the illicit racing."

"True, however." Duncan ticked off the points on his fingers. "We know Bevilacqua needed money. He was skating by on just his other rental income."

"By the way, his repayment agreement for the bankruptcy hadn't been approved. I saw it, though. There wasn't going to be a lot left over for extravagances, and he struck me as the type of man who liked the finer things in life."

"I also found this." He clicked over to another email. "Bevilacqua tells McDonough he's selling the Markleysburg house."

Cavendish stood and searched the piles. A few minutes later, she found what she wanted and handed it to Duncan. "That property originally belonged to Bevilacqua's grandmother. She died in January of this year. He was her beneficiary."

"That's how he ended up with this property in the middle of nowhere. He doesn't know what to do with it in the short term, so he rents it out. But he gets strapped for cash, especially with the pending bankruptcy plan payments, so he tells McDonough it's going on the market."

"McDonough doesn't want to move." Cavendish returned to her seat. "He obtained, or is about to, a greyhound for illegal racing. He offers to cut Bevilacqua in on the winnings in exchange for continuing to rent the house. Bevilacqua could fulfill his bankruptcy commitments and still have money for fine wines and useless tchotchkes." Cavendish tapped her lips. "I like it. It strengthens Bevilacqua's motive." She paused. "You're pretty good at this."

"Thanks." *Progress.* Duncan pointed at the laptop. "If McDonough wasn't forking over his landlord's share of the winnings, Bevilacqua could easily have gone down to persuade him to pony up. The two fight, the next thing you know, McDonough's on the floor with three slugs in his chest. After all, we did find a .38 at the scene today. It'll be interesting to see the ballistics report when it gets here."

"As I said, I like it. One problem." She drained the can of Coke and sent it to the recycling basket with a perfect hook shot.

"What's that?"

"If Robert Bevilacqua killed Otto McDonough over this racing thing, who the hell killed Bevilacqua?"

Chapter Twenty-Eight

ally sat on Jim's bed and watched him change out of his suit. She had received his call while she was en route from Pittsburgh, letting her know Eddie had summoned him for a meeting. She stopped at her apartment just long enough to change and headed to Confluence. During the drive, she thought again how stupid it was to keep her residence in Uniontown. But every time she thought she'd made up her mind to move, the logical part of her brain leaped out to put the brakes on. Deal with the job first. The last time she and Jim spoke of it, she promised a decision "later." Later might come sooner than she originally thought.

Jim pulled a sweater over his head. "So that's that." He had just finished bringing her up to speed on Robert Bevilacqua's death, the gun found at the scene, and the fact that Bethany Carlyle's alibi might not be as good as first thought.

She dangled her shoe from her toes. "You don't know if the same weapon was used to kill McDonough?" Not normal after-work conversation for two people who were dating. *Then again, we're hardly a typical couple.*

"Not yet." He finger-combed his tousled hair. "Ballistics will take a day or two. But six shots missing from the same kind of firearm used in both homicides? What do you think?"

"I'd be thinking it's the murder weapon for both. You said the serial number was filed off?"

"Someone tried. Once I got the call from Eddie, I left, but Cavendish said she would track down the registration."

"Speaking of Cavendish,"—she watched as he went into the bathroom—"how are things progressing? Have you made any headway convincing her you're not just some noob?" Jim had also told her about the rumors surrounding his partner. *How typical. I bet if Cavendish was a man, the story would be very different.*

"I think so. She used my name and gave me a compliment."

"In the same day?"

Jim came back to the doorway, a bottle of mouthwash in hand. "It was. Personally, I was a little surprised." He tossed back a shot of the blue liquid and swished it around in his mouth.

"Is that all?"

He held up a finger, left again, and came back, mouth empty. "No. She was a complete professional all day. She's a damn solid investigator. I think that intimidates some people." He told her about the conversation with Ed Louglin.

"Because she demands a high level of performance, she's a hard ass?" Unbelievable. Or maybe completely believable. She was used to Jim and the way he evaluated people on performance, not skin color, gender, or other aspects of their personality. She was quite sure there were some dinosaurs in the state police who would think a competent woman who expected quality was being difficult. *And they probably don't think the same things about men.*

He grabbed a pair of loafers from under the bed. "Based on that conversation, I think she's had some difficult partnerships. It's not that she thinks I'm unqualified. She's testing me. Trying to see if I'll react the same way some other male troopers have."

"What are you going to do?"

"I'm going to be a mature professional. Based on today, I think she's coming around. I can only hope the trend continues and we wind up with a solid partnership. I know I can trust her and she learns she can trust me."

"See if you pass."

"Yes." He slipped on the shoes. "I'd take you to Eddie's, but I don't think it's a good idea this time."

"Understood." She stood and gave him the once over. Too bad he had business to take care of. *There's always later.* "I'll be waiting for you."

* * *

Fifteen minutes after Duncan departed, he parked his Jeep in the lot at Eddie's place. Unlike last time, there were only two cars there, a dark blue SUV and a gray Lincoln Town Car. He looked at the clock. A minute past five. Earlier than Eddie usually wanted to talk. *He probably doesn't want me interrupting his business.* Duncan walked over to the metal door and banged. He should bring Sally some night when the place was in full swing. It would be an interesting experience.

Barely a minute passed before the eye-slot cover opened. "He's expecting you," Stanley said. The slot cover banged back, and the door opened. "You know where to find him."

Duncan walked down the hallway. The building was silent but expectant, as though it waited for the night's customers to kick off the festivities.

He found Eddie in his usual place, behind his desk, an unlit cigar on the ashtray next to him. A plate with half a grilled chicken sandwich and the remains of a salad also adorned the desktop. "Nice to see you." He indicated the chair opposite.

"A chair? You're making me feel special, Eddie."

"You are. I don't invite just anyone to visit me off hours. Where's Pretty?"

"I left her at home this time."

"What a shame. It was her I was looking forward to seeing."

Duncan glanced around the office. "Why such an early meeting? I could have come later, let you get through your meal."

"You make my customers nervous, Trooper Duncan."

"I was in a suit last time. I'm in street clothes now."

Eddie shook his head, light glinting off his hair. "Face it, Duncan. No matter what you wear, there's no doubt that you are a police officer. You could show up here in pajamas, and within thirty seconds of meeting you, everyone would know you're a cop. It's your posture. And the fact you can't relax in a crowd. I'm sure your girlfriend has told you this."

"Crowds are dangerous." Sally had told him. He ignored her then, and he'd keep doing it. "What did you want to talk to me about?"

"Always right to business." He picked up the stogie, snipped off the end, lit and puffed it to life. The stench of burning socks filled the room. "You were right. There was an attempt to establish an off-the-books dog track here in Fayette County."

"Let me guess. They weren't nearly as rigorous with the rules as an official place."

"Correct. As it was communicated to me, the idea was owners would bring their own animals. Whether the dogs were registered with the NGA was not an issue. No drug testing, no proof of ownership, just six dogs running madly after a bit of fluff on a lure." Eddie snorted. "I cannot for the life of me see why anyone would prefer that to a nice game of five-card stud. Can you imagine the cleanup? All that dog shit."

Duncan drummed his fingers on his thigh. "You said *was*, past tense. Did it get off the ground?"

"No." Eddie puffed. "About the time they wanted to open, the West Virginia State Police, along with representatives from West Virginia animal control, the National Greyhound Association, and a couple of other entities, brought down the first operation, the one in the papers. The people in Fayette County spooked and abandoned the attempt."

"Not to mention that their customers probably bolted for cover."

"Indeed." Eddie studied the burning end of his cigar. "The entire thing imploded at the end of June of this year. Since then, nobody has said word one about illegal dog racing."

"Good to know. Thanks, Eddie." Duncan stood. "As always, I appreciate your cooperation."

"I have a request this time."

Duncan raised an eyebrow. Eddie occasionally asked for things. Usually, nothing major and nothing illegal, of course. Mostly he stayed out of the bookie's way in exchange for information when he needed it. "What?"

Eddie blew a noxious cloud of smoke. "Next time, bring Pretty. She makes you look good. You still get taken for a cop, but when she's on your arm, at least there's a possibility you're here for the entertainment."

Chapter Twenty-Nine

Friday morning, Duncan brought Cavendish up to speed with what he'd learned from Eddie. "Which means after the West Virginia thing was broken up, McDonough wouldn't have raced Johnny. He could have been looking to offload the dog, or he might have had feelers out in other areas, looking for a new location."

Cavendish stared at the whiteboard with a furrowed forehead. "What's our to-do list look like?"

Before Duncan could respond, Ferguson stuck her head through the doorway. "Duncan, Cavendish, update."

Cavendish waved at him.

She's senior. Shouldn't she be giving the report? Of course, Cavendish wasn't the only person he needed to impress. Maybe she was letting him take the lead so their boss could do her own evaluation of her new trooper. Duncan summarized the findings to date.

"What's next?"

He glanced at Cavendish, but she didn't look inclined to speak. "We need to interview Bethany Carlyle, or at least her friend, about what they were doing in Somerset the night of the murder," he said. "We need to catch up with Dan Overbeck and find out if McDonough ever paid for Johnny's Pixelated. Hopefully, we get the ballistics report on that .38 we found at Bevilacqua's murder."

Ferguson directed her next question at Cavendish. "Will it all get done today?"

Cavendish straightened. "Possibly. We should be able to make good progress. I'm comfortable splitting things up if it means we complete the investigation quicker."

Duncan schooled his face. *Splitting up?* More than anything Cavendish had said, the suggestion told him she'd been favorably impressed by his performance over the last couple of days. She'd never have let the rookie go off on his own.

Ferguson slapped the doorframe. "Good job. Keep me updated." She left.

Cavendish turned to him. "Did we find out anything about the owner of the gun?"

It was illegal in Pennsylvania for the government to keep a firearm registry. But all sales and transfers had to go through the Pennsylvania Instant Check System, which was maintained by the State Police. Assuming the gun had been purchased legally, they could find the owner. "We ran out of time yesterday. Let's do that before we leave." He studied the board. "Two more things. We need to talk to Max Renner. And I wish we could shake Kyle Sullivan's tree again."

"Why Sullivan? His gun isn't a match for either killing." She drummed her fingers on the back of the chair. "Besides, his motive for shooting Bevilacqua would be what exactly?"

"I don't know. He didn't tell us he was Mikey Fisher's half-brother, and he lied about why he left work. That bothers me. Besides, you're assuming the same person killed both men. Until we get ballistics, I'd rather not assume."

"You've got a point." She turned to him. "Where do you want to start?"

"Bethany Carlyle and her friend. Then we swing by and check in with Overbeck."

She nodded.

"Do we know when the Malibu got back on the Turnpike?" Duncan asked as he perused the printout in his hand.

Cavendish jabbed a finger at it. "It re-entered the toll plaza two hours after it exited, give or take."

"Two hours and six minutes, to be exact." It would have been a short trip to Markleysburg, but possible.

"They cut it tight for a shooting." She tilted her head. "Guess we'll let them explain the situation. Let's run that gun registration and go."

They went back to the bullpen.

"What's the number?" Cavendish asked as she pulled up PICS, the state gun registration database.

Duncan read it from his notes. "The last number was the most indistinct. Could be a five, could be an eight."

She typed it in and waited. "Nada on the five. Let's try the eight." Another pause. "Looks like it was sold a year ago to a Justin Quincy. He lives in Carnegie. Do you want to call him or pay him a visit?"

"I think we'll have better luck if we talk to him in person." Duncan made a note of the address. "No chance ballistics are back, is there?"

"Ha, surely you jest." She turned off her computer. "I'll call Quincy from the road and make sure he's home. One thing is for sure, though."

"What is that?"

She grinned. "We're gonna log a lot of miles today, so I hope you like driving."

* * *

Sally brought Kim up to date as they stood by the coffee machine. "And that's that." She returned to her office.

Kim's staccato footsteps followed her. "Why do we care about this?"

"Two things." Sally sat at her desk. "One, that money didn't come from Lynn's relative, so where did it come from? Two, I don't think Lynn quit her job, the first one. I'm positive she was fired. I just need someone to confirm it. I could submit a subpoena for the practice's employment records, but I don't want to wait for that. I need to convince another employee, one who liked Lynn, that it's in her best interests to tell me what the real situation was."

"You misunderstand. Why do *we* care about this? Our client is Ciara Delmonico. We can show more than reasonable doubt with the witnesses you've interviewed. We're done."

"You might be, but I'm not."

Kim flopped into a chair. "Want to explain that to me?"

Sally rubbed her eyes. "What is justice?" She fixed the other woman with a stare.

"The guilty being punished." Kim arched an eyebrow.

"Is that it? I'm going to stand up in court and show a jury reasonable doubt that Ciara is guilty. In the process, I'm going to throw another woman, one who most likely has her own addiction, under the bus. Is that justice?"

Kim shifted, and she studied the top of Sally's desk a little too carefully. "It is for our client."

"But not for Lynn Moss."

"Who isn't our client."

"No, she isn't. Kim, look at me." Sally waited until her partner lifted her gaze from the desk. "You wanted me. This is who I am. I cannot and will not sacrifice one woman to save another. I know what you're going to say. Who's going to pay for this? Yes, that's an issue and we should talk about it. But Kim, listen." She leaned forward. "If I'm right, Lynn Moss didn't steal because she's greedy, or to fund her nefarious activities, or anything like that. She stole because she has a problem, one just as serious as Ciara's gambling. Don't we help people with problems?"

Kim's response was unintelligible.

"I didn't hear you."

The redhead rolled her eyes. "God, Sally. You always did have a righteous streak. Fine. Let's help Lynn Moss." She jabbed her index finger at Sally. "But let me be clear. This type of work doesn't keep the lights on. I meant it when I said not every client can be a charity case."

Sally smothered a smile and held up her hands. "I promise it won't be."

Kim's glower said she wasn't convinced, but she said, "Why do we need someone else from Lynn's old employer as a witness? We have the statement from the Dennister woman."

Sally sat back. "If Lynn Moss was our client, how would you explain that?"

Kim pursed her lips. "That she'd finagled a prescription from a doctor at her old job. Yeah, I see what you mean. It's not absolute proof she forged anything." She tapped her nails. "Since this is your crusade, I'll leave you to it. I'll be over there doing work that pays. One of us has to." She shook her head and went across the hall to her own office.

Sally stared at the blank monitor. Where to begin? Supposedly the money that saved Lynn Moss from ruin came from a relative. Did she even have a recently-deceased cousin or aunt? Where to look?

She snapped her fingers. One of those ancestry websites would help. She woke up her computer and navigated to a popular site. She signed up for a thirty-day free trial, then entered as much information about Lynn Moss as she knew from public records. Then she clicked Search.

The result was a plethora of information. Lynn was a middle child, the third of five. Her parents were deceased. Her father only had brothers, both of whom appeared to be childless. Her mother had an older sister, who also had children, but the site didn't give a date of death for any of them. It wasn't the same as not finding a death certificate, but it was good enough for Sally's purposes. That meant it was unlikely the money came from an inheritance, either aunt or cousin.

Sally clicked back to the siblings. It was a painstaking process, but between the ancestry site and Google, she was able to come up with addresses and phone numbers for all of them. Two, an older brother and a younger sister, lived out of state. The others were local. In fact, the eldest, Gerald Kelleher, lived in Fayette County. Sally dialed the phone number.

After three rings, a man answered. "Hello?"

Sally introduced herself. "Is this Gerald Kelleher?"

"Speaking." His voice sounded a bit fussy and a little nasal.

Sally explained the situation, without going into specifics about Ciara. "I'd like to meet with you to talk about Lynn."

A heavy silence came over the line. "I'm not going to get my sister into trouble," he said.

"I'm not asking you to. I think she's in trouble. I might be able to help with that, but only if I get the answers to my questions. Your sister won't give me the information I need, but you can." She paused. "If you need to call Lynn first, I understand."

"I might. Is there anything else?"

"Only that not only can you help your sister by talking to me, you can help prevent another woman from being wrongly convicted of embezzlement."

Another pause. "All right. Since it's for my sister, I'll meet with you. I'm at work, but I can see you for lunch."

"Perfect. If you are near Uniontown, there's a place called Dex's."

"Yes, I know it."

"Then we'll meet there at noon unless I hear from you before that." Sally hung up. "Eureka!"

Kim looked up from her desk, where she'd been reading the paper. "I take it you've gotten good news?"

"I have." Sally gulped the remainder of her lukewarm coffee and decided to get another cup. "And I'm counting on brotherly love to help me move forward."

Chapter Thirty

Duncan and Cavendish made it to Pittsburgh by nine-fifteen. Fat drops splatted on the windshield as a rainstorm sputtered to a start. Duncan drove to the South Side address listed on the EZPass account and the Malibu's registration. "Guy's name is Trevor Shaw," he said.

Cavendish ran the plates on the silver Prius parked in front of the house. "The Toyota belongs to Carlyle."

They got out and dashed to the front door. Duncan knocked. Water dripped off the awning overhang and ran down his neck.

Cavendish maneuvered to stand under the minuscule cover, but a brisk wind slanted the rain, soaking her slacks. "Come on, open up."

The door opened. A college-age male with longish brown hair and a scraggly goatee stood behind the storm door. "Yes?"

Duncan and Cavendish held up their badges. "Pennsylvania State Police. Are you Trevor Shaw?"

The guy nodded.

"May we come in?"

Shaw hesitated. "I didn't do anything."

Interesting. Automatic response to seeing the police at his door or guilty conscience? "We didn't say you did," Duncan said. "We have some questions for you, though. And Bethany, if she'll speak to us. It would be nice not to drown while we talk."

Cavendish nodded toward the Prius. "That is Bethany Carlyle's car, isn't it?"

"Yes. She's a friend," Shaw said. He yelled over his shoulder, "Hey, Beth, c'mere!"

Carlyle appeared. She pulled on a sweatshirt over her t-shirt, leaving her purple hair tousled. "You again. What now?"

"We have a few more questions," said Cavendish. "We'd also really appreciate it if you'd open up and let us in."

"Hold on." Shaw pushed the door shut. Muted voices could be heard through it. The couple was arguing, probably about whether to let their visitors inside.

The rain came at them in sheets. Duncan thought about the trenchcoat he'd left at home this morning. Not that it would provide much protection against a downpour like this. He glanced at his watch. How long were Shaw and Carlyle going to leave their visitors outside?

The main door opened again, and Shaw pushed open the flimsy storm one. "Come in. We'll talk, but only in the kitchen. No walking through the place. You want a towel?"

"Please," Cavendish said as she entered.

Duncan followed on her heels. The decor screamed "college student," with mismatched furniture, a carpet that was flattened and stained from feet and spilled beverages—or worse—and a Pitt flag on the wall.

Bethany disappeared and returned moments later with two raggedy towels. "Here," she said, thrusting one at each trooper. "I'll have you know, this is Trevor's idea, talking to you. I have nothing to say."

"That's fine." Duncan toweled off his face and did the best he could to dry his shoes and wring out his pants. "You said something about the kitchen?"

"That way," Shaw said, pointing toward an open door. "Follow me."

The kitchen's floor was worn linoleum, and the counters had seen better days, but the room was clean. Shaw grabbed the cabinet door pull. "Glass of water, coffee?"

Bethany stamped her foot. "Trev!"

"No, thanks," Duncan said.

Cavendish murmured her refusal.

"Mind if we sit?"

"If you insist." Bethany scowled and leaned against the wall.

Shaw pulled out two chairs. "What is this about?" he asked as he lowered himself into a third chair.

Duncan pulled out his notebook. "Ms. Carlyle, the last time we spoke, you said you'd been in class then a meeting for a club at the University of Pittsburgh last Thursday night, right? That would be the night Otto McDonough was killed."

"Yeah," Bethany said.

"When did the meeting end?"

She shrugged. "No clue. What, are you claiming I lied?"

"No, we've confirmed you were at the meeting," Cavendish said.

"So, what's the big deal?"

Duncan pulled out the EZPass report. "Mr. Shaw, your EZPass was registered at the Somerset toll plaza around six-thirty that evening. Were you in Somerset at that time?"

Shaw licked his lips. He didn't look at his girlfriend. "Uh, yeah."

Bethany pushed off the wall. "Trev, shut the hell up!"

He faced her. "For Christ's sake, Beth. They know the car was there."

"You could have told them you loaned it to someone."

He snorted. "I'm not gonna be an idiot and lie to the freaking state police. You told me the guy was murdered. I said I'd keep my mouth shut as long as no one asked questions. I'll do a lot of things for you. Going to jail for making a false statement during a murder investigation isn't one of them." He turned back to the troopers. "Yes, we went to Somerset. I didn't pay attention to the time, but if the computer says six-thirty, yeah, sure."

Cavendish nodded toward Bethany. "You said 'we.' Was Ms. Carlyle with you?"

Shaw hesitated. "Yes."

Bethany let loose a string of profanity that would make a Marine flinch.

Shaw, however, remained calm. "We went to Markleysburg."

Duncan glanced at his partner. "Why?"

"Bethany wanted to talk to that guy, the one who was killed. I don't remember his name."

"Otto McDonough."

"I didn't know him, but she said something about how he worked at a racetrack in West Virginia, the one with the greyhounds her group had protested at. They'd argued, him and Beth, and she wanted to have another go."

Bethany stormed out of the kitchen.

Duncan flipped the page in his notebook. "Did you see him?"

"No." Shaw rested his hands on the table. "We found his house. Beth knocked on the door, but he didn't answer. Then she shouted, taunted him, threw some baggies of dog shit at the front door. The guy still didn't answer. After about ten minutes, it was clear to me he either wasn't home or wasn't going to open the door, so I dragged her away, and we left."

All that tallied with the exit and entrance times to the Turnpike. "When you were at the house, did you see anything?" Duncan asked.

"A truck, another person, something like that?" Cavendish added.

"Um, no." Shaw drew out the words. "I mean, there were cars and stuff around, but the only car at the house belonged to McDonough. At least that's what Beth said."

"Did you go up to the house, try to look in the windows?" Duncan asked.

"Nope. Well, she did, to knock on the door. She tried to look in the window, but the blinds were down. I told her to give it up. Car or no car, the place was empty." Shaw pressed his hands to the tabletop.

Bethany spoke from the kitchen door. "I think he was in there." She stomped over to the table and yanked out the last chair. The legs screeched on the linoleum, and she flung herself into it.

Duncan chose not to remark on her movement. He wasn't sure why she'd changed her mind about talking, and he wasn't going to ask, just in case she reversed course. "Why do you say that?"

She shrugged. "Just a feeling. When I was pounding on the door, I swear I saw movement at the front window, just a flutter of the blinds. That asshole was in there, probably laughing at us. Then a few minutes later, I heard a door slam, like a metal screen door."

"You didn't see anyone?" Cavendish asked Trevor.

"I told you I didn't. And I didn't hear anything, either," Shaw said. "But I was at the street. Beth could have heard a back door. I don't think I'd have noticed."

Duncan held Cavendish's gaze and wondered if her thoughts mirrored his. It was a bit outside the window, but not ridiculously so. "Think hard. Were there any lights on in the house?"

The two young people looked at each other. "Yeah, in the front. But then they went off," Bethany said. "That's another reason I was convinced McDipshit was there. But like Trev said, nobody answered. I wanted to stay, but he dragged me away." She glared at her boyfriend.

Duncan made notes as she talked. It was going to be a rough night for Trevor after he and Cavendish left, he thought. Lucky for him, at least one of the students had some sense.

"After you heard the door slam, are you sure you didn't see anyone?" Cavendish asked.

"Like Trev said, no one was in the front, not even in the street," Bethany said. "But when I circled around back, there was a guy walking down the road behind McDipshit's. You know, the next block over."

"What did he look like?"

Bethany flipped her hair. "I didn't pay that much attention. He was wearing a plaid shirt and jeans, wore a blue ball cap, and had brown hair. He had his hands in his pockets and walked all hunched over. Between that and the hat, I can't tell you anything else. Oh, he was skinny. I think he was around my age, but that's just my opinion."

Skinny, twentysomething, brown hair. Duncan glanced at his partner, but she maintained her poker face. He stood. "One last question. Did you hear anything that sounded like gunshots? Perhaps you thought it was a car backfiring?"

Trevor and Bethany both shook their heads.

Worth a shot. "I appreciate you taking the time to talk to us." He pushed a business card toward Shaw. "If you think of anything, call me."

He spread his hands. "We didn't have anything to do with him dying. Honest."

The rain had not abated, and Duncan and Cavendish made a mad dash to their car. Inside, she pulled a wad of napkins out of the glove box and handed some to Duncan. "What do you think?" she asked.

He patted water off his face. "Honestly? I think Shaw is telling the truth. Carlyle was too angry at him, and their story fits the timetable of the EZPass records. Plus, I can't see where either of those two would have gotten a gun."

"Agreed. She'd do anything to humiliate someone or deface property. Like the shit-slinging, literally. But shooting a man? That takes balls."

"But they saw the lights go off. And potentially heard a person leaving the house."

"Skinny, young, brown hair. Three things that apply to Kyle Sullivan."

Duncan turned the ignition. "Yes."

Cavendish bit her lip. "But no car. That means the killer parked away from the house."

He drummed his fingers on the door panel. "Or didn't need a car to get there in the first place."

216

Chapter Thirty-One

Duncan stared through the window at the rain, which slacked off the farther they got from Pittsburgh. "What do you think about Carlyle?"

Cavendish tapped her fingers on the steering wheel. "I think she's back to the bottom of the suspect list, if not off it entirely."

"Agreed. She may have gone to harass McDonough, but I don't think she went to kill him." Duncan wasn't one to accept a statement without proof. But Trevor Shaw had been pretty direct and hadn't bothered to deny the trip. Carlyle might have started off recalcitrant, but she'd come around by the end, albeit reluctantly. "I find her sighting of a young white male interesting, though." Equally interesting was Cavendish's slow and steady transformation into a real partner, but he wasn't going to rock the boat there. *I'm sure she has reasons. Once the case is over, I'll ask about them.*

"Indeed. As you said, Sullivan wouldn't need to drive over. I think you're right. We need to talk to him again." Cavendish reached over to redirect the air vent away from her, then pulled out her phone. "Do you want to head there next?"

"No, I think I want to save Mr. Sullivan for last. Why don't we make a big loop. The West Virginia staties gave us the all-clear to talk to Overbeck. We'll hit him, then Renner, and finish up with Sullivan."

"Sounds like a good plan to me." Her phone vibrated, and she tapped the button to accept the call. "Cavendish. What's up?"

Duncan listened to the conversation with half his mind focused on the remaining suspects. Two motives related to dog racing, Renner and

Overbeck. The other one was more personal, the death of Sullivan's half-brother. Normally, he'd be inclined to follow the money. Except...he thought of Sullivan's reddened, watery eyes from the first conversation. Tears of grief? How much had Sullivan loved that little boy? But there was the incontrovertible fact that his .38 was not the murder weapon.

Since Cavendish's side of the conversation consisted of "uh-huh" and "yep," Duncan made a quick call to animal control and asked about Johnny's Pixelated.

"He's good," the woman said. "In fact, we're just about ready to release him to the adoption group."

"Really? He looked on death's door when we found him."

"Just undernourished. We gave him a good grooming and a vet check, neutered him, and he looks much better. Poor guy. I heard he was used in an illegal racing scheme."

"Possibly." Duncan sped up to pass a couple cars. "Something that's been bothering me, though. Shouldn't he have been heavier if he was racing? That freezer was stuffed full."

"Tracks usually don't feed the dogs very good meat, and I'm sure an illegal operation wouldn't spend a lot on chow," the woman said. "My suspicion is he got poor quality meals, added to the steroids and whatever they allegedly doped him with. We had to treat him for worms, too. All of that added up would contribute to the low weight. But he's well on his way to health. He's going to be a beautiful dog."

Duncan thanked her and hung up. Beside him, Cavendish was doing the same. "Any news?" he asked.

She waved the phone. "Ballistics. We were right. The thirty-eight found at the scene of Bevilacqua's murder matches the slugs recovered from McDonough. No useful prints, though. The gun itself is clean. There's a decent partial off the magazine, probably from when the shooter inserted it, but it doesn't match anything in AFIS."

"Let me get this straight. A gun that belongs to a guy who has no connection to our victims was used in both crimes?"

"That appears to be the case."

Duncan let the facts roll around in his head for a moment. "What was his name again?"

Cavendish consulted her notes. "Justin Quincy, address in Carnegie. Do we talk to him before or after Sullivan?"

It was a good question. "Let's do it before. I want to have a bucketful of information before we talk to Sullivan. Right now, there is no connection between Quincy and any of this. If we ask Sullivan about it, I think we're going to get the runaround."

"Agreed." She opened the map. "We talk to Overbeck, dip down to chat with Renner, swing up to catch Quincy, and finish out with Sullivan. That's a long-ass day."

"We might have to break it up." Duncan flicked on the signal to exit the highway. "Then again, no one ever promised us a nine-to-five gig."

* * *

To fill the time before her meeting with Gerald Kelleher, Sally filled out the presigned subpoena form required to obtain Lynn's bank records. She glanced at her watch. It was still only mid-morning. Even though she planned to deliver the subpoena to the bank now, it would be several days before any information would be forthcoming. She needed someone else to verify Lynn's unemployment benefits, or lack thereof.

As she hurried to the bank, the clouds opened up, and she popped open the compact black umbrella she'd thankfully had the foresight to bring along. Thankfully, it only took her minutes to arrive at the local bank branch, where she dropped off the subpoena with a manager. "The faster I get the results, the better," she said.

"We'll do our best," the manager said.

Sally returned to her office. The umbrella kept a good bit of the rain off, but her shoes and legs were drenched by the time she got there. She set the dripping rain gear near the entry and took off her heels.

Kim came out of her office. "You look like a drowned rat."

"Only from the knees down. My top half is dry, and I can go barefoot."

219

Sally set the shoes near her door and walked to the coffee pot. Kim had added cocoa to the selection, so Sally picked a dark hot chocolate. The smell alone was warming. She took her cup and returned to her office.

"You deliver the subpoena?" Kim asked, standing in the doorway.

"Yes, but who knows how long it will take for the bank to get back to me." Sally tested the hot chocolate. Still a bit too warm. "I tried to get them to hurry, but we'll see."

"Doesn't anyone else know whether the woman collected unemployment?"

"Her brother, maybe, but I don't meet with him for"—Sally checked the clock—"another hour. I arranged to meet for lunch at Dex's."

"What about the folks from the dog group?"

Sally thought over the details of her conversations with Pat Dennister and Annie Norquist. "I don't recall them saying anything. I suppose I can ask. But I can't drive up to Pittsburgh, not if I hope to make lunch on time."

"Gee." Kim pointed at the telephone. "If only we had a solution for problems like that." She tossed her mane of red hair and strutted away.

It wasn't Sally's preferred method of communication. But in times like this, beggars couldn't be choosers. She looked up both numbers and dialed Pat Dennister. After saying hello, Sally asked, "I need you to think back. Did Lynn Moss ever talk about unemployment benefits?"

"I'm not sure what you mean. Did she talk about how much she received?"

"Yes, or if she didn't receive payments...anything really."

Pat paused. "I don't remember, no wait. I do recall asking her once if she'd looked into it."

"I thought you said she'd quit."

"Well, that's what I thought at first. But now that I think back, she said she *left*, not how it happened. That's why I told her to check into unemployment because the worst they can say is no. I also suggested talking to a lawyer if she'd been fired because of her back, because that's illegal."

Sally had asked the same question. "What did she say?"

"She mumbled something like she had it all under control, and I shouldn't worry."

Sally thanked Pat and hung up. The next call went to Annie Norquist.

"I don't have anything else to say, and I'm not sure I should talk to you," Annie said after Sally introduced herself.

"Ms. Norquist, I understand. You are in a hard spot. You don't want to get your friend in a bind. But this is critical. If Lynn Moss is in trouble, she needs help. What you say could get her that assistance and keep an innocent woman out of jail." Sally bit her lip as inspiration struck. "Remember, we're talking about your money. You can always speak to the DA about dropping the charges if it turns out that is what you want to do."

A heavy silence hung over the conversation. "What is your question?"

"Did Lynn Moss tell you whether or not she received unemployment benefits?"

"No. I asked, right after she left. She didn't want to talk about it."

"Did she quit, or was she fired?"

Annie's sigh sounded like a gust of wind. "They fired her. She didn't want to talk about that either. I didn't press it."

"Thank you, this helps. It really does."

"Will it help Lynn? She's a good person who has had a rotten run of luck. The divorce, the accident, her back...I want to help her. I've always wanted to, and she kept me away."

Maybe Lynn was ashamed of her behavior. Sally knew many addicts didn't want to admit they had a problem and were too proud to ask for help. That could be the case with Lynn Moss. "I don't know. But I can tell you this. I don't want anyone to get in trouble if she doesn't deserve it."

Chapter Thirty-Two

By the time Duncan and Cavendish pulled into Dan Overbeck's weed-choked driveway, the rain had stopped, and the sun struggled to break through the cloud cover. He got out, stretched, and popped his back. Being a passenger wasn't any easier than driving.

"How do you want to play this?" She jerked her thumb in the direction of the blue saltbox dwelling.

Duncan considered several plans as he studied the house. Neat, the west side a little faded from the glare of the afternoon sun, the grass cut reasonably short. Overbeck didn't waste time on frills, but he didn't live in a dump, either. The garage door was open, showcasing a late-model red Ram pickup. "I don't think we want to beat around the bush. He already said he didn't deliver without payment and hinted he wouldn't take it well if a customer stiffed him."

"We tell him we know McDonough never paid up and see what he says?"

"Exactly." Duncan didn't doubt that Overbeck had, or could get, a .38. But there was no report of his truck at either scene. More importantly, there didn't seem to be a connection between him and the owner of the murder weapon. "I don't think we need good cop-bad cop, either."

"Let's do it." She knocked on the door.

It didn't take long for Overbeck to answer. "What the hell do you want? I already talked to you about McDonough, and I don't have anything else to say."

"We do," Cavendish said. "Can we come in?"

"Hell no."

"Then how about you come outside? The rain has stopped."

Overbeck glowered through the screen.

"Look, we have a couple of questions," Duncan said. Was the man tired of talking to the cops, or did he have another reason for refusing entrance? "You answer them and we'll be on our way."

"If I don't?" Overbeck asked, jutting his chin out.

"We go away and make arrangements to meet someplace less casual," Cavendish said.

"But we will have a conversation," Duncan added. "Where is completely up to you."

Overbeck narrowed his eyes. "Not in my house. I don't want no cops in my place."

Which doesn't make you look suspicious at all. Duncan jabbed his thumb toward the driveway. "Fine. As my partner said, the rain has stopped. We can go over there."

For a moment, Overbeck looked like he was going to slam the door shut, but he came out, went over to the driveway, and whirled around. "You got five minutes. Go."

Out of the corner of Duncan's eye, he saw Cavendish take out a notepad and pen. "The last time we spoke, you said you only sold dogs to buyers who paid in advance. Or if they were vouched for by a previous customer. Is that correct?"

"No payment, no dog."

"You also said you only accepted Bitcoin, no cash."

"Yep."

Cavendish looked up. "You're absolutely positive about that? No exceptions ever?"

"None. I didn't want to meet the buyers except when I delivered the dog, and I wanted the money before I did that."

"Okay, there's where we have a problem," Duncan said, crossing his arms in front of him. "We know for a fact that Otto McDonough didn't pay for Johnny's Pixelated. Bitcoin is hard to trace, but we have very smart people working for us, and they assure me there is no record of a transaction between the two of you."

"Did someone vouch for Otto McDonough?" Cavendish asked.

Overbeck ran his tongue over his lips. "I knew Otto from the track. He wasn't a completely unknown quantity."

Duncan could see the man was on the edge, but not ready to go over it. "You also told us you wouldn't take kindly to someone who didn't pay. Well, you didn't use those exact words, but you insinuated the situation would get pretty nasty. Did it get that way with McDonough?"

Overbeck's gaze darted between the two troopers, a rabbit caught in a coyote's glare. "No, it didn't."

"Why not?" Cavendish asked.

"Shit." Overbeck raked his fingers through his hair. "Because of the friggin' West Virginia disaster."

"Explain," she said.

He blew out a breath, deflating a little. "Otto should've paid me. But then the West Virginia state cops busted the operation. I had to shut everything down. No dogs delivered, and I didn't think it smart to collect any payments, either."

Cavendish was writing, so Duncan took up the questioning. "Then Otto *was* part of that operation."

"Yes and no." Overbeck shifted his stance. "I took Johnny's Pixelated from a West Virginia track, and Otto was going to race him in the existing group. He told me he had a little trouble setting up his Bitcoin account. I granted him an exception because, like I said, I knew him from Blue Mountain, and I could find him any time. Hell, wasn't like he was gonna disappear, right? I delivered the dog. Day after Otto told me he solved his tech problems, I got nabbed. I told Otto to sit tight."

Very understandable, Duncan thought. "Then what?"

"The whole thing in West Virginia took some time to resolve. At least my part did." Overbeck pulled out a pack of cigarettes and tapped one out. "I guess it was, oh, late summer when I got in touch with Otto. Told him it was time to send the money."

Cavendish looked up. "Let me guess. He didn't."

Overbeck lit the cigarette and inhaled. "He said he did." Smoke leaked out of his mouth as he talked. "I checked a day later. I hadn't received anything. I went back to Otto, he said he sent the payment. Even sent me a picture of the screen. But I still didn't see a deposit when I checked my Bitcoin account." He took another drag.

Duncan constructed a timeline in his mind. Overbeck's part in the illegal racing case had been over by July. "You said this happened when?"

"Maybe mid-July?" Overbeck tapped ash from his smoke. "No, closer to August, maybe even as late as the end of the month."

"I'm quite sure you didn't let it slide."

"Hell no. I went to visit the asshole."

"At his house?" No one had reported seeing a red Ram truck. Had they not included a big enough time period in their questions?

"No, at work. I figured he couldn't weasel away from me there. At home, he could always refuse to answer the door." Overbeck inhaled again. "I cornered him in the parking lot when he was leaving. No one else was around so it was perfect."

That explains why no reports of the truck. "When did you do that?" Duncan asked. They'd never asked about visitors at Blue Mountain. An oversight that could easily be remedied.

Overbeck hemmed and hawed.

Cavendish spoke. "When. Did. You. Go. There?"

He hesitated again, and his shoulders jerked. "Late August. The week before Labor Day. I went at a time I knew there weren't any races scheduled so it was less likely I'd be seen."

Duncan shot a glance at his partner. "And?"

"He gave me some bullshit excuse about how it must be an error, or maybe he'd set up the account wrong. We, well, I, said I was done with excuses and I wanted my money. And I might have said something else, I don't remember."

"Stop jerking us around," Cavendish said, a snap in her voice. "We already know you weren't happy. You as much as told us you'd get nasty if someone didn't pay up. Did you threaten him?"

"Do you own a gun, Mr. Overbeck?" Duncan asked.

"And who is Justin Quincy?" Cavendish added.

In the silence, a few birds chirped, drowned out by the hum of an occasional passing car. Finally, Overbeck dropped the cigarette and ground it out with his foot. "I think I want a lawyer now."

Chapter Thirty-Three

S ally arrived at Dex's with five minutes to spare. She went inside and asked for a table for two. She'd only gotten as far as ordering a glass of water and was still considering her options when the greeter showed Gerald Kelleher to the table.

"Sorry I'm late," he said as he sat and opened the menu.

"You're practically on time, Mr. Kelleher." She noted that Kelleher had not jumped to indicate she could call him by his first name. "A friend of mine loves the Reuben."

"A little too heavy for me." A slight man with gray hair rapidly receding from his forehead, Kelleher looked like he could do with gaining a few pounds. His clothes weren't exactly baggy, but they definitely looked to be a size too big. His ears jutted out a little, and his pale gooseberry-colored eyes scanned the menu.

The server returned. Sally ordered a steak sandwich with cheddar. "Have you made up your mind, or do you need a couple minutes?"

"Oh, um," Gerald dragged his finger down the options. "Grilled chicken, no sauce, no tomato, no cheese, and a chef salad with oil and vinegar on the side."

"Do you want anything to drink?" the waitress asked.

"Water, no ice, no lemon, and please make sure the water is room temperature, not cold." He folded his hands on the table.

The woman's face didn't budge. "I'll bring your drinks in a minute."

Sally took a moment to study her lunch companion. Prim, that's the word she'd apply to Gerald Kelleher. Baggy clothes or not, he reminded her of a librarian, more than a little fussy and definitely accustomed to having his own way. "Thank you for meeting with me."

He brushed invisible dust from the table. "I don't know what you want me to say, Ms. Castle."

I want you to tell me what's really going on with your sister. But a frontal assault wasn't the way to go. Sally opened her questioning from an indirect angle. "I'm representing Ciara Delmonico, who is accused of embezzling money from River City Hounds. I understand your sister, Lynn Moss, used to volunteer with the group."

He sniffed. "I don't know anything about the dog people. That was Lynn's obsession. It was ridiculous. They're just animals."

Prim and obnoxious, Sally decided. Even if you weren't a dog lover, wouldn't you believe the greyhounds deserved loving homes after they stopped racing? "I wasn't going to ask you about RCH."

"Then what?"

The waitress returned with Gerald's water.

He held up his hand to stop her leaving. He took a small sip. "Adequate, I guess."

This time the server did give a tiny eye roll as she walked away.

"Your sister's name has come up while I was preparing my defense," Sally said.

"Then why aren't you talking to her?"

"I did. Her answers to my questions were unsatisfactory."

"That's hardly my problem."

Sally tamped down a snort. "Not directly, but let me ask you this. Do you love your sister and want to help her?"

Gerald refolded his hands. "Of course I do."

"You can do both by talking to me, right now." Sally tapped the table for emphasis. "As a bonus, you would help prevent a miscarriage of justice."

He fidgeted in his seat. "What kind of things do you want to know?"

"Last winter, Lynn was in an accident. It left her with a bad back injury."

"That's not a question."

"Let me finish." Sally resisted the urge to dump the glass of room-

228

temperature water over his head. "She left the job she had prior to the accident. I know that much. But I'm getting two stories. She says she quit. Her neighbor and a friend of hers from RCH say she was fired. I asked Lynn about unemployment benefits. She flip-flopped on that answer, too. Finally, she mentioned getting some money from an inheritance from a cousin that helped her avoid losing her house up in Penn Hills. But another source says the money came from an aunt."

He fussed with his placemat. "I don't see what I can add."

"I can't call her as a witness in my client's defense if I'm getting conflicting stories. My hope is you can clear up the confusion. Because I'm sure you understand why I'm not clear on exactly what happened."

"This helps your client how?"

"Because it exposes the truth."

The food arrived, and the conversation paused. After the waitress left, Gerald looked at Sally, his eyes narrowed. "I don't see how this helps Lynn, either. Let's say I tell you about her. Doesn't that land her in trouble? I won't be party to ruining my sister's life."

Except if things were as Sally suspected, Lynn Moss desperately needed an intervention. She bought some time by focusing on her sandwich and marshaling her argument. She needed to convince this man their goals were the same. "Mr. Kelleher, I completely understand your position. If all I offered was swapping my client for your sister, I can see why you wouldn't be interested. But that's not what this is about."

He wiped his fingertips on a napkin. "Go on."

"This is a chance to put things right for Lynn. You know she's in trouble. I know it. If she won't take help from you directly, maybe I can assist you."

"Plus, you get your client off the hook."

"That could be the case, yes. But mostly, you'd be taking care of your sister."

Gerald smoothed his napkin. "Lynn hasn't confided in me, you understand. I'm several years older, and we've never been what you might call close."

Given what Sally had observed over lunch, Lynn probably thought her brother would judge her. Sally motioned for him to continue.

"After Lynn's accident, the doctor prescribed oxycodone and physical therapy. She never did the exercises. The pills took away the pain, she said, and she couldn't afford the copayments for PT. The drugs were enough. I told her that was a short-sighted decision. She ignored me."

Sally pulled a notebook from her briefcase. "May I take notes while you talk?"

He nodded. "I know she asked for a second prescription when the first ran out. The doctor refused. She was furious. She came to me."

"What could you do?"

"I had some dental work done at the end of last year. She knew I'd been prescribed Vicodin and hadn't used up what I had. She asked for it. I told her no." He tapped his fingers on the table. "We argued. She appeared to give in. But after she left, I noticed the bottles in my medicine cabinet were askew. The Vicodin was gone."

Most people wouldn't notice, but Sally would bet money Gerald Kelleher was as fastidious with the organization of his bathroom as he was with his food order. "Did you confront her?"

"Yes. She became very irate, denied the theft, and said I didn't understand. I asked to use her bathroom. On a whim, I checked her cupboard. There was my bottle of Vicodin, along with two bottles of oxycodone. One looked like it had thirty pills, the other seemed half-empty, based on the contents of the first one."

"Two bottles of oxy?" Doctors didn't write refills for narcotics.

"Not only that, they were from different pharmacies, and I recognized the physician as her employer. I brought them to her. We argued again, and I left."

"Then what happened?"

"She lost her job a week later. She told me she'd left because of her back. I asked if she'd filed for unemployment. She said there was no point. She knew she wouldn't qualify. I pressed her for details. She tried to wiggle around me, but eventually admitted she'd been fired for cause. She wouldn't say exactly what the cause was, but if you're fired for criminal behavior, you won't get benefits."

CHAPTER THIRTY-THREE

Sally fixed him with a stare. "What do you think happened?"

He played with his utensils, food forgotten. "She wouldn't admit it, but I believe she stole a prescription pad, or at least a couple of sheets. She then forged the doctor's handwriting and filled them at various pharmacies. That accounted for the bottles I found in her bathroom. After that, she cut me off and wouldn't take my phone calls. Until she came to me for money. I told her I'd be willing to help, but only if she sought treatment." His pale eyes flicked up, then back to the tabletop. "You can imagine how well that went over."

Like a lead balloon. "Did you talk to her after that?"

"I called to check on her a couple weeks later. I knew she'd been under tremendous pressure with the accident, the money troubles, and her divorce. I again told her I was willing to give financial assistance if she consulted a doctor for her problems. She assured me everything was fine, she'd scraped up the money she needed, and my assistance was neither required nor desired. She hung up on me. We haven't spoken since."

"When was that?"

The lines on Kelleher's forehead deepened as he thought. "This spring. May perhaps? Or the end of April. Somewhere around there."

Exactly when the money had been taken from RCH's coffers. "What about the inheritance from her aunt or cousin?"

"We don't have a deceased aunt or cousin."

Sally needed those bank records. "Thank you, Mr. Kelleher. I appreciate your confidence in me."

He looked up, the gooseberry eyes wide. "You will help her, won't you? Lynn doesn't believe it, but I'm very fond of her. I don't approve of many of the things she's done in her life, but that doesn't mean I wouldn't do anything to help her."

Sally put away her notepad. "I'll do what I can, Mr. Kelleher. I promise you that."

Chapter Thirty-Four

From Overbeck's house in Pennsylvania, Duncan and Cavendish headed to Renner's breeding farm in West Virginia, this time with Duncan behind the wheel. While they traveled through lush mountains that were just hinting at fall color, they discussed what they'd learned so far.

"Overbeck. Do you believe him?" Cavendish asked, not taking her eyes from the road.

Duncan mulled the question as he stared at the greenery slipping by. "I have no problem with his story of how payment from McDonough got held up. Even the dumbest criminal doesn't want to be taking money from an illegal sale while there's an investigation going on. Why they missed McDonough, I have no idea."

"I can't believe he sold to McDonough without payment up front. Maybe that's why the West Virginia operation missed him."

"Could be. Remember though, Overbeck said McDonough was a known quantity. Overbeck knew where his customer worked, and I'm sure it wouldn't have taken him long to figure out where he lived. It was a fairly low-risk transaction, at least no higher than any other illegal sale."

"What do you think of him lawyering up?"

"Definitely cagey." Duncan drummed his fingers on the doorframe. "My gut tells me it's the move of a suspect trying to cover his ass, though. When we talk to Quincy, I guess we'll find out if they're friends."

Shortly after one o'clock, they arrived at Max Renner's property. The man was leaving a long, low building carrying a metal pail. "Afternoon. Can I

232

help you?"

Duncan showed his badge. "I hope you remember my partner and me, Mr. Renner. We have a few more questions for you."

"The troopers from Pennsylvania, right? I just fed the puppies. I guess I can spare a few minutes. Can I get you something to drink?" He set the pail next to a coiled hose and mounted the steps to his porch.

Both troopers declined the offer. Renner disappeared inside and returned, holding a long-necked beer bottle. "What are these questions?" he asked as he twisted off the cap.

Duncan gestured at a grouping of cane-bottomed chairs. "May we?"

Renner led them over.

Both troopers sat. Cavendish took out her notepad and pen while Duncan led off the conversation. "The last time we spoke, you said you didn't know Otto McDonough had taken Johnny's Pixelated or his plans for him."

"Correct."

"You also said"—Cavendish glanced at her notes—"you were glad he was dead, because if you had known about the abuse, you'd have been tempted to, and I quote, 'shoot him myself.'"

Renner shifted in his seat. "I don't recall saying that."

She looked up. "You did."

"I was angry. I didn't mean it."

Duncan crossed his legs, laying his ankle on his knee. "We now have a witness who puts you at the victim's house. You said previously you didn't know where he lived."

Renner rubbed his chin. "Who is this witness? When was I supposed to have been at McDonough's?"

"A local. He says he saw you sometime around the Labor Day holiday."

The breeder shrugged. "I honestly don't remember."

Cavendish leaned forward. "I'm sorry, Mr. Renner. I find that implausible, to say the least. This witness says you went to McDonough's residence, argued with him, demanded 'him' back, and got quite angry when the victim refused. How do you not remember that?"

The buzz of insects and the jabbering of some nearby blue jays filled the air as Renner stared off into the distance. He brought his attention back to the troopers. "I went to Otto's house. I'd heard a rumor about Johnny, that Otto had taken him for illegal racing. I went to offer to buy Johnny back."

Duncan focused on the suspect's eyes. "What did Mr. McDonough say?"

"At first, he denied having the dog. But then I heard a greyhound cry. It's a very distinct noise if you're familiar with it. I called McDonough an effing liar. The garage door was down, and I demanded to see what was in there. McDonough refused."

"Did McDonough admit to having the hound?" Cavendish asked, looking up from her writing.

"Not in so many words. But he said since Johnny wasn't mine anymore, that he'd raced, retired, and I'd declined to take him back, it wasn't any of my business what happened to him." Renner again looked off in the distance before bringing his gaze back to his visitors. "The way he said it, I was sure he had Johnny. I told him he had one last chance. Give me Johnny, or I'd take him by force."

"What was McDonough's response?" Duncan asked.

"He laughed at me." Renner slumped in his chair and closed his eyes. "So help me, I wanted to shoot him in the back as he walked away, the bastard. But I'm a rare West Virginian in that I don't own a gun. Never even shot one."

The troopers exchanged a long look. "Mr. Renner, I have to ask," Duncan said. "Where were you last Thursday, especially from four to ten pm?" The time would cover travel to Markleysburg, the shooting, and Renner's departure. The only problem was no witnesses put Renner's vehicle, a new GMC Sierra, at the scene of the murder that night. And Max Renner, with his graying hair and trim but muscular build, was not a slight, brown-haired young man. If he'd been at the scene, surely Bethany Carlyle or Trevor Shaw would have seen and mentioned him.

Renner opened his eyes, but his gaze locked onto a spot over Duncan's left shoulder. "I was at home. By myself. No, no one saw me. I didn't talk to anyone or order pizza. Isn't that what you're going to ask next? It's what they ask on the cop shows."

It was, in fact, what Duncan had been about to say. Instead, he leaned forward. "One last question, Mr. Renner. Does the name Justin Quincy sound familiar?"

This time, Renner locked eyes with Duncan. "Never heard of him," the dog breeder said.

The troopers thanked him and left. The last view they had of Max Renner was him sitting on his porch, staring at the horizon, empty metal pail by his side.

Cavendish once again took the passenger's seat. "If he'd been there the night of the shooting, someone would have seen him."

Duncan drove off down the winding road that led to Renner's front gate, then turned onto the main road and set his course back to Pennsylvania. "Just what I was thinking," he said. "But I'll tell you one thing."

"What's that?"

"We know the weapon in both shootings belonged to Justin Quincy, at least at one point. But no one seems to know him. I'm really looking forward to meeting this guy and hearing what he has to say."

* * *

Sally returned to her office in a pensive yet frustrated mood. Gerald Kelleher had more or less confirmed Sally's hypothesis that Lynn Moss had an opiate addiction. The bottles he found seemed to indicate she'd been fired from her job for forgery and maybe even theft, which would definitely disqualify her from unemployment benefits. But it would seem no one had reported the incident. At least no criminal charges appeared on Lynn's background in Tracer. Which meant it was all hearsay unless Sally could get someone at the office to confirm the circumstances surrounding Lynn's departure.

"Fat chance of that happening," she said under her breath as she walked to the coffee pot.

Kim sidled up beside her. "You're talking to yourself again. What now?"

"Oh, same things." While she waited for the machine to finish, she brought Kim up to speed on Lynn Moss's background and job woes. After the last

235

drops splashed into her mug, she picked it up and added a dash of creamer.

"If we're going to be partners, you need to talk more to me when these things come up. Do less navel-gazing."

"I didn't think you were interested in charity cases."

"Partners have to stay united. Besides, you're right. Justice isn't defending your client by throwing another person to the wolves." Kim selected her own pod, popped it in, and pushed the glowing button. "As far as Lynn Moss goes, sounds like an addiction to me. How much you want to bet she swiped pills?"

"No, the prescriptions were from different pharmacies, remember?" Sally stirred her drink, turning it to a creamy shade of brown. She told Kim about Gerald's idea. "Doctors don't keep samples of opioids. But as an employee at the practice, she'd be familiar with how to write a prescription."

"And doctors' signatures are illegible most times anyway." Kim added sugar and stirred. "You'd think the doctor would prosecute that."

"Maybe they haven't yet. Or someone on the staff felt sorry for her. Maybe they tried to cut her some slack, told her go into rehab, but she balked, so they fired her. Hell, I don't know." Sally leaned against the wall.

"And unless someone at the office decides to tell you, or you get a court order, you're blowing smoke." Kim nodded, one attorney acknowledging another's problems.

"Exactly. Thus my statement. The Pirates have a better chance of winning the World Series than I have of getting a source inside the office to confirm my suspicions."

Kim chuckled. "I have news that might cheer you up a little."

"What's that?"

She gestured toward Sally's office with her mug. "The defense attorney gods have smiled on you, and the financial information you wanted is here. I put it on your desk. You're welcome."

Maybe I'll finally get some answers. Sally strode back to her desk, slit open the envelope, and read. But thirty minutes later, she pushed the papers away in disgust, muttering in frustration.

From her office across the hall, Kim looked up. "Sarah Marie Castle, do you kiss your mother with that mouth? I haven't heard you utter words like that since we were cramming for exams our second year of law school."

"Sorry." Sally fluttered her hands over the sheets of numbers. "This makes absolutely no sense. None."

Kim stood and came over. "What's the problem?"

"There's no...freaking...money. Look at this." She thrust the report at her partner. "First of all, I don't see any payments coming from the state, so no unemployment income. Either Lynn never filed, or she was denied benefits."

Kim scanned the columns. "You suspected that."

"I did. But there aren't any significant deposits at all. Except one big one in June, and I think that's her divorce settlement."

"You're wondering where the cash went."

"Exactly. If Lynn Moss stole the money from RCH to pay off debts, where the hell is it?" Sally slapped the desk. "This is the twenty-first century, for god's sake. Nobody takes massive payments in cash. You don't mail a stack of twenties to pay your bills."

Kim was silent a moment as she paged through the sheets. "What's this one?" She grabbed a highlighter and swiped it through a line.

"It looks like someone sent her money, maybe using one of those electronic services."

Kim ran her finger down the column. "Here's another one." She highlighted another line.

Curiosity piqued, Sally took back the paper and counted six transfers over the course of as many weeks. She'd seen the transactions before and dismissed them, thinking them nothing but a modern way of one friend repaying another. Apparently, that had been a mistake. "Read me those amounts." She grabbed her phone and opened the calculator. As Kim read, Sally tapped in numbers.

"That's the last one." Kim looked over at her. "What's the total?"

Sally tapped the equal sign. "Son of a bitch. The exact amount missing from RCH."

Kim straightened. "Who sent the money?"

"I can't tell. It only says FundEx and a bunch of numbers." Sally checked the payments and pointed. "A week after all the transfers stopped, she made the mortgage payment. Someone funneled her little amounts over time, so as not to draw attention. I can't believe I missed that the first time."

"You didn't miss it. You just needed a sounding board to help you make the connection. See, I told you we'd be great partners." Kim grinned. "Now you have to find out who. Does Ciara have the group's checking account register, or at least a copy of it?"

"No, but I bet I can get Pat Dennister to share her records with me. If these really do correspond to withdrawals from RCH, there should be a record of who made them."

"Can you prove it's the same person who sent the money to Lynn?"

"Not based on this. I'll ask Jim if he knows a way." He wouldn't be able to do the work for her, but he could set her on the right path.

Kim returned to the bank statements. "Did you see this? She went to three different pharmacies in the space of a month."

"Yeah, I noticed. It tallies with what I learned from her brother this morning." Sally drummed her fingers on her desk. "Someone at her employer knew what happened and has to be willing to talk about this."

Kim pushed away from the desk. "Absolutely. Go get 'em. partner."

Chapter Thirty-Five

Duncan drove on autopilot, staring at the West Virginia mountains as they zipped away from the dog breeding farm. What had they just learned?

"Penny for your thoughts," Cavendish said.

"I don't think Max Renner is our guy."

"Unless we learn he and Quincy are best buddies, I say we bump him down the list." She consulted her notepad. "Where do you want to go next?"

"We're definitely on the same page when it comes to Sullivan."

"That his story is weaker than my mom's coffee? Yes."

Interesting comparison. "It would make sense to have as much ammunition as possible the next time we confront him. Metaphorically speaking."

"I buy that."

"Then we go see Justin Quincy." He studied his partner out of the corner of his eye. She had not offered a snarky comment about rookies all day. Should he call her on it? *No, better let sleeping dogs lie.* "What do you think we'll find when we talk to him?"

Cavendish paused, "I'm not sure," she said. "The gun was sold to him. But he doesn't seem to be connected to any of the players."

"At least not thus far."

She tilted her head. "What do we know about him?"

Duncan thought through the notes he'd taken from a quick background check. "Single, never married, no kids. Works as a delivery driver for a Pittsburgh furniture store. Owns a house in Carnegie, taxes paid, mortgage up to date. And that's about it."

239

"No idea how his .38 wound up at our crime scene?"

"None." Duncan watched the trees, with their patches of red and gold, zip by. "He never reported the gun stolen."

"But he doesn't have to. Not in Pennsylvania. Yes, most people do, and it's something that's recommended. But it's not required."

She had a point. But as a police officer and a gun owner, he didn't think much of people who'd let such a thing slide.

Quincy's neighborhood was quiet, the street lined with the type of plain, square dwellings that would have been typical of those put up when coal and steel ruled the Pittsburgh economy. Small yards, no garages, built close together. Most of the driveways were empty, suggesting the owners were places other than home.

Duncan pulled up in front of their destination. He took a moment to survey the house. Blinds covered the windows. Mail in the box. The garage door was down. "Think he's even home?"

"Let's find out."

They approached the door, and Cavendish knocked.

Duncan stepped over to the garage. The windows were clean, and showed off the fact that no vehicle was inside.

She joined him. "No response. What are you looking at?"

He jerked his thumb toward the garage. "It's empty."

"At work?"

"Maybe." He flipped to his notes, pulled out his phone, and dialed Quincy's employer. After identifying himself, he asked, "Is Justin Quincy working today?"

"Is he in trouble?" the young man asked, voice apprehensive.

"No, but his name has come up in a current investigation. My partner and I would like to speak with him."

"Hold on." The line went silent, maybe as the employee put it on hold. A minute or so later, he came back on. "He's out on a delivery run now. He should be back to pick up the goods required for his last stop in, oh, half an hour?"

"Thanks. When he arrives, would you have him hang out until we get

240

there? Thanks." Duncan tapped the red icon to end the call. "He'll be at the warehouse in thirty minutes." He tossed her the keys. "Your turn. I hate city driving."

They navigated the narrow streets to Quincy's employer. When they parked, Duncan saw a white van, with the company logo painted on the side, sitting in the parking lot. The driver, a Black man wearing jeans, a flannel shirt over a white T-shirt, and work boots, was just getting out. "Excuse me, are you Justin Quincy?" Duncan called as he exited the car, Cavendish following.

The man didn't move. "Who wants to know?"

The troopers held out their badges. "Troopers Duncan and Cavendish, PSP. If you're Quincy, we have a few questions. If you aren't, do you know where we might find him?"

The driver pushed the door shut and stuffed his hands in the front pockets of his jeans. "Yeah, I'm Justin Quincy. Is this about the damned gun? I knew I should have called the cops. I'm gonna kick Toby's ass the next time I see him."

Duncan and Cavendish exchanged a look. "Yes, it's about your gun," she said. "When was the last time you saw it?"

"What is today, the seventeenth?"

"The eighteenth," Duncan said.

Quincy counted back on his fingers. "Three, no two weeks ago tomorrow."

"You lost a handgun two weeks ago and didn't bother to say anything?" Cavendish's voice betrayed the fact she had the same opinion of nonreporters that Duncan did.

Quincy ran a hand over his barely-there hair. "Like I said, I'm gonna kick Toby's ass. He's my brother. He told me I didn't have to. I didn't want to make a fuss. It wasn't that valuable a piece. He said I wouldn't get in trouble."

"While your brother is technically right, it's always a good idea to report something like that missing or stolen. Because if it turns up at a crime scene, that's more of a mess than a simple police report," Cavendish said. "The value of the weapon has nothing to do with it."

Quincy blanched. "My gun was at a crime scene? Shit. I had nothing to do with any crime. What was it, armed robbery?"

Duncan clicked open his pen. "Why don't you tell us what happened?"

Quincy glanced at the door of the warehouse. "I went to my club Labor Day weekend. Actually, it's not my club. They offered a two-week trial membership, so Toby and I signed up."

"What club was this?"

"The Western Pennsylvania Shooting Club. It's that new one up in Canonsburg. The flyer listed some sweet facilities, fancier than you usually see, so Toby and I figured why the hell not, right? Might as well check it out."

When he didn't continue, Duncan looked up. "Go on."

"They had a contest for the holiday weekend. I entered, but got beat in the third round. I packed up my stuff and left. Later, when I got home and went to put everything away, I saw the .38 was missing."

Cavendish struck a pose that indicated she didn't buy it. "Let me get this straight. You went all the way home, unpacked, and *then* noticed your piece was missing? You didn't notice the weight was off in your carrying case?"

Quincy twitched his shoulders. "Toby and I use the same box. He has two guns, a .45 and a Glock. Plus, it has space for extra magazines, cleaning supplies, all that shit. Yeah, a .38 is heavier than a paperclip, but with all the crap in there, no, I didn't notice much of a difference. Maybe I should have, but it was a long day, I was beat, and I wanted to get home and have a beer. My bad."

Quincy not only was irresponsible when it came to reporting, he was sloppy in his regular habits. The worst kind of gun owner. But Duncan didn't feel like issuing a lecture. "Then you had it at the club, and it was gone by the time you got home. Toby didn't notice it missing when he packed up?"

The other man shifted on his feet. "He was out by then and had already put his pieces away."

Cavendish rubbed her temple. "Between the time you left the club and when you got home your .38 what, vanished?"

If possible, Quincy looked even more embarrassed and uncomfortable.

"Well, we didn't go home right away. We went back to watch more of the competition. A buddy of ours was still in it. The one who gave us the flyer."

"Where did you leave the case?" Duncan asked.

"In the locker room." Quincy's face brightened. "You wouldn't believe this place, man. They got showers and lockers, just like a gym. It's pretty sweet. The shooting ranges are nice, too."

Duncan knew the answer to his next question, but he had to ask. "Did you lock the case?"

The enthusiasm faded, replaced by the return of shame. "No. I was gonna, I swear. But Toby said the next round was starting, so I just snapped it shut. I figured it was no big deal. Everyone was watching the tournament, and no one was in the locker room. Besides, who would steal a gun at a shooting club? Not like every dude there don't have his own piece, right?"

Duncan stared at the man in front of him. Could Justin Quincy be that clueless? "A person who wanted to commit a crime, that's who."

Quincy gulped. "You never said what kind of crime. Was it like a holdup or something?"

"Murder." Cavendish crossed her arms. "Two of them, in fact."

His brown skin turned ashy. "Are...are you sure it was my piece? Maybe you all made a mistake. I didn't kill nobody."

"No mistake." She narrowed her eyes. "And we are quite sure. It's yours."

Duncan held up his hand. "Mr. Quincy, do you know a man named Otto McDonough?"

Confusion laced through the fear on Quincy's face. "Who?"

"What about Robert Bevilacqua? Max Renner? Dan Overbeck?"

"Nah, never heard of those guys. Are they members at the club?"

Duncan's gut told him Quincy was telling the truth. "One more name. Kyle Sullivan."

"Sullivan, Sullivan." Quincy lowered his eyebrows, the tip of his tongue visible through his lips. Then he nodded. "Yeah, him, I know. He's a member at the club. I watched him. Dude can shoot."

Cavendish uncrossed her arms. "Mr. Quincy, this is very important. Did you, at any time, see Mr. Sullivan in the locker room?"

"Not that I saw."

"Did he ever leave the range?"

Quincy paused. "I didn't see him anywhere except the indoor lanes. I took my turn, missed, packed up my stuff, went back, watched for a while, then left."

"You watched Sullivan?" Duncan asked.

"Yeah. Like I said. Dude can shoot."

"And when you went back to the locker room, your case was as you left it?"

"Looked like it."

Damn it. "Thank you for your time, Mr. Quincy." He held out a business card. "If you think of anything else, please call me."

"I'm not in trouble?"

Cavendish held out her own card. "No, but let me put it this way. You didn't break any laws. However, if it were up to me, and I'm pretty sure my partner feels the same, you'd be surrendering any other guns you might own. Here's some advice. Be more responsible with your firearms from this point forward, yes?"

Quincy took the second business card and swallowed. "Yes, ma'am."

Chapter Thirty-Six

By the time Duncan and Cavendish returned to their car, a thick bank of white clouds obscured the sun. Duncan glanced upward. The color of sky and lack of moisture in the air assured him no rain was imminent.

"What do you think of Quincy?" Cavendish asked as she leaned on the roof.

Duncan spun the keys on his finger. "As a suspect, a witness, or a gun owner?"

She made a sound of disgust. "He's a piss-poor owner. Doesn't lock up his weapons and leaves them unattended? Can't tell by the weight of the case one is missing? Puh-leeze."

He surveyed the parking lot. "I know what you're thinking. Could be Sullivan stole the .38, and used it on McDonough and Bevilacqua."

"But you have a problem with that."

"Several. No prints on the weapon. Nobody can put Sullivan at the scene for Bevilacqua's murder. And, as you pointed out earlier, Sullivan doesn't have a motive for the Bevilacqua murder."

"He's got a hell of a motive for McDonough, though. He went to confront his brother's killer. Administer a little small-town justice."

"We can't put him at the scene. Oh sure, we have a vague description from Bethany Carlyle and her boyfriend of a young guy with brown hair walking behind the house. Want to guess how many young guys with brown hair live in Markleysburg?"

Cavendish scowled. "Party pooper." She yanked open the door and got inside.

Duncan slid into the driver's seat. "I'm not saying you're wrong—"

She waved her hand. "Believing it to be true and making a case are two separate things." She grabbed her seat belt. "My last shooting was a whole lot simpler."

He started the car. "Blame me. I always find the complicated ones." He checked the dashboard clock. "Two-thirty. We still have time to see Sullivan, unless you've got a better plan."

"No, let's go." Her phone rang. "Cavendish."

As Duncan drove, he listened to the one-sided conversation, which consisted mainly of "uh-huh" and "yeah" said at varying intervals, his partner's face unreadable.

At last, she ended the call. "Cross Dan Overbeck off the list."

"Why?"

"That was his attorney." She made a face. "He has an alibi. On the day of McDonough's murder, he was at dinner with a female friend. He spent the night with her. When Bevilacqua was killed, Overbeck was in conference with his lawyer and representatives from the West Virginia gaming commission. Follow-up to the illegal racing investigation."

"It's about time people started taking themselves out of the picture." He navigated the on-ramp to the Parkway West. "I wasn't looking forward to making a connection between Overbeck and Bevilacqua."

"That leaves Sullivan and Renner. I'm not feeling the dog breeder."

"Neither am I. Oh, I believe he'd beat the snot out of McDonough and take his dog back, but why shoot Bevilacqua? It doesn't make any sense. And I think he's telling the truth when he says he doesn't know Quincy."

She shifted in her seat. "I suppose he might be a member at the gun club. Renner, I mean."

"Easy enough to find out. It's on the way to Markleysburg."

* * *

Sally grabbed a bottle of water from the minifridge and returned to her desk.

CHAPTER THIRTY-SIX

She took a gulp, replaced the cap, and flexed her fingers over her laptop. How to approach this? It would be difficult to get anyone to talk. According to Lynn's employment records, she'd worked at her former job for almost five years. Plenty of time to make a friend or two, ones who would want their former coworker to get help.

Sally pulled up the website for the orthopedic practice. On the "Meet Our Staff" page was a list of all of the current members, from physicians and nurses down to the administrative workers. She dismissed the doctors. Even if they'd been sympathetic enough to give Lynn a pass on criminal charges, they wouldn't want to talk about any dirty laundry, especially to an attorney. Would Lynn have been close to anyone in the business office? The office manager was a fiftyish woman, and billing was handled by a man. Not promising.

Sally looked at the pictures of the nurses. Each smiling face was accompanied by a short biography. One man probably in his thirties, one woman who might have been middle-aged, one fresh-faced girl who looked barely out of college, and one woman who appeared to be in her mid-thirties. Which one would have been friends with Lynn outside work?

"Let's see who we've got," Sally said. With simple checks, she obtained enough information to order the list. *This Tracer database is awfully complete.* The male nurse had a wife and three children, all under the age of seven. The girl who appeared young enough to be a recent graduate turned out to be just that. Sally checked her background notes, where she had noted Lynn's age as fifty-one. If anything, Sally found it unlikely the girl would want to hang out with a woman old enough to be her mother.

That left the two other women. One, Margaret Henderson, was a few years younger than Lynn. Margaret lived in Plum. "She's divorced," Sally said as she jotted down Margaret's contact information. She and Lynn would have two topics in common. Work and failed marriages. The other nurse, Karen Slovick, was ten years younger than Lynn, married, and lived in Aspinwall. Because of the difference in age and marital status, Sally didn't consider her as good of a candidate, but it wasn't impossible.

She placed a phone call to Margaret and got her voicemail. Sally left a

247

message identifying herself and saying she wanted to talk about Lynn Moss and her former employment. Then she called Karen.

She picked up on the fifth ring. "Hello?" Her voice sounded groggy, like she'd woken up from a nap.

Sally identified herself, then said, "I understand you worked with Lynn Moss at Steel City Orthopedics. Is that correct?"

Karen's voice became wary. "Yes."

"Are you still employed with the practice?"

"What's this about, if you don't mind my asking?"

"I'm trying to determine the circumstances under which Ms. Moss left." Sally twirled her pen. "I've received conflicting stories, and I'm concerned. I think she needs help."

Wariness turned to caution. "How do you mean?"

"Based on what I've learned, I believe Ms. Moss has a drug problem. I want to get her the help she needs."

"There's gotta be something more, something in it for you. You can't be a friend of Lynn's because I've never heard her talk about you."

The woman was sharp. Sally leaned on her desk. "It may help a client of mine as well, but believe me, I am concerned about Ms. Moss. I hope you are willing to talk to me, off the record, if you wish."

There was a long pause. "No, I don't think that's a good idea. I'm sorry, Ms. Castle. When Lynnie left, we were advised not to talk about it, and I think I'm going to trust my employer on this one. Goodbye." Karen ended the call.

Sally dropped her phone on her desk. "Shit." Karen had been tempted to talk. Sally would bet money on that. She looked at her laptop screen for the time. Two-thirty. She picked up the phone and called Jim. "Hey you," she said when he answered.

"What's up?"

"Where are you?" She heard the murmur of a female voice. "Is that Cavendish?"

"Yes, we're on our way to Markleysburg." He hesitated. "Is there something you need?"

"I just wanted to know if you were going to be home for dinner. Otherwise, I'm getting take-out."

"I don't know. Hold on." He must have held the phone next to something, because although he talked to his partner, no words came through clearly. "Should be. Depends on how long we spend at our next stop." There was another pause while he held another muffled exchange. "Would you like to meet us somewhere?"

"You mean both of you? Aren't you working?"

"We'll be ready to knock off by five. Why don't we meet at Whiskey & Rye? It's been a long day here, and yours has probably been the same. I'm willing to bet neither of us feels like cooking."

"Sounds like a plan." She hung up. Meeting Jim somewhere wasn't an unusual situation. But why on earth would Jenny Cavendish want to join them?

Chapter Thirty-Seven

D uncan tossed his phone in the cup holder. What could Sally possibly want to pick his brain over? Knowing her, it could be anything.

"Problem?" Cavendish asked. "You look like you bit a lemon."

"Probably not. Chances are Sally is after advice, but then again, I never know."

She raised her eyebrows. "I look forward to meeting her. Any woman who can nudge you off balance must be a pistol."

"I'm not off balance. I'm…cautious. She has a knack for getting herself in trouble." *That's putting it mildly.*

Cavendish didn't press the point. "I'll call the club and see if they've got camera footage from the day of the competition. If this place is as swanky as Quincy said, they'll have CCTV. Think they'll make us get paper to see it?"

"Not if we're lucky." Duncan felt confident in his ability to get a warrant signed by any judge in Uniontown, where his reputation preceded him. He didn't want to have to spend the time convincing a judge in Washington County to sign off on the affidavit. Then again, if Cavendish was as good as he thought she was, she had to know people who would be able to grease the wheels.

After Duncan parked at the Western Pennsylvania Shooting Club, he and Cavendish headed straight for the office, where they found a man poring over some paperwork. "Excuse me. Are you the club manager?"

The man looked up. "That's me."

Duncan held up his badge. "Trooper Duncan. This is Trooper Cavendish. We'd like a moment of your time, mister…."

"Collins. Zach Collins. Hold on a sec." He made a tick mark on the sheet in front of him, then focused on his visitors. "What's this about?"

"We have a few questions for you."

"Yes?"

Cavendish consulted her notes. "We understand there was a shooting competition here at the club on September fourth. Did you watch?"

"Most of it," Collins said. "I took a break to go to the bathroom, and we all had lunch around noon, but I was on the range a lot."

"Do you remember seeing a man named Justin Quincy? He was here with a friend for a trial membership."

Collins' pursed his lips as he repeated the name a couple times. Then his face cleared. "Black guy. Not a bad shooter, but he didn't have good luck that day. I don't think he and his buddy signed up. They liked the place, but said it was too expensive."

"We know Kyle Sullivan is a member here," Duncan said. "Did he leave the range at any time?"

"I don't…I think he was there. But I can't swear he never left." Collins shrugged. "I guess he could have walked off when I was in the can."

"Did he come to lunch?" Cavendish asked.

Collins thought a moment, then nodded. "Yes, but I think he was one of the last in. Yeah, we'd run out of roast beef sandwiches, and he made a joke about how next time he'd get his grub first, then take a leak."

"Do you know a man named Max Renner?"

"Renner…no, I don't."

Duncan shot a glance at his partner. "Do you have CCTV coverage?"

Collins' gaze darted between the two troopers. "Of course. Except where there are privacy issues."

"What about the locker room?"

"We have two kinds of lockers. One where you can stash jackets, one where members can shower or change. We have coverage in the former, but not the latter."

Cavendish stepped forward. "We'd be much obliged if you'd show us the footage you have from that camera on the day of the tournament. Assuming you still have it."

Collins drummed his fingers on the desk. "We keep all recordings for a month. I'm not sure I should simply hand it over because you asked, though. I want to see a search warrant."

Duncan kept his face calm but inwardly cursed. "We understand completely." He looked over at Cavendish. "You know who is on warrant duty?"

She already had her phone out of her pocket and was thumbing the screen. "Got the number right here. I brought an affidavit form, too."

Collins swallowed. "Don't you have to go get it signed by a judge?"

"Not these days." She waggled the phone. "There's a procedure for getting approval over the phone. For situations like these."

"There is?"

Duncan smothered a grin and faced the club manager. "We do it all the time. Sit tight. This won't take more than what, five minutes, you think?" The last question was intended for Cavendish, but Duncan kept his eyes on Collins.

"If that," she said.

Collins slumped, a defeated look on his face. "Never mind. This way." He got up and left the office.

Duncan fell into step beside his partner, and they followed the manager down the hall. He leaned over to her. "Were you bluffing?"

"Not in the least," she said out of the corner of her mouth. "My first partner made me write up warrants all the time. I got very friendly with several of the judges. When we have time, I'll tell you the story about the time I interrupted one at his granddaughter's birthday party." She shot him a conspiratorial grin.

Collins led them to a room lined with computer drives and a monitor. He logged on to the system. "You're looking for September fourth you said? All day?"

"We're particularly interested in...." He glanced at Cavendish.

She checked her notes. "Around two o'clock."

252

CHAPTER THIRTY-SEVEN

"One-thirty to three in the afternoon."

Collins nodded and tapped the keys. "You got it."

The image appeared on the screen. The locker room was empty, no sign of Quincy's case. "Can you play it on fast forward for us?" Duncan asked.

Collins obliged, and the tape sped up. Right around two, Quincy entered the room with his gun and a box. He set the box on a bench, put the weapon inside and shut it. Then he doubled-over and rushed behind the wall to the changing area and toilets. A few minutes later, he emerged and left. Nothing else happened until almost two-thirty, when another figure came into the frame, walked over to the case, and opened it.

Cavendish snapped her fingers. "Slow it down."

Collins obliged and the film returned to normal speed.

The figure was slim, wearing a blue shirt and a ball cap. But it was clearly a man. He opened the case, examined the contents, then removed the .38. He checked it, then slipped it in his pocket, and closed the box.

"I didn't know any of this, I swear," Collins said, sweat gleaming on his face.

"Don't delete it. We'll be back for a copy," Cavendish said.

"Come on, turn around," Duncan muttered. A matching build and the possibility Sullivan had left the range wasn't enough. They needed to see his face.

The figure turned and took a few steps, head bowed. He stopped, sneezed, and the cap fell on the floor. He scrambled to pick it up and jammed it back on his head. But not before the camera caught a flash of his face.

* * *

After her failed phone call, Sally turned her attention to the money trail. She didn't use an app to send money, preferring to use her bank's service. She wasn't a Luddite, but this wasn't her area of expertise. Kim might know, but she was out of the office. Who else could give her a nudge?

Tanelsa.

"How much do you know about these cash transfer apps?" she asked once

253

her friend answered the phone.

"Well, hello to you too. I'm fine. Thanks for asking." Tanelsa's voice held a tinge of amusement.

Sally's cheeks heated. "I'm sorry. Hi. How are you?"

"That's better. Always lead with friendliness." Tanelsa chuckled. "Are you finally moving into the modern world, embracing technology and finance?"

"Not quite. It's pertinent to a case. Unfortunately, I know zilch about these apps. I know you've used a couple, and I'm throwing myself on your mercy. How do they work?"

"Pretty simple." Tanelsa paused and the sound of crunching came over the line. "You sign up with the service and link your bank account or a card. Credit or debit, I don't think it matters. Then you can send people money, and others can send to you."

Sally thought a moment. "Easy enough. How does it show up on your bank statement?"

"What do you mean?"

"Say I use one of these apps to send money to you from my account. When I get my statement, does it list your name or what?"

"Oh, I get it. Depends on the service. But I think most of them just give you the name of the app and a string of numbers. At least that's what I always see." There was another pause. "Here, I'll send you an email." A rustle came over the line, then some clicking as Tanelsa typed.

Just like in Lynn's bank statements. Sally touched the trackpad on her laptop to wake it up and went to her inbox. A moment later, a message appeared from Tanelsa. Sally clicked it to view the contents. "What's this link?"

"That'll take you to a page with a list of some of the more popular money transfer apps."

"Thanks, T. I owe you." She hung up.

Sally scanned the web page. "FundExpress. I bet that's it." She went to the site for the app. "Jeez, this is as bad as Bitcoin." At least it seemed to be. Details on the site were light on specifics and heavy on marketing. But it was enough to get the gist. But unless she could match names to account numbers, there was no way she could prove anything. Sure, she could get another subpoena. But chances were good the company would put up a fight.

Sally shook her head in frustration. It would tie up her case for months, and poor Ciara couldn't stay unemployed that long. Or maybe not "poor Ciara." Had the accountant obtained the money for Lynn and sent it to her as a bribe if Lynn knew about Ciara's gambling?

After a moment, she shut the laptop and swept up the sheets of bank information. One of them fluttered to the floor, and she bent to pick it up. It seemed to be a photographic record of checks, each one a small but clear image. Her attention snagged on the one at the bottom of the page. Lynn had deposited five hundred dollars this past spring. Not an unusual action, but the name on the signature line leapt out at her.

Chapter Thirty-Eight

Duncan pulled into Kyle Sullivan's empty driveway in Markleys-burg around four. A quick call to his employer revealed he wasn't at work.

"I'm pretty pissed, to be honest," said the manager.

"Why is that?" Duncan asked.

"He hasn't been to work for the past two days. He hasn't called, either."

Cavendish's phone rang. She answered and stepped away.

Duncan covered his ear so he could focus on Sullivan's boss. "Is that like him?"

"No. He's usually very reliable. But if he doesn't get his ass to work, reliable or not, he's fired."

"I'll tell him. Thanks." He ended his call moments before his partner did. "What's the scoop?"

She jerked her head toward the house. "That was forensics. We may have caught a break."

"Oh?"

"They finished going through all trace evidence from the Bevilacqua murder. One of the prints lifted there matches one from the McDonough scene."

"Not only the same gun, the same shooter. You said no matches in IAFIS?"

"You got it." She glanced at the house. "Shall we?"

They approached the front door, where Cavendish knocked and an-nounced their presence. No answer. Not even the blinds moved.

Duncan walked around the back of the house. He could clearly see the empty kitchen through the back window. No car, no lights, no motion. He returned to the front.

Cavendish banged on the door again. "Kyle Sullivan! State Police. We need to talk to you."

"I don't think he's at home."

"Damn it." She backed away and studied the building. "Where is he?"

"No clue." His gaze traveled the neighborhood.

"Too bad your prints don't stay on file indefinitely when you apply for a gun permit. I'd love to compare them to Sullivan's," Cavendish said.

Duncan turned his attention to the garbage cans on the side of the road. Two big gray ones, and one smaller one marked for recycling. "Why don't you check with the neighbors? Find out if anyone has seen Sullivan today and knows where he might be."

"Sure." She followed his line of sight to the curb. "What are you going to do?"

"Thought I'd try my hand at dumpster diving, domestic style." He pointed at the plastic cylinders.

"You're going to steal Sullivan's stuff?"

"It's the trash. Fair game."

She grinned. "Better you than me. Good luck." She headed off down the street.

Duncan pulled on a pair of nitrile gloves and opened the recycling bin. Not only did he think that would yield better results, he didn't want to sift through rotting food. Inside were several flattened beer cans and one or two food cans with the labels peeled off. And one glass bottle of Rolling Rock beer. "Bingo." He took the bottle to the car and pulled out the fingerprint kit. He carefully brushed powder over the bottle's surface. It didn't take long for him to develop three clear latent prints, which he lifted and labeled. Then he placed the bottle in a bag, in case they decided to try and grab DNA evidence.

Cavendish jogged up ten minutes later. "Any luck?"

"One bottle with three good prints. You?"

She brushed hair off her forehead. "A fat lot of nothing. One or two people do remember seeing Sullivan's truck this morning. One of them even said he saw our target get in and drive off. But the witness assumed Sullivan was going to work and has no idea where else he would have gone."

"But he's definitely not here."

"That seems to be the case. Here's an interesting tidbit. Remember the dog-walker? From the last time we were here?"

He thought a moment. "Henry?"

"No, that was the name of the dog. The owner's name is Ben Hastings. You are so a dog person. You remember the dog, but not the owner."

"Wiseass." This was what he'd imagined working with a partner was like. Whatever he'd done, or not done, Cavendish seemed to have changed her mind about him. "What about him?"

"I talked to Hastings again and showed him more pictures. Want to guess who he recognized?"

"I'm not in the mood to play twenty questions."

"You're no fun." Cavendish sniffed. "Robert Bevilacqua. Mr. Hastings swears he saw Bevilacqua on the night McDonough was murdered. Hastings said Bevilacqua did a slow roll of McDonough's house. Didn't stop, but he turned the corner and drove off. Here's the thing. Remember Bethany Carlyle's statement that she saw a twenty-something guy with brown hair walking behind the scene?"

"Yeah."

"Well, from what Hastings said, Bevilacqua would have passed the guy after he made the turn."

"If it was Sullivan, Bevilacqua might have seen him."

"You got it." She tipped her head at the garbage. "You think those are Sullivan's prints? It is his garbage."

Duncan rested his hands on his hips and tapped his thumbs on his belt. "It would be a pretty wild coincidence if these turn out to match the ones at our scenes, and they belong to someone other than him."

She bit her lip. "Let's run them over to the lab. Then we can find out what your girlfriend wants from us."

258

Chapter Thirty-Nine

Sally parked her Camry in the lot at Whiskey & Rye and scanned the vehicles there. She didn't see Jim's Jeep. She did notice a nondescript dark gray Dodge Charger, parked so it could make a quick exit. She peered at the front grille and spotted the red and blue lights. It was definitely a police vehicle.

As soon as she entered the restaurant, she knew why it was Jim's type of place. The lights were low, but not dim. A gleaming wooden bar took up the far corner, with a blackboard, covered in hand-lettered offerings, behind it. The parquet floor shone. Booths boasting cushy leather seats lined the walls. Tables, most set for four, filled the open eating space. The air hummed with conversation, but not the raucous tones of a bar.

She scanned the room and spotted Jim at one of the tables. She threaded her way through the crowd and over to him. "Is this seat taken?" she asked, leaning on a chair.

He got up. "It is now." He leaned over to kiss her and pulled out the chair. "They have a nice selection of local wines. But then again, you occasionally drink whiskey." His eyes glinted with amusement.

"When in Rome," she said. "But I have no idea what to order. What's good?"

"If you trust me, I'll get you something."

"Of course I do."

"Be right back." He went off toward the bar.

Less than a minute after he left, another woman sat down at the table. "I'm Jenny Cavendish," she said, holding out her hand. "You must be Sally,

Jim's girlfriend."

"I am. Pleased to meet you." *So this is Jim's partner.* The woman radiated professionalism. Her dark slacks and jacket with a white shirt had to be common attire for plain-clothes officers anywhere, at least if TV shows were anything to go on. But Jenny Cavendish wore them well. They weren't tailored, but they fit nicely. Unlike some women who chose not to wear makeup lest they look too feminine for a man's job, Jenny Cavendish's look was subtle, yet polished. She carried herself with confidence and Sally immediately got the impression of a woman who knew she was good at her job and expected others to keep up with her. If they couldn't, or wouldn't, she'd not waste a moment.

"Where'd he go?" Cavendish asked, her blue-eyed gaze cool and steady. *She's sizing me up. Not as a rival, but as a professional.* "Off to get me a drink." Sally reached for a leather-clad menu. "Thanks for letting me crash your party. Got any dinner recommendations?"

"You're welcome." Jenny took a sip of amber liquid. "The food is all good. But tonight's fish special is maple-glazed cedar-planked salmon, brought in fresh this morning."

"Sold." Sally laid down her menu.

Jenny studied her over the rim of her glass. "How long have you known Jim Duncan?"

Straight to the point. "Let's see. Must be almost two years now."

"You knew him before you started dating."

"Oh yes. The classic cop-attorney interaction. His suspect was my client." Jenny ran her finger around the rim of her glass. "What's his angle?"

Sally scoffed. "He doesn't have one."

"Come on. Everybody has an angle."

Sally leaned back and crossed her arms. "Is this why you wanted to meet me? To pump me for dirt on your partner? Because if it is, I'm leaving right now, and you can explain to him why I'm gone."

"You don't pull any punches, do you?"

"No. And you probably don't either. So let's cut the crap, shall we?"

Jenny paused, then laughed and lifted her glass. "Touché." She sobered.

"Listen. I've had a number of partners. Some I thought would be good, some I knew from the first would be jerks. Yeah, I'm digging for information. Do you blame me? This one seems too good to be true. Now, some might say I'm going to the wrong source. That you love him so of course, you're going to give me a good report. I tend to think differently. If you want to know what a man is really like, ask the woman at his side."

"Fair enough." Sally leaned on the table. "I told you. Jim and I were friends before we were involved. Trust me. What you see is what you get. He's fair, honest, loyal, and values hard work. He's also got a bit of a stubborn streak, but don't tell him I said that."

Jenny swirled her whiskey glass. "He spent a lot of time on patrol. Fourteen years. No promotions. What took him so long to switch?"

"You're thinking he wasn't good enough. That's why he stayed where he was for so long." Sally shook her head. "You're wrong. Jim liked his job, he liked his barracks, and he was loyal to the people he worked with. Why did he make the move now? You'd have to ask him, but my guess is that he was ready. Simple as that." She paused. "If you're looking for an ulterior motive, or hidden agenda, I'm telling you now. You can stop. All he wants is to do the job, do it well, and serve with honor. Play fair with him, and he'll have your back, no questions asked."

Jenny tilted her head. "It really is that simple, huh?"

Sally met her gaze. "Yes, it really is."

Jim returned, a glass in each hand. "This looks like a serious conversation. Should I come back later?"

"Nah, we're good," Jenny said.

Chapter Forty

Sally woke and dressed by seven o'clock Saturday morning. She dialed Pat Dennister's number. "Pat, hi. It's Sally Castle."

"Sorry I didn't call you, but I didn't get home until late last night. How can I help you?"

"I'd like to look over your records for RCH, particularly your checkbook register."

"What for?"

Sally debated how much to say. "I'm following a hunch."

"What will it do to Lynn? I know I said I was worried about her, but I don't think getting arrested will help."

"Quite honestly, I don't know. I won't until I see where this idea takes me."

A heavy silence came over the line. "What do you want from me? Can't you get the RCH books with a court order?"

"I can, but it's Saturday. I'd rather not wait until Monday. I think you want this cleared up as much as I do. However, if you'd rather I do it the formal way, I will."

"Aw hell." Pat's sigh sounded like a gust of wind. "I'll do it. Do you want me to drive down and meet you at that coffee place? I'm dropping my dog off for a dental cleaning. That will take all day, so this will give me something to do."

"That would be very nice of you." Sally made arrangements to meet Pat at nine and hung up.

When Sally arrived, Pat was already in the back corner, at the same table they'd sat at for their previous meeting, several piles of paper in front of her.

"Hi. How's it going with Johnny's Pixelated?" Sally asked.

"Good. I expect he'll be ready for adoption by the end of the month."

"That's fantastic. Do you mind if I get my caffeine first?"

Pat waved her off. "Go ahead. I'm still getting everything laid out."

By the time Sally made her purchase and returned, Pat had reorganized all her materials into three piles. "Here's what I have," she said as she pointed to each pile. "These are the official bank statements. These are all our receipts from purchases. This last pile is any invoices I paid. Where do you want to start?"

Sally made sure the snap on the lid was tight and set her cup off to the side. Then she pulled out Lynn Moss's bank records with their highlighted rows. "I'm looking to see if I can match these deposits to payments from your group."

"She wasn't with us, though."

"That's my point. Was someone taking from the group to help Lynn instead of her stealing directly?"

Pat scrunched up her face. "I know I didn't do it."

"But you're not the only person on the group account. Humor me." Sally looked at the first sheet. "My first record is from April fourteenth of this year for ninety-six dollars and forty cents. Is there anything on or around that date?"

Pat paged through her records. "Yes. Annie wrote a check on the twelfth for printing supplies."

One down. "Next one is May first for one-hundred-three dollars and four cents."

"Here. Annie wrote a check for our spring picnic. We gave every attendee a bag with little gifts, like poop bags and a doggie toothbrush, and she bought some of the items."

Over the next half-hour, Sally and Pat painstakingly matched every deposit in Lynn's bank account to a withdrawal from the River City Hounds funds. None of them were excessive, and they were all for seemingly normal items. Every purchase had an associated receipt. All of them had one thing in common. The transactions had been made by Annie Norquist.

Pat scrubbed her hand through her short hair. "I can't believe this. I knew Annie and Lynn were close, but this is incredible. Annie has been with the group for years. She's adopted and fostered over a dozen greyhounds. Why would she steal from us?"

Sally drained her cup. Her heart ached for the older woman, whose anguish was etched on her face. "I don't think she thought of it as stealing. After all, the biggest check she wrote was that one that was ostensibly for the picnic bags. If I'm right, and I believe I am, she saw a friend in desperate need, and this was the only way she could think to help her."

"But she has receipts for all the purchases."

"It could be she bought the supplies for the group with her own money." Sally examined one of the slips more closely. "See here? This is a credit card transaction, not a check. I think she took the cash from the group, gave it to Lynn, and charged the purchases so there would be a paper trail. Maybe Lynn promised to repay her. I won't truly know until I talk to her. Up until now, she's dodged my questions. When I show her the evidence, she's not going to be able to."

Pat pressed her fingers to her lips. "Do you really think the funds went to Lynn? Is there any way this is all a coincidence?"

Sally wished she could reassure the older woman, but she knew it would be better to rip the bandage off and let the healing begin. "If it was one time, sure. But Pat, this is a dozen matches. I suppose it's theoretically possible, but, in my experience, it's simply not probable."

Pat sat in silence, eyes a little wet. "Annie may have been helping a friend, but this wasn't the way to do it. She put Lynn's welfare ahead of the group, our dogs, and an innocent woman. That's not right." She dashed a hand across her face and pulled her piles together. "I want one thing from you."

"What's that?"

"I want to be there when you talk to Annie."

* * *

Duncan wandered about his house after Sally left to meet Pat Dennister. He should have gone with her. That would have at least given him something to do. Maybe he should take Rizzo and go out on his boat for some fishing before the weather turned sour.

The ringing of his phone saved him. He recognized the number as the State Police lab. "Duncan."

"Hey Jim, it's Tony. I'm calling about the fingerprints you dropped off yesterday. From the bottle."

"They're done already?"

"I put in a little unsanctioned overtime."

It was a pleasant surprise. Duncan hadn't expected results until at least next week, maybe even longer. "Why? I mean, you don't work Saturdays. Don't think I'm not grateful, but I can't figure out why you'd do it."

"I was interested. Plus, I never paid you back for that six-pack of pilsner you gave me."

"That was a birthday gift."

Tony huffed. "Do you want these results or not?"

Rizzo barked, and Duncan let him outside. "Yes."

"They match. The prints from both murder scenes and the bottle."

If the prints belonged to Sullivan, and Duncan was willing to bet they did, that hit the trifecta of means, motive, and opportunity. He thanked Tony and called Cavendish.

"This better be good since you're interrupting my Saturday morning," she said, the noise of some type of retail store behind her.

"The prints from the bottle at Sullivan's are a match."

"Damn." Her voice became muffled as she spoke to someone. "Still no proof they're Sullivan's?"

"No, but come on. A bottle at his house matches both murders. What are the odds he had the shooter over for a beer?"

"Not good. What are you proposing we do?"

Duncan thought. "Where are you?"

"Out getting my Saturday morning latte and a pastry."

"Swing by my place and pick me up. I think it's time we found Kyle Sullivan."

* * *

While Sally drove north, Pat called Annie to make sure she was at home. After telling the RCH president to stay there because she had information on the embezzlement case, Pat hung up. "I hope you don't hold this against me, but I want Annie to have an explanation for this that doesn't involve sending money to Lynn."

"I understand." And Sally did. Losing the group's money was bad enough. Learning that a friend had been responsible was something else entirely. "Just remember this doesn't have to end up in court. You could ask for restitution and let it go."

Pat stared out the window. "We'll see."

The sun shone on a perfect early fall day when Sally arrived at Annie Norquist's Shaler home. She and Pat approached the house and Pat knocked. Less than a minute later, Annie opened the door, and Rascal pushed his way to the front.

Pat entered and rubbed the greyhound's ears. "Sorry to barge in on a Saturday."

"Not a problem," Annie said. "I wasn't doing anything. Although the fact you brought Ms. Castle has me a bit nervous."

Sally greeted the dog and turned toward his owner. "Is there somewhere we can sit and talk? Maybe the kitchen?"

"Sure." Annie led the way. Rascal trotted behind them. "Can I offer you anything, coffee, water, soda?"

Pat shook her head. Sally said, "No, thanks."

Annie poured herself a cup of coffee, added cream and sugar, and sat. She pointed at two other chairs around the kitchen table. "Have a seat. What do you want to talk about?"

"It's something we need to show you." Sally pulled out Lynn Moss's highlighted bank statements.

Pat opened her bag to get the RCH check register and statements. "Ms. Castle has Lynn's records. These are my books from RCH."

Annie looked puzzled, but the skin around her mouth tightened.

Sally spread her papers out. Then she explained the situation.

Annie licked her lips. "Coincidences," she said, her voice cracking on the middle syllable.

"Doubtful." Sally fixed her with a firm look.

Annie averted her gaze. "My name isn't on these transactions."

"All I have to do to find the account owner is set the court order in motion. I really don't want to do that." Sally folded her hands. "Quite honestly, I don't believe anyone acted out of malice or ill will. I'm firmly convinced you thought you were doing the best thing you could for a friend. But Ms. Norquist, you need to see this didn't help anyone. Not Lynn Moss, not RCH, and definitely not Ciara Delmonico. I promise. If you come clean right now, there's still a possibility of setting things to rights for everyone involved."

The RCH president stared resolutely at her coffee cup.

"Annie, please." Pat's voice held an unmistakable note of begging. "Did you take money from the RCH account and send it to Lynn? That's all we want to know."

No answer.

"Ms. Norquist, you have to trust me." Sally took a breath. She could see Annie wasn't going to give up her friend, even at the expense of her beloved dogs. Not if all Sally could do was bully. Sympathy and understanding, that's what she needed. "The best thing you can do for Lynn now is tell the truth. What has happened is only putting lipstick on a pig, as my grandfather would say. Her problems aren't being addressed, and your actions are causing other people pain. Is that really what you want?"

Annie sniffled, but remained silent.

Pat reached out and touched her friend's arm. "I'm not mad, honest. We can fix this. Ms. Castle can help us. I want to know. If Lynn is in trouble, she should get help, real help. And think of poor Ciara. Do you want her to go to jail over this, for something she didn't do?"

Long seconds ticked by. The only sound was the click of Rascal's nails as he crossed the linoleum floor and laid his head in Annie's lap. "You're right. Lynn needed money," Annie said, voice low. "Just until she got everything settled and back on her feet, she said. Pat's year-end treasury statement showed RCH had plenty of cash. Lynn swore it was a one-time thing and she'd pay me back."

There was no triumph for Sally in being right in a case like this. "But she didn't."

"No. I put the stuff on my card, I had to pay it off, so I slipped cash out of group's account." Annie wiped her nose with the back of her hand. "She asked again. I lost count of how many times. She always promised she'd pay us back, and I wanted to believe her, so I kept doing it. And then we had the failure to pay, the audit, and...I had to stop. But we still needed to explain where the money went, and I couldn't throw her to the wolves." When she looked up, her eyes shone. "She's a good person, Ms. Castle. She doesn't need prison, she needs detox. But she's not strong enough on her own. I thought, I hoped, that if I could cover her, she'd wake up and get herself clean."

Sally gathered the papers. "What about Ciara?"

Annie stroked Rascal's head. "I'm sorry about that. I never thought she'd get in trouble. Even after the audit identified her as the culprit, I figured the legal system was good enough that she'd be found innocent and everything would be okay."

Pat got up and hugged the other woman. "Nobody's going to jail. I'm sure of it."

Sally looked at the two women. "One last question. Does the name Dan Overbeck mean anything to you, either of you?"

Pat stood behind her friend, rubbing her back. "He used to do transport for us. You know, bringing dogs from the track to our group, especially from West Virginia. I heard he was arrested."

"Do you know of any reason he would have given Ms. Moss money?"

Both women shook their heads, wearing similar perplexed expressions.

"No matter. Well, ladies, this is a step in the right direction." Sally leaned on her elbows. "I need to talk to Ms. Moss. If you don't want to be there, I understand."

Annie took a ragged breath and sat up straight. "No. We'll go with you."

Chapter Forty-One

It was almost eleven o'clock when Duncan and Cavendish arrived in Markleysburg. Once again, they found Sullivan's house apparently locked up tight. His truck was still absent, and a quick survey of the neighborhood failed to turn up any leads.

"What about work?" Cavendish asked. "Maybe he went in to make up for lost hours."

Duncan pulled out his phone and dialed.

The manager told him Sullivan had not shown up. "He's definitely fired now. If you find him, let him know."

Duncan's next call was to Michael Fisher's father.

"Why are the State Police looking for Kyle?" Mr. Fisher asked.

"We have a few questions."

"About what?"

Duncan looked at his partner. "About Otto McDonough and a man named Robert Bevilacqua. Mr. Fisher, if you know where your stepson is, it's in his best interest to talk to us."

"Oh no, it ain't." Fisher's tone was pugnacious. "I know how it goes. You all start asking questions, next thing I know Kyle's in jail. My wife is sick. He takes good care of her. I ain't gonna help you put him behind bars. You want to find him? Do it yourself." He ended the call.

Cavendish walked back to the car. "Let me guess. He's not going to be helpful."

"Can you blame him?" Duncan opened the driver's side door.

"Got any other ideas?" Her voice was genuinely curious, not accusatory.

She's as stumped as I am. He looked around. Where would he go if he was Kyle Sullivan and wanted to avoid notice for a while? "When was Mikey Fisher's accident?"

She thought a moment. "April of this year. Today is the five-month anniversary, come to think of it." She paused. "Where are you going with this?"

"I'm thinking if Sullivan is as distraught as he says about his half-brother's death, upset enough to kill a man, it's a date he'd want to commemorate." He slid in the car and grabbed his seat belt.

Cavendish followed suit. "You want to check the local cemetery?"

"Damn straight, I do."

* * *

At eleven-thirty, Sally, Pat Dennister, and Annie Norquist arrived in Penn Hills. The garage door was up, and Lynn's car was inside. Plump trash bags filled the cans, spilling over the top and onto the ground. Piles of dog poop were in the grass near the sidewalk. Lynn's greyhound, Cassie, bounded up to the gate, reared on her hind legs, and put her paws on the top rail.

Pat went over to greet the dog. "Lynn's home. She wouldn't leave Cassie like this."

Annie twisted her hands. "I agree."

Sally gestured to the house. "Do you want me to knock, or will you?"

"I'll do it." Annie trudged to the front of the house and rapped on the door. Pat left the dog and went to stand by Annie while Sally hung back.

Lynn answered the door wearing a stained t-shirt and ragged sweatpants. "Annie, Pat. I wasn't expecting you. What's up?"

"Can we come in?" Annie asked.

"I'm about to take Cassie for a walk."

Pat shook her head. "You're barefoot, and Cassie is in the backyard. She's not wearing her martingale. This is important. We brought someone with us."

"Who?" Lynn asked.

The RCH board members stepped aside to reveal Sally.

"Sorry to show up unannounced, but your friends are right," Sally said. "We really do need to talk."

A mix of emotions passed over Lynn's face. Fear combined with resignation. "I hope this won't take long. I have errands to run."

Once they entered, Sally noted the deteriorating condition of the house. Dirty plates and cups sat on the coffee table. When they entered the kitchen, the sink held dirty dishwater, in addition to used take-out containers on the counter. The faint smell of rotting garbage scented the air.

They all sat around the table. Lynn chose the chair farthest away from the others. "What's this all about? I haven't been doing any greyhound volunteering. Is it Ciara? I've told you all I know."

Sally pulled the papers from her bag. "No, I don't think you have." She found the highlighted sheets. "These are records from your bank."

"How did you get that?" Lynn asked. She tried for outrage, but instead, her voice was heavy with fear.

"I obtained them with a court order." Sally tapped the records. "I want to tell you a story." Step by step, she went through the whole narrative. As she talked, she watched Lynn's face pale until it was as white as paper.

At the end of it, Lynn bit her lip. "Sounds like you don't need anything from me."

Pat leaned forward. "We understand. It's been rough for you. Ms. Castle, she said we can put this right. But you gotta come clean. Help us help you."

Annie blinked away tears. "Please, Lynn."

Lynn looked away. "What exactly do you want me to say?"

Sally lowered her voice, using the compassionate tone that had worked so often with recalcitrant clients. "I want you to confirm Ms. Norquist's story."

"So I can go to jail?" Lynn's voice cracked.

"No, so you can get help." Sally leaned on the table. "Ms. Dennister already told you it can all be fixed. I might be able to help you. But I can't do anything unless you are honest with me, right here, right now."

Pat reached for Lynn's hand, but she snatched it away. Pat looked at Sally, then back at Lynn. "Look around. This place is a mess," Pat said. "You need to get yourself straight and clean, and it starts with admitting you have a problem. All you need to do is tell us the truth."

Silence reigned in the kitchen, broken only by the hum of the fridge as the compressor kicked on. Finally, Lynn passed a hand over her face. She stood and went to the sink. Once there, she splashed some water on her eyes. Then she grabbed a towel, dried herself, and turned. "It's all true, just like Annie said. Every time I filled a script, I told myself it was the last one. I was gonna quit and go clean. But it was just so hard." She appealed to Annie and Pat. "You gotta believe me."

"We know," Annie said.

Sally folded her hands. "Why did you get money from Dan Overbeck?"

Lynn wiped her nose with the hem of her shirt. "I knew, or suspected at least, something was wrong. Last spring, we were short a dog in one of the batches he brought from West Virginia. A black male."

"Johnny's Pixelated," Sally said. Her heart ached for the broken woman across from her.

Lynn nodded. "It jumped out because I had the perfect adopter lined up, and then we didn't get the hound. Dan fobbed me off with some flimsy story. Then I got a phone call from a friend of mine in Wheeling that Dan was in trouble and the state police were involved. I needed cash and I didn't want to go back to Annie. I told him he had to pay me five hundred bucks or I was gonna tell someone about the missing dog. I didn't feel too bad, since it was likely he was in trouble anyway. He paid, and a couple days later, the whole illegal racing story broke. Frankly, if he was already sunk, I don't know why he paid me."

"Only he knows, but maybe because Johnny wasn't related to the West Virginia operation," Sally said. She'd pass the information on to Jim. Whether it could help him with his homicides, she didn't know. But he should have the information.

"Now what?" Lynn asked. "They'll take Cassie from me, won't they? I'll lose my house, my dog, my job…everything."

Pat got up and folded the younger woman into a gentle embrace. She turned her head to look at Sally. "Is that true?"

She gathered up the papers. "Let me speak to the Allegheny County DA."

Lynn looked up. "You'll help me? Even though you represent Ciara?"

Sally's professional way forward was clear. "I'll do what I can. I may end up referring you to someone else, assuming you need representation. But I can find out what you all need to do so you can put this behind you."

Gratitude shone in Lynn's face, but also some worry. "What's this going to cost?."

"Don't worry. As they say on TV, the first consultation is free."

* * *

Markleysburg only had one cemetery. Duncan drove there, while Cavendish provided navigation. He pulled through the gates and proceeded at a slow speed. "Keep your eyes peeled for Sullivan's truck."

Not two minutes later, she pointed. "There."

The two-tone Chevy was parked half on the grass at the end of a row of headstones. As Duncan stopped behind it, he could see a man seated cross-legged on the grass. Duncan knew it had to be Mikey Fisher's final resting spot.

The troopers exited the car. Duncan unholstered his Glock and held it loose at his side. Without looking, he knew Cavendish had done the same. "Kyle Sullivan," he said in strong, calm voice. "Stand up, hands where we can see them."

Sullivan scrambled to his feet. A half-empty bottle was clutched in his left hand. The right held a black handgun. "You leave me alone. Get away from my brother."

Duncan brought up his own weapon. Behind him, he heard a hiss as Cavendish swore under her breath.

He focused on Sullivan. The bright noon sun beat down. There were no trees to block it. Sullivan squinted against the glare or because he'd had too much alcohol, Duncan didn't know. Either way, he wasn't going to be accurate if it came to shooting, no matter what his performance at the gun club tournament.

"Don't freaking move." Sullivan waved his gun hand in a wide sweeping motion, back and forth between the two cops. "You turn around and walk away. You can wait for me outside the gates, but don't you come near my brother."

Now that Duncan was closer, he could see the shine of tears on Sullivan's face. His voice was slurred and thick, and held an unmistakable note of pain. "Drop your weapon. We don't want to hurt you." *I don't want you to hurt us, either.* Duncan could tell the younger man wasn't really aiming at anything. Drunk on booze and grief, he was a loaded gun, literally, and could probably do more damage than if he was sober as a judge. A far cry from the last time Duncan had faced down an armed suspect. But Sullivan wasn't a hardened criminal, and that made him unpredictable. In some ways, Duncan would have preferred to be facing a pro.

"Yeah?" Sullivan's answering laugh was ragged. "Nobody ever wants to hurt anybody. That's what that prick said. 'Wasn't my fault. I didn't mean to.'" He snorted and dragged the back of his left hand across his nose. "I didn't mean to, either. Look how that turned out."

Duncan heard, rather than saw, Cavendish muttering behind him and knew she was calling for backup. "I said put the gun down." He didn't shout. He kept his voice firm, calm, and in control, willing the suspect to comply.

"What if I don't want to?"

"Kyle, we know about Otto McDonough." *Keep him going.* If he could keep the suspect's attention and talk him down, it would give others time to arrive. Hell, he might even be able to disarm Kyle and bring this to a peaceful end, without shots fired. It would be the best solution for everybody. Duncan had no desire to fire his weapon at another human being again. Once was enough.

Sullivan's gun hand wavered. "You don't know shit about McDonough."

"Then why don't you put down the gun and tell me about it?" *Stay calm, relaxed.* "Kyle, whatever you've done, don't make it worse. Mikey wouldn't want that, would he? Put down your weapon, and we'll talk."

Cavendish moved to a new position, her Glock drawn and trained on

Sullivan. As she passed Duncan, she whispered, "They said fifteen minutes."

Shit, that long? In this kind of situation, fifteen minutes was an eternity. One of the negatives of working out in Pennsylvania's rural areas. There wasn't a police station on every corner. Who knew where their backup was coming from? "Kyle, are you listening? Put the gun down." He paused. "We know you went to McDonough's house. We know about Mikey and the accident. We saw you take the other weapon from the guy at the gun club. Put down the gun and talk to us."

Sullivan kept his watery eyes on Duncan, but he didn't drop the .38. "You think you know everything. Did you know he was drunk, McDonough? Huh, did you?"

"He'd been drinking. It was in the report."

"He was smashed," Sullivan said. "It was raining, he was speeding, and not paying attention. Mikey didn't have a chance. And they let him off."

"That made you mad. I can understand that. I'd be mad, too."

Sullivan stumbled and caught himself on the headstone. But he held on to the .38. "Hell yeah! Not that it would have changed anything, but at least he coulda said sorry. But no."

Duncan risked a glance at Cavendish. She seemed content to let him keep talking. Maybe she didn't want to interrupt the rapport. "You went to see him." The thought that she was seeing him under the most extreme pressure skittered across his mind, and he wondered what her opinion of his performance was. He pushed that aside. The most important thing was he stay focused. The longer Sullivan talked, the more likely the confrontation could be brought to a peaceful conclusion.

"Bet you don't know what he did," Sullivan said, voice sullen.

"Why don't you drop the gun and tell me?"

"He *laughed* at me. But he wasn't laughing when I pointed my piece at him." His voice dropped to a whisper. "Then...pop-pop-pop-pop. And he just...fell over. Stupid surprised look on his face." He blinked. "I didn't mean to kill him."

Duncan couldn't risk a look at his watch to see how much time had elapsed. *Where are they?* "What about the other guy? Robert Bevilacqua. He had nothing to do with your brother." He strained to hear the sound of sirens, but the only thing he could pick out was a faint rustle of leaves as a soft breeze tickled the trees.

Sullivan's right hand drooped ever so slightly. "He saw me. Leaving McDonough's. He called and said he saw me in the back of the house, he knew all about Mikey, and he knew what I'd done. He made me come to his house to see him. He wanted money."

"He told you that, huh?" *C'mon, Kyle, drop the gun.*

"Yeah." Sullivan seemed to look off into the middle distance. "He said he understood why I did it, that McDonough was garbage, but he needed cash. So unless I wanted the cops to find out I'd been at McDonough's crib that night, I needed to pay him. Shit." He hawked and spat.

"Then pop-pop-pop."

"Uh-huh. I didn't mean to kill him either. Why won't people leave me alone?" Sullivan's voice rose as he spoke. He accentuated the last word by jabbing the .38 in Duncan's direction. Completely focused, Sullivan appeared to have forgotten about Cavendish.

Duncan almost felt sorry for him. "Kyle, for the last time, drop the gun. Don't let this end badly for a third time."

Sullivan's gaze sharpened. He licked his lips. "You really know it all, do you?"

"And we have evidence to prove it. Last chance. Drop. The. Gun."

Sullivan sagged. The .38 dangled from his fingers for a long moment, then hit the grass.

Cavendish holstered her Glock and darted in to secure the suspect. "Kyle Sullivan, you're under arrest. On your knees, hands on your head. Slowly."

Sullivan complied, and she cuffed him.

Duncan waited until she finished. After that, he holstered his gun. "You got him?"

"Yes." She hauled Sullivan to his feet. "You're good at talking."

"Thanks. I think." He closed his eyes, waiting for his heart to stop pounding, something he had noticed, but not paid attention to during the standoff.

"Don't forget to grab his stuff." She hustled him off to the car.

"I'll cancel the call for backup, too." Duncan snapped on nitrile gloves before picking up the gun and the bottle, which turned out to be a half-empty liter of cheap whiskey. Then he let dispatch know the additional units were no longer required. He met Cavendish at the car.

With Sullivan in the backseat, Cavendish leaned against the roof. "His story is full of crap. He didn't mean to shoot anyone. My ass, he didn't."

"I know. Fortunately, we just arrest them. It'll be up to the DA to make that argument."

"Thank God. Back to the barn?" she asked.

"Yep, I'll drive. Let's get the paperwork done and close this puppy."

"Then what?"

He opened the door. "I don't know about you, but I need a drink."

Chapter Forty-Two

By the time Duncan and Cavendish dropped Sullivan off to be processed, finished their paperwork, and turned in the state-issued car, it was nearly five o'clock. Duncan spun the keys to his Jeep around his finger. "If you still feel like having a celebratory drink, I'm paying."

"It is my personal policy never to turn down free booze. I'll meet you there." Cavendish headed for the door.

Thirty minutes later, they were seated at Whiskey & Rye, glasses of premium scotch in front of them along with a flatbread topped with mozzarella, basil, and tomato.

Cavendish lifted her drink. "To your first case. Congratulations, rookie."

They clicked, and Duncan took a sip. *What the hell?* "May I ask you something?"

"Go ahead."

"I thought you'd stopped with the rookie bullshit. Or have you put me back on probation?"

She grinned. "Figured it out, did you?"

"It wasn't hard. I'm new to this section. Not stupid. Or do you think I spent fourteen years on patrol because I couldn't hack anything else, and someone finally took pity on me?"

"I wondered." She swirled her whiskey. "Fortunately, that isn't the case. At least with you."

"You could have asked, you know."

"Yeah, and you might have lied through your teeth. I preferred to see you

278

in action." She skimmed her hands over her hair, dislodging the knot. "Ed Loughlin told you I was a hard-ass, didn't he?"

Duncan stared at his drink. "No comment."

"Don't worry. I know my reputation." She pushed aside her scotch. "My first partner was a crusty thirty-year veteran. He worked me like a dog and never gave me an inch. I had to write all the warrants, do all the grunt work. At the time, I thought he was taking advantage of the fact that I was the inexperienced young woman. But after he retired, I realized he'd been the best partner I could have had as a new trooper in this role."

He raised an eyebrow. "Oh?"

She tapped the table. "He taught me how the job is supposed to be done. No cutting corners, no dodging the heavy lift. You want the collar, you do it right. No dancing around."

It reminded Duncan of his experience with his first field training officer. "Sounds like a good guy."

"He was. Unfortunately, the next few guys who rotated through here failed to live up to expectations." She swept her hair back up. "Too interested in having their own way or using the job to burnish their reputation on their way up the chain. I have no use for people like that, and I'm not above saying so."

People like Corporal "Golden Gary" Sheffield. He sipped his drink. "I'm going to assume that didn't make you popular."

"No, it did not. Fortunately, Lieutenant Ferguson is capable of seeing through the bullshit." Cavendish crossed her legs. "And that brings me to you."

"What about me?" He knew the answer, but he wanted to hear her say it.

"What kind of trooper were you? Were you willing to put in the work? Fourteen years is a long time to spend driving a car around Fayette County. Why did you come here? Did you think this was a way to spend the last six years of your career, marking time to retirement? Or were you going to pull your own weight? I couldn't go easy on you. I needed to know right off the bat, not when the shit hit the fan and lives were at stake. Namely mine."

Duncan let the silence hang between them. "Did I pass your test?"

She gave him a lopsided grin. "We're sitting here, having a drink, and toasting your first success. What the hell do you think?"

* * *

Sally returned to Uniontown by five and parked outside the office. She'd called the DA in Allegheny Count to inform him of Lynn Moss's confession, discussed tactics with Annie Norquist and Pat Dennister, and given Lynn the name of a defense attorney. "He's a good guy, and he'll treat you fairly." On the way home, she called Ciara Delmonico and asked her to come to the office at five-thirty.

Ciara showed up at quarter after five. "Is something wrong?" She picked at the zipper on her light jacket.

"It's very right, actually." Without going into too much detail, Sally told her what had happened that afternoon.

"What does it mean?" Ciara asked, her forehead puckered.

"It means you're cleared." Sally reached across the desk. "I've spoken with the DA, he's in the process of withdrawing the case, and you're free to resume your business."

Ciara clasped the outstretched hand. "Thank you. I don't…I don't have the money right now to pay you. But if you need your taxes done, call me. I'll definitely give you the friends and family rate."

"We can work out a payment plan." Sally tightened her grip. "Did you get into a gambling addiction therapy treatment group?"

"Yes. In fact, my first meeting is tonight."

Sally let go and sat back. "Call Monday, and we'll talk. Good luck."

Ciara thanked her again and left, brushing past Kim on the way out.

She stopped in the door. "Ciara looks happy. All wrapped up?"

Sally told her friend about the day's events. "That means I'm ready to move on to something new for you. A client who can pay full rates, if you'd like."

"About that." Kim hesitated and pointed at a chair. "May I sit?"

"Sure." Sally had expected Kim to be thrilled. *Something's up.* When she didn't speak after taking a seat, Sally prodded her. "Spill it. I won't bite."

"Remember the reason I started this?"

"Yeah, you were passed over for partner."

"I got a call from the senior partner at the firm this morning while you were gone." Kim bit her lip. "Turns out, the guy they promoted is moving to Seattle. His wife got some big opportunity at her job, one that's too good to pass up."

"It happens." Sally suspected she knew exactly where the conversation was going.

"Before he left, he suggested a replacement."

And there it was.

"Me. In fact, he said they should have picked me in the first place."

"You're taking it."

Kim's expression said it all. "It's what I want. I only opened my own office because, well, I was angry. I didn't want to leave, but I felt I had to do something. It was too much of an insult to let it pass." When Sally said nothing, Kim hurried on. "I know, it leaves you in the lurch. You quit your job, or at least you said you were, to come here, and now I'm bailing on you. I'll help you find another spot. Maybe the firm will take you on. I can't promise anything, but—"

Sally held up a hand. "I assume you signed a lease for this space? What's the rent?"

"Yes, six months." Kim blinked. "Seven-fifty a month, and that includes electric, heat, and water. Why?"

"I'll take it over from you."

"Sally, you don't have to do that. How are you going to afford it?"

"I've done the math. I've been wondering what I want to do. Ciara's case, and listening to Lynn Moss, helped me figure it out. I want to help the people who have nowhere else to turn. They can't afford the big firms, and they don't qualify for public defense. I'll fill that gap."

"You can't do all *pro bono*, can you?"

"I didn't say all my work would be free. Relax. I made a spreadsheet. I know what I want to charge, and how to structure payments, all of it.

Seriously."

Kim pulled at her lip. "It'll be hard to make enough money alone. You'd do better with a partner."

Sally leaned back, laced her fingers behind her head, and smiled. "I know. And I've got just the woman in mind."

* * *

Monday morning, Sally laid her letter of resignation on Bryan's desk.

He didn't read it. He took off his glasses and polished them on his tie. "Are you sure about this?"

"Trust me, Bryan. I've never been more sure in my life."

He stood and held out his hand. "You'll always have a place here, Sally. Best of luck to you."

She grasped it. "Thanks. Just do me a favor, will you?"

"What's that?"

She grinned. "When you come across someone you can't represent out of this office, give me the referral."

Chapter Forty-Three

One month later

Sally watched as Jim screwed in the last bolt for the swinging gate on the newly installed fence. "Thanks for doing this."

"Not a problem." He tested the latch, then pushed the gate shut. It settled into place with a satisfying clank. "I probably should have installed a fence ages ago. Now I don't have to put Rizzo on the lead. He'll love that."

"I mean, thanks for housing my dog. You didn't have to do that."

"I know. But he and Rizzo will keep each other company." He gathered up his tools. "I wish you'd come along with him. Where are you going to go?"

"I have six months to figure it out." She kissed his cheek. "I just...I want to see what's out there first. I may end up here. Hell, I probably will. But I want to try."

He grinned. "When is Tanelsa's last day with the public defender?" He started to the front of the house and the porch.

She followed. "End of the month." It hadn't taken much to convince Tanelsa to join her new partnership. She only hoped Bryan didn't kill her the next time they met. First, Sally resigned, then she poached his staff. "Have you heard anything about Overbeck?" The information she'd given Jim, including the fact he'd paid off Lynn Moss, had led to another round of charges, this time in Pennsylvania.

"He's going to jail this time. I know that. He identified Otto McDonough as a buyer. The way I heard it, his lawyer couldn't agree to a deal fast enough."

Jim looked at his watch. "When is the dog supposed to be here?"

"Soon." A dark red SUV in front of the house slowed. "I think that's her."

The SUV pulled into the driveway, and Pat Dennister got out. "Hello there. Hold on a minute." She went around back, lifted the tailgate, and waited as a handsome black greyhound leapt out. His coat shone in the sunlight, not a speck of white to be seen. Pat closed and locked the car and tugged the leash. The dog willingly followed, but stopped every few feet to sniff, the whiplike tail wagging furiously.

"He's gorgeous." Sally came down off the porch. "Hey boy, come here." The dog broke off his olfactory investigation and trotted to Sally. He leaned against her.

Pat shook the leash. "Let's get him inside. We'll introduce him to the house, I'll give you his papers, you give me a check, and I'll be on my way." She looked at Sally. "Have you decided on a name?"

"Pixel," Sally said.

Pat clucked her tongue. "Come on, Pixel. Let's go." She climbed onto the porch, and Pixel jumped up beside her.

An hour later, Pat left. Sally went to the backyard, where Jim stood, tossing a ball between his hands. "Your dog doesn't play fetch. All he wants to do is explore and pee on everything." He pointed at Pixel. Rizzo followed his new friend, putting his mark wherever the greyhound did.

Sally sighed. "Men. Dog, human, doesn't matter. Everything's a pissing match."

He ignored the statement and tossed the ball. Both canines ignored it. He turned to Sally. "You good?"

She linked her arm through his and looked around at the sunny yard, blue sky, and the dogs ambling around. "Yeah, I am."

A Note from the Author

I was first introduced to retired racing greyhounds when a friend of mine brought her dog to my kids' summer swim practice. Solomon was a big, beautiful male with impeccable manners. Being a dog lover, I had to learn more.

Experts believe the greyhound breed is 2,000 years old and has changed very little over that time. Pictures that strongly resemble greyhounds are on the Egyptian pyramids. The theory is that the conquering Romans brought greyhounds out of Egypt and eventually to Great Britain as dogs of the nobility used for coursing and hunting small game. George Washington, a noted dog enthusiast, had a greyhound named Cornwallis. The real introduction of the breed to America came in the late 1800s when greyhounds were brought to hunt the jackrabbits that destroyed crops in the Midwest. I have no doubt that racing started when some farmer said, "My dog is faster than yours," but the mechanical lure was invented after 1900 and the first track opened in San Francisco shortly after 1910, which was the birth of the racing industry.

Greyhounds belong to a sub-category of dogs known as "sighthounds." While they have the superior canine sense of smell, their sight is their primary sense. Greyhounds can see up to half a mile away and the position of their eyes gives them a 270-degree field of vision. The dogs can literally see behind them.

People say greyhounds are bred to run, but that isn't entirely true. They are *born* to run. Everything about them is form following function. The head and body are slim and aerodynamic (there's even a notch behind the skull to tuck their ears). They have a flexible spine and an "inverted S" chest shape that allows for more speed. Their paws leave the ground at two points during their stride, meaning the dogs are airborne during the run, and their paws are natural shock absorbers. A greyhound's maximum speed is 45 mph, making him the second-fastest land animal on Earth, and it takes only three strides to reach that pace.

All of this leads people to think greyhounds are energetic, high-maintenance dogs that need a lot of exercise. Nothing could be further from the truth. Affectionately known as "45-mph couch potatoes," these gentle giants want nothing more than to curl up on a cushion, bed, or couch where they'll spend up to 20 hours a day napping. Because of this, and since greyhounds are a relatively quiet dog when it comes to barking, they can thrive in apartment settings.

Due to the efforts of enthusiastic adoption groups, the rate of placement for retired racers in America hovers around 95%. With the decline of racing in America (only four states allow racing **and** have active tracks), it has become harder to obtain retired racers in this country. Sadly, that is not the case worldwide. Greyhound racing still flourishes in Ireland, Australia, and the Far East (notably in Macao, where dogs live and die in inhumane conditions). There is also the plight of Spanish greyhounds, known as "galgos." These dogs, slightly heavier of body, are used for hunting and are usually killed, often in barbaric ways, after the season.

If you would like more information on greyhound rescue, please visit www.ngagreyhounds.com/ADOPT or search for greyhound rescue groups near you.

Acknowledgements

Somehow book five feels like a significant milestone in a series life. As always there are a lot of people to thank.

My critique partners, Annette Dashofy, Jeff Boarts, and Peter Hayes for keeping me honest and pushing me as a writer.

Editor and friend Susan Gottfried for making me do the "hard work" and my proofreader, Kathy Deyell, for hunting typos. Both of these ladies make me look good.

Trooper Forrest Allison of the Pennsylvania State Police for answering my questions on the operation of the Criminal Investigation Division.

Chuck van Keuren for his legal expertise in defense law (who knew the subpoena process was so straightforward)?

Kyle Catanzarite for sharing her knowledge about greyhound racing, from breeding through retirement and adoption. And for her tireless work with Ruth Scheller and Sue Yanakos of Three Rivers Greyhounds to rehome these beautiful, gentle dogs. TRG has ceased operation now, but I will be forever grateful to them for bringing Koda into my life.

Endless thanks to Sisters in Crime and Pennwriters for providing the resources necessary to grow as a writer and the emotional support needed to stay sane.

Book advocate and blogger extraordinaire, Dru Ann Love, who has championed this series from the start and whose "good morning" messages help me start every day with a smile.

The amazing team at Level Best Books—Harriette Sackler, Verena Rose, and Shawn Reilly Simmons. Here's to more books together!

Last, but certainly not least, my husband, Paul, who has been my partner for the last 25 years in all things big and small. I love you, babe.

About the Author

Liz Milliron is the author of The Laurel Highlands Mysteries series, set in the scenic Laurel Highlands of Southwestern Pennsylvania, and The Home Front Mysteries, set in Buffalo, NY during the early years of World War II. She is a member of Sisters in Crime, Pennwriters, International Thriller Writers and The Historical Novel Society. Liz lives outside Pittsburgh with her husband and a ridiculously spoiled retired-racer greyhound.

SOCIAL MEDIA HANDLES:
  @LizMilliron (Facebook and Instagram)

AUTHOR WEBSITE:
  http://lizmilliron.com